V.

The

Mating Game

Keith

from

Janis

December 17

2016

The Mating Game
Published by The Conrad Press in the United Kingdom 2016

Tel: +44(0)1227 472 874
www.theconradpress.com
info@theconradpress.com

ISBN 978-1-911546-10-8

Book cover design and typesetting by:
Charlotte Mouncey, www.bookstyle.co.uk

The Conrad Press logo was designed by Maria Priestley.

Printed and bound in Great Britain by Clays Ltd, St Ives plc

Copyright material used
An extract from *Drink Down* by Kevin Smith (1962 - 2010),
musician and lyricist of The Fling.

The
Mating Game

Jovanka Houska
& James Essinger

I am still a victim of chess.
It has all the beauty of art – and much more.

Marcel Duchamp (1887-1968)
*- he gave up art for chess. At one point his fascination
with the game so demoralised his first wife that
she glued all his pieces to the board*

Hey, open up here comes original sin
Hey, open up here comes original sin
Hey, open up here comes original sin

It's all-right, it's all-right, it's all-right, it's all-right
It's all-right, it's all-right, it's all-right
It's all-right, it's all-right, it's all-right

No one's got it all
No one's got it all
No one's got it all

'Hero of the Story' – Regina Spektor

Vanny's
tournaments

European Chess Championship, Odessa, Ukraine
(ten rounds, one rest day)
Monday, September 12 – Thursday, September 22
(rest day: Sunday, September 18)

Hastings International Chess Congress, England
(nine rounds, no rest day)
Saturday, December 28 - Sunday, January 5

Gibraltar International Chess Festival
(ten rounds, no rest day)
Monday, January 23 - Wednesday, February 1

European Women's Chess Championship
(nine rounds, one rest day), Budapest, Hungary
Monday, March 12 – Wednesday, March 21
(rest day: Sunday, March 18)

The Niklas Bogolyubov World Open Chess Championship
(ten rounds, one rest day), New York, United States
Monday, June 4 – Thursday, June 14
(rest day: Monday, June 11)

The opening

*The first dozen moves of the game, when each player
starts to develop their strategy.*

From *Introduction to Chess* by Ivana Jones
(Checkmate Publications)

1

I suppose if you want to know when it *really* started, I'd need to begin with falling in love with chess when I was a lonely and rather chubby girl at the posh school, Abbey Hall in Devon, where my dad had sent me. But perhaps I ought to go back to the wintry afternoon in Hastings last year - on Thursday, December the twenty-ninth - when I met Sven, and Boris, in the space of a few hours. They've both ended up changing my life, though not as much as chess did.

Hastings is, of course, famous for its battle, which led to England being taken over by William the Conqueror in 1066. That December afternoon, my heart was about to be conquered, in a location as unpromising as the Horntye Park sports centre, where the Hastings International Chess Congress - the oldest chess tournament in the world - was being played. The tournament had started the previous day, four days after my birthday, which is on Christmas Eve, and no, it isn't a great day for a birthday.

I'd managed to win my Round One game. My opponent that afternoon in Round Two, at two fifteen in the afternoon, was going to be a Norwegian player called Sven Olsen. I'd never heard of him before the previous evening, when the pairings went up on the internet and I discovered I was playing him today. Outside the sports centre, the weather was still cold following a big snowfall on Boxing Day. There'd been a bit of a thaw afterwards, but then the thermometer had shot below zero again. I got to the venue at, I suppose, about one o'clock in the afternoon. When I arrived, I spotted Miklos Steiner near the sports centre's entrance.

You'll perhaps have heard of Miklos, who's the second highest-rated chess-player in the world. He was talking quietly, and in a distinctly sinister fashion, to Arpad Bognar, their heads close together. Arpad, like Miklos, is a Hungarian grandmaster, or GM, to use the abbreviation widespread in the chess world. They'd both achieved my most precious ambition, which was one day to become a chess grandmaster. This aim had become my dream ever since a quite possibly crazy moment, in my last year at university six years earlier, when I'd resolved to try to make chess my career. To win the GM title you need three official grandmaster-strength results in tournaments, or 'grandmaster norms', as they're called. I was an international master (IM) already, but that was only a stepping-stone to being a grandmaster. There are fewer than forty female GMs in the whole world. I so much wanted to become one of them. I had only one norm so far.

I tiptoed past Miklos, hoping he hadn't noticed me and wouldn't. But just as I was about to push the sports centre's heavy front door open, I heard his voice switch suddenly from Hungarian (I don't know the language, but I supposed it was that) to English, with irritating mock-gaiety and with a very annoying stress on the second syllable of 'hello'.

'Hel*lo*, Ivana. I heard you von yesterday.'

He spoke as if my winning a game of chess was about as likely as the sun suddenly turning into an orange blancmange.

Wondering whether today in Hungary was *Say Hello Contemptuously to Women You've Slept with and then Totally Ignored* day, I turned and looked at Miklos.

'Yes, I did,' I replied, as levelly as I could.

'Vell done. If you keep on vinning, perhaps soon we vill play each other again.'

I suppose he was thinking *if ve play each other again I shall of course vin, and you'll vant to sleep with me once more.* His English, by the way, was close to perfect, apart from his always pronouncing the 'w' sound as a 'v'.

I don't want to go into great detail about what had happened between Miklos and me on a hot evening the previous September, at the European Championship in semi-tropical Odessa. I still had painful three-month-old memories of Miklos leading me into his bedroom, kicking the door shut, stripping quickly, then glancing at me.

'You take off your clothes now, yes?' he'd said. I'd looked back at him. 'Is that it?' I'd asked. 'Is that your courtship technique?' He'd just shrugged. I'd thought of walking out of there and returning to my own hotel room. But I didn't. Why not? Because I was at the mercy of my silly quirk, which was that I found a man especially attractive if he could beat me at chess, which Miklos had, earlier that evening. Miklos had started sidling up to me on the bed. When he reached me he looked deeply into my eyes, then gently reached behind me and undid my hair-clasp. My hair, which is long, black and straight, fell down around my shoulders. He'd kissed me with a tenderness I hadn't expected. Our kissing had soon become less tender, and more desperate.

Miklos hadn't been in touch with me since then, not once. OK, I didn't really want him to have been in touch, but I wanted him to have at least *tried*.

There outside the sports centre, that winter afternoon, as I was trying hard to think of something witty to say that would make clear to Miklos - without revealing any secrets to Arpad Bognar - that even if Miklos and I did play each other during the tournament and he beat me, there'd be no chance at all of a repeat of what had happened in Odessa, Vladimir

Vladimirovich Vladimirov, aka The Three Vs, who as usual was dressed in black shoes, black trousers, a black pullover and a black leather cloak, appeared on the scene.

The Three Vs looked rather like the goodie terrorist in *V for Vendetta*, which, as anyone on the international chess circuit knew, was The Three Vs' favourite movie. He didn't have a Guy Fawkes mask, no, but his thick black eyebrows, severe mouth that never smiled, and his rather hooked Roman nose, added up to a moderately accurate likeness of the mask. The Three Vs was known for being the maddest member of the international chess tour, which, believe me, is saying a great deal.

Without giving any indication of being aware that Arpad or me were in the vicinity, Vladimir etc. (people refer to him as The Three Vs to save vocal cords and toner) started jabbering to Miklos in guttural Russian. At the same time, The Three Vs began hopping about on his left leg, though staying close to Miklos so Miklos could hear him. Miklos, who was dressed in a dark suit as usual, as if he was attending the prospective funeral of his opponent, seemed completely unfazed by The Three Vs' hopping. I could only think that Miklos was as used to the loony as most of us in the rest of the professional chess world were. Arpad Bognar, who'd also spotted The Three Vs, backed off.

I didn't know any of the Russian language in those days except for vodka, *Gorky Park*, Roman Abramovitch, the Russian names of the chess pieces, *da* (which means yes) and *matrioshka*, the Russian word for those Russian dolls that get smaller and smaller and slot into each other. I suspect this tells us something very significant about the Russian mind; I'm just not sure what.

I didn't say another word to Miklos. Instead, I just walked off, still brooding on how arrogant Miklos was, and amazed that I'd been stupid enough to have gone to bed with him at all. The Three Vs was still hopping.

Feeling I absolutely needed to escape, I decided to head for the chess bookstall inside the sports centre to do a little browsing.

The bookstall at Hastings is at the back of the room where, during the hours of play, a grandmaster takes an audience through some of the top games underway. As play hadn't started yet, the two dozen or so chairs in the room were all empty. I was standing in the doorway, about twenty feet from the bookstall.

A moment later I saw the most beautiful man I'd seen in my entire life.

There was a chess book in his hand. He was absorbed in the book, and was only half-facing me, but enough of him was on show for me to see the full extent of his gorgeousness.

He had a light brown leather biker's jacket slung casually over his left shoulder, yet he looked far too well-scrubbed for anyone to have imagined he'd ever been anywhere near a motorbike.

He was just so beautiful. He was slim and looked muscular in a very nicely masculine kind of way. His face was full of thought, and his lips were wondrously kissable. His stubble was light, his blond hair rich and tousled. He was tall: six two or three. I thought he was about thirty, which would have made him four years older than me.

He put the book back on the stall, then took hold of a white tee-shirt that had the words *THE MATING GAME* on it in large black uppercase letters. After feasting my eyes on him for fifteen seconds or so (there was no-one else in the room except for him and me and the elderly man who ran the bookstall and he was at the far end, absorbed in paperwork), I approached this godly vision of male beauty and, desperate for eye contact, I asked:

'Are you really going to *buy* that thing?'

He holds the tee-shirt up against himself and glances at me. Now I'm only about six feet away from him. He has beautiful, grey, bedroom eyes. 'No,' he says, in a deep, thoughtful, very masculine and very adorable voice, 'I don't think so.' He places it back down on top of the other tee-shirts on the stall. 'Not really my style,' he adds.

He speaks English with a truly attractive accent. Scandinavian, I think. Nothing like Miklos's.

'No, definitely not,' I agree. Smiling at me cautiously, he says: 'You're Ivana Jones, aren't you?'

'Well, yes, how did you guess?'

He gives a restrained Scandinavian shrug. 'Because you are quite famous. I am playing you at two fifteen today.'

Oh my God, I think, *oh my God.*

'You're... you're Sven Olsen?'

'The last time I checked, yes,' he replies, good-humouredly.

I shake his hand, and he tightens his fingers over mine. It's difficult to keep looking him in the eye when my knees feel weak at the mere touch of his hand, but I try my best.

Sven smiles goddishly. 'Please excuse me being so forward. We both know I'll be an easy opponent for you, so I think we should both enjoy our game this afternoon for as long as it lasts.'

'You shouldn't assume you'll be an easy opponent for me,' I say quickly. 'In a chess game, anything can happen.'

It's true, though, that I looked Sven Olsen up on the 'Chessbase' online player directory the previous night and saw that he was a journalist by profession and was rated about 200 points below me. At that time, I was the fifty-second highest-ranked woman player in the world. If you included men as well as women, though, I was only about number 1700. Sometimes I did play in all-female tournaments, though mostly I enjoyed playing in mixed events like in Odessa and Hastings.

'You're very kind,' says Sven. 'On the other hand, I do think you will beat me. I also think women are at an advantage in a game of chess. After all, isn't chess all about an army, led by a queen, trying to kill the opposing king?'

Tom Hardiman, who was in those days my Friend with Benefits, once said much the same thing. I've always felt that Tom's love of chess substantially stems from his fantasy of being dominated by women.

But I know I shouldn't be thinking about Tom now.

I smile at Sven. 'It says on Chessbase you're a journalist?'

'Yes. I'm certainly not a good enough player to make a living from playing. I've recently set up a new Norwegian chess magazine. In Norway we have four and a half million people, and maybe seven thousand active chess-players. Fortunately, Norwegian chess-players will buy more than one chess magazine. After all, chess is not an expensive hobby. You buy a board and set, maybe a clock, some books, and you're happy to buy a magazine or two as well. It's not like golf.'

'And the Norwegian winters are long and dark.'

'*Yes,*' Sven agrees, giving a gorgeous Norwegian husky deep tone to the word. He shrugs, as if winter's too inescapable a fact of life for him to want to discuss it. 'I want the new magazine to earn its reputation by producing features about international tournaments,' he adds. 'So I'm here covering this tournament in Hastings, and next month I'm playing at Gibraltar, and then... we'll see.'

'You're playing at Gibraltar?'

He nods.

'I'm playing there too. But, Sven, doesn't your wife mind you travelling all the time?'

'As a matter of fact, I'm single.'

The tone of his voice doesn't betray any awareness he twigged my pathetically obvious attempt to find out if he's married.

My smile broadens with relief. 'So, you haven't yet got to know Miss Right?'

'Regrettably not,' he says, sadly. 'But why "Ivana"? You're English, are you not?'

'Yes, but my mum Lena comes from Zagreb, the capital of Croatia. The "Jones" is because my dad's English.'

Sven nods thoughtfully. I feel sure I can guess just how wonderful he'd be in bed: intelligent, caring, inventive. *Perhaps a little excessively theoretical, but that could be cured.*

He smiles again. How delicious his smiles are.

'See you at two fifteen,' he says.

'See you, Sven.'

I abandon the plan of browsing the bookstall, give Sven a little wave and head off to the playing-hall.

How I wish, at that moment, I wasn't burdened with my quirk!

2

We chess professionals, or would-be chess professionals, mostly don't earn much unless we're among the top dozen or so players in the world, which I'm not and frankly which I'm never likely to be. Ever since I'd left university, money had been a problem. In July last year, though, about two months before my embarrassing encounter with Miklos, and so around five months before I had the delight of meeting Sven, I played in a tournament in the Slovenian capital Ljubljana, and something happened which I'd hoped would ease the money strain a bit.

The Ljubljana tournament, held in the most difficult capital city in the world to spell (I had to check the spelling just now on google) was sponsored by SlovCos, a Slovenian cosmetics company with a name that definitely needed a makeover itself. After the prize-giving - I'd managed to come equal third - a handsome guy in a dowdy-looking brown suit came up to me. 'I am Goran Novak, SlovCos's marketing director,' he explained, then said he'd like me to be in a TV advert for one of the products his firm sold: a moisturising cream, smelling of orange blossom, called 'Softy-Softy'.

At first, due to the weird name of the cream, I suspected that the whole thing was a joke and he was just trying to chat me up. When I discovered that the name of the cream was real but silly, I was surprised, then flattered, then scared. I mean, I had no idea *at all* what I'd look like on screen.

I agreed to do it, though.

The filming took place two days later and lasted just one morning, in time for me to play my game in the tournament round being held that afternoon. I had to be at the studio at seven in the morning. Goran paid me 1,000 euros cash in hand as a fee (I subsequently declared it on my tax return, I'm horribly honest about that kind of thing) and promised me another 250 euros each time the ad was shown on television. That 250 euros didn't seem very much, but I'd decided I'd not bother negotiating with Goran, especially as he'd told me that all I had to do was scoop some cream out of the pot, breathe in the orangey fragrance for a few moments, then smooth the cream sensuously on my face and say *Za mladostni videz koze uporabljam kremo Softy-Softy*.

In case you don't speak Slovenian, this means *I use Softy-Softy to keep my skin looking really young*. I had to learn this by heart and try to pronounce it as well as I could. I don't think I let Goran down as far as speaking Slovenian in a bad accent was concerned, though I presume I managed to get it right enough for SlovCos to be OK about using the footage. Actually, Slovenian sounds quite a lot like Croatian and while I didn't know more than a smattering of Croatian by that time, maybe having a Croatian mum helped me a bit. So far the ad had been shown nine times.

When I was a little girl, I never spoke to Mum in Croatian beyond a few words. My dad, Godfrey Jones - a forceful northerner with a face like an overcooked baked potato who, at the time I met Sven, lived in Monte Carlo with his fifth wife Larissa and their little boy Piotr on a rather rundown yacht named after me - only wanted us to speak English at home. Mum told me she and Dad argued over that a bit, but eventually Mum caved in as usual.

How did Mum meet my dad? You may well ask. She was in England, working in Halifax at the offices of a food wholesaler, when she got to know him. He regularly bought vast numbers of cucumbers from her boss for his company,

Jones's Condiments Limited, to convert into Jones's Delicious Halifax Pickled Gherkins. (I was born in the back of Dad's gold-coloured Rolls-Royce because he was sorting out a problem at one of his three pickle factories before the Christmas shutdown and had headed for the hospital with Mum too late, so she delivered me herself on the way to the hospital).

Mum and Dad were married for eight years, then Dad left her for a Bulgarian woman, also called Ivana, who became his second wife. Dad's always been partial to Eastern European women.

3

As I reach my seat in the Hastings Chess tournament hall, and on the Black side of board four, at about five past two, there's no sign of Sven yet.

I'm at one of the five boards that are in front of the spectator seats in the playing-hall. Each of these boards has a TV screen behind it, the demonstration screen as it's called, which displays the positions of ongoing games for the benefit of spectators. It's impossible when spectating at a chess tournament to see very much of what's happening on a board as you're at least ten feet away and at the same level as the players, so that's why display screens are used.

A red rope, supported by wooden posts, ring-fences the five top boards from the dozen or so rows of spectators' seats, most of which are occupied by now. There are about sixty boards but only the first five face spectators, so playing at one of the top boards is regarded as a privilege. After a few rounds the privilege has to be earned, because only the top-scoring players play there. But as we'd only played one round yesterday and there have been lots of winners, I'm playing on a display board for simple reasons of luck. Miklos will be there at a top five board because of his high ranking, though. Most of the boards are linked electronically to the Hastings event's website, so people can follow the games live on the internet.

By ten past two there's still no sign of Sven.

I scan the playing-hall for familiar faces. Big chess tournaments are like a moveable feast; we all just move around from one tournament to the other, and we can easily be in

East Sussex one month, then Gibraltar the next month and Edinburgh the month after that.

Most players are already at their tables, nervously fingering their pieces, writing the number of the round, their own name, and the name of their opponent on their score-sheets.

A moment later I spot The Three Vs coming into the playing-hall wearing his trademark jet-black cloak, just like the one the terrorist V wore in *V for Vendetta*.

Suddenly Miklos strides into the playing-hall.

He really is *striding*. Today, as always, he's wearing his dark suit. The players and spectators who are so foolish as to be standing in Miklos's way part like the Red Sea for Moses. As usual, Miklos is followed at a respectful distance by his manager, an American guy whose name I never remember but who has a little white beard and white hair, which altogether makes him look like Colonel Sanders, the former KFC man.

Miklos glances at me, then sits down on the White side of board one. He's still staring at me as he settles in his chair. I decide to force a smile back at him, teasingly flicking my hair out of my cleavage and leaning forwards. His face seems to go blank then, and his eyes lock on me even as his prospective victim - an American international master – sits down opposite him. Hearing his opponent clearing his throat, Miklos seems to snap out of whatever reminiscence he was having, then reaches decisively forwards to shake hands with the American.

I look away - and see Sven.

He's heading over towards our board at a fairly leisurely pace. His long arms and long legs and long yummy bod look all relaxed, as if he's coming to have a coffee with me rather than engage with me in mortal combat (on the chess board).

He reaches me.

'Hi, Ivana,' he murmurs. The softness and ultra-sexiness of his deep voice, enhanced by my own nervousness, make my toes tingle. I look him in the eyes for a moment, only for a moment, and I see yet again just how lovely he is.

Hi darling, I think. 'Hello, Sven,' I purr in return. Our legs brush under the table as he sits down opposite me. I can even feel Miklos' eyes on me again as I smile apologetically at Sven and slowly slide my legs away.

Sven is so close to me now I can detect the curiously attractive smell of his leather jacket, which he takes off and drapes over the back of his chair. I'm aware of a soapy just-washed scent about him; and something minty too, presumably he's only recently brushed his teeth.

I clear my throat, trying to calm down, and feeling glad that being able to read minds isn't something even sex gods have learned to do yet.

The spectators' seats are all completely full now.

I look hard at my pieces on the black side of the board. There they all are, waiting to leap into action at my touch. My sixteen friends: eight pawns, two knights, two bishops, two rooks, a queen and a king.

One of the many mind-blowing things about chess is that even after only about fifteen moves or so, almost every game is unique and has never been played before. And the number of possible games? With about thirty options in any position for either side each time that side has the move, and with most games lasting about thirty moves or more, the number of possible games is ultra-vast. Tom Hardiman says there are more possible games of chess than there are atoms in the observable universe. That's just the sort of weird fact he enjoys getting his head around.

I glance at the electronic clock, which is sitting, squat and grey, to my right and Sven's left. Sven and I, like all the players in the Hastings tournaments, each have two hours for forty moves. You don't need to make a move after any specific period of time; instead, you have a bank of time you can use as you please. But if you don't manage to make your forty moves in your two hours, you lose the game as surely as if you'd been checkmated.

For a few seconds Sven and I look hard at each other, then he extends his right hand towards me. I put mine out too, and we shake hands. How delightful that physical contact with him is.

I smile at Sven faintly, then our hands gently separate, mine very reluctantly.

He glances down at his pieces.

The lady tournament controller's firm, crisp voice, announcing the start of the round, is audible but somehow seems very far away as she says the magic words: *Please start White's clock.*

4

Sven presses the button in the middle of the clock. Instantly, the 2:00 on the digital counter on his side becomes 1:59. He stares intently at his pieces for a few moments, worry lines on his lovely forehead, then plays his first move, *pawn to king four*, moving the pawn in front of his king two squares forward. That was my fave first move back then too, when I was White.

Sven glances at me, I look back at him unflinchingly, and push my queen's bishop pawn forward one square, supporting the move pawn to queen four, which I plan to play next. The chess defence I most like, the 'Caro-Kann' as it's called, swings into action. This defence was invented by two nineteenth-century chess-players: Horatio Caro and Marcus Kann. I don't suppose either of them got out very much.

Our game starts to intensify. Now I'm completely in concentration mode myself, though I'm still totally aware of Sven's lovely face, minty smell, and gorgeous physical presence. A few times, as the game continues, we accidentally touch our shoes against each other's underneath the table. Each time, this feels utterly electric, at least to me.

Sven and I play on, launching attacks on opposite wings: mine on Sven's queenside, Sven on my kingside.

It's all a question of whose attack will force checkmate first. I'm so excited I can feel my heartbeat throbbing in my ears. My mouth's dry. I glance at Sven. He doesn't meet my glance; I suppose he's much too worried about his position. I see tiny beads of sweat on his forehead.

And then... suddenly I know *Sven's mine*, or rather... his king is. I see a forced checkmate in just two moves. There's no defence. I can checkmate him by sacrificing not another pawn, but my *queen*.

Even Miklos, having condescended to look up from his own game, is paying some brief attention to the demonstration screen that displays to the spectators the game Sven and I are playing.

I play the move I've spotted: *queen takes rook check*. I draw a breath. Sven looks at his position in dismay. There's not a trace of self-confidence in his expression now. I feel I've sucked all his manly strength from him. Sven takes my queen with his knight: he has no choice.

I'm Ivana the queen, and I've won.

I play rook takes knight, checkmate.

Game over.

Applause crackles out from some of the spectators. That's frowned on, forbidden really, but just for once the tournament controller, who's nearby, doesn't shoosh the audience.

Sven holds his hand out in my direction to indicate his resignation.

I stretch my own right hand across the table.

Sven's hand feels clammier than it did just before our game started.

I glance at our clocks. He's consumed twenty minutes, but I've only used twelve. The whole game took only just over half an hour, yet it was so exciting it only seemed to last about five minutes.

It was a quickie.

5

According to the regulations there at Hastings and at most tournaments, Sven and I have to sign each other's scoresheets. I tear off the little piece of paper at the foot of the scoresheet where I fill in our names and the result - *Sven Olsen 0: Ivana Jones 1*. His name's first because he was White.

I go over and drop this slip of paper into the results box – the bottom half of a clear, clean, plastic food container – on the controller's table. I glance back at Sven, who's still sitting, looking bewildered, at the chess-board. I smile at him, he glances back at me a trifle awkwardly, as men usually do when I beat them. A few moments later, Sven gets up and follows me out of the playing-hall. Once the door's shut behind us, I smile at Sven and, hoping he'll say yes so I can spend more time with him, I ask:

'Would you like to look over the game with me in the analysis room?'

'Ivana, that would be most pleasant, but I really should be getting back to my hotel. I have a piece to write for the magazine, you see.'

To hide my disappointment, I say quickly, 'Oh, what's it going to be about?'

'It'll be a personal report concerning the events of today.'

'What kind of things will you be saying?'

'I'm not entirely sure yet, but I like to make my tournament reports quite personal, so I think my article will begin something like... *Dette var den største kvelden i min sjakk karriere. Hvorfor? Fordi i runde to i Hastings Masters var jeg satt opp til å spille mot*

den legendariske og vakre Ivana Jones, og jeg var fast besluttet til å
sette hennes Caro+Kann på prøve.'

He grins. 'Sorry to tease you.'

I smile as beautifully as I can. 'No problem. But unfortunately my Norwegian's not too hot. Apart from "Oslo", "Abba" and "fjord" I'm in big trouble.'

'Actually, Abba are Swedish.'

'Sorry, I didn't know that. But what was it you just said in Norwegian?'

'That this was the biggest afternoon of my chess career, because I was drawn in Round Two of the Hastings Masters against the legendary, beautiful Ivana Jones, and I was planning to put her Caro-Kann to the test.'

'You're very kind.'

'Thank you. I failed the test, of course.'

'It's only a game, you know,' I point out, quickly.

'That's what chess-players like to think when they lose. If they say it when they win they never mean it. Well, goodbye, Ivana.' He reaches out his lovely pale right hand, and I shake it. 'Good luck in Round Three.'

'You too,' I tell him. Chess tournaments aren't usually knock-outs like Wimbledon; every contestant in the main Hastings tournament who stays to the end plays the full nine rounds. The pairing method is known as the 'Swiss' system, where you play an opponent who has the same score as you, or close to it. So in Round Three I'll play someone who's also won their first two games.

'See you around, Sven.'

'See you, Ivana.'

He smiles, turns, and heads toward the exit.

I turn down the corridor to return to the playing-hall so I can see how my very best chess chum, Jasmine (though I usually call her Jaz) Duval is getting on in her game. Just before

I open the door that leads into the playing-hall, I glance back at Sven, to see if by any chance he's turned round to glance at me.

He hasn't, but I can't help hoping he already did and that I didn't notice.

6

Coke.

Not the type you get from drinks dispensers or which is made from coal. The other kind.

That was what Jaz's eighteen-year-old brother Desmond used to sell for a living seven years ago, when Jaz was just fifteen. Or at least he did until, one May night, a couple of spaced-out junkies he was visiting down a lane near a garage in Camberwell didn't have any money. So instead of paying him they took turns stabbing him with their knives, left him bleeding to death, then had a big binge on the cocaine he'd brought with him.

Desmond was found dead the next morning by a guy out walking a dog. The two junkies had fled, but were found, spaced out on coke, in a bedsit close by. They still had their knives, with his blood on them, tucked into their trouser belts. Talk about smart. They're both serving life sentences at Gartree Prison in Leicestershire.

'Desmond being murdered almost destroyed my family,' Jaz had told me. 'After his death, Mum just used to sit on the sofa, staring blankly ahead as if she was seeing the murder actually happening over and over in her mind. Then my younger brother Brandon started playing truant and got arrested a few times, but fortunately I managed to sort him out and persuede him to go back to school. I think I'd have gone off the rails myself, but I was lucky.'

'Yes,' I'd said, 'you got into chess.'

Jaz and I had had this particular chat over a cosy Chinese buffet supper in London's Chinatown, only a month or so after we first met, which was about five years before that day in Hastings when I first met Sven. I have an especially vivid memory of that supper with Jaz, despite the distance of time since it took place. I'd left uni the previous summer, having scraped a Second in my law degree. At the time I still harboured notions of going to law school and combining playing chess with being a solicitor, but I never actually went to law school; I just focused on chess.

I'd given Jaz several lessons by then. We were getting to know each other better, but she was still calling me 'Ivana' rather than 'Vanny'. Over our cheap and cheerful Chinese supper that evening I asked Jaz how she got into chess.

'A few weeks after the murder,' Jaz said, 'I was wandering around Brixton, still in a total daze, when I came across a couple of old black guys playing a game of chess on a bench in a small park. It was one of those awful little parks you get in parts of London, all graffiti and empty beer cans and dogshit and a few bits of dirty grass. I remember their names, Sonny and Charlie. They lived in a lodging-house nearby. They didn't have jobs, so they used to come to the park and play chess.'

Jaz fell silent for a moment, her eyes full of something big, inexplicable, kind of mystical.

'And I just watched them, Ivana, and after a while one of them asked me if I knew how to play chess, and I said no, but I'd like to learn, and they taught me. And every day for about a fortnight, including the weekend in the middle, I went back there and played chess with them. I told them everything, too, how my elder brother had been killed and how his murderers had been caught and were going to be tried. I told Sonny and Charlie all about it and about other things they managed to get out of me, such as how I'd been studying for my GCSEs, but had stopped going to school after Desmond's murder. Oh, Ivana, they were *so* cross with me about that.'

'They were?'

'Yes. They were furious with me, but... in a sort of friendly, caring kind of way. Sonny said "education's the most important thing there is." "Yes," Charlie agreed, "but chess... it's pretty important too."'

Jaz drew a quick breath. 'I didn't forget their advice. I went back to school and caught up, and every Saturday I used to go to the park and play chess with them, and then I joined a chess club in Brixton, and I found I just kept getting better at the game, and about nine months later I got spotted by an ECF selector at a blitz tournament in Streatham, and she said she'd find me a coach.'

I smiled. 'And that's when you came to my attention.'

When I met Jaz, she was still at school and living at home in Brixton, and I was living in a ground-floor flat in Churchill Gardens, sharing it with Charlotte Richmond (Lottie), who was my best friend of all. The third person in the flat was a viola player friend of Lottie's called Annabelle. Lottie was trying to make a mark as a pianist, though she earned most of her money from organising chamber music concerts - she seemed to be on her mobile phone most of the time. Her dad Sir Rupert Richmond - a zillionaire industrialist - had bought the flat for her, though Lottie paid rent and of course Annabelle and I both paid Lottie.

By the time of that Hastings tournament last winter where I met Sven, Jaz was twenty-two and living at the flat on Churchill Gardens with Lottie and me. Annabelle had moved out about a year earlier so she could live with her boyfriend in Baron's Court.

Jaz wasn't a professional player yet, but she was on her way. She already had one international master norm, which she'd got at a tournament in Munich, so she just needed two more to win the title. For the time being she had a day job in the sales department of Chess and Bridge, which publishes the magazine *Chess*, the most popular chess magazine in the UK. Jaz liked her job, as it at least meant she could earn a living in the chess world she adored, though she'd much rather have been working as a chess-player full-time.

When I got to Jaz's board that day at Hastings after beating Sven, I saw that Jaz was doing seriously well as White against her own Round Two opponent. Jaz was playing White, and her opponent - an almost bald, stocky middle-aged bloke with glasses and some serious stubble (he looked more like an all-in wrestler than a chess-player) - was looking stunned and completely dismayed at being totally outplayed by:

- a girl
- a *black* girl
- a King's Gambit he'd obviously accepted. Like Tom Hardiman, Jaz loves playing the King's Gambit when she's White. It's a swashbuckling, incredibly aggressive opening.

A few moments later, Jaz's opponent resigned. As he shook her hand, he had that unmistakable, castrated, look men usually have when we girls beat them. Or I should say, as most men do, because Sven had been different: he'd looked somehow noble in defeat.

It was clear that Jaz's crestfallen opponent wasn't going to be in the mood for going over the game with her: we call this a *post mortem* in the chess world. Jaz, sensing this - she's a kind and sensitive girl - didn't ask him. He whispered a quick thanks to Jaz for the game, then slunk off, and if he'd had a tail it would certainly have been between his legs.

Jaz gave me a terrific and winning smile: her beautiful brown face and her big, deep brown eyes lighting up. She stepped away from the neighbouring boards and moved into the aisle, where I was standing.

'I saw your game, Vanny,' she whispered breathlessly. 'It was just *so* fantastic. I've always dreamed of winning with a queen sacrifice like that.'

'Thanks,' I whispered back. We shared smiles with each other. Jaz and I love each other tons as friends. We'd both won so we were doubly happy.

7

Jaz and I were both staying at the Imperial Hotel on the seafront. Like most of the hotels in Hastings, it's seen better days. Yet its rather pretentious posh decrepitude has a certain appeal to it, with the downstairs rooms being quite high-ceilinged and spacious and the bedrooms also posh in a dated sort of way. My hotel expenses were being paid by the ECF (the English Chess Federation), so I had my own sea-view room at the hotel. Jaz only got a small contribution from the ECF towards her expenses, so she was sharing a twin room with a girl called Danuta, one of three young Lithuanian chess-playing women - all reputedly lesbians, though Jaz had reported no attempts on her person so far - playing in the Masters. To be honest, I'd sometimes wondered a bit if I might be a little susceptible to liking women myself; at school at night I sometimes used to think about cuddling and kissing Lottie, but anyway... it wasn't something I really thought about any more.

A few minutes later, when Jaz and I stepped out of the playing-hall into the cold, overcast afternoon that our victorious hearts were immune to, I heard a man's voice from behind me calling, 'Ivana Jones?'

His English was fluent, but the voice had an unmistakable Russian accent. I turned round.

There was a clean-shaven man standing about ten yards away. I supposed he was about forty. He was wearing a black, very well-tailored and expensive-looking overcoat that had two strips of sleek black real or artificial fur at the collars. His hair was dark brown. On his head he wore a dark brown fur hat, like the one Lee Marvin wears in the old movie *Gorky Park*, which I'd seen with Tom on his DVD player and which was one of our favourite films. I wondered whether the hat was made of sable too.

The man was handsome, and looked sleek and prosperous, yet somehow not in an unpleasant way. I noticed that his eyes - I was too far away to see their colour - had, even at that distance, a piercing sort of look, as if he knew all there was to know about me. Around his neck he wore a white scarf - of silk, I thought - and his trousers were jet-black, like his shoes.

'Yes,' I said. 'I'm Ivana Jones.'

He smiled, revealing gleaming white, even teeth, then took a couple of long strides toward Jaz and me. Now I saw that his eyes were dark blue.

He stuck out his right hand toward me. I shook it with mine. His hand was dry, his handshake firm and decisive. He glanced at Jaz, and shook her hand too, before again turning to me.

'I saw your game today,' he said, in the same fluent Russian-accented English. 'Your queen sacrifice was inspired, and unforgettable, Miss Jones.'

'Thank you,' I replied, then politely added: 'Are you playing in any of the events?'

'Alas, no. My business interests leave me no time for participating in rather long tournaments such as this. Besides, I am not a particularly strong player. My international rating is barely 1800. I am afraid, against you and your talented friend, I would have no chance at all.'

'I see,' I said, briskly.

I quite often get people I don't know approaching me, and not just people from the chess world, either. I find it best to be polite to them, but not over-friendly. As for ratings, well, being 1800 doesn't mean that you're the 1800th best player in the world and that the person with a rating of 1 is the best. That's how things work in tennis, not chess. No: in chess, the higher your rating the better a player you are. So the world champion would be about 2850, a very strong grandmaster around 2600, a normal grandmaster 2500 or so, an international master like me approximately 2400, and a strong player from a local club maybe 2000. So 1800 is the rating of someone who can play a decent game, but isn't ever likely to have a chance of even scraping a draw against a professional unless the professional were to make some terrible mistake.

'Perhaps I might introduce myself?' the man asked. 'My name is Boris Bogolyubov. As you may know, the Russian for "God" is *Bog*, and my name means "one who loves God".'

'I see,' I said. 'Well, it's good to meet you, Mr Bo-gol-you-bov.' He looked surprised I could pronounce his surname properly, but in the chess world you need to be able to pronounce foreign names. 'Now, my friend and I are heading back to our hotel, so we'd like to...'

'I quite understand,' Boris Bogolyubov returned. 'Of course, you will want to relax after your games, and celebrate. Please, I do not wish to intrude.' He looked hard at me for a moment. 'Miss Jones, I have a letter for you, and I think... indeed I hope... you may find it of interest. All I ask, please, is that you do not open it here, but only when you are back wherever you are going. That really is all I request.'

'What's in the letter?' Jaz demanded, with lovable solidarity. 'Nothing embarrassing for Ivana, I hope?'

'No, of course not. I assure you both, I am a gentleman.'

Having said this, he reached into the left inner pocket of his overcoat, drew out an ordinary white DL envelope, then handed the envelope to me. On the front of it, in a rather gorgeous flowing dark blue script, there was written

Ivana Jones, International Chess Master

I glanced at Jaz, who shrugged. Then I looked back at the envelope.

'All right,' I said to him. 'I'll take it. Thank you.'

'It is I who should thank you for accepting it,' he said.

He certainly was a gentleman. He gave each of us a little bow, first me, then Jaz. Then he said, 'I wish you both a most pleasant evening.'

'Thank you, Mr Bogolyubov,' I replied.

He started heading towards the sports centre, and Jaz and I began walking down the path that led away from the venue.

'Open the envelope,' said Jaz, in a hissed whisper, once we were some distance away.

'Jaz, I'm dying to, but... let's go back to my room at the hotel, and open it there.'

8

The moment we reach the reception of the Imperial Hotel, we dash up to my room. I quickly take my coat off and throw it onto the bed. Jaz doesn't even bother to remove her jacket, but sits down on the long edge of my bed, looking intently up at me.

Grabbing a blue ball-point pen from the desk, I use the sharp end of the pen to slit the letter open.

There are three pieces of paper inside. Two of the pieces of paper, stapled together, are obviously a letter, written in the same lovely flowing dark blue handwriting, with the salutation 'Dear Miss Jones' on the front.

But I don't start reading the letter at once.

Why not? Well, because in the envelope there's another piece of paper.

It's about the size of a banknote.

Except it isn't a banknote.

I hold it up in front of me and look at it for a moment. Jaz can't see what it says because she's behind it. I stare at this other piece of paper in total amazement, then, breathlessly, I glance at Jaz over the top.

'What *is* it, Vanny?'

I say nothing. I can hardly breathe. I go and sit next to Jaz on the bed. She budges up a bit to give me room. Still not saying anything, I glance at her and hand her the third piece of paper.

She just looks at it.

'*Oh, my God,*' she murmurs.

The third piece of paper in the envelope is a cheque drawn on the Russian Fiduciary Bank.

The cheque is for one million US dollars.

It's payable to 'Ivana Jones'.

Me.

9

'Vanny, it can't be real, can it?'

'No, I'm sure it isn't.'

'He must be a madman.'

I nod sadly. 'Yes, I suppose so.'

'What... what does the letter say?'

Jaz still has the cheque in her hand and doesn't seem to want to put it down anywhere, for all her conviction that it isn't real.

I pick up the letter and start reading it aloud to her.

The Royal Suite
The Royal Victoria Hotel
St Leonards-on-Sea

My dear Miss Jones

Late in the afternoon of a cold day in November, about six weeks ago, I found myself in a hotel during a business trip to the beautiful city of Ljubljana, capital of Slovenia, with the entire evening in front of me. In an idle moment of leisure while deciding how to spend the evening, I flicked on the television. But I could find nothing worth watching, and was about to turn off what I believe is known by some as the goggle-box, when suddenly the commercials came on.

There you were. Of course, I did not realise it was you at that moment. I merely saw a woman of preternatural beauty and charm.

'What's peter natural mean?' asks Jaz.

'It's preternatural, actually. I don't know exactly but I suppose it means extraordinary, or something like that.'

'I think he ate a dictionary for lunch. Anyway. Go on, Vanny.'

You were promoting a brand of face cream to which the manufacturers, acting on the assumption that when selling to a non-Anglophone audience it is legitimate to commit any degree of mutilation upon the English language, gave the name 'Softy-Softy'.

My dear Miss Jones, I have been a complete and devoted admirer of yours since that moment in my hotel room in Ljubljana six weeks ago.

I am a single man. I have no existing romantic attachments, and no 'baggage', to use that cumbersome and infelicitous expression. A man in my position is inundated with offers from beautiful women of their persons and destinies, but I assure you, and I lay my hand on my heart as I say this, that I do not have the slightest interest in any other lady than you.

I am an ardent fan of chess, even though I only have a very limited ability at playing it. Perhaps I could become a better player if I had the time, but my business interests - which include oil, aluminium and steel, the ownership of one of your leading British banks and a Finnish healthcare innovations company - allow me little time for relaxation.

I am, however, proud that I have the same surname as one of the best Russian players of the early part of the twentieth century!

Now... to the point of this letter.

Miss Jones, I would like to ask you, with ardour, passion and sincerity, to become my wife.

I am thirty-six years old. I have never been married, nor do I have any children. It is true that I am somewhat older than you, but I am young in heart and indeed I think my entire outlook on the world has remained suffused with youthful optimism.

If you would accept my offer to become my wife you would want for nothing that love, my warm heart and my prosperity could offer you.

I glance over at Jaz, give a shrug, but say nothing.

'Vanny, that's terribly romantic, isn't it?'

'Well... yes, I suppose it is. And his English is very good.'

Jaz nods. 'It's marvellous. Unless, of course, someone helped him write it. But that would be pretty creepy, so let's hope no-one did.'

'I agree,' I say.

'Go on.'

By way of providing a small token of my sincerity, genuineness and earnestness, I am enclosing, as you will see, a check with this letter. It constitutes a gift that is entirely unconditional and which I merely offer to show you the sincerity of my feelings.

The check is for you, to spend as you wish and to enjoy as you choose.

If I never hear back from you, I shall at least have the gratification and pleasure of knowing that I have helped you to pursue your career, perhaps in greater comfort than you would otherwise have been able to pursue it.

But should you wish to contact me, my dear Miss Jones, should I be that fortunate, I append my mobile telephone number below. I shall be remaining here in Sussex for the forthcoming week. I shall sometimes be visiting London on business, but my address is the Royal Victoria Hotel in St Leonards-on-Sea. I hope to pay some further visits to the tournament.

Please rest assured that, having expressed my feelings and my proposal to you in this letter which I intend to give to you, I shall under no circumstances embarrass you by coming to see you thereafter unless you expressly first speak to me.

With fondest affection

Boris Niklovitch Bogolyubov

10

'*Bloody hell,*' gasps Tom Hardiman.

He puts Boris Bogolyubov's letter down and glances across the table at me. I'm sitting next to Jaz, and opposite Tom, at the Golden Pagoda, our favourite Chinese restaurant in Hastings.

Tom, Jaz and I adore Chinese food. If we were suddenly all simultaneously to die and, due to a clerical error in St Peter's office, made it to heaven and the waiter came round to take our orders for dinner, we'd skip the manna and nectar. Instead we'd go for e.g. sweet and sour chicken, duck with black bean sauce, fried seaweed, special fried rice and banana fritters.

'*Bloody hell,*' Tom gasps, again.

'How very articulate you're being,' I tell him.

'*But… but… Boris Bogolyubov's proposed to you and given you a cheque for a million dollars.*'

'Goodness me,' I say, 'I'd never have guessed if you hadn't told me.'

'But Vanny, it's *Boris Bogolyubov,*' says Tom with an even bigger emphasis.

I frown at Tom. 'You sound as if you know him.'

'Know Boris Bogolyubov?' Tom echoes. 'Of course I don't *know* the guy. But I've heard of him. Haven't you?'

I shake my head. 'Not until this happened, no.'

Tom leans over the snow-white tablecloth toward me. We haven't ordered yet, so the cutlery and place-settings are all clean and neat, ready for action. 'I googled Boris Bogolyubov after you phoned me in my room,' Tom goes on, 'in an even more hyper state than you usually are, to tell me about the letter. Boris made most of his money from oil and aluminium, or *a-loo-min-um* as our friends across the Pond say. He's one of Russia's youngest oligarchs.'

'Olly what?' Jaz asks.

'It's a name used for Russian billionaires,' replies Tom, 'who managed to grab hold of a big chunk of Russia's national assets. Vanny, I think you should take the cheque off the table and put it away before it gets covered in soy sauce.'

Suddenly feeling flustered, I take hold of the cheque, fold it and slip it away in my purse.

I look at Tom and then at Jaz. 'Why has he chosen *me*?'

'Because you're beautiful and wonderful,' says Jaz.

'I'm serious, Jaz.'

'It's the truth,' she says.

'We can, of course,' Tom puts in, 'assume he doesn't know about your little fetish.'

'Which one?'

Tom smiles faintly. 'Yes, fair point. I mean the small problem that you only want to shag guys if they can beat you at chess.'

'Oh, do say it a bit louder, please,' I tell him. 'I think there might be some people over there on the far side of the restaurant who didn't quite hear you.'

'Not that that's going to put Boris off, anyway,' says Jaz, thoughtfully, and keeping *her* voice down.

Tom nods. 'Definitely not,' he says, but lowering his own voice this time. 'A guy like that, rich enough to do absolutely anything he wants to do... and used to having people running around to obey his every whim, he'd most likely just see your strange little quirk as a challenge. The important question is, what are you going to do?'

'I'm not going to do anything. Listen, I don't love him, for Bog's sake!'

'Bog's sake?' says Tom. 'What are you on about?'

'*Bog* is Russian for God,' Jaz explains. She turns to me. 'You must admit, girls don't get proposals like this every day. Especially not chess-playing girls.'

'I wish,' Tom adds, 'some billionaire woman would propose to *me* and send me a cheque for a million dollars which I don't even need to give back if I don't want to marry her.'

'Tom does have a point,' says Jaz. 'At least you can keep the money, even if you say no to Boris's proposal.'

'I'm *not* going to keep the money whatever I decide. Who do you think I am?'

'Vanny,' Jaz says, '*pleeeeease* don't do anything rash. It's a... it's a *fortune*. It would solve your financial problems for ever. You could do tons of things with it. He doesn't even insist that you marry him. It's a fortune,' she repeats in a wistful tone.

'Maybe just tell him the truth,' says Tom. 'Tell him about the thing you have with men.' Tom smiles with an evil glint in his eye. He can look like a bit of a piratical romantic rogue when he smiles, Jack Sparrow without the silly outfit and the bad teeth. 'Tell him that the only way to win your heart - temporarily at least - is to beat you at chess.' Tom pauses for a moment, then gives a shrug. 'Alternatively, maybe the best thing to do would be to get therapy for your... problem, and then at least you could make a kind of normal sort of decision about whether or not to marry him... or somebody else.'

'*I'm* being told to get therapy by a guy who has a six-foot orc in his bedroom and calls his two pet goldfish Frodo and Gandalf?'

Tom gives an embarrassed shrug. 'OK, fair dos.'

'Where did Boris Bogolyubov learn to write English like that, anyway?' asks Jaz.

'Boris Bogolyubov's not just a rich bastard,' explains Tom quietly, 'but a brainy bastard too. He has a degree in English from Moscow University, then he did a PhD - his subject was Shakespeare's sonnets - at Babbage College, Cambridge. According to Wiki, he lectures after that for a couple of years in English at Moscow University, then suddenly gives it all up and goes to work in Siberia, selling oil futures. Obviously he decided making money was more fun than teaching literature. Anyhow, that's how his business career started.'

'He does sound rather interesting, doesn't he?' Jaz puts in, more loudly than she probably intended.

Not for the first time, I can't help thinking she wishes the letter had been addressed to *her*.

11

It was past nine o'clock by the time we left the restaurant. I offered to pay the bill, but Jaz and Tom insisted on paying for themselves. 'We don't just love you for your money, Vanny,' Tom said, with a grin.

Once we'd paid, we all went back to Tom's room, two floors above mine at the Imperial Hotel, and started playing five-minute chess (that is, each player has just five minutes on their clock for the whole game; it's frantic fun), with the loser giving up their place to the next person. Tom won most of the games, though I won some too.

Later, around ten thirty I suppose, I excused myself and said I'd go back to my room, to chill out a bit.

'Jaz, you're playing really well. See if you can beat Tom. You would have done just now if you hadn't forgotten about the back-rank checkmate.'

'Yes,' said Jaz, 'that's a problem I often have, and not just on the chess-board. Vanny, what are you doing to do about the cheque?'

'I haven't decided yet.'

'For God's sake, don't do anything hasty,' said Jaz.

'Oh, he won't mind,' I said. '*He'll* want me to keep it.'

'What?' Jaz asked.

I smiled. 'Jaz darling, leave Dad out of it.'

My father Godfrey likes to be called God and calls himself that.

'Ha ha. Well, at least sleep on it, anyway,' Jaz suggested.

'Yes, I definitely recommend that,' put in Tom. 'It'd be a good way of keeping the cheque safe.'

'He's got a point, Vanny,' said Jaz. 'You could put it under your pillow.'

'I remember reading somewhere that that's what lottery winners are advised to do with their jackpot-winning tickets,' Tom said.

'Actually,' I smiled, 'I might just do that.'

I said goodnight and left them both still playing.

The list of Round Two results, and the pairings for Round Three, was already up on the website for the Hastings tournament. Miklos headed a list of (I counted) fifteen people – including Tom and me – who had a maximum two points out of two, meaning two wins. Miklos was scheduled to play the Cornish international master Andrew Greet in the next round. Andrew (known to his friends familiarly as 'Greetings') has a reputation for giant-killing, which I really hoped he'd put into practice against Miklos.

Jaz, with one and half points so far, faced a tough third-round pairing, Black against Mark Hebden, who had two out of two. But because there was an odd number of people with that score, someone had to be floated down to play someone with one and a half, and that person was Mark.

I'd been paired in Round Three against the Polish international master Wladek Kruza. His rating, at 2460, was a bit higher than mine, but at the last Gibraltar tournament, the only time I'd played him before, I beat him. Having beaten someone who's never beaten you always scares them. Also, I was going to be White, and when I won against him in Gib I was Black.

Sven had been drawn against a Hastings junior, who'd also lost one game, and whose rating was some way below his. I was sure Sven would have a decent chance of winning.

I lay back on the bed and thought about Sven and about the mysterious Boris Bogolyubov. What was the deal with Boris, anyway? Did he really think I could be *bought*?

I had a bath, with lots of my favourite lavender bath oil in the water. As I was having the bath I decided on a plan.

After the bath I got nice and comfy and dry, then went to bed, thinking of Sven until I fell asleep.

12

I assemble a Cool but Assertive outfit for my mission: skinny blue jeans, grey suede knee-high boots, and a navy-blue overcoat with gold-coloured buttons. After a bit of thought I also choose a nice slouchy dark green felt hat.

The Royal Victoria Hotel turns out to be, as I suppose the name suggests, an old-fashioned-looking place with an impressive stone front and a vintage, seriously posh revolving door made of some polished brown wood. At around eight fifteen that morning, I go in through the revolving door, taking care not to get brain damage as I do, and say to the lady behind the reception desk, 'I'd like to see Mr Bogolyubov, please, if he's available.' She nods and politely asks me to wait there in the lobby. I sit down on a nearby armchair, next to a low wooden table that has a copy of the *Daily Telegraph, The Times, Financial Times* and *Daily Mail* on it, and also a copy of *Country Life*. Erk. I hear the lady speaking very quietly into the phone, but I can't make out exactly what she says.

A few minutes pass. I'm about to pick up one of the four newspapers and have a read when a double door at the far end of the reception area opens and Boris Bogolyubov steps through the lobby.

He's wearing an obviously expensive black suit and carrying his dark black overcoat in one hand. He has on a sky-blue silk tie and a white shirt. His shoes are black and polished to a shine.

Walking next to him is an absolutely ginormous man who must be at least nine inches taller than Boris B, and Boris B is himself certainly at least six feet tall. This other man's shoulders look close to three feet wide. This much bigger man's suit's grey and he's carrying, not an overcoat, but a brown briefcase. He has very short fair hair and a stocky face with darting, unfriendly, eyes. He's frowning as he comes through the doorway, and he goes on frowning after setting eyes on me.

The bodyguard, maybe? After all, I think we've established that Boris B. is heterosexual.

In contrast to the huge man, the moment Boris B. sets eyes on me, he smiles a friendly, white-teethed smile at me.

'Miss Jones,' he says, heading toward me. He speaks the words with an emphasis that sounds entirely sincere and warm-hearted. 'Thank you so much for coming. In truth, though, had you taken refuge behind an email or a phone call, I would have been disappointed.'

'Really?'

'Yes. I can tell you are a woman of spirit. I was expecting you would come in person, and you have.'

The huge man lags behind. Boris B. and I shake hands. Keeping my voice down, I say, 'Mr Bogolyubov, could we have a word in private?'

He nods. 'Yes, yes, of course. Let me think where.' A moment later he says, 'I have an idea. Will you follow me, please?'

Before I can reply, he turns to the huge man and says something to him in, presumably, Russian. I wish I knew what it was. The huge man replies *'Da, da,'* in a harsh yet respectful voice, and goes to sit down in chair close by a grandfather clock.

Boris B. turns around smartly. 'Please, Miss Jones, this way. We will not have much time, alas, as I have a meeting at half past nine in the City of London.'

'*Half past nine?*' I glance at the time on the nearby grandfather clock rather than take my mobile (which I had put on silent) out of my pocket. It's twenty-two minutes past eight. I know that Hastings is about sixty miles from London. 'Do you drive a jet-propelled car, Mr Bogolyubov?'

'Not exactly, no.' He pushes open the double doors he'd come in, then stands back to let me past. We're now in a luxurious wood-panelled corridor. We walk down it for ten yards or so, then arrive at a door he opens. This leads out to a courtyard containing a pond with a little island in the middle featuring a grey stone statue of Pan playing his pipes.

We walk out into a big car-park which has several large shiny posh black cars in it. I also notice that at the back of the car-park, on the edge of a grass field, there's a big bright red helicopter.

Boris B. points out towards the car-park. 'We can talk in there, if you like.'

'Where? In one of the cars in front of the helicopter?'

'*In* the helicopter.'

I glance at him. 'I'm sorry, but I'm not getting into a helicopter with you.'

'Why not? It is private, and very peaceful, as long as the engine is not switched on.'

'What if you do switch it on and try to abduct me?'

He looks at me calmly and confidently. 'Miss Jones, I asked you to marry me. I assure you that I have not the slightest desire to try to win your heart, so to speak, by compulsion. However, I have a little time before I must leave for London with Alexander.' *Yes, the bodyguard*, I think. 'You and I can talk, in the helicopter, in private,' Boris B adds.

'OK, I'm happy to do that. You can call me Ivana, by the way.'

'Thank you.'

'But I'm not going with you to London.'

'Ivana, there really is no question of me thinking you would wish to do so.'

'And anyway, if you take time to talk to me, how can you possibly expect to get to London for nine thirty, even in the helicopter?'

'Well, this particular craft cruises at an airspeed of 186 knots, and the weather on the route north to London from here is good. I checked with Heathrow Air Traffic Control a short while ago. It is true I may arrive a little later than scheduled, but my bankers are unlikely to complain.'

'Why won't they?'

He gives a casual shrug. 'Because I own their bank.'

'Oh. Oh, I see. And Alexander... he's your bodyguard, I suppose?'

'*Da.* Yes.'

'He looks terrifying.'

'Oh, Alexander is all right. It is true that if anyone had malicious designs upon my person they would find him a most formidable adversary, but otherwise... his bark is worse than his bite, as you English say.'

'You speak English very well.'

'Thank you. I have had a love affair with the English language ever since my teenage years. Tell me, do you know the sonnet that begins *Shall I compare thee to a summer's day?*'

'I don't know the whole sonnet but I've heard that line, yes.'

'What about the one that starts *Let me not to the marriage of true minds admit impediments?*'

'I don't know that one, Mr Bogolyubov.'

'It is, I think, my favourite. Perhaps one day I shall recite it to you, though not this morning. But will you please call me Boris? I much prefer that.'

I nodded. 'All right. Thank you, Boris.'

He leads me to the helicopter, goes round to the far side, gets in, leans across, opens the other front door and beckons me inside, up two metal steps, and to the seat on the left next to his pilot seat on the right. There are three other rows of seats, each with two adjacent places, all empty.

As I sit there with Boris on my right, I'm careful not to put my hand on the gleaming polished trimmings - made of walnut wood, I think - in case I leave a hand-print. My hands are clean, but all the same, even the idea of touching those fittings seems completely socially unacceptable. Boris, on the other hand, looks very much at home in the beautiful, soft beige leather upholstered seat. His expensive lemony aftershave goes rather well with the lovely, luxurious smell of new leather.

So there we are, sitting next to each other in his helicopter.

I look at the various dials on the control panel in front of him. I don't understand any of them, really, except perhaps for a dial with a horizontal line in the middle. I suppose that's what you look at, when you're airborne, to keep the helicopter, you know, straight.

Ivana Jones, helicopter flying expert.

I look straight ahead at the car-park for some moments in silence, then turn to my right and look intently at my suitor.

'Boris... how can I marry you?' I ask. 'I don't even know you.'

'That is true, of course. But... we could get to know each other.'

'Well, yes, I suppose we could. But... really, can't you see that writing such a letter to me to propose to me was... well, a rather strange thing to do?'

'I accept that it must have seemed so. In this age of mobile phones and emails, physical letters are usually either junk mail, utility bills, or requests for money from charities.'

'Speaking of money,' I say, 'the cheque was a very strange gift, too, and not *at all* appropriate.'

'I'm sorry you see it like that. I merely want to be of assistance. I'm aware that the life of a chess professional can be financially difficult, because the world, in its stupidity, does not value chess as highly as it should. If you were, for example, a pop singer or a super-model - and you are certainly more than beautiful enough to be either - my gift would not seem so disproportionate. In any case, it only amounts to about one week's earnings for the totality of my business interests. So you really do not need to feel under any obligation to me. I did my utmost to make that clear in the letter, to endeavour to remove any possibility that you would feel awkward about accepting the money.'

'I know you did. But I'm sorry, Boris, I can't keep the cheque. I have it in my purse, and I'd like to give it back to you.'

'Ivana, please keep it. If you don't wish to enjoy the money, you are obviously free to destroy the cheque or... I suppose you could refrain from banking it and could pin it to your kitchen wall as an amusing memento. But please, don't give it back to me. Now, tell me... would you like to take a short flight around Hastings bay?'

'What, *now?*'

'Yes. But if flying in this craft would make you feel uncomfortable, I apologise for suggesting the idea.'

I have a quick think. How often do I get a chance to fly in a helicopter with a Russian billionaire?

Partly to stall for time, I say: 'But you have to go to London?'

'Indeed, but as I say, they will wait for me. I only suggest a short trip. I know you have an important game today, and that you will want to prepare for it.'

'Yes, I do.'

'Then let's say no more than ten minutes?'

'Well... all right, yes, but... so you can fly the helicopter yourself?'

'My dear Ivana, of course. Why else would I suggest a flight? I have been a trained helicopter pilot for more than twelve years. I am licensed for most kinds of helicopter. I also have licenses to fly several types of fixed-wing aircraft, including the Boeing 737.'

He suddenly looks harder at me. 'Is there a reason why you can't contemplate marrying me? Do you have a boyfriend, for example?'

I shake my head. 'No,' I murmur.

This isn't a lie. After all, Tom Hardiman was my Friend with Benefits, not my boyfriend.

Boris nods. 'I see. Well, do you think I am physically unattractive?'

I smile faintly. 'No.'

'Well, that is good to know,' says Boris.

I make no reply.

'So shall we fly?'

I can't help liking the way he phrases the question.

I nod. 'OK.'

He smiles, takes some jangling keys on a key-ring out of his pocket, sticks one into a little switch in the dash-board that's like the ignition switch of a car, and turns it.

At once I hear the sound of an engine starting up overhead. In a few brief moments the noise has become very loud indeed.

Boris turns and smiles at me, for all the world like a little boy proudly showing me the toy he'd just got for his birthday or for Christmas (which in my own case, as you know, are pretty much the same thing).

I've never flown in a helicopter before. I always vaguely imagined that inside a helicopter cabin there'd be a fairly gentle humming sound. I didn't expect this appalling din.

Boris takes a pair of headphones from a hook on the back of the door to his right and hands them to me. I put the headphones on. I'm grateful for them right away, because they immediately muffle the roaring noise.

Boris grabs a pair of headphones for himself from another hook on the back of the door, and puts them on, then fixes first my seat-belt and then his. He reaches over me (I've realised by now that being in a helicopter with someone is even more intimate than playing chess with them) and he makes sure my door is properly shut.

He checks his own door too, then sits up and takes hold of a lever with his left hand that's on his left and my right, in the place in the helicopter where you'd expect a car's hand-brake to be. He moves his hand up to what looks like a red throttle at the end of the lever, the kind of throttle you can turn. As he turns it, the engine noise becomes even louder, even with the headphones on. But then he starts to speak to me, and I can hear him well through the headphones.

'Cloud cover this morning is at around two thousand three hundred feet, so we'll stay at two thousand. Hang on to your breakfast, Ivana!'

Boris puts his feet on two pedals that I only now notice on the floor. Then, taking hold of another handle that's in front of him, a sort of curvy one, he gives the lever on his left a gentle lift.

I'm expecting the helicopter to start rising slowly, but that's not what happens at all. Instead, I get the feeling I'm in an elevator that's gone psycho. The helicopter shoots up so fast that almost at once we're looking down on the Royal Victoria Hotel as if it were an increasingly small hotel in a model of a village.

'Feeling OK?' Boris asks politely through the headphones.

'Yes, this is *great.*'

It is, too. Great, but scary. I mean, it certainly doesn't feel like being in a plane. Sometimes in a jet airliner you're hardly aware of being airborne at all, especially if it's dark outside and you're having dinner and watching a movie or playing through some chess game on your iPad or on a magnetic set. But really this is like proper flying: sort of like being on a magic carpet that's just got him and me on it.

We gain more height. I watch the circular dials on the dashboard and notice how the one I'd seen before, the one with the line in the middle, moves gently up and down around the horizontal. There's another dial that has hands like a clock's that are going round too fast and a digital display in the middle with numbers that keep going up and up. It occurs to me that this must be giving the altitude.

To my amazement, after only about twenty seconds we're more than a thousand feet up. Now Boris adjusts the curvy lever. The helicopter, which has been going forward only very slowly as it went up, lurches powerfully into fast forward motion. We go on gaining height. Maybe just half a minute later we're up to fourteen hundred feet. I look out of the window. Far below I can see the promenade, the pier, St Leonard's and Hastings, as well as the great wintry expanse of sea that vanishes to the horizon.

For the next ten minutes or so - I suppose it's about ten minutes, anyway, but somehow it's hard to gauge time up here - Boris takes me on an amazing trip high above the sea and the towns, an experience that somehow makes me think I'm temporarily a soaring goddess blessed with the power of flight. By now I'm scarcely aware of the din of the engine, just of the excitement of being up there. We climb higher, above two thousand feet, and now there are wispy clouds around us, but Boris soon levels out and the clouds stay above us.

'You OK?' Boris asks me, through the headphones.

'Yes, this is wonderful.'

'Would you like me to make her do something even more exciting?'

'Looping the loop, you mean? I'm not sure my breakfast will stay down if...'

'No, I wouldn't loop the loop today. The cloud cover's too low. I've something else in mind. Tell me, do you trust me?'

Our eyes meet.

'Yes,' I reply, surprising myself. 'Yes, I do trust you.'

He smiles. 'Good'. Then he reaches for the ignition key and turns it.

After a few jabbering protests, the helicopter's engine cuts out.

13

I can't speak. I think my heart might have come close to stopping. I watch as Boris pushes the lever on his left all the way down.

Staying horizontal, the helicopter starts to drop towards the ground.

My heart turns over in my chest.

'Turn the engine back on!' I shriek. 'We'll die!'

Boris shakes his head quickly, and looks at me in a sort of disappointed way, as if surprised I'm not willing to trust him. 'No, no, don't worry. It's called autorotation.'

'Auto *what?*' I yell.

'Autorotation,' he replies calmly. 'The main rotor shall carry our weight down.'

'But we're falling really fast!'

Still perfectly calm, through the headphones he says: 'Yes, this model of the Brewster Speedbird – the BS9, which is as you see an eight-seater - autorotates at about fifty miles an hour.'

'Fifty miles an hour!'

'Yes,' he murmurs, absently. He isn't looking at me, but focusing on the dashboard and making careful adjustments to the levers and the pedals. We just go on falling... but now I notice, with utter and enormous relief, that while we're still coming down fast, the descent feels somehow controlled.

'I've reduced the collective to zero,' Boris says, speaking quickly in a calm, measured way. 'The collective - this control here on my left - governs the angle of all the rotors. I've made them completely flat, to maximise rotor speed and wind resistance. Let me see if I can guide us back to where we took off.'

'Don't you... don't you know if you can?'

'I think I probably can, yes,' I hear him say in my headphones. And he adjusts the curvy lever, and I realise that even during this still-fierce descent he can steer us.

'But won't we crash if we hit the ground at fifty miles an hour?' I protest, still panicking.

'Ivana, please stop worrying, we won't hit the ground at that speed. When we're about forty feet from the ground I'll flare: that is, I'll increase collective pitch to give us a sudden burst of lift; then we'll go down on a cushion of air.'

'Why... why don't you give us the lift now and we can go down more slowly?'

'Because if I flared now,' says Boris, giving a shrug, 'we would enjoy some lift for half a minute or so, yes, but we'd pay a price, because we'd consume all the kinetic energy in the main rotor, which would then slow down and probably stop.'

'And... what would happen then?'

'I would need to switch the engine back on.'

'And if you couldn't?'

'We'd fall like a stone and die,' he replies, in a matter-of-fact way. 'Now, please, trust me and don't worry.'

So I force myself to shut up.

The dial says nine hundred feet. I look below: Hastings seems to be rising up to us much too quickly. I try to breathe slowly. *He knows what he's doing, he knows what he's doing, please God he does,* I keep repeating inside my head. *And he's a billionaire. He doesn't want to die any more than I do.*

Boris steers us down, and now to my amazement I see that the Royal Victoria Hotel has swum into my field of view some way ahead. The helicopter appears to be heading straight for the car-park. Boris's guiding us down carefully, adjusting the curvy lever this time, but... *we're still coming down much too fast.*

I wonder feverishly whether the helicopter's cabin would give us any chance of surviving an impact (*into the tarmac of the car-park*, I think with a surge of panic) at fifty mph.

The ground shoots closer and closer towards us. Then, when we – and I really mean this – aren't much higher than the top of the hotel itself, Boris pulls on what he calls the 'collective' lever.

Instantly, gloriously, there's a wonderful lifting sensation. Suddenly it really does feel like we're on a cushion of air. The helicopter's floating effortlessly.

A few moments later, Boris lands us in the car-park as gently, silently and calmly as a falling leaf settling on the ground.

He undoes his seat-belt, and looks at me. 'Well, did you like it?'

There's something strangely sexual about the question, as if we'd made love together in the air.

I want to tell him he's insane, and to never expect me to trust him again. But at the same time I have to admit that he kept true to his word; we're alive, and the delicious adrenaline rush is still pumping through me, so I just nod – though more as a *thank you for not killing us* than as a response to his question.

'So, Ivana,' says Boris with a victorious air about him, 'perhaps we could spend some more time together here in Hastings, and see how we "get on", if I might use a phrase that is so widely used, yet seems entirely inadequate to express the marvellously infinite complexity of how human beings forge mutual rapport and affection with each other.'

I love the way he talks. I look into his eyes, hoping he'll understand. 'Listen, Boris, please, I don't want you to take this the wrong way. Despite you having a really strange way of courting women, I still think you're an absolutely amazing man, Boris. You really are. But, I – I really *can't* marry you.

He frowns, and his blue eyes slowly lose their lustre.

'Not... not even after we've autorotated together?' In his Russian accent the word 'autorotated' sounds very sexy, as if autorotation was not only a new way of making love, but even an improvement on the traditional way.

'Really, I loved the flight, scary as it was. The reason I can't marry you is, because, well... there's no way I'm ever going to marry someone unless I adore making love with them, and I'm afraid I'm only ever turned on by a man if he can beat me at chess. In a proper rated game, I mean, not blitz or rapid-play,' I add hastily, anxious for him not to think I'd just go to bed with any moderately fanciable guy lucky enough to beat me in a five-minute game in a pub, because I'd accidentally lost my queen e.g. through a silly Bacardi-fuelled blunder.

Boris hasn't stopped looking at me. *'Are you serious?'*

'I'm afraid I am. Look, just let me give you the cheque back.'

'Keep it.' He smiles faintly. 'You may need some of it, to buy yourself some beautiful clothes for our wedding.'

'Our wedding? What d'you mean?'

'I mean I'm going to learn to play chess better. Please give me six months.'

'Boris, if you're asking me not to date anyone else or see anyone else during those six months, I'm afraid I'm not agreeing to that.'

'I'm not asking you to do that or make any commitment to me at all. I simply said that I shall try over the next six months to become a much better chess-player.'

We don't really say anything more, though he does ask me for my email address 'so I can keep you in touch with my progress in chess', as he puts it. After only hesitating for a moment, I give it to him. I expect him to fish out his iPhone and key it in. Instead, he just tells me he'll remember it.

A few minutes later I head out into the fresh morning air on wobbly legs, looking up at the sky. Then I hurry along the promenade, in the bright, cold winter morning, back to reality.

14

Well, when I sit down to play Wladek Kruza a couple of hours later, the helicopter flight is still soaring inside me.

That afternoon I feel a mysterious fire burning inside me, maybe some fire from the sky-world where I dwelled for a while that morning.

I dispose of poor Wladek Kruza in thirty-two moves.

The day doesn't go so well for Jaz, who loses to Mark Hebden. I'm glad to say Jaz isn't too despondent about her loss to Mark: she knows she's been outplayed by a better player. I hope she'll just see the defeat as part of her learning process. What really matters is that I know it will make her even more determined to learn to play as well as Mark does.

Tom wins in that same third round against a British international master. I suspect that the way things are heading, we'll probably be playing each other before long.

Despite my hopes that Sven will win in this round, he loses again. I chat with him after the game. I feel even more madly in love/in lust with him than ever. While I'm with Sven I even manage to stop thinking about Boris, the helicopter flight and the cheque.

Sven isn't disappointed (or at least, doesn't give the impression of being disappointed) about his second loss in succession. Indeed, he even seems quite relieved that, with just one point from three games, he's now realistically out of contention in the tournament and can focus on the article for his magazine.

Of course, I don't say a word to Sven about the marriage proposal I received from Boris.

Sven asks me how 'your friend Jasmine did in her game'. I'm impressed he remembered her name. I tell him and he says he's very sorry to hear she lost. I just want to spend more time with him. I take him to see Jaz, who's very chummy with Sven from the outset. Sven also says he wants to buy us tea and mince pies, so we go up to the canteen on the first floor of the Horntye Park sports centre and he does.

Over the tea and mince pies, Sven wasn't exactly witty, but he did his best to amuse us. He even told us two Norwegian jokes. I was surprised that there were any at all.

'So,' said Sven, 'Olaf goes to a bar with Erik to drink lager. They just drink and say nothing. After two hours they are still sitting there, drinking in complete silence. Another hour passes, then finally Olaf turns to Erik and says, "nice bar, isn't it?" Erik glares at him. "Hey," he says, "did we come here to *drink*, or to *talk?*"'

I felt mildly amused. Jaz laughed.

'Also,' said Sven, apparently encouraged, 'we have many jokes that make fun of Swedes... the people, I mean, not the vegetable. For example...' and he glanced at Jaz, 'how do you get a one-armed Swede down from the top of a flag-pole?'

Jaz shook her head. 'I don't know.'

'You wave at him,' Sven explained.

It was fun to have tea with Sven, though admittedly I spent most of that tea-time wondering how nice it would be to make passionate love with him. I wanted to keep on being there with him and Jaz, all of us drinking the fine strong tea they serve in white foam cups at Horntye Park, and eating the delish icing-sugar-coated mince pies they serve there. We all had two mince pies each. But unfortunately when I offered to get us a third one, Sven replied:

'I'm so sorry, Ivana, but I have to go and write my daily report in my room.'

'But not all the games have finished yet,' Jaz protested.

'I know,' said Sven, 'I'll follow them on the tournament website.'

'Oh, yes, of course,' said Jaz.

It was hard letting Sven out of our sight, but I managed to. I had a lot to tell Jaz about that morning, after all.

The best news of Round Three was that Miklos was held to a draw by Andrew Greet. This was a serious setback for Miklos in his bid to win Hastings. Andrew was on the defensive for much of the game, but soon after Jaz and I were back in the playing-hall we were totally agog to see Andrew find a sudden brilliant tactical resource, forcing Miklos to accept a perpetual check or be checkmated. Not surprisingly, Miklos chose to accept perpetual check, which is a draw.

Miklos looked totally p'd off. *Excellent*, I thought. After he'd briefly shaken Andrew's hand, the World Number Two stormed out of the playing-hall followed by his manager.

On the morning of Tuesday, January the third - the day of Round Seven of the Hastings tournament (I made a note of the date in my diary) - I took the cheque into the Hastings branch of my bank. I couldn't bank it the day before, which was a bank holiday. The bank manager - a pale young man who looked totally flustered when the girl cashier showed him the cheque - told me they'd have to 'negotiate' the cheque for me as it wasn't a sterling cheque and was such a large amount. The bank said that this negotiation would take fourteen days, and that the money wouldn't start earning interest until it had cleared into my account. I was told that the cheque would clear on Wednesday, January the eighteenth, after ten business days. Despite everything Boris had said, I didn't think it would really clear. I expected him to put a stop on it.

Miklos's failure to win in Round Three had thrown the whole tournament open, like when the first seed gets beaten at Wimbledon in Round One.

I only drew in Round Four but managed to win again in Round Five, so I went into Round Six with four and a half points out of five.

By now I knew that the grandmaster norm for me at Hastings was likely to be seven and a half out of nine or eight out of nine, depending on the strength of my opponents in the rest of the tournament. You see, the number of points you need to score to get the norm isn't fixed, but depends on the strength of the opponents you face, and their ratings, as you progress through the tournament.

In Round Six I had a horribly tough fight, as Black. I played the Caro-Kann defence again, against the Spanish grandmaster Jaime Quinteros. In the end I was left with a bishop and knight (and my king, of course) against his lone king. It's a doable but difficult checkmate. But as a professional, being able to checkmate with bishop and knight is just something I need to be able to do. Jaime Quinteros resigned one move from being mated.

Unfortunately, in the next round I could only draw again. Then, in Round Eight I had to play Tom, who at this point had the same score as me: six out of seven. Miklos was leading the tournament by now with six and a half; he'd won all his games since being held to a draw by Andrew Greet.

Tom beat me.

I played the Caro-Kann yet again. It was, I realised almost as soon as I'd played it, a mistake. Tom knows too well how much I love that opening. He launched a really cunning kingside attack I hadn't seen before.

He seemed really, really keen to win for some reason.

15

I suppose it's time I told you something more about Tom.

I first got to know him on a weekend in August, just over a year before I stupidly succumbed to Miklos.

Tom and I met over the chess board, in Round Three of a five-round weekend tournament in Leicester. Tom, who's an extremely aggressive player, beat me quite quickly with a kingside attack he pursued mercilessly, just as he did that day in Hastings.

Despite my being very cross in Leicester that Tom had beaten me, I was happy about it in one definite respect. I couldn't wait to try to seduce him. He was and is very attractive. He was twenty-nine when we met but he looked about twenty-five, and still does. I suppose a life of complete lack of responsibility keeps him young.

Tom's playfulness, hyper intelligence and general bonkersness were things I really liked about him from the start. There in Leicester we had great banter about e.g. whether giving King Richard III a proper and decent burial in Leicester Cathedral had induced Richard's ghost to bless Leicester City Football Club and help make them Premier League Champions; what to add to Sangria to make it more fun; what women like in bed compared to men, and so on. It was also fantastically obvious that we were incredibly attracted to each other. Seducing Tom was about as difficult as drinking a glass of Pimms. From the start, though, he somehow seemed to me more like a mate, a chum, one of the girls in a way – someone to hang out with like

Lottie and Jaz – rather than a potential husband. Still, he was certainly a really attractive guy.

In a curious, sleek kind of way, Tom's actually very masculine. He's got a lean, wiry frame – you'd expect him to be weak but despite his hungry-artist look, his limbs are rock-hard with muscle. He has a nice face, with thoughtful hazelnut eyes, framed by jet-black hair. Tom, by the way, is just three inches taller than me: five eleven to my five eight.

We went for a drink in a nearby pub, The Daniel Lambert, which was named after a famous Leicestershire character from a couple of centuries back, who was extremely fat.

In The Daniel Lambert, Tom and I discovered, among other things, that we lived quite close to each other in London. Tom told me he had a flat on Gloucester Road itself, not far from Gloucester Road tube, which in turn was not far from where I lived on Churchill Gardens, near Earl's Court tube. Tom also said he made more of his money from playing online poker and from some shares he'd bought in the chess dating website www.chessmates.com than from chess, and that he adored snooker and wished he was as good at it as he was at chess.

That night I slept in Tom's room rather than mine. Up to that moment, it was the most passionate night I'd had in my entire life.

Apart from a two-month gap from February to April last year when Tom went to New Zealand to coach the national chess team and indulge his ambition to visit the locations of that beautiful, alternative-universe country which Tom mostly called 'Middle Earth' because *The Lord of the Rings* movies were filmed there, he and I had basically been Friends with Benefits ever since our first meeting in Leicester. We met on average about once a fortnight. I'm not quite sure why I'd only ever thought of a Tom as a friend I could have sex with rather than as a man I might marry, but anyway, that was how I saw him.

We often did moderately kinky things, including tying each other up, spanking each other with our hands or ping-pong bats, and naked mixed wrestling, which Tom seemed especially to like but which I always thought was a bit silly, though I admit it was sort of fun too. As well as our regular meetings for naughtiness, we also usually had a night together after he'd beaten me at chess in any of the tournaments when we found ourselves paired against each other. He didn't always beat me; I won maybe one game out of five, then maybe a couple were draws and the rest he won. Tom wanted me to spend a night with him even if I beat *him*, but I never allowed that even though I knew I'd have liked it. I stuck to my principles.

I was pretty sure Tom would have liked to have seen me more often than we did, but I didn't let that happen. This was partly because I thought that if we saw each other too often we'd get bored of each other, and seeing each other only about once a fortnight meant we never did. In any case, both of us were often away at tournaments, and frequently not even in the same country. We had a sort of unspoken deal that it was OK to sleep with other people if we wanted to. I didn't, in fact, do that very often, though, and when I did it was usually a disaster e.g. Miklos. I always used protection, by the way.

Tom's other big interest in life - apart from chess, internet poker, snooker, and going to bed with me whenever he had the chance, or even half the chance – was reading fantasy novels. The novels mostly had pretentious titles like e.g. *The Moons of Ormrod*, *Children of the Amulet*, and *The Guardian of the Sword*, to name just three of the novels I'd seen on his bookshelf. They generally featured characters who had extremely silly names. The names were, indeed, so silly that you often couldn't easily pronounce them just by reading them on the page. For instance, here are two I once noted down from *Children of the Amulet*; 'Auvwhää-Kennôðð, king of the Kennôðð folk', not to mention his 'beautiful and wild queen Auvwhää-Kennôðða'. That's fantasy books for you.

My loss to Tom totally put paid to my hopes of getting a second GM norm at Hastings. Of course Tom knew how desperately I wanted that norm, but he also knew I'd have lost my respect for him if he'd not tried very hard to beat me. We lived by the code of chess gladiators. That was the code at the heart of our lives.

I knew Tom would expect to claim the spoils of the victor that night, but meeting Sven and then Boris on the same day, and getting the outrageous cheque, had thrown me. I really wasn't in the mood for horizontal naughtiness. I told Tom so very plainly, though in a friendly enough way. He was OK about it. Oh, I could tell he was disappointed, but he was OK. I suppose he assumed there would be other opportunities.

Jaz and I shared my double bed that night. We gossiped until very late. Danuta, the Lithuanian girl she was sharing with, had asked her politely whether she (i.e. Jaz) might be able to sleep somewhere else for that night. Danuta had booked herself a tryst with a blond German girl called Heike. I heard later, on the grapevine, that Heike had a fiancé in Hamburg. Well, I suppose that night Heike wanted to take a hike into the world of girls. I must say, I did wonder what exactly Danuta and Heike had got up to.

Anyway.

I managed to win in the final round, so I finished with seven out of nine - six wins, two draws and one loss. This was enough to come in equal fourth with two others, ironically including Tom, who got utterly hammered by Miklos in the last round and also finished on seven points.

So Miklos won the tournament. Still, at least I'd not had to play him, though I would have had to if I'd beaten Tom. Equal fourth prize was £260 (chess tournament prize money doesn't remotely compare with the worlds of golf or tennis unless you're one of the top half-dozen players in the world, which I certainly wasn't), but I won the women's prize, too, £2,000. The £2,260 cheque seemed much more real than Boris's $1,000,000, but it didn't make up for my not getting a second grandmaster norm. And despite all Boris had said, I still didn't really think the cheque would clear.

Jaz was frustrated with her tournament performance, too. She finished with five and a half points: a point below the international master norm. Jaz lost in the last round in a game she was winning from the start, but she blundered horribly because of nerves.

That evening, after the prize-giving, I invited Jaz out for a drink. I wasn't sure she'd want to come. I knew how upset she was at losing in the last round, which is always (of course) the worst round to lose in as you can't restore your spirits by winning the following day and so the last-round loss just stays with you.

Yet Jaz seemed in surprisingly good spirits, and as we were drinking our ciders at *The Pig in Paradise* (the most chessy pub in Hastings, which organises informal chess events most evenings during the tournament, such as pro-am fifteen-minute chess), Jaz said, 'Of course I'm disappointed for myself, but I'm so happy for you, Vanny. You did really well! I'm sure you'll get your two more GM norms this year.'

'Thanks. You're so sweet, Jaz.'

She smiled and sipped her cider. 'There's something you need to know.'

'Tell me.'

'It's about Tom.'

I smiled. 'I think I can guess what it is. I've always said you should ask him out.'

Jaz shook her head. 'I like Tom, and I hope he likes me, but there isn't any chemistry between him and me, there really isn't. Besides, do you know he's totally into you?'

'Who, Tom?'

'Yes, of course.'

'How d'you know he's totally into me?'

'I can tell. That night when we were playing five-minute chess and you left us... he talked about you all the time, even when we were playing, so in the end I even had to tell him to shut up.'

'You're sure it was me he was talking about and not his own ego?'

'Yes, yes, it was you.'

'Definitely? He wasn't talking about Auvwhää-Kennôðða, queen of the Kennôðð folk?'

'*Who?*'

'Oh, never mind.'

'The point is, Vanny, I think Tom is in love with you.'

'But Jaz, he *can't* be in love with me. He's just my FWB, that's all.'

Jaz shook her head. 'I don't think that's how he sees it.'

I didn't say anything to her for a moment. I went to the bar to order another half pint of cider for each of us, and to give myself a chance to think about what she'd said.

If what Jaz said was true, emotionally things in my life were obviously going to get even more complicated than they were already.

Jaz and I would probably have discussed Tom more, but while I was paying for the drinks I saw Sven come into the pub and look around in the way people do when they're not exactly scheduled to meet anyone but are trying to see who's there without making it too obvious that's what they're doing.

My seeing Sven instantly turned my insides into a maelstrom (they have them in Norway, don't they?) of colly-wobbles.

Jaz waved at Sven and he came over to see us.

We spent the first fifteen minutes or so drinking cider with him and talking about the tournament, then we went to the Golden Pagoda for supper. I'd agreed with Jaz that we wouldn't tell Sven anything at all about Boris and the cheque, so we didn't. Most of what we talked about in the restaurant was chess and our experiences at the tournament, but while he was drinking Chinese beer, Sven told us about something else.

It happened after Jaz had asked him where he lived.

'In Oslo now,' Sven replied, in his lovely, sensuous voice, 'but I was born in a small town called Mandal, on the east coast of Norway. After doing my national service in the Norwegian army - where I learned to fire guns and to trek, to be honest I quite enjoyed being in the army - I studied European History and English at Oslo University and I've lived in Oslo ever since. Right after university I started working as a reporter at *Aftenposten* - the main daily paper in Norway.'

'Oh, OK. Cool.' Jaz leaned towards him over the table. 'So how about telling us something about your love life?'

Jaz has always been just so subtle. For the first time, I saw Sven blush.

'Well, now I am single, as you know,' Sven said, glancing at us a little uncomfortably. 'Though of course I have had relationships, but I do not imagine either of you would be very interested to hear about them.'

'No, no, that's what Vanny and I *reeeaaallly* want to know,' Jaz said.

Sven just stared at us in Norwegian, then finally said: 'What do you want to know, Jasmine?'

'Well, f'r example, Sven,' replied Jaz, brightly, 'have you ever been married or engaged or anything?'

'Married?' Sven shook his head. 'No, never. But, I was engaged for a few months until the spring of last year – no, the year before that.'

'*Who to?*' I gasped, wondering who the incredibly lucky woman was.

'Her name was Finna,' Sven replied, keeping his voice low. 'She was twenty-seven when I met her. She had recently joined *Aftenposten* as a reporter. By this time I was features editor of the newspaper, though I was already planning to leave at some point and to set up a new Norwegian chess magazine.'

'Were you in love with Finna?' I asked.

Sven nodded, rather sadly, I thought. 'Oh, yes, very much... very much.' His voice suddenly grew quiet, even mournful. 'Finna was... somehow wild, and looked almost like a pixie, in a way, and yet... she was a mentally strong and very sorted person, not at all weak and frail. She always wore green,' Sven went on, 'that was her favourite colour. Her hair was a very beautiful yellow colour, so green went well with it. Her clothes were all different shades or hues of green, and her handbag was green too. She even had green ink in her fountain-pen.'

Yes, and all this is making me green with jealousy, I thought.

I drew a slow breath, but even after taking it I still felt I lacked air. 'You were really crazy about her, weren't you?'

'Yes, very much. I was full of joy at her being in my life. I planned a future with her, I was... utterly in love. After we had known each other for only three weeks, I asked her to marry me. She said yes. I bought her a diamond solitaire engagement ring. For four months I was so happy it seemed impossible to believe that such happiness could be attained on earth. But then, with no warning at all, she... ended it.'

We stared aghast at him.

'*She* dumped *you?*' I gasped.

'Yes.'

'Why?' I said. 'Was she mad?'

Sven shrugged, though his face showed a certain appreciation at what I'd implied. '*Nooooo,*' he countered in a suddenly alarmingly deep voice, 'Finna was just following her heart, as I was. She left me for a busker, from Bergen, who played Cat Stevens songs near the block of flats where she lived. Finna and he are now married, have a baby girl, and have moved to a small town called Karasjok, in Norwegian Lapland. They run a health-food store and a vegetarian café together. Finna still sends me postcards sometimes, and I would say we are now friends, though to start with...' he drew a quick breath, 'it was very difficult for me. But now time has passed, and so it is easier.'

I felt truly sorry for him, but also amazed anyone would dump this god. Sven didn't ask us about our own personal lives, I suppose he was too much of a gentleman to do so, though at some point Jaz did slip in that she was single. Sven also told us more about Norway and how beautiful it was in winter and about his childhood growing up in Mandal. In return, Jaz told him about her life growing up in Brixton. Sven seemed really sorry when he left us at about ten, after putting the money to pay for his meal on the table (he wanted to pay for Jaz's and mine too but we wouldn't let him) and after saying he had to get up early in the morning to catch a train to Gatwick airport for his flight back home to Oslo. Gatwick's the closest major airport to Hastings, but even so it's about forty miles away.

Sven kissed Jaz and me goodbye on the cheeks. I watched him leaving the restaurant and felt very happy that all being well I'd be seeing him in Gibraltar.

What I felt uneasy about was what the little slip of paper inside my fortune cookie said. I've still got that slip of paper.

I never eat fortune cookies: they're too crisp for my liking and let's face it, they're pretty tasteless. I don't normally take too seriously the little snippets of fortune-telling, or wisdom, you find inside them, either.

This one, though, which was in the wisdom category, I kept. As usual in the case of those snippets, the wisdom was in a sort of concentrated English that rarely bothers with the definite or indefinite article.

It said (and, as it's still in my purse now, says) *making dreams come true costs great price.*

That had never occurred to me before.

The time would come when I would know just how true it was.

16

Jaz and I checked out of the hotel after breakfast the next day and left for London Charing Cross from St Leonards Warrior Square railway station.

I'd passed my driving test the previous summer, but I'd never been able to afford a decent car and I didn't want to drive some old jalopy, so I was car-less.

During the rail journey, Jaz and I played friendly chess games on my pocket magnetic set. We reached Victoria station mid-morning. I felt fairly flush with my *real* £2,260. At least I knew that cheque would definitely clear in a few days, so I paid for a cab for us from Victoria to Churchill Gardens.

When Jaz and I got back to the flat, we dumped our cases in our bedrooms, then went to find Lottie. She was in the kitchen, making coffee and talking on her mobile. Lottie was on her mobile a lot of the time, occasionally chatting to friends but more often organising concert events, which she did as a lucrative sideline to her piano-playing. She didn't earn a real living yet from playing the piano, though she was hoping she would before long.

Some people are kind enough to say I scrub up well, but Lottie was absolutely lovely. Five feet eight, so the same height as me, she was a willowy, natural blonde with wonderful creamy skin. She had a truly wholesome look to her and in fact she always looked so blond and healthy and nice that she always somehow reminded me of milk or cream. I remember I'd thought of her in that milky way, if you'll forgive the galactic pun (and also she inhabited the social stratosphere while I stumbled around on the ground) the very first time I set eyes on her at Abbey Hall school, where to start with I was so desperately homesick, friendless and unhappy.

Lottie was only nine days older than me; her birthday was on December the fifteenth, she was Sagittarius and I'm Capricorn. If she'd been born seven days later she'd have been Capricorn, like me.

Meeting Lottie was one of the most wonderful things in my life. Among the many reasons why I adored her is that she didn't live off her dad's money, even though he was a gazillionaire businessman. It's true that the flat she, Jaz and I lived in was Sir Rupert's, but Lottie insisted on paying him a proper rent for it, and Jaz and I each paid a third. Lottie's dad Sir Rupert is a friendly, kind, charming, businesslike kind of person who, I'm sure, would have been disappointed if Lottie *hadn't* insisted on paying him a proper rent for the flat.

Lottie was their only daughter now. A few years before I met her, the family had suffered a terrible tragedy when Lottie's sister Mandy, who was only thirteen at the time and flying unescorted to New York to visit an aunt of Lottie's who lived there, was killed in the Fraserburgh air crash. The big two-engine jet she was travelling in had developed a fire in the left-hand engine. Due to a faulty indicator light, the first officer shut off the wrong engine, the one that was still working fine, and the plane crash-landed in a field near the coastal town of Fraserburgh in Scotland. The captain had tried really hard to land the plane safely by gliding it into the field, but at the last moment it stalled and nosedived into the ground, killing the captain and first officer, everyone in first class and about a dozen people in the middle of the aircraft too. Many of the rest of the people in the middle of the plane were injured but they all survived, and everyone in the cheapest seats at the back did. I knew from Lottie that the family believed that if they hadn't been so rich, and if Mandy hadn't been travelling first class, she'd most likely still be alive.

Later, after getting to know Lottie, I discovered that she always tried to avoid flying if she possibly could. The reason she didn't fly wasn't because she was actually scared of flying, but because she didn't want her parents to worry about her.

Lottie had a brother called Hugo. He was a few years older than her and worked for Sir Rupert.

Lottie smiled at us, said, 'I've got to go, Mum; Vanny and Jaz have just got home,' and she pushed a button on her phone to end the call, put her mobile down on the kitchen table, and Jaz, Lottie and I all flew into each other's arms. About ten minutes later Lottie knew absolutely everything about what had happened during the time Jaz and I spent in Hastings i.e. everything I've told you.

Lottie stared at me. 'So... you put it into your bank account?'

I nodded, a bit breathless. 'Yes.'

'And in three weeks it'll have cleared?'

'Yes,' I said, 'if it clears at all.'

'Well, I hope it does,' Lottie replied. 'Vanny, please tell me you're not going to be crazy enough to try and give it back to him again! For goodness' sake keep the money. Judging from what you've told me, there aren't any strings attached, and it sounds to me as if he nearly killed you in his helicopter, so the cheque's the least he could do for you.'

'But it's for a *million dollars*,' I said.

'Darling, I should hope so,' replied Lottie. 'He's a billionaire, after all. I just hope he doesn't turn into a stalker.'

'It's a bit difficult to stalk people if you're in a helicopter,' Jaz remarked. 'Tends to make you a little conspicuous.'

'Actually,' I said, 'despite Boris being slightly insane, he's quite a sweet man. I don't want to marry him, but I don't want to be horrible to him, either.'

'He really did vow to improve his chess so he could beat you in six months?' asked Lottie. Of course she knew about my quirk.

'Yes,' I replied. 'But anyway, how's Ade?'

'Oh, Ade's fine. Still wishing he was as good as Steven Juselius.'

Adrian, Lottie's cellist boyfriend, knew the great cellist Steven Juselius quite well and saw him as a sort of deity.

'As a matter of fact,' Lottie said, 'I ought to call Ade. We had a bit of a tiff last night while we were practising. He kept coming in late. I think he'd had too much Strongbow. I'll go and call him from my room in case the conversation gets a bit naughty, which most likely it will.' She smiled very warmly at us both. 'Hey look, shall we have a party soon? Maybe around the middle of the month? I'm feeling a bit post-Christmassy and deflated, and my two sweetest friends are back home, and Vanny won £2,260 *and*,' she added roguishly, 'may soon be the wife of a billionaire...'

'Unlikely,' I said.

'Oh, who knows how things'll turn out?' Lottie replied.

17

I suppose it was fairly extraordinary, really, that I ended up at the same school as Lottie at all. Basically it happened like this.

After Dad abruptly dumped Mum, she was left alone to bring me, an only child, up. Dad was generous with Mum and gave her a good divorce settlement, but Mum's never worked since her marriage and wouldn't have much idea what to do for a job nowadays, even if she did want to get one.

Almost from the moment Dad left us, Mum's money began to slip away.

I still remember us moving from the huge house on the outskirts of Halifax to a flat in the centre of the town. Even though it was a big and comfortable ground-floor flat with a long garden, it all seemed very small after the house with its private spinney, and the nearby fields where I'd loved to play for hours. As part of the divorce settlement, Mum agreed to give up her claim on the house. No, I don't know how Dad managed to wangle that, either.

That move from the house to the flat was one of the biggest upsets of my life. I still remember crying and crying, and asking Mum where Daddy was and Mum crying too.

Not long before we had to move out from the house, Dad told me he'd come and pick me up every Friday and I could spend every weekend with him there. He promised.

But he didn't come.

I remember looking forward so much to him fetching me that first time, but then Mum got a phone call and told me that

Dad had said he couldn't come that weekend because he had to go to London.

I cried even more.

Dad didn't come to fetch me the next weekend either, in fact basically he never did, except every Christmas Eve, when he'd invite me to his house for my birthday and I stayed overnight. But he always took me back to Mum in the morning, after I'd had my presents, as otherwise Mum would have been alone for Christmas Day.

Then my father suddenly, impulsively, like the way he generally does things, again started taking a real interest in me.

I was eleven at the time, and going to a state junior school and living with Mum in a little flat in Pimlico, less than a mile from my school. We'd moved south to London from Halifax when I was nine. Mum said she wanted to live in London and was bored with Halifax, but in a strange way, even though she wasn't married to Dad anymore and didn't see him socially, I think she wanted to be nearer Dad, who had sold his pickle business by then and was living in Knightsbridge with Marina, wife number four. The next wife along was Larissa, whom Dad met when he moved to Monte Carlo a few years later after he and Marina (he mercifully didn't have any children except me with my mum and his little son Piotr with Larissa) were divorced.

Dad still gave Mum and me some financial help in addition to the divorce settlement, but Mum had never been very good with money and we were always hard up. My school uniform wasn't exactly threadbare but it was always scuffed and never looked smart. I was constantly darning my socks and making do, and when there were school excursions Mum usually couldn't afford for me to go and was too proud to apply to the school charity fund to help.

So that was what our lives were like. I did quite well at school, but I wasn't happy at all, and I was overweight too (I even got called Fatty Vanny by my fellow pupils) from eating comfort food and from Mum's cooking. I don't know if you know much about Croatian cuisine, but believe me, with its focus on meat, potatoes, steamed puddings and heavy sweet pastries, it's not exactly a weightwatcher's dream.

Then, one day in June, Dad totally unexpectedly came to visit Mum and me when he was in London. He didn't even phone; he just turned up at the flat and rang the bell.

Mum was frosty towards him at first. In fact, to start with, when he announced himself on the intercom, I wasn't even sure she'd let him in. But she did, so then suddenly there Dad was in our flat, with his suit and his briefcase and his big, baked-potato face. Before I knew it he was hugging me and telling me how much he'd missed me, and that he was sorry he'd always been busy and that, 'whatever anyone else says, our Ivana, you've always been my favourite daughter'. (In those days he often used to say 'our Ivana' when he met me; that's how people talk in the north of England.)

I knew that in a strange, sad way, Mum was very glad to see Dad. I always thought she'd basically stayed in love with him. By the way, did you know that in the Croatian capital Zagreb, there's actually a museum called the Museum of Broken Relationships? Mum's been to it, though I haven't been to Zagreb at all.

Mum spent most of the time during that visit of Dad's bringing us tea and her usual heavy Croatian sweet pastries, and crying; it was all pretty intense. Finally, Dad explained the point of the meeting: that in the autumn he wanted to send me to a 'lovely' (he pronounced it *luvly*) girls' public school he'd heard of in Devon, and that of course he'd pay my fees and give me an allowance.

To start with, I completely detested my new school.

Its full name was Abbey Hall Manor School for Girls, though it was basically called just Abbey Hall, and it was in the Devonshire countryside not far from Totnes, which, as I discovered on an excursion there, is a pretty but rather weird little town full of New Age people and shops selling New Age stuff like moonstones, wind chimes and model dragons etc.

The school was incredibly snobbish. I still had a Yorkshire accent, and some of the girls used to take the mickey when I said e.g. 'oop' instead of 'up' and 'book' with a 'boo' in the middle. Not surprisingly, I did my best to lose my accent as quickly as I could.

We all wore a posh dark purple uniform (Dad paid for it, so for what felt like the first time in my school experience I wore a uniform that wasn't scruffy), and we had to play a game called lacrosse, which is a sort of combination of football, tennis and murder. The racquet, which is called the lacrosse, is basically a small net on the end of a stick and you can run with the ball in it. If that sounds ridiculous, it is. But if it sounds as if the game would be fairly peaceful, it isn't, because the ball leaves the lacrosses at about three zillion miles an hour. Later in my school days I found out that lacrosse is played in the USA too, though a bit more sensibly and with less shouting; also, the Americans have the sense to wear crash helmets, but we played without them so we continually risked brain damage. Not that that would have been a problem for most of the girls at Abbey Hall, who didn't have much in their brains to damage apart from thoughts of:

- money
- more money
- platinum credit cards
- ponies
- lacrosse

- who they've recently injured at lacrosse
- Labradors
- show-jumping
- how rich Daddy was
- where they'd been on their 'hols'
- *Country Life* magazine. The school library had oodles of copies of this; the library could have supplied Britain's dentists' and doctors' waiting-rooms with old editions of the mag. Quite a few of the girls subscribed to it, and the way they talked about it, anyone would have thought it was the only thing worth reading that had been written since the dawn of time. I tried to enjoy *Country Life* but I found it difficult to relate to its articles about posh lords and their even posher houses, or its accounts of shooting a load of harmless little birds that were just harmlessly flying around enjoying their day, until they got blasted to bits.

Despite my efforts, most of the other girls weren't that keen on being friends with me. I wasn't even upper middle-class let alone upper-class and to start with I had my accent. Also, I was quite keen on my studies, which was seen as uncool. I didn't have a horse, a Labrador, a boyfriend called Toby or indeed a boyfriend called anything, or an interest in lacrosse, so topics of conversation quickly dried up. Also, I thought show-jumping was boring to watch on TV and quite dangerous, though I admired the athletic capacity of the horses that did it. I thought the sport would be more fun without people. And even if I'd shown an interest in these things there were still the insurmountable obstacles of my being overweight, having a foreign-sounding first name and a working-class surname, so of course, the other girls didn't want to take the risk of appearing uncool by hanging around with me long enough to get to know me.

Early one December evening, a few months after I'd started at the school, I went into the games room and found I was the only one there. The games room was quite small and not seen as fashionable or trendy. It was the sort of place that overweight, lonely losers went to e.g. me.

I still remember how I thought of playing Monopoly against myself before I miserably tugged out a dog-eared box that had a picture of a horse on the front. But it wasn't the kind of horse you saw in *Country Life*. It was a white chess piece.

Intrigued, I opened the box and found a similarly dog-eared chess board made out of cardboard, and lots of plastic chess pieces.

There was also a crumpled slip of paper which gave the rules of chess, and used diagrams to show you how the pieces moved. I discovered that the piece like a horse was called a 'knight'.

I set the pieces up and began moving them around kind of randomly, then read the rules more carefully and moved the pieces as it said they should move: the king one square in any direction, the queen anywhere diagonally or along a rank or file, the rook only along a rank or file, the bishop only diagonally, the knight in a strange way two squares in any direction then one square to the right or left, and finally I learned that the pawns moved one square ahead, or two when they made the first move. But if pawns captured they did so diagonally and forwards on either side.

I was utterly, utterly fascinated.

The next thing I knew, the bell had rung to tell us it was time to go to our dorms. I'd been playing with the pieces and studying their moves for about two hours, and I hadn't noticed the time passing.

That was the start of a new life for me.

Somehow, I'd found myself.

I was a chess-player.

And, as none of the other girls played chess (or if they did they didn't talk about it), I was instantly the best chess-player in the school.

Chess was something I could be good at.

Then, just before the end of the autumn term, I met Charlotte, so as well as having a new hobby I was bats about, I had a wonderful new friend, too. Very soon I secretly became bats about her. And I was happy, and didn't rely on food so much to cheer myself up, and so soon I lost weight.

Almost from the very start I called her Lottie. She was in a different form, but in my year. I'd heard about her before I met her, because people talked in hushed voices about a girl called Charlotte Richmond, whose older sister had been killed a few years earlier in an air disaster. I felt fairly sorry for Charlotte, even though I didn't know her then, though before I met her, I supposed she'd be like the rest of them i.e. a stuck-up cow.

But she turned out to be absolutely super instead.

18

Lottie, Jaz and I decided to hold our party a week on Saturday, January the fourteenth. As usual Lottie was responsible for the entertainment; Jaz for the food and me for the invitation list. Lottie and I would pay for the party; we only asked Jaz to chip in with a tenner.

Later that same evening when Jaz and I got back from Hastings, I went on-line. I'd not looked at my emails very often during the tournament, and now I had, as far as I remember, about 120 unread ones, about half of which were spam, including several offering to increase my penis size, which would certainly have been a major medical breakthrough. The three most interesting emails were from God, from Tom, and one from... the email address chairman@russfiduciarybank.com

My dear Ivana

I trust you arrived back home safely after your successful participation at the congress in Hastings, and your no less successful initiation into the excitement of helicopter flight!

I'm writing to tell you that I've decided to sponsor an international chess tournament in New York this summer, probably to be held in June. The venue will be the Manhattan Ambassador Hotel. I would be delighted if you would play: perhaps you could let me know when convenient what professional engagements you have in June and I can then ensure that the timing of the event will be suitable for you?

I've chosen New York as the venue because I have many business interests there, including the Finnish healthcare innovations company I mentioned in my letter. The company was founded in Finland but nowadays its main research and development facility is in upstate New York.

The Manhattan Ambassador Hotel is within my property portfolio. One reason I bought it was because of its splendid view of Central Park. You would be accommodated there with my compliments, in the Presidential Suite, the most lavish suite in the hotel. The suite has its own Japanese water-garden, an aviary containing humming-birds, and a private swimming-pool. You would, I think, be very comfortable. I shall of course pay your air fare. When we met I quoted from my favourite sonnet by the immortal Bard of Avon. Perhaps you might enjoy the entire sonnet; here it is for you. Ever since I first saw you, in the Softy-Softy advertisement, I think of you every time I read this sonnet:

Let me not to the marriage of true minds
Admit impediments. Love is not love
Which alters when it alteration finds,
Or bends with the remover to remove.
Oh, no, it is an ever fixèd mark
That looks on tempests and is never shaken;
It is the star to every wand'ring barque,
Whose worth's unknown although his height be taken.
Love's not time's fool, though rosy lips and cheeks
Within his bending sickle's compass come;
Love alters not with his brief hours and weeks,
But bears it out even to the edge of doom.
If this be error and upon me prov'd,
I never writ, nor no man ever loved.

I am already taking steps to improve my chess. I have an excellent coach and am working hard on all areas of my game. So we shall see! I am an eternal optimist.

And in case you are wondering whether the check I gave you is a joke and won't clear, may I please say that while I joke about some things, I never joke about money.

The check is a good one and, as I have mentioned, comes with no strings attached. As our American friends say: enjoy!

Yours, Boris

PS: Should you wish to participate in another helicopter flight, this time with yourself as the pilot, you might enjoy the website www.flyyourownwhirlybird.com

I read the email again, including the sonnet. Finally I wrote a reply.

Dear Boris

Many thanks for your lovely email.

The sonnet's beautiful. I don't understand it all, but I think I understand some of it.

That line 'love is not love which alters when it alterations finds' is wonderful. I think it means that love is only love if it stays there even after you find out that the person you love is different from what you thought they were, or what they become through getting old, or ill, or both.

Boris, I do appreciate your great fondness for me (and no I won't call it love, because as you pointed out in your own letter, love is something two people create together.) You are so sweet, and even though I hardly know you, I do think you're a super person. It's really kind of you to invite me to the amazing tournament in New York. I accept (thanks) and any time in June would be good for me as that tends, in fact, to be a fairly quiet month in my chess life.

It's also really kind of you to offer to pay my air fare and to let me stay in the hotel. As you are kind enough to invite me to the tournament, I'll accept the invitation to stay at the hotel, but I'll certainly want to pay my own airfare from some of the money you gave me, though I really don't feel comfortable about spending more than a very small amount of it on myself. But honestly, there's no need to put me up in the Presidential Suite, wonderful as it sounds, especially with the humming-birds which I've always liked though I've never seen any in real life. As far as the hotel is concerned, an ordinary room would be fine!

Boris, let me please ask you a question, which seems appropriate as it was, after all, you who very kindly gave me the cheque.

What do you think I should do with the money?

Yours sincerely

Ivana

Next I opened the email from Dad.

Vanny, when are you coming to see us?

Dad's emails always tend to be short and sweet like that. In fact, by his standards this was quite a long one.

The best way to reply to Dad's emails is to be pretty short and sweet myself, though never quite as much as he is.

What I wrote back was:

Hi Dad, thanks for your email. I'd love to come and see you and Larissa and Piotr but it will have to be after

Gibraltar, where I'm going on Sunday January 22 to get ready for the tournament, which starts the following day. The Gib event goes on until the end of January and in February I've got quite a bit of coaching to do. But maybe I could come in the first week of March?

Oh, by the way, a Russian billionaire has fallen in love with me and given me a cheque for a million dollars. I'm not really sure what to do with it yet. Any ideas? I haven't yet decided what to do about him, either.

Lots of love, Ivana xxxxx

Once I'd sent Dad this email I clicked on Tom's. The subject bar was: *I've got an amazing CD.*

Vanny, you must come and listen to a CD I have featuring songs by Kevin Smith, a great singer and song-writer from Kent. He recently died tragically and much, much too young. I saw him perform in a pub in Broadstairs last year when I was playing in the East Kent Open. I've been trying to get hold of one of his CDs ever since. Then suddenly I heard on a music website that he'd died and they gave an email address where you could get a CD of him. His death is a total tragedy; he was a majorly brilliant musician. When can you come? Tom xx

I sat and stared at my computer. While I did, a little envelope icon appeared in the top right hand corner of my screen.

It was, again, from chairman@russfiduciarybank.com

My dear Ivana, in reply to your interesting question, and in view of your remark that you do not feel comfortable about spending more than a small amount of the money on yourself (though personally I wish you would spend it

all on yourself), may I perhaps suggest that you use at least
some of the money, in whatever way you think appropriate,
to advance the interests of the kind of love that doesn't, as
the sonnet has it, alter when it alteration finds,

Yours very cordially, Boris

Brooding on this intriguing reply, I typed the link www.flyyourownwhirlybird.com into my internet's browsing bar.

The website was seriously cool. The home page was full of great visuals of helicopters taking off, flying and landing, all different kinds of helicopters – helicopters with just one overhead rotor, helicopters with two, ones that looked really snazzy and ones that looked more old-fashioned, including the kind you see in old Vietnam War films that seemed to be mostly made of glass or Perspex or whatever it is and looked like a flying aquarium.

You could choose which kind of helicopter you wanted to fly. I chose the eight-seater Brewster Speedbird BS9, because I remembered it was the one Boris had flown me in.

I clicked on a really lifelike image of the chopper, and then *Cockpit Point of View* and right away I was back inside the cockpit of Boris's helicopter, only I was now sitting where he'd sat.

On the left side of the screen there were instructions about what buttons to press on your keyboard to make the helicopter you were flying do stuff. The website recommended you used a X3000 joystick, which I didn't have.

I found after a while that I could fly the virtual Brewster Speedbird BS9 reasonably well, though I did have a couple of crashes when I forgot about something called 'yaw'. It said on Help that yaw was when the helicopter turned from side to side as it was flying.

The next hour or so was incredibly enjoyable. Who needs a real life when you've got internet and a virtual Brewster Speedbird?

But, well... one does need a real life too, of course.

I grabbed my mobile and called Tom.

'Hi, Vanny,' he answered.

I think he loves you, Jaz had said.

'Hi,' I said. 'I got your email. The CD sounds great. I'm so sorry about the musician who died.'

'Yes, it was horrible, what happened to him,' Tom replied. 'But... want to come round?'

'Yes, I'd like to. But not tonight, I'm really shattered. How about tomorrow?'

'Great. When?'

'Seven?'

'Perfect. See you tomorrow.'

'See you,' I replied, and pressed the button to end the call.

That's how easy it is to organise a date with a Friend with Benefits.

19

I arrive, on foot, at Tom's flat on Gloucester Road, at about a quarter to seven the following evening.

Well, a girl can be early if she wants to as well as late, can't she?

Under my beige cashmere coat (a birthday/Christmas present from Lottie the Christmas before last) I'm wearing a scarlet pencil dress, very clingy. Underneath it I have on a new Victoria's Secret ensemble, including suspenders and stockings. And if that wasn't enough, I've dabbed on some fresh and sparkly *Oh Lola!* Marc Jacobs perfume.

I've stashed my high-heeled glossy black boots in a Harvey Nichols bag. Like all of the best-looking high-heels you can find, they're practically impossible to walk in except across a carpet and into a bedroom. I'll sneak them on once I'm in the hallway, and never mind what any of Tom's neighbours might think.

His flat (the top floor of a three-storey flatblock) is above a kebab shop and about a hundred yards from Gloucester Road tube station, on the same side of the street. He's actually managed to buy somewhere to live rather than renting; his gran on his mum's side died a few years ago and left him enough to put down a deposit on a flat.

The strange thing about Tom is that, despite him being fairly wacky in most areas of his life, he's actually quite sensible with money. He never seems to be short of it, though he doesn't make a fortune from his portfolio of occupations. Tom enjoys his bohemian freelance life of playing in chess tournaments when he wants, playing poker when he wants, doing chess journalism when he wants and going to bed with me when *I* want.

The door leading into the hallway of the flatblock where Tom lives is just by the kebab shop, which is busy tonight. I press Tom's button (so to speak) and a few moments later the door buzzes. I push it open and go into the downstairs hallway.

The hallway is pretty charmless even by the general standard of London flatblock hallways. There are the usual recently-dropped free newspapers scattered on the threadbare carpet. On an old white wooden table nearby are yellowing dog-eared flyers advertising things like laundry services and take-away food, and there are also a few tackily-printed cards of local call girls with little silhouette images of slim shapely girls striking provocative poses.

The hallway smells strongly of kebabs. Sometimes Tom's flat does as well, though mercifully not too often. He doesn't mind too much if it does; he sometimes goes for days living mostly on kebabs and chips from the shop. They give him a ten percent discount as he's a neighbour. I've told Tom that a kebab-based diet was great if having a heart attack was his prime health objective, but he said that sometimes he doesn't have time to cook or to go out, and anyway that the kebab shop provides all major food groups i.e. 1) kebabs 2) chips 3) Coke.

Once I'm inside the hallway I close the door behind me and start padding up the three flights of stairs. It isn't the grade of flatblock that would have its own lift. Reaching the third floor, I quickly swap my trainers for the high-heels. I put my trainers into the bag and knock on Tom's door. I'm expecting to find it opened by a hang-dog Tom all sweet and loving and vulnerable and so completely unshaggable. But what actually happens is that the door opens very suddenly and very quickly, and I hear a loud blast of music in my ears. After opening the door, Tom, instead of greeting me, hurries back into the living-room whose overhead light is half dimmed, so it's kind of dusky in there. Tom starts doing a kind of gyration that owes a little to Elvis and a lot more to an electric eel on acid. The music is pacy, nautical and sexy and tuneful too.

Tom's wearing a long white button-up cotton shirt, unbuttoned about half-way down, and a pair of blue denim shorts. I know he thinks he looks cute in this outfit, and to be honest, he does.

So, far from Tom being all lovelorn, he's in spaced-out mode. Still, it confirms my suspicions that Jaz had maybe been exaggerating in what she'd said about his feelings for me.

I put the bag down, take my coat off, hang it up in the tiny hallway between Tom's front door and the living-room, and advance into the living-room in my scarlet pencil dress and my boots.

Tom only gives me the quickest of glances, then rushes into his kitchen and dashes back barely half a minute later (by this time I've plonked myself on the sofa) with a glass of Merlot, and one for himself too. He always keeps several bottles of wine in his food cupboard, which doesn't otherwise have much in it apart from an approximately quarter-full bottle of soy sauce, a few packets of biltong, a usually more or less empty container of Bisto gravy granules, a dozen or so cans of different Baxters soups and a roll of Ann Summers' own-brand black bondage tape.

The sofa's next to an antique walnut table (his gran left him some nice furniture, too) on which there's the goldfish tank containing Frodo and Gandalf. The tank's quite big, about three feet wide, two deep and a foot across and has its own filtration system and a piratical theme containing props such as a plastic treasure chest and a sunken pirate ship featuring a skull and crossbones flag and miniature skeletons of drowned pirates.

I always hope Frodo and Gandalf aren't too psychologically disturbed by all this.

Tom flops down on the sofa next to me. 'Listen, Vanny. The next track's the best.'

I sip my Merlot and listen. The track starts with a beautiful jaunty riff on a mouth-organ, followed by vigorous, stumpy, melodious vocals:

I'm travelling down unseen roads, fear of life inside of me
Taking time whenever I can, to free this filling load,
And it's a drink down, drink down, lads, remember all the
times we had,
Drink down, drink down lads, remember the times we had.
On my back a rucksack, in my head an empty map,
My feet are bruised, and blistered too
To walk this muddy track.
And it's a drink down, drink down, lads, remember all the
times we had,
Drink down, drink down lads, remember the times we
had.

Tom and I listen to the end of the song. Then he gets up and switches off the CD player, glances back at me and places a hand theatrically on his hairy-but-not-too-hairy chest.

'That track gets me right here, Vanny. It's just so ace. I saw the guy who wrote it, Kevin Smith, singing it last year in the Tartar Frigate pub, when I was in Broadstairs for the East Kent Open.'

Tom's voice has suddenly got all sad and thoughtful. 'Kev was a genius musician, brilliant singer, great on all the instruments he played - the fiddle, guitar, banjo, mandolin, and those were just the ones I remember. He was pure talent. I heard there was a CD coming out and that it'd be available on a website devoted to Kent music. I had an alert on the website to get notified when the CD was available. The alert got triggered last week, but it also said he'd died suddenly just before Christmas: he was only forty-eight.'

Tom nods sadly, as much to himself as to me, I thought. 'So that was it. All that talent gone. Life is just so cruel, so unfair.'

'Not always,' I say. I put both of wine glasses down next to the fish bowl and lead Tom to his bedroom. Still wearing our clothes, we stumble onto the bed. He gently pins me down, trailing his lips down my neck and along the straps of my dress, then undoes the straps and exposes my breasts. I gaze up at the ceiling as Tom starts gently kissing them. Strangely enough for the bedroom of a supposed grown man, the ceiling's painted yellow with silvery glitter in it. I've always found it funny that we do what we do in a room that looks like it belongs to a socially maladjusted sixteen-year-old – not that I want to be impolite to socially maladjusted sixteen-year-olds. Basically Tom's flat's an interior decorator's nightmare. The bedroom wall behind the infamous life-size orc is painted a garish purple, while the opposite wall hosting his shelves full of fantasy books is painted black. The other two walls are sky-blue and dark green, respectively.

I flop down onto the bed, I turn all the way around now facing the sky-blue wall. As he runs his eager fingers down my back, I gaze at the reprint of a promotional poster for *Casablanca* that's pinned to the wall, with Humphrey Bogart, Claude Rains, Paul Henreid and Ingrid Bergman all pointing their intense, dramatic expressions at me. Next to it is a poster of that student room classic, the weird and dream-like painting *The Persistence of Memory* by Salvador Dali, with the bendy clockfaces. Tom gives me some firm but not excessive spanks and I gasp, turning my head a little so I'm facing the far left corner of the room, where the blue and purple walls meet.

Tom's desk fits into that corner, hosting his laptop at which he toils on his chess columns or other writing, surfs the web, and plays internet poker.

He encourages me to sit up, and as we kiss he gently pulls me towards the edge of the bed. Pushing my legs apart, he gives me a wicked smile and kneels on the floor. The first thing that enters my field of vision as Tom goes down on me is that six-foot orc, the centrepiece of his bedroom, complete with its horrible skull-like face, twisted pointy horns, vile yellow tusks, rusty breast-plate, and great battle-axe in its claws. Its gnarled and terrible outfit is hung with trophy skulls of its victims, and with various knives and swords and other weapons.

The orc is a delightful sight to greet you in the morning, or when you are still half-asleep, in the only-relieved-by-the-street-lamp-outside darkness, groping off to the loo for a pee at night.

Suddenly Tom looks up at me and clears his throat. 'Vanny, can we…' He smiles shyly. 'Can we, uh… try something a bit different this evening?'

'What d'you mean? Have you been to Ann Summers again?'

'No, but I've been reading a really brill book called *Elvira, Warrior Princess.*'

'And who's she, exactly?'

'An amazing warrior queen. She can fight dragons, warlocks, demons and forest-elves and all other sorts of baddies, because not only is she an incredibly good fighter, and ravishingly beautiful, but she can read her adversaries' minds and anticipate their next moves. Also, she kills male warriors in unarmed combat.'

'Don't tell me; she's really sexy, and her favourite method of disposing of guys is to strangle them with her legs after she's sexually exhausted them?'

'How did you guess?'

'Female intuition.' I draw a breath. 'And so you want us to have a fight where I'm Elvira and you're a warrior she's trying to kill?'

'Yes, please,' says Tom.

'You're a complete pervert, Tom, you really are. Actually, I've always suspected you of having a secret fantasy of being beaten up by a beautiful girl... or maybe even killed by one.'

Tom goes corroboratively red.

'Or perhaps even better by a number of girls,' I add, rather to my surprise finding myself warming to my theme. 'In our world where everything can be personalised, if capital punishment was ever brought back, condemned people would probably be allowed to choose exactly how they were executed. I suppose most of us girls would choose death by chocolate! But I'm sure you'd just love being wrestled and then killed by, say, five... no *six*,' (I add, suddenly realising that there'd need to be one for each limb, and two more) '... really gorgeous women, all between the ages of twenty and twenty-five, all naked, and working as a team.'

Tom looks thoughtful, and purses his lips, perhaps to try to conceal that he's started to salivate. 'What am I being executed for?'

'Having lustful thoughts about a woman.'

'Vanny, if *that* was a capital offence, most of the men in the world older than about thirteen would be on Death Row.'

'Stop being so literal. This is a fantasy.'

'All right, all right.' He just stares at me. 'Why are there six?'

'To ensure you can be continuously overpowered, of course.'

We often imagine fantasy scenarios.

'At first there are only five of them,' I murmur. 'Five stunning naked women, who start by breaking your resistance. They pummel you, push you, and throw you around. Then they trip you and force you onto the big, wide, king-size bed, plenty big enough for everyone.'

I pause for breath. I'm starting to feel rather heated myself.

'The bright crimson satin sheets and covers are cool and smooth against your skin as you grapple with the women. But working together they're much stronger than you, and they quickly break down your resistance, and overpower you, each taking control of a different limb, and they beat you up a bit. They're the execution team, you see.'

'They are?'

'Yes,' I say, with a nod. 'Executing men is what they do, and they're very good at it. In fact, they're the best. Now, stop interrupting. OK, so they're all naked, and ohhhh so cute,' I lean over and run my hand from Tom's shoulder down his arm to his right bicep. He shivers. 'You're bruised and helpless, but still fully dressed. You being fully dressed won't do at all, so they... well, they strip your clothes forcibly from your body, leaning their naked bodies over you as they do. Lying on top of you, they use the weight of their bodies to hold you down. They're touching you all over.'

I want to make it more real for Tom, so I take hold of the bottom of his shirt, and pull it (Tom doesn't protest) over his head. Then I grab Tom's legs, unzip his denim shorts and tug them off, and then I remove his sexy black boxers and his not-so-sexy black socks, and throw them onto the carpet.

I'm still wearing all my clothes, which seems an unnecessary hindrance, so I quickly strip completely, letting my dress fall to the carpet. To torment Tom still further, I quickly bend down and take him into my mouth for a few seconds, then I stand up and push him back down onto the bed, spreading his legs, and kneeling on the bed between them.

'Don't move, or I'll stop,' I say, breathlessly. Tom nods and gasps. I clear my throat and lower my voice. 'So now you're naked,' I say huskily. 'They throw your clothes on the floor, and with total abandon, display their luscious bodies, teasing you with light touches,' I run my hand over Tom's panting chest, 'but making sure you can't get up. There's always at least three of them holding you down.'

Tom hikes himself up on his elbows, so he can watch what I'm doing as I talk. Slowly and sensuously, I'm running my hands over my arms and my legs, before moving up to my tummy and breasts.

It seems a shame to stop, really, as Tom is gasping with excitement and his face has gone all red, but I need to get on with the story.

'Two of the girls each grab one of your ankles in both their hands. They're strong. No matter how much you kick out, you can't break their tight grasp.'

I take hold of both Tom's ankles, and I lick him along his shins to his knees, following my lips with my hands until they cup his knees, then smooth their way to the top of his legs, teasing between them, and back down again. 'Though, in fact, you can't kick out now, because another girl is sitting naked on your thighs. You can feel her warm bottom holding down the top of your legs. You can't move at all.'

I grab hold of Tom's wrists and move to pin them to the bed with my own hands. He resists briefly, but obviously doesn't really mean it. He lets me pin him down, and I give him a long, lingering kiss on the mouth before I continue. 'There's a girl sitting on both sides of the bed, each clamping one of your hands down.' Tom closes his eyes briefly, then looks to me as if he's about to faint with pleasure. I'm virtually purring as I murmur, 'you're totally helpless. You struggle, and try to escape, but all five of them work together and are just too much for you. Spread out there on the bed, in their clutches, it's like you're being… sexually crucified.'

Tom's face is flushed and his chest rises and falls quickly with shallow breaths. 'It's at this point,' I say, 'that the sixth executioner, the team leader and the most beautiful of them all, which is saying a lot, pads into the room.'

'She does?' Tom gasps.

'Yes. She's the most beautiful of all. She has a wonderfully pretty face, and gloriously long, glossy chestnut hair and wonderful dark brown eyes with long lashes. She's completely naked too, of course, all except for a beautiful, bright crimson neck scarf around her throat. She runs her hands down her hips, then back over her tummy and she cups each breast with her back arched and her chest forward. Then she stretches over the bed towards you, and gives your manhood nice long strokes with her warm, sensuous fingers.'

I lean over the bed so my heavyish breasts are close to Tom's face, while I reach out and open the top drawer of his bedside table. I take out the container of white musk massage oil from its usual spot, leaving the drawer open. There are other things in there too e.g. yet more Ann Summers' black bondage tape. Flipping open the lid of the container, I squirt oil over Tom's chest, noting his pleasurable flinch as the coolness surprises him. After placing the bottle on the bedside table, I first use my hands, then my own chest, to spread the oil, sliding along his body as I do so. His hands can't resist reaching out and rubbing my breasts, as I knew they would. His breathing deepens.

'Please... please go on,' Tom gasps.

'Don't worry, I will. OK, well you're trapped there with all six girls working together in co-ordination, and you're their victim and are totally helpless.' I pause for a moment. 'And then, still stroking you, the chief executioner kisses you on the lips.'

I kiss Tom on the lips too, at first teasingly, tracing his lips with my tongue, then deepening the kiss, letting my tongue slip inside his mouth to play against his own tongue. He can't resist that. His arms circle me and pull me down on top of him. We kiss deeply for a while, and his hands wander down my back. He grasps my bum gently but firmly.

'At this point,' I murmur close to his face so he can feel my breath, 'the chief executioner, still kissing you, caresses your neck and your throat with her bare hands.'

Tom shivers. 'Does she?'

'Oh yes,' I nod wickedly. 'So, there you are, utterly at her mercy, at the mercy of all of them, and all their various perfumes are mingling around you and through their perfumes you can smell the scent of their beautiful, oil-slick bodies. You might wonder whether such glorious goddesses could possibly carry out their jobs and kill you at all. And maybe you imagine in a desperate fantasy that the chief executioner might have fallen in love with you, or maybe they all have, and they won't carry out the execution at all but, believe me, they are good at their job. They are going to give you the sexiest experience you ever had, or are ever likely to ever have, and you'll die happy.'

Again I pause to give myself time to imagine what happens next. After a few moments I lean towards the drawer again and grab the bondage tape, while he takes advantage of my right nipple brushing his face to grab it with his lips and suck. A shock of electricity runs through me as he tugs gently. I suddenly find myself enjoying two lovely orgasms in quick succession. I can't help but rest the hand holding the tape on the bed for a moment and let Tom work his tongue first round one nipple, then, pulling me closer, round the other nipple. I'd like him to keep on doing what he's doing, but this is a story I'm concocting for Tom, so I get back to it.

'And now the chief executioner caresses your throat more firmly. Are you scared? Can you feel her strong, long-fingered hands round your throat?'

I put the tape down next to me while I circle his throat playfully, and his lips part as he pretends to gasp for breath. Then I pick up the roll of black tape, find the end and unravel a strip. The spindles on Tom's iron headboard are perfect for this. I guide his hands above his head and bind them to the post.

'While the sixth executioner, with the crimson scarf, caresses your neck and kisses you, the others are making sure you can't move.'

I manoeuvre myself off the mattress and go down to the foot of the bed. I quickly tie Tom's legs apart to the iron frame at the foot of the bed. Now he's really at my mercy, and I feel great power run through me. I can do anything to him, and there's nothing he can do about it. Like in my story, he's helpless and vulnerable.

He's mine. I'm totally into the role.

'You must realise by now that the women have done this before. They've executed men many times. You really are going to die. Now, you can try to resist as much as you want,' I run my hand up and down his erection, '*but you can't escape*. It's no use struggling. No use at all. We women are too strong for you, and we know what we're doing. The women holding your feet and hands have done this job many times before. They're not going to let you go, however hard you struggle to break free. You can struggle all you want, but it's no use, we have you trapped. You are in our power.' I say these last few sentences in a very seductive tone.

I spot Tom peeking between his eyelashes. There's one more thing I want to do, so I can complete the story. Again, I lean over and grab something out of the drawer. It's the blindfold. I don't want him to spoil the role-play with reality. I lift his head and place the stretchy blindfold on him. No more eye contact.

I lay my hands back on his neck, and intermittently kiss him, as I speak. 'And now, the chief executioner's hands and fingers are around your neck, getting stronger and stronger. I can feel your fear. You know I'm going to kill you, don't you? I can taste your lips. Can you taste the sweetness of mine? I have on your favourite perfume, and that tickling you feel is my long, brown hair brushing over your body. If I remove my hands from your neck, like this, maybe you think I really like you after all. Maybe you think I'll give you a reprieve.'

'And will you?' gasps Tom.

'No, but you're hoping I will. And maybe you feel a sense of relief, or at least you do until the chief executioner – me – sits up on your chest, and slowly, enticingly, removes the scarlet silk scarf from round her lovely swan-like neck. She signals to the woman by your thighs to start her work, and I see her running her hand up and down your erection, simultaneously kissing and licking the head.'

Tom can't hold back his moans now. 'And now,' I tell him, 'you're even less able to resist, so weak and helplessly are you at our mercy. I have the scarf in my hands.' I look around for something to use as a scarf – finding nothing, I unclasp my stockings with one hand, keeping the other on his erection. 'The scarf's purpose has been fulfilled many times before, and it craves another neck to hold tight and squeeze until it stills the life of the person whose neck it is. And though you are feeling the absolute pleasure now of being mastered by a woman, in a short while you will feel fear as you've never known it. Absolute pleasure and absolute fear combined...'

'Is that possible?' Tom gasps. 'Absolute fear and pleasure combined?'

'Yes, definitely. Well, you know me, don't you? And now the scarf of the chief executioner is in my hands, and I've made a loop of it, and am slipping it over your neck. Can you feel the scarf round your neck? Can you feel it when I pull it tighter round your throat? That's the feeling of death. There's nothing you can do to stop us now. The girls are holding your hands too firmly for you to stop me pulling the scarf a little tighter, like this, and a little tighter again... Can you feel death coming for you? Can you feel the ecstasy of your heightened senses combining with your terrified thoughts "is this is it? Is this is the way I will die?"'

I lean towards him and kiss his lips passionately with my eyes closed. I press my hot, completely naked body against his, our skin surfaces touching all over, our sweat mingling together just like our breaths are mingling already. I feel his hardness pressing against my firm right thigh, so I lift myself slightly and move a few inches to the right. He gasps with excitement. I quickly get a condom out of his bedside drawer, open the packet and slip it on him. He gasps some more. I'm very wet, and he's very hard, and a moment later, very naturally, he slips into me. I twist the stocking around his neck. 'And now... and now I, the chief executioner, and my beautiful naked executioners, will take your life according to the sentence,' I somehow manage to say. I can feel Tom writhe beneath me as I twist the stocking again and again, my eyes closed so I could feel his shuddering become uncontrolled and final. He screams out with pleasure as he comes inside me.

Then, suddenly he goes still, and I know my job is done. I open my eyes. I see at once his face is the wrong colour; it's a dangerous shade of red, and his legs are twitching irregularly under me.

Oh my God, have I really killed him?

20

'Wake up, Tom, wake up!'

He doesn't.

I slap his cheeks twice, both of them, then his face.

He still doesn't move.

Oh God, oh God, oh God.

I rush to the kitchen at the speed of light, grab a saucepan, turn the cold tap on full, fill the saucepan and dash back. Thank goodness, when I get back to the bedroom, Tom's groaning and moving a bit. I fling the entire saucepan of water at him (taking care to keep hold of the saucepan).

Tom blinks, gazes at me and sits up on the bed, water fountaining all over him.

'Bloody hell,' he murmurs. 'You almost did it, Vanny. *You almost killed me.*'

'*I'm sorry I'm sorry I'm sorry I'm sorry.* I got carried away. Oh, God, I'm so sorry.' I'm almost psychotic with relief.

I fling myself on him in a sort of affectionate ecstasy of relief that he's OK. I know he's just my Friend with Benefits, but I actually feel very loving towards him at that moment.

We make love vigorously for quite some time.

That night, sleeping deeply next to Tom, I dream about strangling him to death with my legs.

'I just don't get it, Vanny. Why would a Finnish healthcare innovation company have its main research and development facility in New York?'

It's the morning, maybe about half seven. I sit up in bed, still completely naked. 'I see you've a bee in your bonnet about that company I told you about, the one Boris mentioned to me in his email.'

'You bet I have. Well, let's check it out,' Tom murmurs. He hops out of bed, naked as - though hairier than - the day he was born, puts on his black boxers, and goes straight to his desk. He switches on his laptop. Once his laptop's booted up he hunches himself over the keyboard and starts tapping away.

I wonder what he's doing.

Three or four minutes later, he spins round in his swivelly chair and says: 'The company's called Henki Oh Why.'

'Why's it called Hen-key Oh Why? What kind of name's that for a healthcare company?'

'Not Hen-key, but "Henki"- H-E-N-K-I. It says on google that it's Finnish for "soul", "mind, or "spirit". And the "Oh why" isn't like in "Oh, why is Vanny so gorgeous?" but...'

'You slipped *that* in rather well.'

'Yes,' Tom smiled wickedly. 'Just like earlier.'

'Don't be lewd. What were you saying about the "oh, why"?'

'I was saying that "Oh Why" means the letters "O" and "Y". It seems to be the Finnish abbreviation for Limited. I got that from Wiki, too.'

'So now we know. Come back to bed.'

Tom gets off the swivelly chair and sits down next to me on the bed. He's looking very thoughtful. 'According to this, your Russian admirer's an executive director of Henki Oy and owns ninety-three percent of its shares. There aren't any details on Wiki or anywhere else about the kind of innovations Henki's been producing, and their website is also ultra-cagey about that. All it says is that Henki is "pioneering state-of-the-art developments in patient care". In other words, typical corporate guff.'

'But why would anyone invest in it if there's so little information about it?'

'Maybe that's the idea. Perhaps he doesn't want any more investors. Could even be that the seven percent he doesn't own is held by some of his own associates.'

Only now, Tom hops back into bed next to me. He still looks terribly thoughtful.

'You're not going to let this go, are you?' I say.

'No, I'm not. I'll do some more research later. But anyway, what are *you* going to do about Boris?'

'You already know. Nothing.'

'OK... but what about the money? Are you going to take his rather weird advice he gave you in the second email and create a fund for the love that... what was it...?'

'*Doesn't alter when it alteration finds.* I haven't decided yet.'

'Well,' said Tom, 'whatever you decide, he doesn't sound like a quitter to me. After all, it sounds like he's arranged the tournament in New York just for *you*.'

'That isn't necessarily so. I mean, it certainly isn't clear from his email.'

'Maybe not, but it seems pretty obvious to me. Anyway, can you get him to invite me?'

'I'm very happy to ask him to invite you. I don't know if the hotel offer is for everyone, though.'

'Vanny, the guy's a billionaire. He gave you a cheque for a million dollars as if it was just a bouquet of roses, *and* he sent you a Shakespeare sonnet. He'll hopefully do anything you want. Just don't tell him about our relationship.'

'You and I don't have a relationship,' I remind him. 'We're basically just friends.'

If this disappoints Tom he doesn't show it. 'Dead right. We should be "just good friends" again. How about tomorrow evening?'

I shake my head. 'Too soon. Soon, but not that soon.' Wanting to change the subject I say, 'what's so good about an X3000 joystick?'

'The X3000? Oh, they're absolute state-of-the-art. Fantastic response speed, full simulated biofeedback. Why d'you ask?'

'You remember the helicopter flight I told you he took me on in Hastings?'

'How could I forget?'

'Boris sent me a link to a rather cool helicopter flight simulator game and I've been having a go. Only it's hard doing it only with the keyboard and the mouse. It says you need a X3000 joystick. Oh, and foot pedals for the helicopter's foot controls, but I've ordered those from Amazon already.'

'I'll see what I can do about the joystick.'

'Tom, you don't need to buy me one.'

We get all nice and cuddly and close again. Sometime during our happy toil, Tom, with me on top of him, his hands pressing against each of my buttocks, and with him deep inside me, starts to murmur in his ecstasy a favourite quotation of his, from a batty philosopher called Wittgenstein, who is Tom's favourite philosopher:

'If we take eternity to mean not infinite temporal duration,' Tom breathes, *'but timelessness, then eternal life belongs to those who live in the present.'*

I smile as I look down at Tom's dishy face. His eyes are closed, his lips parted in happiness, his breath's coming fast.

'And d'you think we're living in the present right now?' I ask.

He nods wordlessly.

'Me too,' I whisper.

21

I saw Tom again two days later, on the Wednesday evening. I wanted a platonic evening, though: I was just feeling like that. Tom seemed OK about it. I think we were both still exhausted after Monday.

'Your admirer's got a big stake in a really mysterious company, if you ask me,' Tom said.

'What d'you mean?'

'Just what I say. I'm talking about Henki Oy. I've used every search engine I can and I can't find anything else about it at all. I even phoned up their head office in Helsinki and their research and development facility in upstate New York.'

'Goodness, you really are making progress.'

'I pretended to be a journalist interested in their work,' Tom said. 'I got nowhere when I phoned their Helsinki office at all. They took ages to answer my call. When they finally did, I found myself talking to a middle-aged morose-sounding Finnish bloke. I asked if I could speak to the public relations department, but he said he was the only person there, and that he was just a caretaker, and that if I had any questions I should phone their office in the States. I asked him for the number, but then the line went dead before he'd given it to me. Pretty suspicious, don't you think? I phoned again of course, but this time just got voicemail. So I decided to check out the website and see if I could find the US phone number that way.'

Tom had been talking really fast. He drew a quick breath. 'The phone number of their facility in the US isn't on their website: it's one of those really irritating websites that don't provide any phone numbers. But I managed to get the number from international directory enquiries.'

'So you phoned them? What happened?'

'That's where things got really weird. I mean, I just couldn't get to talk to anyone. The telephone answering system was fully automated - that's pretty normal for the States, and very irritating, but if you try hard enough with an automated system and are persistent you can usually get to talk to *someone*. But not when you phone Henki Oy. You get about eight options, and each one of the options has various sub-options, but not one of those sub-options gives you the chance to actually *speak* to anyone, and believe me, I tried every bloody option. It's actually pretty spooky.'

Tom stared at me in the intense way he sometimes does. 'Vanny, why don't you ask Boris what is it that Henki Oy really does?'

I shook my head. 'I suppose I could, but it'd just put him on his guard, wouldn't it? Besides, I wouldn't feel comfortable asking him a question like that. We still have a pretty formal relationship.'

Tom gave a wry smile. 'Oh, it's "we" now, is it?'

'Of course not. Don't be silly.'

'OK, well it's none of my business, I suppose, but I think there's no way we're going to find out anything more about it unless you *do* ask him. Why not just send him a sweetly curious email?'

I told him I'd think about it.

A couple of days after the evening when I invented the execution scenario for Tom, an X3000 joystick arrived in the morning by special delivery. I didn't need to read the accompanying note to be able to guess who sent it, but of course I did read it. The note read, *'thanks for blowing my mind. Now you can blow yours.'*

22

It was the evening of our party. There were about twenty of Lottie's musical friends there, and roughly the same number of chess friends of Jaz and me. I don't remember all the chess-players who came, but of course Tom did (he and I always took care in public to avoid giving any indication of what we got up to when we were alone). Stuart Conquest came along too, with three gorgeous Spanish women. He tends to divide his time between Britain and Gibraltar. That trusty Cornish giant-killer Andrew Greet was there too. So was David Howell and his beautiful sister Julia.

We used the living-room for dancing. At about nine o'clock in the evening, Lottie and Adrian would be doing their party piece: their 'rocked-up' version of Pachelbel's *Canon*.

The performance of the *Canon* did go ahead, but it all happened quite a bit differently from what we'd planned, because the party had a Surprise Celebrity Guest.

Lottie had told me Ade had mentioned the party to the famous cellist Steve Juselius, and I knew there was at least a remote possibility Steven might come as apparently he didn't have a professional engagement that evening. But all the same, you know how it is with celebrities: by definition they're in demand and...

Steve arrived.

I'd never met him before in the flesh, though I had seen him a few times on TV. I was coming out of the kitchen in my party outfit (another pencil dress but an orangey-yellowy one this time), and in the corridor I saw a guy, mid-thirties, in a black jacket, a grey button-down shirt, no tie, and grey trousers. His face was slightly lined, but handsome because of this rather than in spite of it. There was... I don't know... a tremendous amount of intelligence in his eyes and in his expression. His hair, which was jet-black, curly and unfashionably long, gave him something of the look of a Renaissance nobleman, and....

Then I recognised him.

'You're Steven Juselius!' I exclaimed, in my habitually subtle way. 'I'm Vanny.'

He gave a faint nod, and reached out his right hand to shake mine. 'Hi, Vanny. Ade's often mentioned you as Lottie's best friend. Pleased to meet you.'

'Thank you.'

'I wasn't sure I could come; I had a dreary dinner in Chelsea with some music critics, but they all seemed to pass out after passing the port, so I skulked off and got a cab here. Ade promised there'd be some lovely women here, and,' Steve smiled, 'he wasn't joking.'

I seriously blushed. 'Thanks. I think you're a sort of a god of the cello.'

He shrugged. 'Oh, I just move the bow about and hope for the best.'

I'd liked to have talked to Steve more, but at that moment Lottie and Ade appeared in the corridor (I supposed Steve had texted them to say he was on his way) and there was a sort of explosion of greetings and hugs. We all went into the living-room and had drinks and the people there who did know who Steve was whispered to the others who didn't.

Well, what happened next was that Ade offered to let Steve play his cello part in the performance of the *Canon*. Lottie was ecstatic at the prospect of playing a duet with Steve and agreed so quickly I even wondered if Ade might have secretly been a bit disappointed. But if he was, he certainly didn't show it, and yielded his place about as readily as Tom would agree to being tortured by an all-female Swedish hockey team.

I did wonder how on earth the performance was going to work, though, as I knew Lottie and Ade had been doing quite a bit of practising for their party piece. So how was Steve going to learn it with about half an hour's notice, especially as the *Canon* wasn't written for the cello, so he wouldn't know the piece by heart?

How little I knew about what brilliantly talented musicians can do! Adrian went off in a huddle with Steve to talk about the piece. While they did, I headed off with Lottie to her room to help her button up the lovely sequined pink dress she'd be wearing for the performance. While she was in her underwear and fishing the dress out from her walk-in wardrobe (she was the daughter of a millionaire, after all), I asked Lottie if she had the music for the cello part, as I didn't see how Steve could play it without that.

Lottie smiled. 'No, Vanny, dear, Ade and I have just learnt it together from listening to it; we haven't written the music down.'

'But then how can Steve play it?'

'Oh, darling, he's practically the best cellist in the world. He won't have a problem, really he won't. And besides, of course he does know Pachelbel's *Canon.*' Lottie started putting her dress on. 'Ade's going through what we've done with the chords and the rhythm and stuff.'

'So you mean Steve can basically just turn up here and play something he's never played before?'

'*Of course.* He's a musical genius. All right, can you do the buttons up at the back now?'

How wonderful music is. I remember something Hogwarts headmaster Dumbledore said in the first Harry Potter book, about how music was better than all the magic they ever did at

Hogwarts. I always liked him saying that. I bet J.K. Rowling agrees with him.

Oh my God, that performance! How can I ever forget it?

I was sandwiched on a sofa between Ade and Tom, and with two other girls on Tom's left. Tom seemed particularly happy about sandwiching me. Most of the other guests were sitting around, on chairs and bean bags or just on the floor. Ade had lent Steve his cello: Ade's was only quite a cheap one by cello standards; it had only cost a few thousand pounds. Steve's usual cello, Lottie had told me, was a Strad and worth a fortune, but he didn't have it with him.

Lottie was sitting at the Steinway grand piano that stood in the living-room. And there on Lottie's left, with Ade's cello, sat Steve Juselius, his hair combed into an approximate semblance of order.

Then they began playing.

Steve opened with some wonderful low notes, then after maybe ten seconds or so Lottie came in on the piano with some of the most exquisite, quick, light-fingered, stunning high notes I'd ever heard her play; so lovely, so sublime, they were like the ringing of bells in heaven. It was spellbinding, wonderful beyond wonder. I was already practically in tears.

Steve went on playing these marvellous gravelly low notes as an undercurrent to Lottie's playing. Then after maybe half a minute, Steve, his eyes half-closed, his whole expression lost in the ecstasy of the music, began to play the main melody of the *Canon*, while Lottie accompanied him with lovely scaley bits.

A minute or so later, they changed tempo and went into a rocked-up version of the piece, and it really worked, and we clapped to the beat, and the whole room was full of music and happiness. After a while the piece grew more stately again, and this time Lottie had the main melody, while Steve was just sort of counterpointing her, if that's the right word, which it probably isn't. So their version of Pachelbel's *Canon* went on thrilling us, with lightning-quick changes of tempo, swift alternations between who carried the melody, and utterly full of life.

We all applauded for ages when they finished.

Afterwards, the CD player was switched on again and most of the guests started dancing. I followed Lottie into her bedroom. I knew she'd need help getting her dress off so she could put on something more suitable for dancing. Once I was in the room I was astonished to see Lottie glance fiercely at the door, as if it had done her some personal injustice, and then to my horror kick it shut. She flung herself onto her bed, and cried and cried and cried.

It must have been some minutes before she began to tell me what was wrong.

By the time she did, I was so upset about her weeping I was crying too.

But of course, I listened hard to what she said.

A few minutes later I was still wondering what it could all mean, when there was a sharp knock on the door.

I opened it. Standing there were Ade and Steve. I somehow felt Lottie needed to tell them, her fellow musicians, what she'd told me, and I realised I shouldn't be there when she did. So I gave Lottie a big hug, used a corner of one of her bedsheets to dry her eyes, kissed her on the forehead, and left the room.

I hurried to find Tom. He was in the kitchen talking to David Howell.

'Tom,' I said, 'can I talk to you for a moment in private?'

I glanced at David. 'Sorry, Dave.'

David smiled. 'No problem, Vanny. When the urge takes you, best to act on it.'

I grinned. So did Tom. He followed me out of the kitchen and into the corridor.

'Come into my bedroom,' I said.

'Bloody hell, you really are insatiable.'

'Keep your voice down, and don't be silly. That's not why I want to talk to you. You know we never do it here, anyway. Hurry up. I need to tell you something.'

Tom was fortunately sensitive enough and sensible enough not to say anything else until we were in my room. When we were, he only said, in an adorably completely serious voice, 'All right, so what's the problem?'

'It's Lottie. She's in a terrible state. I wouldn't have left her, but Ade and Steve turned up after she blurted out some strange things to me. She cried all the time; I couldn't stop her crying, though I did my best. She was crying just so much. She said that she hadn't been playing well... for a few weeks she said. She told me that the fingers of her left hand weren't doing what she wanted them to do. She said... Tom, she said she'd thought it had all been her imagination, and that she had really been hoping the reason was she'd been getting distracted by her outside work – you know, all the event organising she does – and that it'd all be OK when she was performing. But then, she said the same problem had happened: just now when she'd been performing, about two minutes into the piece, during a fast scaley passage, her fingers all fell over one another.'

'I don't understand,' Tom said. 'The performance was great.'

'Tom, I told her so too. But she said very likely no-one had noticed, but that was only because Steve had been so good at covering her up and adapting to the new tempo.'

Tom grew instantly deeply thoughtful. For a few moments he rubbed his chin with the thumb and forefinger of his right hand, which suddenly made him look like an ancient sage from one of his fantasy books.

'I told Lottie I thought maybe it was carpal tunnel syndrome,' I said, 'but she told me, really tearfully, that she'd looked it up on Wiki and that the symptoms of carpal tunnel syndrome didn't seem at all like what was happening to her at all. She said she was going to see her doctor.'

Tom nodded. 'Good. Glad to hear it. Yes, she needs to do that. Vanny, you should go back to the party. Lottie obviously needs some very good medical advice. Meanwhile, you've got guests. And besides, they're playing "How Deep is Your Love". I'd really like a dance to that with you.'

'We can't dance to that, Tom. I don't want people to guess.'

'Guess what?' he said, suddenly all innocence.

'You know what I mean.'

'All right, then I'll find someone to dance with who appreciates a good man.'

Suddenly, for some reason which I didn't understand, because this wasn't typical of me as far as Tom was concerned, I reached out my right hand and stroked his forehead.

'I appreciate a good man, Tom. You know I do.'

He drew a quick breath. 'I know. Come on, let's not get gushy. I know you hate it when I make you feel gushy.'

I nodded. 'You're right, I do.'

I wiped my eyes, then I went back to the living-room. Tom followed me only after half a minute or so; this was our brilliant plan so that (hopefully) no-one would guess anything.

The moment I was back in the living-room, I saw Lottie dancing with Ade to "How Deep is Your Love?" I don't think anyone would have guessed, from the way Lottie and Ade were dancing, that she'd been so horribly upset less than half an hour ago.

Steve Juselius was dancing with one of the three Spanish women Stuart had brought along. But Tom and I didn't dance to it.

23

Four days after the party, first thing on the morning of Wednesday, January the eighteenth, when I was still in bed, I used my iPad to log onto my bank's internet banking site. I was by myself that morning in the flat, but my heart was beating almost as fast as it did after a particularly vigorous bout of naked combat with Tom.

Jaz had left for work. Lottie, who'd had some headaches the day before, had booked herself a doctor's appointment for eight thirty that morning.

I keyed in all the passwords to get to my current balance. Finally, the screen with the balance in my savings account came up.

My balance usually teetered around the £2,500 mark, and that was when I was having a good month. There'd been a slight positive hiccup in my account when I came back from Hastings and banked my £2,260 prize, but much of that had gone: two months' rent at £425 a month (I'd been a month in arrears), on some new clothes for myself and on helping Mum out with some of her household expenses.

Then I found myself staring at the amount in my Instant Saver account.

Boris's cheque had cleared.

Now, I just looked transfixed at the six figures.

£673,010. Plus forty-six pence.

What was in my account consisted of the sterling equivalent of the million-dollar cheque plus the remnants of what I'd had in there myself.

Had I really expected the cheque to clear? I suppose by now, to be perfectly honest, I had, but that absolutely was *not* the same as being prepared for how I'd feel if it did.

I didn't know what to do, or what to feel. This massive financial windfall was so totally undeserved.

I put my iPad on my bedside table, lay back in bed and tried to get myself together.

It wasn't easy.

Yes, I'd been imagining that this might happen, and I'd imagined that preparing myself for it might have made it easier to have handled it, but it didn't feel any easier to handle *at all*.

I lay there for a few more minutes, allowing the warmth of the bed to comfort me. Then I got up. I was a great believer in those days that every problem had a practical solution, or at least that most did anyway.

But that was before I really knew what grief and loss really were.

The middlegame

The phase of a game between the opening and the endgame, in which the main strategies introduced in the opening are developed and expanded.

From *Introduction to Chess* by Ivana Jones
(Checkmate Publications)

24

'The *love fund*?' Jaz said, when she came in from work, early that evening.

I smiled. 'Yes. Only, it needs capital letters really, because it's so important.'

Jaz nodded. 'So what exactly is the Love Fund?'

Lottie hadn't come home yet. I supposed that after she'd been to the doctor's she'd gone to practise at one of the various music studios with which she has connections, and where she can practise on grand pianos and bash them as loudly as she likes.

'Don't you remember? Boris's cheque? It cleared today.'

'It did?'

'Yes!'

'Oh my God, oh my God,' Jaz said. 'I mean... I knew today was the day, but... I honestly don't think I ever thought it was going to clear, really. I haven't even mentioned it, I suppose because I didn't want to tempt fate, and... what's in that envelope, anyway?'

She asked this because I had just that moment handed her a brown envelope.

I hadn't sealed the envelope by licking the gluey bit, but had just tucked the flap in. Jaz picked up the envelope, pulled out the flap, then reached in with her index finger to retrieve the contents.

I just watched her.

Jaz glanced at me, then at what she'd just fished out from the envelope, then at me again.

'What's this, Vanny?'

'It's a cheque,' I said. 'It's a cheque for ten thousand pounds, payable to... Lucretia Duvall.'

'*Mum*. Oh, Vanny... what can I say?'

'Don't say anything, please.'

'Oh Vanny, this is just so generous of you.'

'Not really,' I said. 'I didn't earn the money, I just got it, so it's easy to be generous with it. My mum gets one too. Ten thousand pounds. The first two contributions from the Love Fund. I'll explain what it is later, but basically it's for people I love and for people who love life. There's an envelope on your bed with a cheque for ten thousand pounds in it. It's to help you. I'm giving myself ten thousand pounds too, because I want to and I never said I was a saint, and also I've bought myself a treat. The rest is staying in the fund – I've opened a special bank account for it at Santander and the money will be for people who I think are true and good and also for charities that I think can really use some of it. There isn't much money really if you think of all the terrible amount of suffering in the world, but I'll do my best to try to stop some of that suffering.'

Jaz looked at me, and again at her mum's cheque. Suddenly she began to cry.

So did I.

Presently, Jaz wiped her eyes with an edge of the table-cloth, and I wiped mine with a paper napkin 'Oh,' I said, 'and I've also decided I'm going to give twenty thousand pounds to the English Chess Federation to help develop junior chess.'

'Vanny, that would be *so* marvellous. It would... well, it would transform junior chess in this country.'

I smiled. 'Good.'

'So... what's this present you've bought?'

'I'll show you after you've finished your tea.'

'You can't show me now?' Jaz asked.

'No, I'm afraid not.'

'Why not?'

'Because,' I smiled, 'she's parked in the street downstairs.'

Jaz screamed. I screamed. Jaz put down her cup, stared at me, screamed again, grabbed me by the right hand, and led me out of the flat, down the stairs and out into the street. There, close by a street-lamp, I felt proud and yet also a bit mercenary as I showed Jaz my brand-new, gleaming metallic red Fiat Femina, complete with alloy wheels and a sun-roof which obviously wasn't open at the moment, it being a cold, dark, January evening.

There'd been several red Fiat Feminas at the showroom, but I'd chosen one which had the letters 'SAL' at the end of its number-plate. I'd already decided to call her Sally.

I'd bought Sally earlier that afternoon for £12,999, after managing to negotiate a discount from the list price of £15,000.

Jaz just gaped at the car.

'Oh my God! My God! It's just *beautiful*,' she said. Then she smiled. 'I've heard about Fiat Feminas. They're specially designed for girls, aren't they?'

'Yes, they are. You've got to call her Sally though.'

'Sally?'

'Look at the number-plate.'

Jaz's smile widened.

I thought back over what the salesmen had told me that afternoon, then I said: 'She's got extra room in the ergonomically designed boot for shopping, plus wine bottle holders. Extra space in the glove box for all our personal things. Special contoured driver's seat for maximum comfort for our more rounded shapes. The salesman seemed a bit embarrassed to mention that one, but he did mention it. All her controls are designed to be extra-responsive to a more gentle touch. Mirrors on the back of the driver and passenger sun-shades.

Central locking, so no struggling with shopping and unlocking doors. Oh, and the built-in SatNav specially highlights major shopping centres and clothes shops, including charity shops. Honestly, anyone would think Sally's designers think we women never do anything but shop!'

'As if,' said Jaz. 'Well, Vanny, you're the one who bought a car whose entire design is based on gender stereotypes. Don't go complaining about it now.'

I laughed. 'Come on, let's take her for a spin.'

I opened the central locking and we both got in, me in the driver's seat and Jaz next to me.

'How does your seat feel?' I asked her.

'Wonderful. It's almost like my bum's being massaged.'

'Your bum *is* being massaged. Yes, mine feels like that, too.'

We closed the doors and I switched the electrics on so I could use the heater; it was quite cold outside.

I was about to turn the key in the ignition, but then I saw Lottie on the pavement, walking towards us, and I gave the horn an impulsive parp to get her attention.

Lottie looked in our direction, but didn't seem to register that she'd seen me.

I realised at once that my dear friend looked so, so unhappy. I glanced behind me and after checking the coast was clear I opened the door on my side, turned the ignition key half a turn to switch the electrics off, then got out of the car. So did Jaz.

Lottie had seen the car, but she didn't look pleased for me or indeed pleased about anything. She was wearing a lovely, well-cut light brown cashmere coat. Her blond hair was tied back in a single ponytail. But she looked weary and sad, too, and as she got closer to us, I saw under the street-lamp that her eyes were sad as well.

She forced a smile. 'So, I suppose the cheque cleared.'

I nodded. I wanted to tell her about the Love Fund, and that I wasn't planning on spending all the money on myself, but somehow I could tell from the expression on her face that she wouldn't welcome me going on about anything at all, at least at that moment.

I gave her a hug, but she wasn't responding to it. 'What's wrong, darling?'

'Yes, what is it?' said Jaz.

'I don't feel well,' Lottie said. 'I've had a headache practically all day. And yesterday, too.'

I quickly went to get the key from the car, shut the driver door and pointed the keys at the car to lock it. Jaz, Lottie and I all began walking back towards the entrance to the flat.

'What did the doctor say?' I asked.

Lottie shrugged. 'He thinks it's a migraine caused by stress. He gave me some tablets.'

'Did you tell him about your loss of finger control while you were playing?'

'Yes,' Lottie said. 'He told me that was probably caused by stress too. He told me to take it easy for a week and take the tablets and see how things go. But how can I take it easy? I've oodles of calls I need to make tomorrow.'

We'd reached the street entrance to the flat by now. I opened the door with my key.

'Well, maybe I could help you with your work this week,' I said.

'But Vanny, you're busy too,' Lottie said. 'You're going to Gibraltar on Sunday and you need to train for it.'

'Yes, but I can help you as well. I don't want you getting stressed, darling. I'll help you.'

I made the three of us all a nice, simple meal; my version of spaghetti Bolognese with not too much mince (Lottie, Jaz and I all eat meat, but tend to prefer vegetables) and plenty of chopped tomatoes and peas and chopped carrots and then lots of grated Parmesan on top. Of course, half the fun of spag bol is the challenge of eating it, and avoiding getting the sauce all over your face and your clothing. It was a really delish supper. We didn't have any wine though, as Lottie told us that it said on the side of the migraine tablets bottle you had to avoid alcohol, and if Lottie couldn't drink, Jaz and I didn't want to. So we all stuck to water. Afterwards we had white Magnum ice creams and decaf coffee.

Lottie finally seemed to relax during the meal. She took one of the anti-migraine pills. She could take two a day, and she'd already taken one and by the time we were onto the Magnums she said the headache had stopped, which I was of course really pleased to hear.

'I'm not sure if it's the pills or the company, or both,' Lottie said, 'but I do feel much better.'

Jaz nodded. 'Or maybe it was the spag bol.'

Lottie smiled. 'No, I'm sure it was the company. Though, it was *such* a lovely supper, Vanny, it really was.'

After we'd had the coffees, Lottie went to the music room to practise on her electric piano using headphones. It was really good to see her go off to practise: I knew that whenever she was really down she couldn't play the piano, so the fact that she could had to be encouraging.

I went to my room and wrote an email to Boris to tell him about the Love Fund and that as the cheque had cleared today, I'd made the first donations.

I decided not to tell him about my car.

But I did mention Tom's name to Boris, in a casual sort of way. I said in my email that I had a friend called Tom Hardiman who was a grandmaster and would really like to play in the New York tournament. I asked Boris if he'd consider arranging for Tom to have an invitation. I also added a few lines about my new hobby of virtual helicopter flying.

I ended the email like this:

I'm looking forward to running the Love Fund, which I'm sure will be a truly illuminating and interesting experience.

Oh, by the way, how's your chess coming along?

Very best wishes, Ivana

Then I wrote an email to my father.

Hi Dad

Thanks so much for your seven emails telling me to marry Boris. Dad, I don't want to because I'm not in love with him. Many thanks to you and Larissa for inviting me to Monte Carlo in the first week of March. I think I'll come down on the morning of Thursday March 1 if that's OK, and stay until Tuesday or Wednesday.

No, Dad, I wasn't joking about the million-dollar cheque. It really exists and actually I would have made more fuss about it, but I wasn't sure until today if it was even going to clear, but it has, so right now there's more than £600,000 in my bank account.

I've given myself a special treat and bought myself a new car with some of the money - it's a Fiat Femina called Sally – and I'm going to keep £10,000 for myself. But actually, I'm certainly not going to spend all the money on myself as you suggest. I don't want to spend more than a very small part of the money on myself as I didn't earn it. But fortunately I've thought of a really good cause and will be giving some help to that cause, as well as to British junior chess.

Anyway, looking forward to seeing you both soon.
Lots of love to you dad and to Larissa and Piotr.

Hugs from Ivana xxxxx

Dad, who's sixty-three years old, had lived in Monte Carlo for about twenty years and been married to Larissa, who was forty-two, for eight of them. Their lovely little boy, Piotr, my half-brother, was six years old.

Later that evening, just before I went to bed, I knocked on the door of the music room. Lottie called out to me to come in. I did.

She was sitting at her desk, doing emails. She looked up and smiled at me.

'Thanks, darling. Guess what? I played the piano part earlier from the Pachelbel piece Steve and I performed at the party. My fingers didn't seize up at all.'

I went up to her and kissed her on the forehead. 'I'm so, so glad, I really am. How d'you feel now?'

'Better. Much better. But... still not a hundred percent.'

'Well, you only started taking the tablets today, so I'm sure you'll feel better once they really start to kick in.'

Lottie smiled. 'I'm sure you're right, darling.'

I smiled back, kissed her on the forehead again, then went off to bed.

As I lay there, though, waiting to go to sleep. I suddenly felt worried about Lottie, and in fact so worried that my sudden elevation to undeserved wealth didn't mean much to me.

Lottie wasn't the sort of girl to say she didn't feel a hundred percent; in fact, I couldn't remember her ever having said that to me before.

I went to sleep promising myself I'd keep a careful eye on her all the time until I had to leave for Gibraltar, and I did.

As the week progressed, Lottie seemed to me to keep on getting better, though the headaches never completely went away. More positively she was often on her mobile in her room, and I sort of got the idea that something new and exciting was happening in her life. But I didn't ask her what it was: Lottie always liked to tell me in her own good time about new things that were happening to her. I was sure I'd know about it sooner or later.

25

Jaz and I flew to Gibraltar on the following Sunday, January the twenty-second. I've played in the Gibraltar Tournament for the past four years. It's a great event to play in, because of its high prize-money (not long ago, David Howell came second in Gibraltar and won £20,000) which attracts lots of extremely strong players. Jaz and I were both getting an appearance fee (I got a bit more as I was an IM) and our hotel expenses including breakfast and dinner. We each had our own rooms, though rooms are allocated fairly randomly to players, and Jaz and I (and, as things turned out, Sven) all had rooms on different floors of the hotel where the tournament takes place. This is the Caleta, which is spectacularly built into an eastern-facing cliff-face, overlooking the Strait of Gibraltar and the Mediterranean. The rooms are comfy, but with so much going on chess-wise and socially at the Gibraltar tournament, no-one uses their rooms for much else than sleeping unless they get lucky.

Now I don't know if you've ever been to Gibraltar, but I need to say right away that it's a definitely wacky place, and as you've already seen that my life is pretty wacky itself, you'll know that when I use a word, I really mean it. Gibraltar's one of those places that, if you were to read about it in a novel, you wouldn't believe it could exist.

One moment you're in Spain (the nice warm southern part) and the next minute you cross a nice friendly border (well, it's friendly enough at the moment anyway) and suddenly you get this feeling you've come to England, not modern England but a special, weird kind of old-fashioned England. An England where things happen quite slowly, and where all the signs are not only in English, but in that familiar English font which you see on roadsides in England itself.

So there you are, in Olde Worlde England, except it's hot and sunny and Spain's just across the border and there's this amazing mountain (the word 'rock' really doesn't do it justice) towering over you. I mean, it must be weird enough to be in Gibraltar anyway, but it's even stranger when you're playing in a hotel built into the side of a mountain, and full of chess-players.

I got my air fare paid by the tournament organisers, but Jaz didn't, so I'd treated Jaz to her air ticket, and instead of flying from Stansted with BudgetJet as we usually did, we flew with British Airways in premium economy.

Rather than eat at the hotel that first evening, Jaz and I walked over the border into Spain, our passports in our pockets if anyone asked to see them (no-one did) and we had supper in the Spanish town of La Linea, which is where you arrive once you walk out of Gibraltar. We like going to La Linea. When we'd gone there for supper the year before, which was Jaz's first time playing at Gib, we'd discovered a really great *tapas* bar, where we had among other treats, *boquerones* (fresh anchovies marinated in vinegar, garlic and parsley) that quickly became Jaz's favourite tapa. I love *boquerones*, too. They make you less kissable but they're completely delish. The tapas bar was still there, and we had a lovely supper there.

Tom wouldn't be arriving till the following morning, in time for the start of Round One, as he was doing coaching over the weekend.

Jaz and I got back to the hotel at about ten o'clock that evening. We went into the bar for a drink, and practically the first person we saw was… Sven, who was in a corner of the bar near a roulette machine, talking to Stuart Conquest.

I didn't *want* to feel as I did the moment I saw Sven, I really didn't, I didn't *want* to be completely heady and hopeless the moment I set eyes on him, but I did. He was wearing a V-neck blue jumper and a very cute white and blue checked shirt, well-polished and quite formal brown shoes and smart navy jeans. Sven looked absolutely divine in this: thoughtful, poised, tall and even more delish than the *boquerones.*

I'm not sure Sven noticed Jaz and me come into the bar, though I think he may've done. Jaz and I went to order drinks and as we ordered them, we were only about five yards away from Stuart and Sven. We ordered two glasses of Sauvignon Blanc and moved away from the bar in the opposite direction to where Stuart and Sven were. I noticed Jaz kept giving Sven little glances, but I supposed that was only because she knew all about my feelings for Sven and found him curious.

After five minutes or so, I noticed Britain's number one player, Mickey Adams, go up to talk to Stuart. Sven drifted away, and came over to us. By now Jaz and I were sitting at a table in a secluded corner and talking about Lottie and how happy we were that she was feeling better.

When I noticed Sven coming over to Jaz and me, I tried my best to seem really calm and deeply engaged in conversation with her, i.e. to pretend I was totally unamazed at the prospect of seeing Sven again. But basically it didn't work: I gave him a single glance, and then I was caught, sitting there staring at him and undressing him in my mind as he loped towards us.

Sven had a glass of lager in his left hand. When he was only a couple of steps away from our table I instantly, so to speak, put his clothes back on. He finally glanced up at Jaz and then at me; I presumed he was too nervous to look at me first.

'Good evening, ladies,' he said very formally. Jaz, just to break the ice, got up and pulled his tall, slender, goddish, Norwegian form into a very British hug.

'Great to see you again,' he said to her as he stood there all awkwardly, then she sat back down, glancing at me as though saying, *you'd better be glad I'm doing the work for you.*

I got up, smiled at him nervously, and we exchanged a touch-of-the-shoulder type of hug. Then we made room for him, exchanging pleasantries as he set his beer down on our table. I reminded myself that Sven still didn't know anything about Boris.

Sven glanced at me. 'It is great to see you again, too. Perhaps, Vanny, we will play each other again at the tournament.'

I smiled back. 'Yes, perhaps we will.'

'I know Vanny will be happy for you to beat her, if you could,' said Jaz with a grin.

'Why would she be willing to let me beat her?' Sven asked, obviously genuinely puzzled.

'Oh, I can't possibly imagine,' said Jaz, sipping her wine, and making eye contact with me over the top of the glass as she did so.

I let my eyes linger on hers for a moment, telling her off telepathically, then turned back to Sven. 'How's the magazine coming along?'

'Very well, thanks, but it is extremely hard work. Even now, regrettably this can't be anything more than a brief hello, as I'm booked to interview the tournament organiser Stuart Conquest. I'm sorry, but I look forward to seeing more of you both during the tournament.'

I was personally completely sure just how much of myself I would have been very happy to show him... and who knew how things would work out between him and me during the ten rounds of the tournament?

Jaz and I said goodbye to Sven. He smiled at me and then shook Jaz's right hand with his own. I saw his long white Scandinavian fingers momentarily clasp Jaz's smaller dark brown hand with its elegant slender fingers and red fingernails. Then their hands were apart again, and Sven, having first left his empty glass on the bar rather than on our table, loped off towards the exit.

I glanced at Jaz. 'He's a complete dish, isn't he?'

'Oh God, yes. I shouldn't say this, Vanny, because I so much want you to win the tournament, but I really hope he beats you so you can tell me what it's like to go to bed with him. I'm sure it would be pretty amazing.'

In Hastings I can expect to have a few relatively easy games in the beginning, but that doesn't happen in Gibraltor, where every game's a tough one. In this particular tournament, the field included thirty-two GMs.

To the amazement of absolutely everyone at the event, Tom beat the brilliantly talented Estonian grandmaster Matti Ots in the very first round. True, Tom was White, which always gives a player the advantage of the first move, but Matti Ots was at the time about three hundred rating points above Tom and the result was a complete shock to the chess community.

Once Tom beat Matti, Tom instantly became the celebrity of the tournament. Press coverage of the Gibraltar tournament is major and extensive. Following his victory, Tom was so courted and feted by Spanish and Gibraltarian TV stations and journalists that I hardly saw him, apart from on the exalted top boards that were viewed by spectators. Tom was doing so well in the tournament that he was on those boards all the time.

Yes, Tom was on a roll. He drew with Fabiano Caruana in Round Two, and astonishingly beat Lev Aronian with Black in Round Three. In Round Four, to my delight, Tom even managed to beat Miklos. Tom won his next two games too, and so, with four rounds to go, Tom had an astonishing five and a half points out of six and was leading the tournament.

My own week had been rather different.

I'd won my first two games but in the third round had to play the Finnish grandmaster Kimmo Kinnunen with Black and I lost quickly after missing an ingenious tactic he found. Demoralised by this, I lost in the fourth round too, to Serena Duttagupta, an Indian lady grandmaster against whom I'd normally done quite well in the past.

In Round Five I was paired against a promising British sixteen-year-old boy, who'd been having a good tournament. I was all over him (I mean chess-wise), but I overlooked a move that gave him a perpetual check, and so after five rounds, the half-way point, I was left with just two and a half points.

I was so, so disappointed at how I was doing, and while it was great that Tom was playing really well, I even felt (in a weird, secret, selfish way) that he was being disloyal to me by playing so brilliantly when I was playing so badly.

In Round Six I was drawn against Sven himself.

Even now, thinking about that game makes me feel ill. I mean, it was all very well for me to have fantasies about Sven beating me, and therefore being able to go to bed with him, but we have fantasies about things partly because we don't necessarily want them to happen in reality, don't we?

And you can bet anything that after finishing Round Five with just two and a half points I absolutely *did not* want to lose to Sven in Round Six.

But that's what happened. Maybe I was just too focused on him or whatever, but anyway I did something I've not done more than just once or twice in my chess career and ignored or more likely just forgot about the fact that he was attacking my queen (with a knight) and I *lost my queen! Erk. Erk.*

Even after that disaster, I managed to counter-attack (I was playing White) but Sven had just too much material and we reached a point where he still had the advantage of a queen over a knight and my counterplay had ground to a standstill like a frozen Norwegian lemming in the heart of winter.

I couldn't face the awfulness of my position anymore and I resigned. We'd been playing for about four hours, it wasn't a quickie this time. So now I was demoralised *and* shattered.

I can be incredibly inconsistent. Having told you how much I'd hoped in my fantasy that Sven would beat me at chess, now the thing had actually happened, and having the sort of score - two and a half out of six - that many of the weaker players had managed to achieve, I felt totally demoralised by how badly I was doing in the tournament, and sex with Sven was the last thing on my mind.

Sven, gentleman that he was, didn't ask me whether I wanted to look through the game with him. Instead, he asked me out for an early evening supper, and I said yes, though I didn't eat much and I didn't say much either. During that supper Sven and I often found ourselves eating in silence, yet somehow I didn't find it awkward and I don't think Sven did either.

The restaurant Sven and I went to was by the sea, and only about a ten-minute walk from the Caleta Hotel. As we headed back to the hotel later, and as the street wasn't especially well lit and as I was now feeling more philosophical about my pathetic performance in the tournament so far, I was starting to feel quite keen on Sven again. I wanted him to hold my hand. On one occasion I thought he might have been about to, but he didn't.

The closer we got to the hotel the more I wanted him to spend the night with me, and I was relieved my room was on the second floor whereas his was on the fourth so there was a fair chance he'd walk me to the door of my room to say goodnight. I was fairly confident that once he was there, it would be easy-peasy to invite him in on some pretext, however fake and dodgy.

We went up in the lift together. We were the only ones in the lift, which was a little suprising as while it was close to midnight now, the hotel was still busy with people finishing dinner. The evening meal is usually eaten late in Spain.

When we reached the second floor, I walked with Sven down the corridor with its reproduction of Old Masters on the walls and the gentle yellow illumination coming from small cup-like lights positioned every few yards on either side. The corridor had that calm, otherworldly quality, with that slight background hum you get in hotel corridors late at night.

We reached the door of my room. I knew it was perfectly likely that Sven would simply bid me goodnight and head up to his sex god eyrie high above me. So, cunningly and pretextually, I said:

'There's a new book out on the Caro-Kann Defence. You want to see it?'

Sven gazed at me in that enigmatic way of his, as if he had me all figured out and it amused him to play my little game, instead of taking the more direct approach and pushing me up against the wall and having his Norwegian way with me like an amorous Viking. 'Yes, of course, if you wish. I would be very interested.'

A few moments later he was inside my room and basically at my mercy. There was the double bed at the far side – I always ask for a double bed if I'm staying in a hotel by myself, because there's just so much more room to stretch out in one. There was a table and a sofa too. I put just one bedside light on, and the room was bathed in a gentle and seductive illumination.

I could feel Sven's eyes on me as I went over to my bedside table on which the pretext reposed, next to the teabags, the cups and the small hotel bedroom kettle. I picked the book up, went back to Sven and handed it to him. The book was called *Winning with the Caro-Kann!* Sven opened the book, then glanced at me, still with that amused glint in his eye, as if the book had confirmed his suspicions.

'Vanny, it was published two years ago, so I think it is not so new.'

'Well, it's sort of new, anyway. Compared with the nineteenth century, at least.'

He smiled. 'You can be very wicked.' He said the word 'wicked' with a very deep, manly intonation that made my toes totally tingle.

I smiled wickedly. 'I know.' I gently took the book from him. 'Enough chess for one day.' I tossed the book carelessly onto a nearby armchair. Unable to keep calm any longer, I very impulsively but happily stood on tiptoes and kissed him.

I put my arms around him and we kind of walked over to the double bed together and sat on the edge of it while kissing, his hands on my waist, mine around his neck.

It was curious, I'd never kissed a sex god before, and I hadn't been prepared for what the experience would be like.

It was wonderful, just wonderful, and I felt myself losing control, but... as I did, another feeling came over me, too... that somehow it just didn't feel right.

I broke the kiss, and looked him in the eyes. I didn't know what to do, but Sven did.

What he did was smile, and the moment he did I felt better.

'Ivana,' he murmured, 'somehow I don't think this is what either of us want, is it?'

I said nothing. I felt sad, but somehow strangely relieved too.

'Oh, I don't know what I want, Sven,' I said. 'But never mind me. What do you want?'

'I want to know you, Ivana. I want to be friends with you. Of course I think you're one of the most beautiful women I've ever met. You're also a lovely person. But somehow... I don't think it would be good for us if I were to fall in love with you.'

I didn't know what to say, or what to do. But again, Sven at least knew what to do at that moment. He took both my hands in his and squeezed them gently. I felt electricity surge through me, but it felt like the kind of electricity you feel *after* you've made love with someone you really like, rather than before. I meant it was a friendly sort of electricity, not an incandescent one. That really was just the point.

'I should go back to my room,' said Sven. 'You do not need your beauty sleep, but you do need to sleep.'

'Sven...?'

'Yes?'

Then I whispered, 'I want you to stay here tonight.'

'Vanny, you know it is best that we don't...'

'I don't mean for sex. I mean just because I'd like to sleep with you. We can have a cuddle, but... nothing else. I'd really like to spend the night with you.'

Sven looked thoughtful. 'All right,' he murmured. 'But the condition is, we never tell anybody.'

I hadn't expected this sudden burst of desire for secrecy from Sven. Of course it was an enormous turn-on.

'All right,' I said.

I would have agreed with anything he said. I just wanted him to be there that night, with me.

He went to his room and he came back down about twenty minutes later. I knew he'd've had a shower and brushed his teeth. I'd given him my plastic cardkey so he could get back in. He was still wearing the clothes he'd gone out in. By that time I was in bed, in the left side of the bed by the dressing-table that had the tea on it. I was completely naked, but I'd pulled the duvet up to my throat so that he couldn't see that I was. Also, I'd put all the lights off in the room except for the shaded lamp on the little bedside table.

When he saw me in bed, he gave faint smile.

'Just take your clothes off and come to bed,' I instructed.

'Ivana, I have to keep something on, for the sake of decency.'

'No you don't.'

For a few moments he stayed where he was. Then, as I watched him naughtily from the bed, he slowly began taking his clothes off, averting his gaze from mine. Finally, he removed his socks and then his black underpants, and for the first time I saw his lovely and quite large manhood. His balls were large too. Then he stepped towards me, looking at me a little shyly. He already wasn't so limp any more. He was circumcised, which surprised me a bit. Apparantly casually, but in fact with a very clear purpose, I shifted so that the duvet slid down to reveal my bare left shoulder.

I watched him as he came over to his side of the bed, not looking at me. He stripped with his back to me, revealing the dips of his waist and the impressive musculature of his shoulders. Then he got into bed on my right, and he was finally there next to me, all naked and manly and just-showered and his breath smelling minty from his tooth-brushing. His skin had a lovely fresh scent to it.

We lay on our backs next to each other.

'How are you?' I asked him.

There was a silence, then he murmured:

'Fine. I am fine. How about you?'

'Fine too. Happy, as well.'

He turned to glance at me. 'So am I,' he murmured.

We lay there in far more comfortable silence for a while, then he said, in a deep, Scandinavian voice as deep as the deepest Norwegian forest:

'Good night, then.'

'Good night,' I said.

He turned his lovely naked broad back to the right, away from me. After a few moments I turned the same way. I stared at him for a while without daring to touch him. His body heat spread under the sheets, enveloping me, until I could hardly resist any more. Really really hoping he wouldn't push me away, I moved closer, touching the back of his legs with mine. He tensed a little, but said nothing, so I snuggled closer to him, pressing my bare belly and breasts against his warm back. He seemed to be holding his breath. I wondered if he could feel my heart pounding against him. I reached round gently with my left hand and found that now he had quite a big erection. As his manhood was big anyway, this was definitely saying something.

I decided to try to improve it even more. I gently took him in my left hand and stroked the underside a few times, then I gently stroked his balls and brought my hands back up to carefully touch the tip of his erection.

Sven moaned gratifyingly.

I lifted my mouth closer to his left ear. 'Don't move,' I murmured. 'Or at least, don't move more than you need to. If you turn towards me, I'll stop.'

'I won't move,' he breathed.

'Good,' I said, and kissed the top of his left ear. 'This doesn't change anything. We're still just friends.'

'Yes,' he gasped. 'Just friends.'

I held his now even more considerable erection concertedly in my left hand and gently started feeling my way around it again slowly, exploring first its tip, then all along the shaft.

Then I let my hand linger this time on his rather heavy balls. He moaned louder as I felt them again.

I hadn't been sure what I wanted to do, but once I felt his balls I was sure I wanted to make him come.

He moaned divinely as I touched him in the very very sensitive place below his erection, and I kissed his left ear-lobe and the back of his neck. He didn't turn round; he was following Vanny's orders.

I just kept stroking his balls and the underside of his erection, then I held his entire manhood in my hand and finally I resumed stroking him in the ultra-sensitive part beneath his balls until I could feel, and could hear by his panting breaths, that he was approaching the point of no return.

I gently bit into the back of his neck while finishing off what I was up to. Now my fingers were gliding all over his hot erection.

When Sven finally came, he gasped and cried out. I couldn't resist reaching my fingers forward and catching some of his come on my fingers.

'That's for being a super friend,' I whispered in his left ear, when his gasping had died down and his breathing had returned to something approaching normality. 'And for beating me.'

'What... what would happen if I won the tournament?' he asked in a sort of breathless groany murmur.

'You'd be richer and you'd boost your rating,' I said. 'Now, my dear sex god, you can turn round.'

'*Sex god?*' he echoed. 'Is that what you think I am?'

'Yes,' I whispered. 'And I want you to turn round and look at me.'

He obeyed. I leant towards him, gently pulled him towards me, lovely man that he was, and I gave him a long, three-or-four-minute kiss to remember.

Finally, grudgingly, I broke the kiss, and I whispered into his right ear:

'Now, Sven, go to sleep.'

I've never told anyone else about any of this.

26

I woke up early that Sunday morning in Gibraltar, suddenly absolutely certain that I wanted to make love with Sven after all, but there was a slight obstacle to this plan: he wasn't there. He'd left a little note on his pillow using a hotel black biro and a paper napkin from the tea, coffee and biscuit tray.

Dear Vanny, thank you very much for everything. It was lovely to sleep with you. I hope you slept well, and that you win today. Sven

No 'xx' or even 'x', but then he was, after all, just a friend. So what did 'it was lovely to sleep with you' mean? Nothing, presumably.

I sat up naked in bed. His side of the bed still smelt of him, the lovely sweet smell of his sweat, and still a trace of the scent of his come.

But enough of me for the moment. Let me tell you about Tom, who was heading for his greatest tournament result in his chess career.

He ended the Gibraltar tournament with eight and a half out of ten. So did Matti Ots, who had bounced back after his first-round loss to Tom and who joined Tom in equal first place. There was a quickplay chess playoff (each player had twenty minutes for all their moves) to determine who would be the winner. Unfortunately, Tom, obviously exhausted from his incredible success and effort, wilted in the blitz games and lost both of them, but it didn't matter: he'd still gained more than a hundred rating points and had had by far the best result of his chess career, and he'd won £20,000 for gaining outright second place.

But... I didn't see him get his prize, nor give all the interviews he gave to the various Eastern European chess-mad TV and radio stations which had been following his progress with such excitement.

You see, I wasn't there for the last two rounds of the Gibraltar tournament.

I wasn't there because, at just before twelve noon on Monday, January the thirtieth, which was when Round Eight of the Gibraltar tournament was being played, I got a phone call from Lottie, and then Steve, on my mobile.

I was in my hotel room at the time, preparing an opening for my afternoon game.

Lottie was crying so much during the call I had a job to make out what the poor thing was saying.

Finally, when I still wasn't sure what she was telling me, she handed her mobile phone to... Steve Juselius.

He told me, in a voice hoarse with emotion, that he and Lottie had fallen in love and that Lottie wasn't with Ade any more. In an instant, everything about Lottie's phone calls in her own room fell into place, but there wasn't time for me to focus much on this major development in Lottie's personal life, because... because Steve then told me why she was crying.

2 7

I checked out of the Caleta Hotel less than an hour after getting that phone call. My hands fumbled the clasp of my case shut as I finished quickly stuffing all my things into it. I wiped the tears from my face before leaving my room and showing my face to the world. I'd withdrawn from the tournament. I told Stuart Conquest that an emergency situation had come up and I had to return to the UK right away. Stuart, empathetic fellow that he was, told me he completely understood, and said that he hoped the emergency situation sorted itself. I said I hoped so too.

I managed to catch the 14:25 British Airways flight from Gibraltar to London Heathrow. It was expensive booking so late, but I didn't care in the least. I just wanted to be with Lottie.

Steve had told me on the phone that Lottie had 'a serious neurological problem' and that she was desperate for me to come home and be there with her at the appointment she was having a with a specialist at six o'clock that evening in Harley Street.

I hadn't thought twice about leaving Gibraltar. Would I have been so willing to withdraw from the tournament and come home if I'd been doing anywhere near as well as Tom was? I honestly don't know, but I hope I would have come home anyway, because the Gibraltar tournament would be there next year and Lottie was ill and needed me.

Throughout the flight - it was a grey day, where even the sky *above* the clouds had a greyness and dismalness about it - those words Steve had said to me echoed in and out of my mind. They were like a fragment of a horrible song I couldn't get out of my head.

Serious neurological problem.

What exactly did that mean? I really couldn't guess. But I was still convinced that whatever had happened to her, it *would* only be temporary and that she'd be totally back to normal before too long.

The flight from Gibraltar to Heathrow lasts just under three hours. With the benefit of the time difference, I landed at some time around half past four in the afternoon, UK time. With only cabin luggage, I cleared customs at about a quarter to five. As I came out of the Arrivals exit where happy people were embracing and hugging each other, I saw a chauffeur dressed in a grey uniform with a peaked cap holding a piece of white card with my name hand-written on it. This was the driver Sir Rupert Richmond himself had arranged. Steve had texted me to tell me I'd be met at Heathrow.

In a sleek white BMW, the chauffeur drove me and my worry about Lottie into London, along the great big, ugly, arterial roads that lead into West London through Hammersmith and then along the smarter roads of Kensington and Knightsbridge and left up Park Lane towards Mayfair and the fabled Harley Street, into the heart of the London medical world.

I tried asking the chauffeur if he knew anything more about what had happened to 'Miss Richmond', but he'd said that he was sorry, he didn't.

By the time we reached Harley Street, darkness had fallen completely. The car slid elegantly and smoothly to a standstill outside a building that was very different from the other ones nearby. Instead of being a grandiose four-storey old-fashioned house, it was maybe seven or eight stories high, a modern building with quite a lot of glass and silvery metal in it that reflected the evening street lamps. Somehow, I found the scientific modernism of the building reassuring.

There was a swing door on the ground floor which opened into a large, brightly-lit reception room. On the right was a counter with a stocky black security guard sitting behind it. Behind him on the wall was a list of floors with names of consultants and the numbers of their rooms.

It must have been about six o'clock by now. I thought perhaps Lottie and the others hadn't arrived yet. Carrying my case, I went up to the security guard.

'Hello... I'm meeting a friend, Charlotte Richmond, and her parents and a friend of hers, Steven Juselius. They're seeing a consultant called John Hamelin.' On the plane, I assumed it was spelt like the Pied Piper, which I wasn't sure was a good or bad sign.

'Are you Ivana Jones?' the security man asked, in a deep, well-spoken voice.

I nodded.

'They're already here,' he said. 'They've gone upstairs. Yes, they're seeing Mr Hamelin.'

'He isn't a doctor?' I asked.

'Consultants are usually called "Mr" rather than "Dr" if they're surgeons,' the guard explained, with a helpful smile.

'Oh, I see. I didn't know that.'

'Don't worry, not many people do. You want the fourth floor, room 412.'

I nodded my thanks.

I was the only one going up in the lift, whose motor purred so quietly I could scarcely hear it. My small suitcase in my right hand, I reached the fourth floor in ten seconds or so, and found myself in a brightly-lit corridor, with metal fittings everywhere, and white walls.

The room in front of me was 400, and had the name 'Mr Ahmed Yanni' below it, on a little name-plate consisting of gold coloured letters on a light grey background. The room next to it on the right was 401. I walked down the corridor and soon reached room 412, whose nameplate bore the name 'Mr John Hamlyn'. *So that's how it's spelt*, I thought.

I knocked on the door. It was opened almost immediately by a lady nurse who I thought was about thirty, with dark black hair, high cheekbones and an efficient look about her. She smiled. 'You must be Ivana Jones?'

'Yes.'

'Do come in. They're all in the waiting room. Mr Hamlyn will be seeing you all them very soon.'

She stood back and I stepped into a smallish reception room, with a low, glass-topped table on the left between two long modern, IKEA-like white sofas. She showed me to another room, through a light brown door. The room had bookcases on the right and the left full of what looked like journals of some learned medical society, all bound in dark blue and with gold lettering.

It was in that room that I saw Lottie, her parents, and Steve Juselius, who were all sitting on old-fashioned-looking dark brown wooden chairs. Lottie was in a plain grey dress, her hair in a beautiful ponytail, her face pale. She looked as lovely as always, but very stressed and very scared. Steve was there too, obviously desperately worried but, I thought, trying to appear calm. Sir Rupert and Lady Richmond, whose name was Elizabeth, simply both looked terribly worried.

I ran up to Lottie, put my arms around her and kissed her on the forehead.

The nurse murmured, 'Mr Hamlyn won't be a moment,' then stepped back and closed the door quietly behind her.

Lottie stood up and we went on hugging. Steve stood up too. He was wearing a very smart dark blue suit, a white button-up shirt, and a crimson tie.

'Thanks for coming at such short notice, Vanny,' he said.

'I got the next plane out,' I said, still holding Lottie in my arms.

After a few moments Lottie and I unwillingly broke our embrace.

Sir Rupert, whom I'd only ever met twice before, looked like the wealthy man he was. He was, I knew, sixty-three, with silver-grey hair, a substantial but not excessive frame, and was wearing a City-type grey pinstripe suit. His shoes were jet-black and shone almost like mirrors. Sir Rupert and Elizabeth had got to their feet now, and were shaking my hand. Elizabeth had rather long blonde hair, which was swept back from her forehead. She was wearing a dark blue blouse and a long white skirt.

'We're here to give all the support we can,' Sir Rupert explained to me. 'Lottie's already told us she'd rather go in to see John with Steve and with you, Ivana.'

'We're good friends of John's father,' Lady Richmond explained, quietly.

'Yes, indeed,' said Sir Rupert. 'John's one of the best neurologists in the country. He's a brain surgeon. He saved the life of the boxer Martin Dodson last year.'

I'd vaguely heard about how Martin Dodson had nearly died after a vicious and exhausting fight a few years ago against Sinclair Brown, but I wasn't really paying much attention to anything but the one question in my mind: *what's wrong with Lottie?*

But then I didn't need to go on speculating, because there was a knock on the door, and it opened and John Hamlyn came in.

He was, I'd say, about forty-five: a youthful and definitely good-looking man, with very fair hair and spectacles.

He greeted Sir Rupert and Elizabeth with handshakes, and then Sir Rupert introduced him to Lottie, Steve and me. John, who had an earnest-looking caring smile, shook Lottie's hand first, lingering for a few moments as he did so, in recognition of her being his patient. Then he shook Steve's hand and mine in a briefer, more professional manner that was accompanied, all the same, by a smile.

'Lottie, would you and Ivana and Steve follow me please?' John said, in a gentle, friendly, medium-pitched voice.

Lottie went and gave her mum and dad a hug, then joined Steve and me. John's consulting-room was the next but one room along down the corridor after the waiting-room.

I'm not sure exactly what I was expecting the consulting-room to be like, but I suppose I vaguely imagined it would be really old-fashioned and even with preserved foetuses in bell jars on shelves, with lots of even more ancient medical tomes in the bookshelves. But John Hamlyn's consulting-room was nothing like that. Instead, it was modern simplicity itself: white walls, a wide pine-wood desk on the left with a comfortable-looking black leather chair behind it, and three chairs in front – specially placed for us, I thought – that were pretty identical to the ones in the waiting-room.

To the left of the door as you went in was a white examining couch, with the headrest at about forty-five degrees. There was a curtain rail around the examining couch, and a white plastic curtain which was bunched up against the wall.

Steve, Lottie and I all went into the room and sat opposite John in three chairs on the other side of his desk from where he was sitting. Lottie had sat in the middle chair; Steve to her left, and I was in the other chair on her right.

John cleared his throat quietly then opened a beige cardboard folder in front of him that contained typed notes. Without leaning forwards, I tried to read them upside-down, but I couldn't.

'Ivana,' John began, calmly, 'I gather you've left a chess tournament in Gibraltar to be here, is that right?'

'Yes,' I said, quietly, 'but it's not a problem. Being here is more important to me than being there.'

My voice sounded very hoarse. I barely recognised it as my own.

John nodded. 'Well, I'm very grateful for you coming to be supportive of Lottie this evening, Ivana. I realise that you and Steve will both love Lottie in your own ways, and I think it's really great you're both here this evening. Of course it's also very good that Rupert and Elizabeth have come along too.'

John was silent for a moment, then glanced at Lottie. 'Lottie, you had your first symptoms just sixteen days ago, at your party. You told Dr Baxter about those symptoms. I believe you felt a loss of control in your left hand when you were playing the piano at the party?'

'Yes, that's right,' Lottie murmured.

'I see,' said John. 'You also reported headaches which have come and gone. Early last week, a brain scan was arranged for you and this took place last Friday at the Cromwell hospital in Kensington.'

John looked down at his notes, then glanced up at us all again and went on:

'Dr Baxter saw the results and referred you to me right away. As you know, I'm the son of Dr George Hamlyn, one of your parents' friends, and of course I was more than willing to inspect the scan at very short notice. As it happened, I was operating last Saturday morning at the Cromwell hospital, and after I left theatre, I spoke to Dr Baxter on the telephone and then went to see the scan myself.'

None of us said a thing. My mouth was dry, and I felt absolutely dizzy with worry. But I knew I mustn't show anyone how I felt, as that was just my feelings, and all that mattered right now was Lottie, and her feelings.

'So that's what's been happening so far,' John said, quietly. Raising his voice somewhat, he added: 'I'm a neurologist with a particular specialisation in the brain. I'm a brain surgeon too.'

He glanced down at the notes again. This time a slight frown appeared on his face and then became more pronounced in only a second or two, as if, I couldn't help thinking, with a yelp of terror in my soul, he would have done pretty much anything to have changed whatever it said in the notes. He looked at me, Lottie and Steve in turn, then glanced at Lottie.

'I'll come straight to the point. I'm afraid there is a serious problem.'

I wondered if I was going to faint.

'What is the problem, John?' Steve asked, quietly but firmly.

John looked intently - and, I noticed, very kindly - at Lottie, then he drew an audible breath and spoke softly to her:

'Lottie, you're suffering from what I believe is a Grade Four brain tumour. By Grade Four I mean that it appears to be of the type we call a glioma, which is malignant, and so it will continue to grow if we don't do something about it.'

John fell silent for several moments, looking down at his notes. Then he glanced up at Lottie again, and speaking as softly as before, said:

'It's true that this diagnosis cannot be confirmed beyond doubt until there's been a biopsy of the tissue, by which I mean that a small sample of the tumour is extracted and examined in a laboratory. However, I think it would be very unfair to you

Lottie, and also clinically irresponsible of me, to delay giving you the likely diagnosis simply because the biopsy hasn't been performed yet. Biopsies of brain tumours aren't easy to carry out, and can involve risk. Also, it would be cruel of me to provide you with any hope that the tumour may be benign, when all my experience makes me as certain as I can be, that what we are dealing with here is the type of tumour I've mentioned to you. Furthermore, the sooner we start some treatment for you, the better.'

I glanced at Lottie. She was breathing fast, and she had gone even paler. Her hands were on her knees in front of her. Steve now took her left hand in his right.

John cleared his throat again, a little more loudly this time, but still in a delicate manner.

'I understand this is a lot to take in, Lottie, but there are a range of treatments available. We could undertake surgery and remove the tumour, but I need to explain that there would be the risk of a possible mental deficit.'

'What does that mean exactly?' Lottie asked.

I felt horribly sure I knew what he meant. I was still thinking it was perfectly possible I might faint at any moment.

'What I mean is,' said John, 'that in order to extract the tumour, we may have no alternative but to take the risk of damaging some healthy brain tissue and causing some loss of brain function. Also, the position of the tumour being what it is, there's a danger that if we operate, it will affect your eyesight, possibly to the extent of leaving you with severely impaired sight. There is also radiotherapy available,' he added quickly, 'but I need to say that even with all the resources of modern medical science at our disposal, radiotherapy is only relatively experimental as far as gliomas are concerned.'

John glanced at the notes in front of him again, and then at Lottie once more:

'There's another possibility I ought to mention to you, though I'm afraid it may be frustrating for me to do so. A drug called Ditrexican has been developed in America. In experimental trials, the drug demonstrates an ability to shrink gliomas. There's no evidence it can cure them completely, but shrinking them is obviously extremely important.'

'Why's that?' I asked, impulsively.

'Because,' said John, 'a major problem with brain tumours is that as they grow, they cause increased pressure within the head. However, at present, as I say, the drug is only at an experimental, test stage.'

'How can we get this Ditrexican?' Steve asked, at once.

John gave a brief nod. 'I have some contacts in America, and I was told shortly after Christmas that while it's likely to be three or four years before the drug's released for general use, there's the possibility of some of my patients taking part in the experimental trial. Unfortunately, I don't know at this stage whether this possibility will become a reality soon.'

There was a long silence.

My mouth felt even drier.

'What'll happen to me if you don't try surgery or radiotherapy and if I don't get this drug you mentioned?' Lottie asked, the words sounding forced out through some terrible dryness in her throat.

John didn't reply at once. Finally he said, 'Lottie, the human body is a remarkable thing, and sometimes has astonishing abilities to cure itself. However, it's unfortunately the case, and regrettably I do need to say this, that while many forms of cancer may involve sudden and inexplicable remissions, such spontaneous remissions in the case of Grade Four gliomas are rare.'

Lottie looked him straight in the eyes. 'Is there… is there any possibility, any at all, that there's been a mistake with the diagnosis? Maybe my X-Ray got mixed up with someone else's? Or perhaps the tumour's benign after all?'

John was silent for some moments before he replied, 'I can... well, yes, I can understand why you would ask those questions. But please believe me that I wouldn't pass this news to you if I wasn't pretty certain the diagnosis was accurate.'

Lottie nodded slowly. 'Then how long have I got?'

'Lottie, I can't answer that question with any precision. If we can get you onto the drug, it may well extend very considerably the period of relative health you enjoy, but I think if you elect not to have surgery or radiotherapy, it's unfortunately likely that within three to four months, your health will start to deteriorate significantly. With surgery, I would expect the time-frame to be doubled, but there would, as I said, be the danger of deficits.'

I still felt I could hardly breathe, but somehow I managed to say, 'I don't understand why surgery wouldn't completely cure the problem. That is, if Lottie is willing to take the risk.'

'The difficulty,' replied John quietly, 'is that experience has unfortunately shown it's not possible to remove the entire growth during surgery, because the tumour sends out microscopic fibres that tend to lead to the tumour gradually regrowing.'

Again, there was a silence. Then Lottie said:

'Why me?'

John shook his head. 'I'm afraid I don't know.'

'Is it... is it because I used my mobile phone too much, do you think?' asked Lottie, giving a sorrowful shrug.

John shook his head quickly, evidently happy at least to be able to deny this. 'There's no reliable evidence that use of mobile phones is a factor.'

'I see,' said Lottie. She said nothing for what must have been, I think, a full minute at least, during which time neither John, nor Steve, nor me said a word.

Then she murmured:

'John, what treatment do you recommend I have?'

John Hamlyn was silent for some time, then said:

'I think I would elect not to have surgery, but to see if we could get hold of this drug.'

Lottie nodded slowly. 'Can you please all wait here while I go and see Mummy and Daddy?'

'Of course,' said Steve.

Lottie stood up, glanced at me and Steve quickly, then went to the door, opened it, left the room and closed the door gently behind her.

I didn't look at either John or Steve; I looked down at the floor instead. I didn't know what to do. Part of me wanted to go and be with Lottie now, but I realised I had no place in what would be happening in the waiting-room. Much as I loved Lottie, and I think Lottie loved me too, I wasn't part of her family.

Even though the waiting-room was only two doors down from the consulting-room, it was too far down the corridor for us to be able to hear anything spoken in there.

After maybe two or three minutes, Lottie returned to the consulting-room with Sir Rupert and Elizabeth on either side of her. Elizabeth was crying. Lottie was not. Elizabeth took two quick steps into the room, leaving Lottie and Sir Rupert at the door, and went up to John behind the table. 'We've already lost one daughter,' she said.

'Mandy,' John said, quietly. 'Yes, I know.'

'John, why is this happening to Lottie?'

He shook his head. 'I don't know, Elizabeth, I don't know. It shouldn't be. It's not fair. I know it's not fair. I'm so sorry.'

Elizabeth went on crying, and now I found I couldn't stop crying either. Lottie came up to me and we just hugged, Lottie standing up over me, her arms around my shoulders and my own arms around her waist because I was still sitting down.

It was as if I was the one who might be going to die, not her.

28

From: lottiejrichmond@speedymail.com
To: ijones2412@chessmail.net
Subject: Hi Vanny darling
Saturday, February 4   16.24 GMT

Darling Vanny

Sorry I've been so quiet all week.

I just keep bursting into tears, and then feeling calm and even philosophical, and then I burst into tears again.

I've been here at Steve's as you know and I haven't wanted to do anything much, but he has a piano here and sometimes I play something. I've been listening to 'The Humming Chorus' from Madam Butterfly too often and Steve's asked me not to any more. He's right; it's beautiful, but too haunting and depressing.

I saw the X-ray on Wednesday in John's office. What I've got is horribly big, about the size of a golfball with a kind of extra little lump at the top. I can't even now completely believe that my own body would become a traitor to me like this but that's basically what's happened, isn't it?

John told Steve and me when we saw him on Wednesday that he didn't think radiotherapy would make any difference to the 'outlook', which is how he puts it, apart from buying us a few weeks possibly. He said that radiotherapy would make me feel really ill, and that it might cause deficits itself. So I was about as keen on that as I am on having surgery i.e. not keen at all.

John's making lots of enquiries about that drug he mentioned, Ditrexican, but he still doesn't know yet if he will be able to get me onto the experimental trial. He doesn't think any other of the chemo treatments there are will be likely to help me.

I emailed Ade yesterday and told him about the diagnosis. He emailed me back within an hour telling me how sorry he was and how much he loves me. I'm not sure how to reply. I don't think I will for the moment. I'd already told him about Steve and me.

Steve and I make love every night. The idea of going into the darkness where no-one thinks or feels or makes love and never seeing Steve again is just so dreadful, dreadful, dreadful.

So is the idea of never seeing you again Vanny darling because I...

Love you to bits
Lottie xxxx

From: ijones2412@chessmail.net
To: chairman@russfiduciarybank.com
Subject: A very big favour – urgent!
Saturday, February 4   17.10 GMT

Dear Boris

I hope you're well and studying chess hard!
I am well myself.
Unfortunately, Boris, my very best friend isn't. Her name is Charlotte Richmond, though I call her Lottie.

She's twenty-five, so a year younger than me.

Boris, she's been diagnosed with a brain tumour; a glioma. Her medical consultant, Mr John Hamlyn of Harley Street (I can give you his contact details if you'd like them) has told her that she may not have more than about four months before her health starts to get much worse. He says if she has surgery she may get twice that time; but that surgery itself causes problems including brain damage which may lead to mental deficits.

Lottie's been my very best friend since I was at school. I'd do anything to help her.

There's just one hope. There's a drug called Ditrexican which is in experimental trials in America, and has been found to have some success at shrinking gliomas. I've researched it on Wiki. The active ingredient in Ditrexican is an amino acid peptide, called chlorotoxin, found in the venom of the deathstalker scorpion. Chlorotoxin is known to destroy cancerous glioma cells. The chlorotoxin in Ditrexican has been chemically modified so it isn't dangerous to the patient being treated, but it still retains its power to destroy cancerous glioma cells. Ditrexican is one of the first-ever drugs that can be used to treat brain cancer.

Lottie told me earlier today that John Hamlyn told her this morning that the United States drug company Pharbos, which developed Ditrexican, has reached its limit of the number of patients who can take part in the trial.

I was wondering if you could help us? You told me in the letter you gave me at Hastings that you own a Finnish healthcare innovations company. Do you by any chance have any contacts in the pharmaceutical world?

Lottie's father, Sir Rupert Richmond of Richmond Enterprises plc, is well off (though not, I suppose, as rich as you) but anyway, if money can help in any way, it's available.

Can you help, Boris? Please?

I don't like to beg, but I am begging now. Lottie may not have more than a few months to live. If there's any way, any way at all, you think you might be able to help get this drug, that would be marvellous. I'd do anything to make that happen.

Yours sincerely
Ivana

From: ijones2412@chessmail.net
To: lottiejrichmond@speedymail.com
Subject: Boris might be able to help!
Saturday, February 4   19.34 GMT

Lottie darling

I emailed Boris. He's got back to me and sent the following email, which I'm forwarding to you.

I'm hopeful. Boris is the kind of man who makes things happen.

I'll let you know just as soon as I hear from him.

Love you so much.
Vanny xxx

From: chairman@russfiduciarybank.com
To: ijones2412@chessmail.net
Subject: Re: A very big favour
Saturday, February 4   19.09 GMT

My dear Ivana

Many thanks for your email.

I have, some minutes ago, asked a team of my people to investigate every avenue they can identify for obtaining some supply of this experimental drug Ditrexican.

Ivana, I am very sorry indeed to hear about your friend Lottie.

I shall be in touch again as soon as I have news.

My very best regards to you.
Boris

From: lottiejrichmond@speedymail.com
To: ijones2412@chessmail.net
Subject: Boris might be able to help!
Saturday, February 4   20.27

Darling Vanny, what can I say? Thanks a million times for asking Boris to help. Just please don't get yourself more entangled than you already are with him and his money for my sake. I don't want you having any kind of debt towards him because of me. Watch out for yourself, please. But of course if he can help us, that would be simply wonderful.

Love you so much.
Lottie xxxx

From: lottiejrichmond@speedymail.com
To: ijones2412@chessmail.net
Subject: Horrible news about the biopsy
Tuesday February 7   09.12 GMT

Vanny darling

> I've just now had the result of the biopsy.
> I am afraid John was right.
> It's a Grade Four brain tumour.
> It's called a malignant astrocytic glioma.
> Three terrible words.
> Can't speak today.

Lottie xx

From: chairman@russfiduciarybank.com
To: ijones2412@chessmail.net
Subject: Ditrexican - a breakthrough
Wednesday February 8 07.22 GMT

My dear Ivana

I have it! I have secured a supply of the Ditrexican drug for Lottie. It was not easy. Pharbos was initially unwilling to broaden the experimental trial beyond the United States, but they have caved in with a little (in fact a lot) of persuasion from me. They're allowing Lottie to be an overseas participant in the trial. This is all in the strictest confidence, please, they don't want a leak on this. Lottie can have an initial six months' supply if you can please give me her consultant's address. He will have it by air courier and can start treating her at once. Lottie will need to sign a disclaimer that states very clearly that she is taking the drug at her own risk.

Ivana, I think it is of great importance that you and Lottie realise that the drug is still experimental and that its side-effects are not yet fully known. But if she is prepared to take this risk, the Ditrexican is hers.

My very best wishes to you, Ivana.
Boris

PS. This is not the right time to tell you this, I know, but I am still working hard at improving my chess in what leisure moments I find myself having.

From: ijones2412@chessmail.net
To: chairman@russfiduciarybank.com
Subject: Re: Ditrexican - a breakthrough
Wednesday February 8 08.14 GMT

Boris, I don't know what to say. I am crying, really. Thank you. Thank you from the bottom of my heart. Ivana, xxx

PS: I LOVE the helicopter simulation website and am becoming a bit of a pro at flying!

From: tom.hardimanCHESSGM@googlemail.com
To: ijones2412@chessmail.net
Subject: Greetings from Helsinki!
Wednesday, February 8   22.31 GMT

Hi Vanny

How are you? Why have you still not told me why you went home so abruptly?

Bet you'll be surprised to hear where I am right now. I'm in... of all places, Helsinki, Finland, playing in an all-play-all GM tournament. So far I've one and a half out of two; there are seven rounds altogether.

Finishing Gibraltar equal first, even though I lost in the playoff, has sort of skyrocketed my chess career (I realise you'll probably think 'resuscitated' a more appropriate description, though). I was offered three wild card entries after the Gib event finished. One tournament was in Las Palmas in the Canaries, which was very tempting as it's like early summer there now. The other was in Dublin; interesting and Irish but chilly.

The tournament I chose was here in Helsinki: it's marginally the strongest of the three tournaments.

The organisers paid my air fare from Gibraltar, and they're also paying my hotel costs and even giving me 200 euros a day for out-of-pocket expenses; bloody hell, I could get used to this chess celebrity lifestyle!

The only thing missing is YOU.

Vanny, will you come and visit me? This weekend would be perfect: pleeeease say you don't have other plans? I'm very happy to pay your air fare. When you're here it won't cost you a penny; my 200 euros a day can easily support us even in pricy Finland, and you can stay in my room; it's an enormous twin bed room at the Scandia Marski Hotel and of course... twin beds can always be put together!!!

There's another reason I'm here; it's not only for the chess.

You remember I was looking into Boris's weird company Henki Oy for you? Well, I didn't give up and through doing lots of searches on google, Facebook and Twitter I've made contact with a fairly weird Finnish guy called Jussi (he won't tell me his surname) who actually worked at Henki Oy a couple of years ago. He lives here in Helsinki. I've been texting him and I'm hoping to meet him while I'm over here. If you came to see me, maybe we could meet him at the weekend?

Looking forward to hearing from you, gorgeous.

Tom xxx

From: ijones2412@chessmail.net
To: tom.hardimanCHESSGM@googlemail.com
Subject: Re: Greetings from Helsinki
Wednesday, February 8 22.54 GMT

Hi Tom

Many thanks for your email. You did brilliantly in Gibraltar and deserve the great things that are happening to you. Finally you're taking your chess seriously!

Tom, I'll come but no sex, OK? I'm a bit confused about you and me right now and I don't want sex to start making me even more confused about us.

There's something else I want to tell you but I'd rather tell you it face to face. It's about Lottie. Don't ask me to tell you any more until we meet please and please DON'T ask Lottie herself or Jaz. Let me tell you.

Let me know if you're OK with the no-sex rule; if you are, I'll see if I can get a ticket for a flight out this Friday. Thanks for the offer to pay for my air fare but I'll pay my own fare.

I'll stay in Helsinki until Sunday evening. I have coaching sessions to give on Monday and besides, I need to start thinking about training for the European Women's Championships in Budapest, which as you probably know, starts on March 12.

All best from Vanny x

From: tom.hardimanCHESSGM@googlemail.com
To: ijones2412@chessmail.net
Subject: Can't wait to see you
Wednesday February 8 23.05 GMT

I can't wait to see you, Vanny.

OK, OK, no sex.

I won't ask Jaz or anyone else about Lottie.

I'm playing in the tournament on Friday. Play starts at 11am over here local time - the Finns tends to be early risers, unlike some people I could mention - so the round should be over by about 5pm at the latest. You'll fly into Helsinki Vantaa airport. I'd like to meet you at the airport ideally so please let me know what time your flight gets in. If it's earlier than 5pm I'll try hard to win quickly!

All best
Tom xx

From: lottiejrichmond@speedymail.com
To: ijones2412@chessmail.net

Subject: Finland
Thursday February 9   10.14 GMT

Darling of course I want you to go to Finland to see Tom! I wonder though how long your resolve is likely to last...

As I know only too well from my own experience, it's all very well making that kind of resolve when one's by oneself and feeling all pious and chaste, but it's a very different matter when you're in a warm hotel bedroom that's softly lit and you're all nicely showered and feeling very relaxed and amorous, and a yummy man who's just fresh from his own shower starts towelling himself down in the bathroom with the door open a bit so you can see him.

How am I feeling, Vanny darling? Well, strangely enough not too bad, actually. The prospect of getting the Ditrexican has given me hope.

I do cry a lot though and often I just wonder why this is happening to me at all, someone who loves life as much as I do.

Anyway, I mustn't start thinking about things or I just end up feeling awful. Thanks for letting me know when you're going to Budapest. The concert Steve and I are giving will be on March 10, which is a Saturday. We haven't decided on the venue yet but I hope to firm it up soon. Central London, definitely.

Enjoy Finland, Vanny darling and please give my love to Tom and my regards to Santa Claus.

Love you lots
Lottie xxx

29

As Lottie had predicted, my resolve not to have sex with Tom in Finland didn't last very long. You might have imagined that the Finnish winter might have cooled our ardour, but while I did stick to my no-sex rule for the first night we spent together, in twin beds maybe four feet apart, for the second night we moved the twin beds together.

It was a romantic evening walk around the old, Russian-built, district of the stunning city of Helsinki that did for my resolve, a glorious walk beside stately pastel-coloured buildings and Tom and I listening on his iPod to Sibelius's melodious masterpiece *Finlandia* as we walked along, eventually walking hand-in-hand, and finally a wondrous supper at a Russian restaurant called *Shashlik*, in an especially pretty part of Helsinki, which is surely one of the prettiest cities in the world. Tom and I had one of the most passionate and sexy nights we'd ever had, and this time I didn't need to simulate his execution at the hands of six gorgeous women.

Of course, throughout the few days I spent in Finland I never forgot Lottie's terrible news, but I also somehow and sometimes managed to push it to the back of my mind. After all, I knew Lottie wanted me to do that.

I cried gently quite a lot on the flight back from Helsinki. I cried quietly to myself and thought of Lottie, and of Tom of course. Not that Tom had any need of my tears as far as his chess was going: he was doing really well in the Helsinki tournament too.

When I was quietly crying, and also when I wasn't, I remembered a meeting Tom and I had had on the Sunday morning, in the bar of our hotel, with the Finnish guy Tom had been contacting and who had finally agreed to meet us. He was a very strange guy: he pronounced his name 'Yussi', with the 'y' like in 'you'.

Jussi was scruffy, with blue denims that had a torn hole in the right kneecap, a dirty black overcoat and three or four day's beard growth. I'd say he was about forty, and he was going bald. His teeth were mostly browny-yellow, and he smelt of cigarettes. He was even about to light one up in the bar, but the barman said something to him in Finnish which made him grudgingly put the cigarette and the lighter away. I supposed smoking wasn't allowed in Finnish hotels, like it isn't in English hotels and plenty of other places. Not Eastern Europe though. There, they mostly still smoke there as if smoking were actually *good* for you.

Jussi didn't give either of us the privilege of knowing what his surname was. He didn't stay with us very long either, no more than about fifteen minutes, during which Tom bought him three beers and two double vodkas, all of which Jussi downed without even a thank you. Our guest spent a fair amount of those fifteen minutes ogling me with barely disguised lustfulness. I knew that we needed him more than he needed us, so I chose to ignore it.

Tom and I sat close by Jussi at a table with chairs near the bar to keep the conversation confidential and so Tom also had to put up with Jussi's stale smoky breath, though whenever I could I sat back in my chair to try to get out of noseshot.

Jussi explained in short bursts of brusque English, which usually dispensed with anything as mundane as a definite or indefinite article (I thought maybe Finnish didn't have them), how he'd been hired by the Helsinki office of Henki Oy a couple of years ago and had worked for them for six months as an IT technician until, as he succinctly put it, 'I get boot'. He tended to ignore the concept of the past tense, too. He had a deep, sinister, psychotic voice.

Tom asked Jussi why he'd lost his job.

'Because I am piss-artist,' was Jussi's deep-voiced succinct and at least honest answer. In his voice it came out as *peece-artist*.

Tom and I had nodded at Jussi with pretended sympathy. 'My friend here and I are trying to find out what kind of research they did at Henki,' Tom said, quietly.

Jussi drank a long swig of beer, then lay down his glass and said in his deep voice: 'What they were doing there was state-of-the-art, OK? Big stuff. Yeah, real state-of-the-art. All top secret.'

'What exactly were they doing?' asked Tom.

'I don't know,' Jussi said, then looked blankly at us.

Tom discreetly took his brown leather wallet out of his inside jacket pocket, removed a pale orange fifty-euro note from inside and lay it on the table. Jussi reached out, picked up the note and pocketed it casually, then ogled me for a bit before glancing at Tom and saying:

'I don't know anything too detailed about what they doing, OK? Like I say, it all secret. Finnish office only admin place anyhow; all big work done in the States. But this I will tell you for your fifty euros; their clients mostly sports stars.'

'"Sports stars?"' repeated Tom.

'Yeah, big sports names, plenty famous people.'

'Will you tell us any of their names, or any names of Henki's other clients?' Tom said.

'No. No way, no matter how many euros you throw at me. I not want to wake up one morning with my dick cut off.'

'You mean there are people you think would do that to you?' asked Tom. Thinking of Jussi in the morning even with all his anatomy intact was not pleasant.

'Yeah, maybe,' said Jussi. 'Henki Oy was OK, I think, but some very bad people want technology they're developing. I don't know why. I was just in IT department, making sure computers run OK.'

'This place Henki where you used to work sounds really weird,' said Tom, thoughtfully.

'Yeah, it was,' Jussi agreed. 'That's why when I get boot for coming to work pissed, I not too worried.'

That was basically all we managed to get out of this fountain of information. Still, I suppose what we had managed to find out was better than nothing.

The next thing Jussi did was glance at Tom, indicate me with his dirty-looking right thumb, and ask Tom, in quite a loud voice, 'you screwing her, yeah?'

'Not at the moment, no,' replied Tom, quietly and calmly.

I pressed my lips together to stop myself saying anything.

Jussi got through his next two beers in as many minutes, while keeping on ogling me and asking us about the Pet Shop Boys, who he said were his favourite band. He seemed to think that as Tom and I were both English we would know Neil Tennant and Chris Lowe personally. After Tom and I had both assured Jussi that we didn't, Jussi, who looked extremely disappointed at the news, drank the rest of his vodka in about four seconds, asked Tom and me to promise not to mention to anyone that we'd met him (we promised), then Jussi said goodbye, gave me a final ogle, stood up, farted quite loudly, and loped off into the night.

I thought of Lottie, and Tom, and of the meeting with Jussi, as the Finnair Airbus sped me home.

Tom had ended up tying for second place in the Helsinki tournament with two other grandmasters, and was immediately snapped up by an almost-as-strong tournament in Moscow, which started on Saturday, February the eighteenth. The Moscow tournament was a ten-round event, and wouldn't finish until the very last day of February, which - as this year is a leap year - was the twenty-ninth. On Thursday, March the first, the day after the leap year day, I was going to Monte Carlo to see Dad.

Not surprisingly, after the collapse of my platonic intentions in Finland, Tom was eager for me to come and spend time with him in Moscow. He sent me several emails, in ascending hierarchical order of pleading, asking me to do precisely that. But I replied that I thought succumbing to him in Finland, enjoyable as it had been, was not really what I'd intended to do, and that I didn't want to add another country to the list of those where I'd failed to keep my resolve.

In that same email Tom wrote something else, which didn't seem significant at the time but does now:

Miklos Steiner is here, that guy you had your mistake with. He's not playing too well, he seems distracted. I often see him talking in Hungarian in a private, sinister kind of way to Arpad Bognar, who smokes those cigarettes that produce a really vile-smelling smoke. Oh, and The Three Vs is often in their vicinity for some reason. By the way, do you think Arpad Bognar goes on holiday to Bognor Regis?

You'll have gathered from this that I'd confessed to Tom about Miklos.

Henki Oy remained a major puzzle.

But there was nothing puzzling about the strength and power of the love Lottie and Steve had found together. On the last Saturday in February, the twenty-fifth, almost two weeks after I'd come back from Helsinki, Steve proposed to Lottie over a romantic lunch *à deux* in Harrods' famous Georgian restaurant at the very top of the department store. Lottie said yes.

That same evening I tried, without success, to imagine myself married to Tom, and us going to bed every night with the orc watching us. After Tom's success in the Helsinki tournament he was doing well in Moscow too. Tom's chess career was suddenly blossoming, but that didn't make it any easier for me to believe in him as a potential husband.

30

The next day, the Sunday, Lottie came to visit me at the flat. Jaz was out. I gave Lottie a big hug, and offered Lottie all the help she might want from me with arranging the wedding. However, she smiled and said, 'you're an angel, Vanny, but Mummy's been looking forward to planning my wedding and making it happen ever since I was born and most likely before too, and even though the circumstances aren't what she was expecting, I know she'll be organising the wedding as if they were. She and I'll do what needs doing, and she has loads of ladies who lunch who are close friends of hers and who'll help. So please don't worry about the wedding but go and see your dad in Monte Carlo like you arranged and have a lovely time.'

I arrived at Nice International Airport at around three o'clock local time on Thursday afternoon, the first of March, after the flight of about ninety minutes. I'd had a rather strange text message from God the day before to say he had 'some news' for me and that he'd meet me at the airport.

Dad drives a rather rusty dark blue Ferrari nowadays and still thinks of himself as something of a playboy even though, overweight and with that baked potato face of his, he doesn't actually look like one, even assuming he ever did, which I rather doubt. I'd restricted my luggage to my Samsonite carry-on case again. I was only going to be there until Tuesday; I wanted to be with Lottie late on Tuesday afternoon as she had another scan that day. Also, I had a lot of work to do to prepare for the tournament in Budapest. It was the European Women's Chess

Championship and a really great opportunity for me to try to get that second grandmaster norm I needed. Goodness knew, I could hardly play more badly than I had in Gibraltar.

At first, I didn't spot Dad. All I could see, as I walked the last few yards out of Customs and then out of the airport, were the usual conglomeration of chauffeurs, some in uniform and some not, carrying name-bearing signs. But finally I saw Dad somewhere in the back of this melee and our eyes met and I ran up to him and gave him a hug.

'Lovely to see you, Dad! How are Larissa and Piotr? I'm really looking forward to meeting them.'

Dad nodded, to my surprise, gravely. 'Ivana my love, I need to speak to you about something serious,' he announced in his northern accent that's persisted down the decades. He started walking towards the exit. He'd already put his hand out to grab the handle of my wheeled case and I let him have it, since he liked to be gallant.

I tugged at his shirt until he stopped walking.

'What kind of news, Dad?'

He nodded, his expression set in a deadly serious frown, as if he were a northern ironmaster who was about to close one of his biggest factories, condemning hundreds to unemployment.

'I think we'd perhaps best go to a café, love,' Dad said, in a funereal voice. 'I don't want to talk about it here amid the general throng.'

I glanced at him. 'Something really is wrong, isn't it?' I said.

'Let's go to that coffee shop over there, and I'll tell you.'

I didn't say anything else until we were sitting down in the coffee shop, which had a view of the central concourse of the airport. It was one of those fancy coffee shops you often get at French airports, where there's waiter/waitress service. Dad and I sat at a rather charming pine table and I looked at him and he looked at me. No waiter or waitress had come over yet.

'OK, Dad, what is it?'

Dad stared hard at me for a moment, then said: 'Ivana, Larissa has bloody left me.'

31

I just stared at him. Then I narrowed my eyes suspiciously; Dad's always been a bit of a prankster. 'You're joking, aren't you?'

'Of course I'm not bloody joking.'

'Dad, please keep your voice down.'

'All right. Yes, I am bloody serious,' he repeated, but this time he did keep his voice down, a bit. 'She's left me. She's taken Piotr with her of course and I miss them both very, very much.'

I was still staring at him in bewilderment. 'When did this happen?'

I could hardly believe it. Dad had regularly dumped other women but nobody had ever dumped him, at least not as far as I knew.

'When did it happen?' Dad echoed, raising his voice again. 'About three weeks ago.' I decided not to ask him to keep his voice down this time. After all, this was his local airport and he lived down here. I was just a visitor.

'But how did it happen? I mean, women don't leave you, do they? It's you who leave them, normally, I mean.'

'Don't get funny with me, Ivana. That's not a very nice thing to say. Any minute now you'll be telling me I deserve it.'

'I'm not being funny,' I said, a little stung by how brash he was being. 'It's just how things happen with you, that's all. I know you. Was it you who did something inappropriate then, or was it her? Did you sleep with another woman, for example?'

'No, I did NOT sleep with another woman, Ivana. I'm sixty-three, and let's face it, I'm not exactly in the full prime of my life. I was very happy to settle down with Larissa and I that would be it. Yes, all right, I've had four other wives and I've divorced them all, but Larissa was the one for me and our little lad's the apple of my eye, he really is. But to answer your question, Larissa met a bloody Russian multi-millionaire. His name's Leo. He made his fortune in oil and I wish he was bloody boiled in it. She met him when she was, get this, visiting a bloody book shop in Monte Carlo just before Christmas. She likes reading novels in English by Wilbur Smith, and she'd finished all the books of his she had so she went to buy another one. She met this fellow there. Turns out he's a bloody Wilbur Smith fan too.'

'Is he some sort of oligarch or something? The fellow she met, I mean, not Wilbur Smith.'

'If you mean is he a billionaire like your Boris, no he isn't. It seems that the only person who's got a knack for meeting billionaires is you, lass. But he certainly has plenty of cash and he's got a yacht in the harbour that's about four times the size of mine. That's probably true of his appendage too, for all I know. Anyway, Larissa came back from the bookshop and she was really strange all that night and asked to sleep in the spare room. And the following morning, she went out early without telling me where she was going, leaving me looking after Piotr and taking him to school. And then at tea-time she came back to the *Ivana* and said to me that she was leaving me.'

'What was the reason she gave for leaving you?'

'She told me she'd met someone else and she was completely in love with him and couldn't live with me anymore. I asked her when she'd met him and she said, the previous afternoon. I told her she was crackers. She looked at me in a blazing kind of way and said, and I remember this word for word: "Godfrey, if I'm crackers as you say, it's only because I've put up with you for as long as I have. Now, I'm leaving you and going to live with Leo." The way she was talking to me, Ivana, you'd never have thought that she once told me she loved me and that we got married. I couldn't believe it.'

Now it was my turn to try to keep my voice down. 'So you really hadn't seen it coming? What have the past few years of your marriage been like?'

Dad looked down gloomily at the cafe table in front of him. 'Well, it's not been great all the time, I will admit. We do OK for money but it's been a bit tight sometimes because the interest rates for savings in Britain have gone down even lower than they were a few years ago. So we haven't been able to have all the fun we used to have when we first met. Also, a bloody young idiot at a hedge fund where I had a fair chunk of my money invested lost about thirty thousand pounds of my money speculating in Indian commodities. I've taken my money out of that hedge fund so I can't lose any more that way, but losing that thirty thousand was bloody painful, I assure you. All the same, Larissa and I had plenty of fun, or at least I thought we did, and I was a good dad to your little half-brother Piotr, I really was.'

'Where's Larissa living now?'

'She's basically bloody moved yachts. She now lives with Leo on his massive thing and my poor little *Ivana* is bereft of us all now.'

'What do you mean?'

'I can't live there by myself. It's just too lonely. I tried it for a week and it almost drove me stark raving mad. So I've moved to stay at a hotel not far from a casino. It's called Hôtel Anglais and it's comfortable and cheap. Of course I'm not going to stay there forever of course. I'm looking into renting an apartment. Frankly without Larissa and Piotr to support, life will be a lot easier financially, though I'm going to be bloody lonely. It's a nice hotel, I suppose, but why they call it Hôtel Anglais when hardly any of the staff there can speak a word of bloody English beyond "good morning" and "good evening", and "how would you like to pay your bill?" is completely beyond me. Now, I've made arrangements for you to stay there too. I'll pay for you. The hotel's pretty full right now so your room will be on a different floor to mine, but you'll be comfortable. We're going to go there now.'

The waiter came over to us, having not been in any rush to do so first, waiters in the South of France not tending to be known for their speed at serving people. But in the mood Dad was in, he seemed almost to welcome this. Dad looked up at the waiter sternly. 'We're going, now, young fellow,' Dad said, in english, of course. 'If you'd come a bit earlier you could have sold us each a coffee and maybe a pastry too. Lateness doesn't win customers.'

The waiter didn't apologise as he might have done in England but gave Dad a look of contempt and me a disdainful glance and then swept away to another table.

'Bloody idiot,' Dad said when we probably weren't out of earshot and heading for the airport exit.

'Dad, please don't be horrible, and stop swearing. In all fairness we weren't there very long and if he'd come over right away as soon as we'd arrived, you'd have probably said he was being too hasty. Don't start becoming a grouchy old grump just because you're by yourself. You need to meet someone else anyway, you can't be here alone in Monte Carlo for the rest of your life, it'll drive you bonkers.'

'You're right, love, I'm sorry, I'll try to be nice.'

'Please do.'

'Now for goodness' sake, Ivana, please tell me you've not spent all that million dollars on giving to charities and all that sort of thing?'

'No I haven't. I've spent some of it on good causes and I intend to spend some more of it on good causes, too. I've put it into a special account at Santander because it didn't feel right to keep it in my bank account.'

'How much have you spent on yourself?'

'I bought a Fiat Femina car and I'm going to keep ten thousand pounds for myself, and even that I feel a bit guilty about.'

'You're the one who's bloody crackers, Ivana. You should keep the whole lot for yourself. This kind of financial good fortune only comes along once in a lifetime.'

I didn't tell Dad I'd already given fifty thousand pounds to a charity that funds research into brain tumours; I knew he'd've asked me why that particular charity and I wasn't quite ready to tell him about Lottie yet, though I knew I would soon.

'Well, anyway,' said Dad, 'let's go and rescue the Ferrari from the car park before some not-so-nice vandal from Nice pinches it.'

Well! This trip to Monte Carlo was not, to put it mildly, going according to plan. I'd been expecting a relaxing and jovial time with Dad, Larissa and Piotr, but instead I felt as if I'd been dumped as well.

Dad drove us in his somewhat battered Ferrari to the Hôtel Anglais and I checked into my room, which was large and comfortable and turned out to have a very nice view of the main square of Monte Carlo and the casino. I took a shower. When I was getting dry I saw a text on my phone from Tom:
I hope you had a super journey, Vanny, and that you have a great time with your dad, Larissa and Piotr. xx

I texted back: *Just got here. Larissa's left Dad for a Russian multi-millionaire. Dad's quite depressed about it and I'm afraid it's going to be a difficult weekend. xx*

I almost added *Wish you were here*, because at that moment I rather did.

I got dressed, went to Dad's room to get him and we had coffee downstairs in the café of the Hôtel Anglais which was deserted apart from him and me. Dad grew a bit sentimental. He told me how much he loved me, and how much he missed me, and I sat there looking at the tablecloth.

'You really are my favourite child, you know.'

'Yes, Dad, I know. Thanks for feeling that and saying it.'

The tea was brought to us soon by an extremely pretty, reserved-looking waitress, with tanned skin and beautiful long glossy black hair that was frankly, quite a bit like mine. Dad thanked her courteously and obviously very sincerely, added a tip when he signed the bill, and I watched in admiration as she expertly dealt with his flirty comments. He usually didn't do that, flirt right in front of me, but I suppose men feel the need to assert their manliness and romantic nature when they've just been dumped, or even when they haven't. Or, perhaps he was letting himself go a little more than usual, because of his situation: mostly all he talked about over tea was how betrayed he felt by Larissa, though at one point he looked me firmly in the eye and said:

'I'm so proud of you, my darling girl. You're a true expert in your profession, you write very well when you write your chess articles, and I just know that before long you're going to be a grandmaster, with all the kudos and status and extra money that will involve. But you do bewilder me sometimes. I mean, why not use the money that billionaire gave you to bring yourself some financial security? Why bother with this ridiculous notion of the Love Fund? After all, who said life would be fair? Keep the money and enjoy it and bring yourself some financial security. Stop being such a saint all the time. You are a saint to me and everyone who meets you thinks you're wonderful but, you really need to be a little more selfish sometimes.'

I forced a smile. 'Dad, I know what you mean and I know why you're saying it. If I'd made the money from winning lots of chess tournaments and maybe getting some sponsorship it would be another matter. But this is completely different. I didn't earn the money. And more importantly, I was given it by an infatuated man - the man I mentioned, Boris - who thinks I'm the queen bee's knees and says he's the only woman he would ever consider marrying.'

'Where did he get to know you, anyway?'

'Oh, he saw me in the television advertisement that was broadcast in Slovenia.'

'You mean the *Softly Softly* one?'

'No, that was an old TV police show. You mean *Softy-Softy*.'

'It's bloody confusing, Ivana.'

'I know it is. It's true that I've got to know him much better now and in fact he really is a gentleman. What I haven't told you yet is that one of my very best friends, Lottie Richmond – you met her once when you came to London a couple of years ago...'

'Yes, I remember. Beautiful girl.'

'Yes, she is. Dad, listen... she has a brain tumour - a malignant one - and I just don't know what's going to happen to her. I worry about Lottie most of the time. Fortunately, there's an experimental drug which seems to be effective against the kind of brain tumour she has. I told Boris about it, and he managed to get a supply of the drug for Lottie; he has connections to the medical profession. So right now I'm very indebted to him, so that's another reason why I'd rather not just use his money unthinkingly.'

'Oh my goodness. The poor lass. The poor lass.'

'It's terrible, I know. But fortunately Lottie isn't letting herself become negative about it at all. And Dad, there's something else. Lottie's getting married.'

'She is?'

'Yes. The wedding's on April the fourteenth. She's marrying a famous and incredibly talented cellist called Steve Juselius.'

I waited for a moment to see if Dad's expression would convey any recognition of the name, but it didn't.

'Steve only proposed to her last weekend,' I went on, quickly. 'It's all happening very soon because frankly we don't know how long Lottie is going to live, even with the Ditrexican.'

Dad nodded thoughtfully. 'She's obviously a very brave young woman.'

'Yes, she is,' I said. 'But there's nothing much I can do for her this weekend apart from not forget her. Let's talk about plans. What would you like to do this evening, for example?'

Dad shrugged despondently. 'I haven't exactly given it much thought.'

'Well, I'm your daughter, I love you and I'm here, aren't I? So we can't spend the whole evening just talking about how Larissa finished with you and has left you or how Lottie is so ill. So now let's try to do something memorable with this evening.'

I suppose we did, really. I suggested to Dad that we get a cab to Nice and have supper and see a show. We had a very good early evening French supper at a restaurant called, not very imaginatively, Nice Times, but I thought maybe it sounded wittier to French speakers. Afterwards we just turned up at Nice's national theatre and were lucky enough to find that a French-language version of the musical *Evita* was playing. I'd seen the film, and I saw the show in the West End some years ago, so even though Dad hadn't seen either the movie or the show on stage and it was being sung in French, I could give him an idea beforehand of what happened in the show without spoiling the ending for him. Besides, the musical's so theatrical that you don't need to understand the lyrics to get a good idea of what happens.

Dad, to my delight, loved the show. Afterwards he was buzzing with excitement and pleasure and seemed almost to have forgotten that Larissa had left him, though as the cab we took home approached more closely to Monte Carlo, his despondent frame of mind slowly started to return.

'Fancy a drink in the bar with me, lass?' Dad asked, after I'd paid the cab and we were walking up to the hotel's swing-doors. 'I'd be glad of your company; I'm really not in the mood to go to bed.'

'Dad, I would but I'm pretty shattered. It's been a big day. I'll see you at breakfast. And listen, I love you to bits and I think either Larissa will come back soon or if she doesn't she'll let you see Piotr when you want to. Either way, you deserve someone who is capable of appreciating all that you can bring them, so don't beat yourself up about her.'

Dad smiled soberly at me. 'You're a wonderful daughter, and the apple of my eye. Sleep well.'

I did, eventually, sleep well but not at once, because a little later that evening, in my room, something very strange happened which ended up sort of changing... well, what did it change?

Just about everything, really.

32

As I headed up to my hotel room, I was looking forward to making myself a cup of tea using the facilities I expected to find there. But as soon as I was in the room, I saw that there weren't any tea-making facilities, so I phoned down and asked the man who picked up for some tea. Once I'd hung up, I took my shoes off, and flopped down on the large and unnecessary double bed. I started thinking about Dad and about me. He didn't seem too good at sustaining a relationship, and I didn't seem to be any better.

The awfulness of this realisation made me suddenly feel terribly despondent. I even started to cry. I was still crying when a knock came on the bedroom door. I wiped my eyes quickly and got off the bed, made my way clumsily over to the door and opened it.

The woman standing there was the beautiful woman, with tanned skin and long black hair, who I recognised immediately as the waitress who had served Dad and me earlier that day in the hotel café. I let her in, keeping my eyes down so she wouldn't see the state of my face.

'Your tea, madam,' the woman said as she came in, carrying a silver gilt tray with tea things on it.

'Thanks,' I mumbled. 'Can you – could you just put it on the table, please?'

'Yes, of course,' she said, and she laid the tray down on the low table, glass-topped table in the middle of the room. Once she had, she glanced at me, and of course she saw I was in tears.

'Is everything all right, madam?' she asked, softly and gently.

I coughed back my tears. 'Please, don't call me that. I'm not married and I very much doubt I ever will be.'

'Oh,' she said, and when I looked up, I saw that she was standing a few paces away, hands set awkwardly on her thighs as she stared at the carpet and searched for something to say. 'I'm sorry, I didn't mean - '

'No,' I said. 'No, that was completely rude of me. I'm so sorry. I'm just upset.'

She smiled at me. I didn't understand why. I tried to force down the lump in my throat.

'You know, English guests have always been my favourite,' she said. 'There's something very sweet about how you apologize all the time. The French tend to be too - *comment on dit "têtu" en anglais* - yes, "headstrong", to say sorry, even when they should.'

I smiled faintly. 'I suppose we English are honest about being fundamentally very stubborn people, so we have the decency to apologize for it. I'm Vanny, by the way.'

She smiled beautifully. 'I'm Hélène,' she said, 'oh, Vanny, you're too hard on yourself.'

'You think so?'

She smiled. 'Yes,' she said, and I don't know whether it was the way she said it - in that soft, caring tone that I could easily imagine Lottie using, perhaps tacking on a *darling* - but I found myself crying again before I could even think of something to say in reply. I brought a hand up to my face while she stared at me. I felt so utterly pathetic for breaking down in front of a stranger that I just wanted to drag the bedcovers over myself and hide from her.

'I'm sorry,' I muttered. 'I'm so sorry.'

'See? You're doing it again.' Then there was a tinkle of jewellery, and then she was sitting next to me. I found myself leaning against her, not realising I'd been craving a hug this much. I didn't know her at all: I knew what was happening was completely inappropriate, but at that moment, at that time, it just felt, somehow, so, so right.

'I don't usually cry in public. God, I'm so embarrassed,' I sighed, the words hardly audible as I mumbled into her hair, but she shook her head.

'It's fine.'

'I don't want to inconvenience you – '

'*Arrête, ma cherie,*' she whispered.

She ran her fingers through my hair as I furiously tried to sniff back my sobs. Somehow I found physical contact with her so affectionate, innocent and comforting that I held onto her more tightly, infinitely grateful for her being there. She didn't even ask me any questions, just ran her hand through my hair, and my chest heaved as I let out a ragged sob. I didn't even know now why I was crying – for a stupid and inadequate reason, surely – but her embrace was so comfortable that I let myself go, not even thinking about how embarrassed I would be when it stopped. I leaned against her warm bosom like sinking into a cushion, and I felt her tense a little as my breasts pressed against hers, which were slightly larger than mine.

I moved away instantly, mumbling *sorry* once more, but she clicked her tongue.

'You say sorry again and I'll make you regret it,' she said, but in a light-hearted tone and with a bright smile.

'You will?' I said, but now with a smile.

She smiled back. 'Yes. I wrestle, you know.'

'You *wrestle?*'

'Yes, and I do jiu-jitsu. I can do quite a lot of holds and even some chokes. I could even kill someone with a choke. All women should learn a form of martial arts.' Then she pressed me against her again.

'You can talk to me,' she murmured. 'I mean, if you like.'

My heart started pounding on hearing her intimate tone. I didn't say anything, though.

'So what's bothering you?' she asked. 'Did you and your father have an argument, perhaps?'

I shook my head. 'It's not about my father.'

I drew a breath.

Part of me wondered why I would tell her about my feelings at all, but perhaps it was because she was a total stranger and she wouldn't, I supposed, do anything with the information, that made me think I could trust her with it. Also, well, she looked rather like me. I felt very close to her already. 'Recently I've just had so much on my mind,' I said. 'I just - I've especially been wondering about the role that – that sex has, in my life, and I feel like I've been just trying to live up to everyone's expectations, rather than living for myself, you know?'

'Oh believe me, I know,' she replied. 'I had to play a role for most of my life, and pretend I liked men just so my friends wouldn't be uncomfortable around me. When you're pressured into thinking that everyone else's comfort depends on you correcting *your* attitude, rather than *them* getting rid of their prejudices, it can be very confusing.'

I looked at her for a moment, realising that my heart was pounding even harder. 'Do you mean you're gay?' I asked her quietly.

She gave me another of her gentle smiles. 'Yes, I am.'

'Does that confession make you feel uncomfortable?' she asked a few moments later.

'No,' I said, gently, calmly and truthfully.

There was quite a long silence now. Then she murmured:

'Have you ever been attracted to a woman?'

The question overwhelmed me, but somehow I felt grateful for having been overwhelmed by it.

'I've only ever felt attracted to one woman,' I said. 'I mean,' I added, in a murmur, 'I've only ever wondered about, well, about making love with this one particular woman. And the stupid thing is, I never let myself try while I had the chance. She's getting married now, and – '

My throat tightened again, and I tried not to choke as I forced the words out. 'And she's got a brain tumour, and I think she might die, and while I've often told her I love her to bits, I've never really told her in such a way that she knows I really mean it.'

She nodded slowly. 'Were you afraid she would stop wanting you as a friend, if you revealed to her how you felt?'

I thought for a moment. 'I don't know. I can't really imagine she and I not caring about each other,' I said quietly, then thought about Lottie, all small and frail in John Hamlyn's consulting-room, being told the terrible news. I couldn't help it; I cried some more, as if all my sorrow about what had happened to Lottie and all my hatred of the tumour that was threatening her life was only now spilling out of me.

I sat there wiping my face furiously with the back of my right hand, wondering how pathetic I must seem to this woman, this beautiful woman, with long glossy black hair, who looked a bit like me, who didn't even know me and whose name I didn't even know.

'I'm keeping you from work, aren't I?' I said half-heartedly.

She shook her head. 'It's all right. There are others in reception who will deal with calls. We cover for each other,' and then she was hugging me again, her body against mine and I felt sparks in my lower back, shooting through my belly and making me feel light-headed. 'It's going to be all right,' she whispered.

Her hands cupped my face as I mumbled miserably into her hair, and in the next couple of seconds she turned her face so she could lean her forehead against mine. I could suddenly feel her on my lips, her breath, her proximity, and I couldn't even move any more.

'*Tu es tellement belle,*' the woman said, her lips touching my tear-slick mouth. 'Lottie would, I think, have been very happy to have made love with you.'

I didn't know what to say, still less what to do. I just felt I needed to stall for time.

She waited. She breathed against my lips, making my skin tingle.

'Tell me to stop,' she whispered, 'if you want me to stop.'

'I don't want you to stop,' I whispered back, closing my eyes miserably.

She kissed me on the lips.

Her lips skidded over my tear-wet ones and I tasted salt on her tongue as I let her kiss me, my hands feeling cold and empty as they hovered uncertainly in the air. Her own hands were in my hair, then they were trailing down my neck, down past my collarbones and over my breasts, feather-light, the heat on my nipples making me sigh.

'I don't want you to stop,' I said again, more firmly, and I finally let myself touch her, gently pulling my hair away from her face and holding the back of her head as I deepened the kiss. Her mouth felt just so soft and yielding, and her own hair, like black silk, covered my forearms and tickled my face as it fanned around me. It got in my eyes but I didn't care, I was too giddy with the taste of her and the feel of her lips against mine to care.

'Vanny,' she murmured again, as though she was too moved to say anything else. Then she was kissing me again, and pressing her right thigh between mine, and I forgot about time.

33

In the morning, the bright Monte Carlo sunshine was streaming into my bedroom around the edges of the closed yellow curtains.

We'd made love for about half an hour. It was the strangest, and also sort of the most wonderful, experience of my life. At the end, she'd kissed me goodnight in such a passionate and prolonged fashion I'd come close to passing out.

Now, in the morning, I lay in bed feeling stunned and thinking about her. I hoped one of her colleagues had covered for her. The last thing I'd have wanted was for her to get sacked because of me.

I didn't know what to say, or think, or even what to do.

All I knew was that I just so wanted to see Hélène again.

I picked up the phone and dialled reception. The call was answered by a man, not Hélène, and not the man who'd taken my order for tea the previous evening, either. This man I spoke to now, true to what Dad had said, really *didn't* speak English. I asked, speaking in French very slowly and methodically, whether I could speak to Hélène. But after much verbal kerfuffle (which included an attack of furious impatience on his part), he told me that she was now off and would not come back to work until Wednesday.

I felt infinitely disappointed. I even wanted to cry. *'Elle a peut-être laissé une message pour moi?'* I asked in my feeble French, with, I realised even as I said it, pathetic hopelessness, then even more pitifully added, *'je suis Vanny, dans chambre trois deux sept.'*

'*Non, madame, elle n'a rien laissé pour vous,*' he said.

'*Je comprends, monsieur. Pourriez-vous me dire son nom de famille, s'il vous plait?*'

'*Oui, c'est Dubois. Hélène Dubois.*'

'*Merci bien.*'

Unfortunately, I discovered during the next ten minutes of searching for Hélène on Facebook that the surname 'Dubois' is one of the commonest in France, and that there are about a zillion Hélène Duboises on Facebook, well more than a hundred anyway. I looked at all their thumbnail profile photos when they had them, but unfortunately not one of them was 'my' Hélène. I could only suppose she wasn't on Facebook. So, as I was having my morning shower and brooding on how I could possibly get back in touch with her, I realised I didn't have any choice but to phone her when she was back at work, embarrassing though the phone call would obviously be if someone else answered.

I had no idea of what to make of what had happened at all.

I thought about Hélène so very often during the next few days. Every time I walked into the reception of the hotel I expected, ridiculously, to find her there, even though I'd been told she was away until Wednesday – still, after all, for all I knew she might have changed her shift pattern.

On the morning after I'd made love with Hélène, Dad and I had breakfast together on the hotel terrace, which overlooked the casino. Obviously, I didn't tell Dad a word about what had happened. For his part, Dad told me, in a sudden burst of optimism (he's very prone to those) that he was going to phone Larissa later on and see if she answered and if she did, tell her how I was in Monte Carlo and wanted to meet her. Dad seemed quite taken with this fairly obvious plan. He phoned Larissa later that morning and as a result that afternoon, at about five o'clock, Larissa, Piotr, Dad and I all met on the *Ivana*. Larissa asked Piotr to stay in his bedroom belowdecks while we all had our conversation on the bridge (it's funny how on board ship you quickly get used to using nautical terms). It was a somewhat frosty meeting, because Larissa, though she was very friendly to me, confirmed to Dad that she had decided to leave him and wasn't coming back. But at least she said she'd make sure he could see Piotr whenever he wanted to.

Later that evening Tom texted me *I miss you* and I nearly texted back that I missed him too, but instead, more calmly, I texted that I was looking forward to seeing him at the concert on March the tenth, the following weekend. Tom texted back: *Yes, see you then, but it's a long time to wait. I really miss you, Vanny.*

I knew he missed me. And I suppose I missed him too. I missed lots of people really. I missed Sven, I missed Jaz who had often been out socialising somewhere I didn't know about over the past few weeks and of course I missed Lottie too; she was mostly staying at Steve's flat nowadays. But I was looking forward to the concert and I felt that the rest of my stay in Monte Carlo was likely to be a reasonably enjoyable one.

And so it proved to be. Dad and I went apartment-hunting for him on Saturday afternoon and found somewhere nearby that was a bit smaller than he wanted – he'd aimed to rent an apartment with three bedrooms but this one had only two. The location overlooking the sea-front was great.

Dad arranged to rent the apartment for six months and to move in there in the middle of March. He'd be staying at the Hôtel Anglais until then. We spent the next couple of days doing Monte Carlo-y kinds of things such as having long lunches and strolling along the promenade (it was warm enough to do that) and we even went into the casino despite Dad saying he didn't want to do so. Neither of us had any luck there, but we didn't bet much money and so we didn't lose much either.

I left the Hôtel Anglais at around eight o'clock on the Tuesday morning.

Dad drove me to Nice airport. My flight home was departing sometime around two in the afternoon.

'You're a wonderful daughter, Ivana,' Dad said, as we said goodbye at the security gates where you go airside.

'I'm not sure about that, but I try my best, Dad.'

'You try and you succeed.'

'Thank you.' I took a cheque out from my purse. 'This is for you,' I said, handing it to him.

'What is it?'

'It's a cheque for fifteen thousand pounds from the Love Fund. It's half of the thirty thousand pounds you lost.'

'Ivana, I can't take it.'

'Yes, you can. The way I see things, I was given this money to do good things with it, and I will. So, yes, take the money.' I smiled, quickly made a little tube of the cheque and pressed it into the gnarled crevice between his meaty right thumb and index finger.

'Goodbye, Dad. See you soon.'

'Goodbye, Ivana.' Thank goodness, he didn't try to give me the cheque back.

I saw he had tears in his eyes. I kissed him briefly on the lips, then I moved fairly fast into the security queue, which was fortunately pretty fast-moving.

Dad just stood there, waving slowly to me, until I was through passport control.

34

Later in the afternoon of that same Tuesday, March the sixth, when I flew back to Britain, Steve, Lottie and I were in John Hamlyn's consulting rooms in Harley Street. John pointed with his right forefinger to a sort of white blobby mass roughly in the centre of the transparency. 'That thing there, is, as you will imagine, Lottie's tumour. Yes, it's still visible; but obviously the smaller it is the better and what I'm absolutely delighted to tell you is that it's now a full twelve percent smaller than it was the last time we did the scan. If it continues to shrink in this way, then it is not impossible that Lottie may have several years of good health to look forward to, and maybe a lot longer.'

Steve grabbed one of Lottie's pale hands impulsively, sighing in relief. But Lottie was contemplative. 'It seems like a miracle,' she murmured.

John nodded. 'Yes, I agree. If Ditrexican turns out to be as amazing as it certainly appears to be so far, treatment of all brain tumours will have been revolutionised. And of gliomas especially. But I don't want to speak too soon, because ultimately my job cannot be, and must not be, to give people false hope, for all that I hate disease more than anything else in the world. I would do anything, anything, to wave a magic wand and cure you of this problem at once, Lottie.'

'John, you are so kind and sweet,' Lottie said.

'Would it make sense for Lottie to increase the dosage, just slightly?' Steve asked. 'She's currently taking thirty milligrams a day of Ditrexican, ten grams in the morning, afternoon and evening.'

John nodded slowly. 'Yes, I was going to say that I think increasing the dosage to forty milligrams daily would be a good idea. I suggest you ratchet up the evening dose to twenty miligrams. I need to monitor this very carefully, because after all we don't know about side effects and we don't know whether increasing the dosage will give us any significant reduction in the glioma.'

John went over to Lottie and made to shake her hand, but she smiled, reached out and gave him a hug.

'I'll see you at the concert,' John returned.

'Your ticket's complimentary, John,' Lottie replied, 'and we've allocated you a seat on the front row. I hope you enjoy it.'

I'd decided not to tell Lottie, Steve or John Hamlyn about the £20,000 I'd given from the Love Fund to a charity that supported research into brain tumours.

I didn't know what shift pattern Hélène worked, but it seemed reasonable to assume it was afternoons and evenings, which was after all, when she'd been at work on the Friday when I'd met her. I decided to try calling her sometime around the middle of the Wednesday evening as maybe she'd be less busy then.

'Allo?'

It was the voice of a man I'd never spoken to before. I was calling at some time just after eight on the Wednesday evening, so it was just past nine her time.

I tried English. 'Good evening. Can I talk to Hélène Dubois, please?'

'She is in a store-room. She will be back in maybe ten minutes,' replied the man, in surprisingly good English, considering what my father had said about the hotel.

'OK, thank you, I'll phone back.'

'Thank you. Shall I tell her who called?'

My heart flipped over a couple of times. 'Yes, it's Vanny.'

'I'll tell her.'

'Thanks.'

I hung up. I could only assume that the Hôtel Anglais had had some sort of recruitment offensive to recruit charming people.

Goodness knows the agonies of self-doubt I went through in those ten minutes! I asked myself dozens of times if I should have told him my name after all, as that obviously gave Hélène the opportunity not to take the call if she didn't want to talk to me. But I managed to persuade myself that if she really didn't want to talk to me, then I was wasting my time anyway.

Those next ten minutes in fact seemed as long as a week, but they finally passed.

I drew some deep breaths, found they made me feel dizzy, then rang again.

I heard the Monaco ringing tone - longer and lower in tone than the British one - six times before a voice I knew so well said, more quietly than I'd expected:

'Hello?'

My heart thumped and thumped. 'Hello, Hélène, it's me, Vanny.'

'Vanny, hi. Pierre told me you'd be phoning.'

Her tone was only level, nothing more.

'Can you talk for a moment?' I asked, feeling totally disappointed.

'Yes, but not for long, sorry. It's quite busy here at the moment. Have you got a pen?'

The question was so unexpected I didn't register it at once.

'Pardon?' I said.

'You have a pen? *Tu as un stylo*?'

'Oh, yes. Yes, of course.'

'Look, I give you my mobile number, OK?'

I was breathless. 'OK.'

She quickly gave it to me and I wrote it down on the inside back cover of my very well-thumbed copy of Danny Gormally's book *Insanity, passion and addiction - a year inside the chess world*. I love Danny's book. I wrote down Hélène's number with the neatest, most accurate handwriting I'd done since I was about eight years old, so there was no danger, no danger at all, of my taking the number down inaccurately.

'OK, I've got it,' I said.

'*Bon*. I am on duty all night, but by midnight most of the guests will have gone into their rooms. Vanny, you can call me on my mobile at midnight, at least if you will still be awake then.'

'No problem,' I said, 'I'll still be up. That's only eleven o'clock over here anyway. So I will talk to you later.'

'*Parfait*. Your father is well, by the way. I have been talking to him. He is a lovely man.'

'Thanks. I was going to ask you how he was. But... you haven't been talking to him about us?'

I heard her give a very nice little laugh. 'No, of course not. Vanny, listen, I can't speak much more now, but I want to tell you something.'

My heart thumped again, even harder.

'What's that?' I murmured.

'*Je suis si heureuse...* I am so happy you phoned me. I was hoping you would. I know that you asked when I would next be at work and were told that it would be today, Wednesday. I thought, "if she phones me, it will be today".'

I felt just so excited, and suddenly I realised that I wasn't especially nervous any more.

I heard her hang up.

At eleven o'clock, spot on, again feeling totally nervous, I phoned Hélène from my room.

'Hello again,' she said.

'Hello.'

'I'm in the staff room. I asked Dimitrios – he and I are on tonight – please not to disturb me for twenty minutes or so and to take up any drinks himself. He is a good man and mostly does everything I say. So we can talk.'

'That's super.'

There was a brief pause, then she said: 'Do you feel embarrassed by what happened between us?'

I heard myself clear my throat.

'A little, yes,' I said. 'But... it was wonderful. I... I really would like to see you again.'

'Well, that is good, because I would like to see you again too.'

I could hardly speak. Finally, I found myself blurting out, sort of crazily:

'Could you get a few days off the weekend after next?'

There was a silence, then she said:

'So you are coming to Monte Carlo again to see your dad?'

'No, no, I'm not, or at least not yet. I don't actually know when I'll be coming back to Monte Carlo. Oh, I will at some point, but I can still do the things I want to do for my father when I'm here, in England.'

'Then where do you suggest we meet?' she asked, in her gentle, light-hearted voice with its lovely accent.

'Hélène, something I've not told you is that I'm a professional chess-player. Next Sunday I'm travelling to Budapest to play in the European Women's Chess Championship. It's one of the biggest events in my chess year.'

'Budapest, the capital of Hungary?'

'Yes. If you can take the weekend after next off, maybe you could come to see me there. There are flights from Nice to Budapest. I've looked it up, and the quickest flight is via

Vienna. It only takes three hours altogether, including the connections.'

'You've looked up the flights already?'

'Well, yes.'

'Oh, Vanny I think that is so romantic! But listen, please, it's a lovely idea and maybe I can get the time off from my job, but... you see, I'm afraid I don't have much money. I live with my mum; she is Portuguese. The money I earn here at the hotel helps to support us; it isn't much but it is something. My dad was French. He left us when I was a little girl and I don't have any contact with him. My mother works as a cleaner and I work in the hotel. I go to college one day a week and study Hotel Management. One day I want to have my own hotel.'

'That day will come, I'm sure of it, Hélène. If you'd like to see me in Budapest I could pay. I can buy the ticket and you can pick it up at the airport. Oh, and do bring some warm clothes. It'll be cold in Budapest. I really really hope you can get the time off.'

'It's a very nice idea, but I'm not sure I feel comfortable about you paying for my air ticket, Vanny, though. I will ask my boss about my schedule. Yes, I have plenty of warm clothes. My mother and I lived in Paris until a few years ago, which can be really freezing in the winter. We came to Monte Carlo mainly for the sunshine. We talk tomorrow evening same time, is that OK?'

'Yes, that would be lovely.'

'Listen, Vanny, I really like you, you know?'

'I... really like you too,' I murmured.

'Vraiment?'

'Yes. Really and truly,' I said.

35

The concert Lottie and Steve had organised for the evening of Saturday, March the tenth at the Benjamin Britten Hall on Wigmore Street was now starting to feel like a celebratory event after Lottie's very positive new scan, though Lottie didn't plan to make any announcement about her health condition at the concert. Her illness was still a secret to anyone except her family, her closest friends, and of course the medical people.

The concert lasted around two hours altogether, not including a twenty-minute interval. In the first half, Lottie herself played for about half an hour, then Steve did a couple of solos, and afterwards Lottie and Steve played the marvellous version of Pachelbel's *Canon* they'd played at the party. Lottie looked joyous through the entire performance; her demeanour seemed to me to be a great victory over her stupid and evil brain tumour that the Ditrexican was shrinking. I don't remember what all Lottie's solo pieces were, but the one I do remember was the 'Romance' movement from Mozart's Piano Concerto in D minor. I think that entire piano concerto by Mozart is one of the most delicious pieces of music any human being has ever composed and it's one of the few pieces I can imagine listening to all the way through at a concert without my mind starting to drift.

Lottie was accompanied by a CD playing the orchestral part, so it really was like a concerto. The Romance movement is just so incredibly lovely, with enormous precision being demanded of the performer because a lot of the Romance movement is just single piano notes played like a torrent of sublime droplets from a celestial waterfall. The orchestra of course is still present but very much in the background.

I thought how strange it was that I was all emotional and thinking of all sorts of things to do with what was happening in my life right now, and of all the hundred and fifty or so people there, no-one had any idea what I was thinking about. Jaz was on my right in the second row of seats. In the same row as us were Sir Rupert and Lady Elizabeth and also Lottie's older brother Hugo, as well as Steve's parents and his two younger sisters, Fiona and Imogen. There were also three journalists there, on the same row, from classical music magazines.

Hélène and I had spoken on Thursday night at midnight, and on the previous night, the Friday, also at midnight. Hélène told me on Friday that she wouldn't be able to speak on Saturday and Sunday nights as they were very busy at the hotel but that she'd speak to me on Monday, and let me know if her boss would let her have the following weekend off.

'I'll keep my fingers crossed that he does,' I said.

'When are you going to Budapest?'

'At just after ten o'clock on Sunday morning.'

'I think you have a very exciting life, Vanny. Me, all I do is work here in this quiet small hotel in Monte Carlo.'

'Well, Monte Carlo's a lovely place to live, and... as you know, I really hope we can meet in Budapest.'

'Oh, Vanny, I hope so too.'

By now there was a definite date for Dad's move into his new apartment, March the twentieth, which was a Tuesday and when I was scheduled to play the eighth round - the last round but one - of the European Championship in Budapest.

In the interval, Tom, Jaz and I met with Lottie and Steve and their parents. Tom was his usual urbane, courteous and good-mannered self: the Tom I liked so much. We all had a glass of wine and some rather delicious nibbles that were being served by elegant caterers wearing black tie if they were men and black dresses if they were women.

There came a point later in the interval when, predictably enough, Tom and I found ourselves tête-à-tête close by a pair of large, heavy, half-open dark blue curtains, that were hanging down from a window at the very far end of a very long corridor, so quite a way from the concert hall. There was no-one else nearby. I couldn't help thinking it was just like Tom and me to end up sort of automatically finding some secluded place.

It was dark outside, the switch to British Summer Time not being due until the end of the month. I was vaguely gazing through the window when I became aware that Tom was close by me and wanted to speak. We hadn't had a chance to before, at least not before the concert started.

'I've missed you,' Tom said.

I smiled. I wrapped him in a tight, friendly hug right there. 'I've missed you too.'

He held onto me for a few moments, then we broke away from each other and stood apart.

'How've you been?' I asked, then blurted out, 'Have you learnt any more about Henki Oy?'

Tom shook his head. 'No, not since we met that charmer Jussi. Oh, well, I did manage to find an email address in New York for enquiries to do with investing in the company. It all sounds like a really strange organisation. I wish you'd ask your Boris more about it.'

'Tom, he's not "my Boris" and in any case you'll appreciate it's a bit difficult at the moment for me to do anything that looks like it might be pressurising him. We're incredibly lucky he managed to get Lottie on the American test for Ditrexican - it may have saved her life - and her health is right now a lot more important to me than Henki Oy is. Still, I'd like to know more about the organisation and what they're really up to. Maybe I'll find a way of asking Boris about it at some point but not at the moment.'

Tom nodded. 'I understand.' He smiled. 'Hey, Vanny, it's just so great to see you again.'

'Well, it's great to see you again, too.'

I glanced around. There were quite a few people milling about at the other end of the corridor but they must have been close to fifty yards away from us. I grabbed hold of Tom by the right shoulder and pulled him behind the closest of the heavy curtains. It reached all the way down to the floor; we wouldn't have been visible at all.

There, with Tom behind the dark blue curtain, I suddenly felt we were lost together in some mysterious deep ocean world, where you could breathe and were dry but were otherwise as close and intimate and cut off from anyone else as you would be if you were deep under the sea.

36

As well as being terribly beautiful, Budapest is a really rather unusual place. It's basically two cities joined together: Buda, which is on the western side and consists mostly of a tall hill that has a wide range of stunning buildings built on it. The Danube flows magnificently at the foot of the hill and on the other side is the town or city of Pest, where my hotel was, and where the tournament was going to be held at the Budapest Exhibition Centre about half a mile farther into the town. Pest is almost literally as flat as a pancake and has all the important state buildings on it.

Budapest was all snowy and wintry. I paid the cab that had brought me from the airport, then I checked into the hotel. I felt in a strange but also strangely comforting environment. It also occurred to me that if Hélène *did* visit me, this hotel would probably be where we... well, anyway. My fifth-floor room had a view of the river and of the elevation of Buda on the opposite side. It was a nice big room with a large double bed and old-fashioned foreign-looking wooden furniture including two armchairs and a nice old-looking wooden desk. I was impressed. I thought of Hélène being there with me, and grew nervous. What if her decision was yes and she actually came to see me?

I had a shower in the bathroom, which was very clean but smelt of some foreign and sour disinfectant. As I was getting dry, my phone emitted a single beep and I saw I'd got a text from Tom. It said:

I hope you got there safely. By the way, are you feeling Hungary?

I texted back:

Your puns don't get any better. Yes, I'm feeling very Hungary at the moment to be honest. I intend to go out this evening for some goulash or something which I quite like in the evening, though I remember from the past that they sometimes serve it for breakfast here yuk.
I'm not going to say wish you were here because I do but if you were here it would raise all sorts of questions about us I suppose. All the same, it would be great if you were.
Vanny xx

I did wonder how sincere I was being in the last line. Would I have rather have shared the room with Tom, or Hélène?

I didn't actually know the answer to that question.

Tom replied almost at once:

You mean questions like whether we move the two single beds in your room together assuming there are two single beds in your room? Or maybe there are some nice heavy curtains?

I replied:

Actually there's a very large double bed.

Tom's reply was:

What a waste.

I reminded myself he had no idea I'd invited Hélène to Budapest. I texted back:

Yes, I suppose it is. In fact I definitely think it is. OK, must finish unpacking now and go out for dinner. Xx

Tom replied:

Enjoy dinner and I hope you won't be Hungary after it. xx

After texting Tom *Goodnight xx*, I waited a few minutes out of respect for him then texted Hélène:

Hi Hélène, I've arrived safely here in Budapest. It's cold but not too cold, and there's no snow. The city's as lovely as I remember it being! I hope you are well. Looking forward to talking to you tomorrow evening. Vanny xx

I was irrationally disappointed that she didn't text me back at once. But after thirty-seven minutes she did.

My dear Vanny, how belle it is to have hear from you. I am so glad you have arrived into Budapest safely. I have been looking up some photos of it on google and it looks like a city of much beauty. I so much hope I can come to see you! I will know about my work schedule tomorrow evening so please can you call me at midnight Monte Carlo time? Love from Hélène xx

I loved this text, and the grammatical error in the first line I simply found endearing. I texted back:

Thanks so much for yours. I know it's expensive for you to text abroad so please don't feel you have to reply to this one, but yes I'm looking forward to our chat tomorrow and I really really hope you can come. xx

A minute or so later, Hélène texted back:

I really really hope so too. xx

I decided not to reply, as I thought there was a danger that if I did, she might think I was a bit obsessive. Perish the thought. I'd never told her anything about Tom or Boris.

I was being careful not to let myself think too much about what things might be like if Hélène came to see me, and I was still being careful now not to let my thoughts dwell on something that, after all, might still not happen.

37

The next day, March the twelfth, was Round One of the European Women's Chess Championship.

I'd been (probably unjustifiably) optimistic about turning in a good performance at the event, but my first game was a *total* disaster. I played Black against an Israeli international master, Embeth Rosen, and I just couldn't find my way at all. She launched a very strange early wing attack involving an early advance of the king's rook's pawn and I was stupid enough to castle kingside because I felt I could probably deal with her attack. Castling is the only move in chess that involves more than one piece; you move your king and one of your rooks to hide your king away near the left or right-hand corner.

Alas, I couldn't deal with Embeth's attack and after twenty-seven moves I was busted. Six moves later, when I was about to be checkmated, I resigned.

I felt utterly terrible about losing this first-round game. When I lose a game in which I've played badly I just feel completely miserable and annoyed and wish I was doing anything other than playing chess professionally.

So rather than texting or Facebooking or communicating with any of my friends at all that Monday evening, I buried myself in my chess preparation in my room with my laptop and using the hotel's Wi-Fi system to log on. I think Tom may have sent me a text to see how I got on, I don't quite remember but in any case I certainly didn't answer it.

By nine o'clock that evening I knew from the tournament website who I was going to be playing the following day. My opponent in Round Two would be a fifteen-year-old French player, who wasn't even an international master, called Sabine Duvalier. She'd lost in the first round as White in only seventeen moves to one of the women grandmasters, and I felt that being White against Sabine the following day would give me a chance, all being well, to chalk up an early scalp and to do better.

By the time midnight came round, I was feeling quite sleepy, and also rather overwhelmed by a mild, but not unpleasant, dizziness that often came over me when I spoke to Hélène.

'Vanny?'

'Yes, yes, it's me.'

'I can come!'

'Oh, my God. Really?'

'Yes. I am free from Saturday until Tuesday evening, when I must be back at work.'

'Oh Hélène, that's such lovely news.'

'You are pleased?'

'You know I am.'

'I am pleased, too,' she said. 'Nervous, but pleased.'

'*You're* nervous?' I asked.

'Yes, of course I am.'

'I'm nervous too,' I admitted.

'Good. That is very good.'

'Why?'

'Because it is. It is nice we are being nervous. So how are you doing in the chess?'

'Not too well. I lost today, or rather, I mean yesterday.'

'Oh, no.'

'Yes, I'm afraid I did.'

'Well, never mind. I am sure you will do better later today.'

'I'll try my best to.'

'And when I come to see you, I will give you strength to play even better, I hope.'

'But Hélène, there are four more rounds between now and then!'

'Well, I send you strength over the phone now.'

'Thanks. I really appreciate that. I'll sort out your flights in the morning and email you the details. I'm just so looking forward to seeing you.'

'So am I.'

Despite my terrible loss in my game that day, I was trembling with excitement, pleasure and anticipation when I reluctantly ended the call.

In the morning I made all Hélène's flight arrangements. I didn't go for the cheapest flights I could find, but chose the ones that would have the most convenient change; there were no direct flights from Nice to Budapest. After looking at lots of possibilities, I worked out that Hélène travelling via Slovenia was even better than going via Vienna, so I booked her on an Air Med flight that left Nice at 08.35 the following Saturday and was scheduled to arrive in Ljubljana at 09.55. I also booked her on a Slovo-Air flight that left Ljubljana at 11.20, which I thought would give her plenty of time to collect her bag (assuming she had any hold luggage), get a coffee and pastry or something and then board the plane in good time.

After I'd made all the arrangements, I sent Hélène an email giving her all the details. After I'd written the email, I read through it and realised it was more businessy than I wanted it to be, so I ended it *sorry this is all pretty serious. Am so looking forward to seeing you! Xx* Then I pressed Send.

38

Round Two started at two fifteen that Tuesday afternoon in the Budapest Exhibition Centre. Playing White against Sabine Duvalier, and with thoughts of Hélène ringing in my mind, I was hoping for - and actually rather confident of - a quick win.

In fact, the game started off going my way, then something totally unlucky (well, for me, anyway) happened. As I was making a move that was going to improve my position, I accidentally did something I haven't done for ages, which was touch a piece – my king - I didn't intend to move.

In chess, the rules say that if you want to adjust a piece on its square, you need to say the formula *j'adoube* ('I adjust') which is one of the many phrases the French language has given to the world, and I suppose it would have been appropriate after all, as I was playing a French woman as well as looking forward to the visit of a French-Portuguese one.

I didn't say *j'adoube* when I accidentally touched my king because I had no intention of moving the wretched thing. But Sabine, being a young player and eager for any kind of advantage, which wasn't surprising considering the position she was in on the board, immediately said, in what I have to admit was rather beautifully accented English from under her low-hanging fringe of black hair (the rest of which was cut in a rather irritatingly cute bob around her face):

'You must move your king now. You didn't say *j'adoube*.'

I shrugged, I knew she was right and that rules are rules. The problem was that the only square I could move the king to was one square ahead; a truly terrible square which blocked my queen and basically immediately ruined my position. The game didn't last much longer. Little bobbed hair Sabine's unpleasant Black pieces gradually over-ran all my defences. On move thirty-five, faced with inevitable mate in only three or four moves, I resigned.

I shook Sabine's cool little bony hand, signed the score sheets really quickly, tore off my own copy, and literally stormed out of the playing-hall.

I went to find a café, thinking that if I had a glass of some nice Hungarian wine maybe I'd feel better. They served me a glass of something called Bull's Blood which was a strong dark red wine and which initially did cheer me up a bit but then I made the mistake of having a second glass and the alcohol in the two glasses kicked in quite soon after I'd finished the second one and I started to feel even worse than I had before. I'd forgotten that, as Tom once told me, alcohol is basically a depressant and I just wanted to be by myself somewhere dark and secluded and sad and just spend my time crying.

It was then that my mobile, which I'd switched back on after I'd stormed out of the torture chamber that was called the playing-hall, started to ring.

I could see that the caller was Lottie. 'Hello, darling,' I murmured to her, keeping my voice down as there were maybe a dozen other people in the café at the time and I wasn't keen on them knowing my business.

'Vanny, I'm really sorry about your game.'

'You mean the one yesterday?'

'Yes, I do mean the one yesterday but also the one you lost, today. I saw it on the internet.'

Lottie did this sometimes: follow me on the internet when I was playing in a tournament or at least glance at the tournament website. She could play chess a bit though she wasn't a strong player but she could follow a game and have an idea of what was going on in it. Like all major tournaments, the European Women's Championship has it's own website and you could see live games as they were being played which chess-player surfers can watch on their own computers and enjoy the pleasure of trying to guess what move the player whose play they are following would make next.

'Vanny, listen: there's something I want to say to you.'

'Yes?

'Oh, Vanny, darling, please don't be so sad. Listen. I want to say this. *I want you to win this tournament for me.* I don't know if the Ditrexican's going to cure me; I know it's making things better but I don't know what will happen over the next few months. For all I know, and I don't like saying this but I have to say it because it's true, this might be the last European Women's Chess Championship you play in while I'm alive. This might be my last chance to see you become the European Women's Chess Champion; it really might be. Vanny, like I said: *I need you to win this tournament for me.* I can see from the tournament website there are seven more rounds left, is that right?'

'Yes.'

'Right, well, I really need you to try to win every one of your next seven games. Can you do that?'

'I'll try my best.'

'Not good enough. Are you going to win them all for me?'

'Yes.'

'REALLY?'

'YES!'

'Good! Then go ahead and win them, Vanny, and make my dream come true. And remember, I love you to bits.'

'I love you to bits too. Thanks for the call, darling. You've really cheered me up.'

'I'm glad,' said Lottie. 'I'm just so glad.'

39

After I got back to the hotel, at about eight o'clock, I spent what was left of the day studying chess. Towards the end of the evening, when I'd been studying for at least three or four hours and needed a rest, I went onto the helicopter website and flew a helicopter around the city of New York, though only on my laptop using the mouse and the laptop controls, not the joystick and foot pedals as I didn't have them with me. The visuals on the helicopter website were really brilliant and the ones of New York were particularly good. The whole thing was so spectacular and accurate it really did feel like flying over New York itself at about three thousand feet which means I was flying above all the buildings, but I was careful not to descend close to any particular building.

I badly wanted to talk to Hélène, but I still felt utterly annoyed and low-spirited about losing two games in a row, and I was worried that if I spoke to Hélène she would detect my horrible mood and might even be put off from coming to see me. After all, we hardly knew each other really, and when you don't know someone well it can be dangerous to show them too much of your passionate side or your dark side as you don't know how they're going to react. So instead of phoning Hélène at midnight, I sent her the following admittedly pretty feeble text, which at least, had the advantage of being honest, even if I understated my distress:

Dear Hélène, I hope you've had a good day. I'm afraid I lost again today, but I should have a good chance of winning tomorrow. I'd love to talk to you but I feel quite annoyed with myself for losing today and I don't think I'd be very good company this evening. So can I phone you tomorrow instead? Lots of love, Vanny xx

Hélène's reply came only a few minutes later:

Dear Vanny darling, I'm SO SORRY you lost today! Yes, I do understand that you would rather talk tomorrow and that is all right for me (though I will miss talking to you) as we have a lot of guests from German who arrive tomorrow and tonight I need to make sure their bedrooms are all tip-top. Lots of love and BONNE CHANCE demain!! Hélène xx

By 'German' I knew of course she meant 'Germany'. Her little language slips really were very sweet, but as soon as I thought that I reminded myself that her English was about a zillion times better than my French. Still, at least I knew what *demain* meant.

I was amazed at how cheered-up hearing from Hélène made me feel.

Well, it might have been the inspiration Lottie had given me, or Hélène making me feel much more positive, but I actually managed to win my next three games, so that by the Friday evening, the day before Hélène was due to come, I had three points out of five. On the Saturday morning, when I woke up, I felt dizzy, excited and somehow disturbed for several moments before I realised why I felt like that.

Then I remembered: *Hélène's coming today.*

I lay in bed for a while, trying to work out what I felt about her coming to see me. Had it all been a crazy mistake? What was I doing, inviting a *woman* to spend the weekend with me?

I showered, dried myself and had some croissants for breakfast in the minimalist hotel café. I wasn't too hungry. I had the very clearest memory of the very first time I'd seen

Hélène carrying the tea on a tray, and how lovely I'd thought she was with her long, straight, glossy black hair, her very white teeth, her olive-coloured skin and strong, feminine features, and her amber-coloured dress, which I remembered now she'd removed very calmly and neatly when she was in my room later and placed over the back of a chair before devoting herself to me. And I'd remembered how strong and beautiful her body was.

I finished drying myself, put on some of my favourite *Oh Lola!* Marc Jacobs perfume, and dressed casually in blue jeans, a blue top, a pink cashmere pullover, my black boots and my white sheepskin jacket. I just hoped she liked my outfit. I was too excited and nervous to have more than a croissant for breakfast and a cup of decaf latte.

Finally, at what must have been about ten fifteen, I went out into the cold Budapest morning to a nearby taxi rank to get a cab to the airport. I knew I was going to be early, but I wanted to be. I sort of felt that the sooner I got there, the sooner Hélène might arrive.

The traffic was pretty chokka that morning, but Budapest airport is only about twenty kilometres from the centre and even with the cab often being stationary, it got there in less than an hour.

I've always found time passes quite quickly in an airport anyway, and somehow waiting for Hélène made the time pass even faster. In a weird kind of way, I didn't want the excitement to end by Hélène actually arriving.

I waited, breathless with excitement and happiness. I don't think I've ever felt more alive in my whole life than I did during that time when I waited for Hélène at Budapest airport.

Finally, the details on the electronic information board all shuffled as the board updated itself. Among the new information now being displayed, it said that Slovo-Air Flight 617 from Ljubljana had landed at 12.23.

40

I saw Hélène before she saw me. She was looking around at the other people waiting by the international arrivals exit, but her eyes began combing the area from left to right, and I was standing on the far right. She wasn't moving her head very fast, and so I had maybe four or five seconds to see her, a smile already on my lips to welcome her, before she spotted me.

Her lovely black hair was tousled and unbrushed from her flights, but I liked it looking wilder than it had at the hotel. Her hair was also longer than I remembered it being, and not quite as glossy, but it being less glossy somehow made her seem more real and I liked that too. She was wearing skinny black jeans, black boots not unlike mine, a partly unzipped fake silver fox jacket and a grey woollen jumper. With her right hand she was pulling a small black case on a carrying-handle, and slung around her left shoulder was a glossy red bag.

Then she did see me.

She smiled, hurried over to me, and kissed me perfectly blatantly and openly on the lips. In an instant, I felt all my doubts and nervousness fleeing away like mischievous ghosts scattered by a beautiful enchantress.

'*Chérie*, what time do you start playing?'

I smiled. 'At two fifteen. I thought we'd get a cab back to the hotel and you could have a rest there, and I'll come and see you when I've finished my game.'

'But I want to watch you play! I didn't know anything about chess, but I have been learning a little about it from the internet, and least I know now how the pieces move.'

I smiled. 'You've learnt something about the game and you want to watch me, really?'

'Of course I do!'

I loved that she wanted to watch me play. I smiled at her again. 'All right, we'll go to the venue together, and back to the hotel after my game.'

Outside, it had started to snow. Hélène took out a black beanie hat from a left-hand pocket in her jacket and put it on. Some snowflakes settled on her beanie hat almost at once.

As the cab drove away from Budapest airport, with Hélène sitting on my left in the back and with our luggage in the boot, and as I watched the snowflakes through the cab's windows, I felt her right hand reach towards my left hand, and the gentle but persistent touch of her cool, smooth fingers as they entangled themselves into mine.

I glanced at her, and our eyes met for a few moments before we both resumed looking straight ahead.

We sat there together, hand-in-hand, as the cab headed smoothly towards the tournament venue.

When we reached the venue and after the cab driver had unloaded our baggage and I'd paid him and he'd driven off, Hélène and I stood next to each other next to our luggage, as if we had to adjust for a few moments to being alone together again.

It was only about twenty past one; we'd made good time. There was a roof over the entrance to the venue and this protected us from the snow. A trickle of competitors was coming into the venue, but I knew that most wouldn't be arriving for another half hour or so: chess-players tend not to arrive too early at venues to avoid getting more stressed than they're likely to be anyway.

Walking into the tournament hall with Hélène next to me, I felt relaxed, happy and dizzy. That's the great thing about being a girl; you can have another girl as a close friend and hang out with her as much as you want and no-one's likely to ask any questions, as after all you could just *be* good friends. I pulled Hélène's case for her into the tournament hall and installed her on the nearest seat to my board, so she could glance over and see where I was and what I was doing.

I went to sit next to her. 'Welcome to your first chess tournament. Of course, there aren't many players here yet, but it'll start filling up pretty soon.'

Hélène smiled. 'It's good to be here, at your workplace! After all, you have been to mine. So, who are you playing this afternoon?'

'Her name's Francesca Nolan. She's an Irish international master. We've got a similar rating.'

'*Qu'est-ce que...* what does that mean?'

'It means a number which basically gives an idea of how good you are. Francesca and I have about the same number.'

'So the game will be equal, a draw?'

'Maybe, but I definitely hope not. I absolutely need to win my game this afternoon if I'm to have any chance at all of giving any challenge to the leaders.'

'I see, so you must win today. Do you think you will?'

'All I can say is, I'll try. Fortunately, I've got a good track record against Francesca; I've played her twice and won both times. Also, I'm White today, which is bound to help.'

'White moves first, yes?'

'Yes, and that's where White's advantage comes from.'

Hélène nodded. 'I see. Good. So, now, Vanny I think very much you should stop talking to me - it is nice to talk to you but I am thinking of you having the best chance to win this afternoon - and you should go for a walk and forget about me for the moment and think about winning your game.'

I nodded, smiled, held her hands in mine for a quick moment, then squeezed her hands gently but firmly before heading outside the playing-hall and outside the venue and into the calm and fluttering snowfall.

I let the snow fall on my hair, and on my nose and my eyelids, let it fall softly all over me as I stood there, inhaling the cold air and welcoming the snow gently pecking at me with its frosty breath.

I stood out in the snow for five minutes or so, thinking about the game I was about to play but thinking more about Hélène and wondering - not only with a lot of excitement but also with sheer practical curiosity - what exactly was going to happen later, when we got back to my hotel room.

Finally I headed for my board. As I sat down, I noticed Hélène. She was only about twenty feet from me. She gave me a little wave, and I saw her mouth *bonne chance* at me.

A few minutes later, Francesca arrived at the board. She was in her mid-twenties, had reddish hair and, to my surprise, that afternoon she was wearing a pink tee-shirt that had the words *THE MATING GAME* on it in large capital letters. So Sven hadn't bought one of those tee-shirts but she had. I didn't make any comment about the tee-shirt, though: talking to your opponent very much or even at all before the game starts is frowned upon and can even be regarded as deliberately attempting to distract them, which in some circumstances can cost you the game.

Francesca and I shook hands, then we avoided each other's glance until the tournament controller, a very plump Hungarian lady, announced in broken English from the front of the playing-hall that this was Round Six and could White (she meant the player playing White) please start the clock.

I did, and so did all the other players who were playing White.

I don't want to sound like big-headed Vanny, but I think my excitement at Hélène being there with me really made me play in fiery fashion that afternoon. Francesca resigned on move twenty-seven after we'd only been playing for just over an hour, so our game was one of the first to finish.

Francesca and I shook hands.

'Good luck in the rest of the tournament,' I said.

'You too, Vanny. Win the next three rounds and you could win the championship!'

'I know… but it won't be easy.'

'I'm sure it won't. But if anyone can do it, you can.'

'Thanks, Francesca.'

'You're welcome, Vanny,' she said in her charming Irish accent, and went off towards the tournament cafeteria. I walked in the opposite direction, to the table where the tournament arbiters were based, so I could drop off the signed score-sheets.

'You weren't too bored?' I whispered to Hélène, when I got back to her. The playing-hall was absolutely silent, and even by the spectators' seats you had to whisper.

She shook her head. 'No,' she whispered back. 'I loved watching you concentrating, and with your head in your hands as you studied the board! You looked very beautiful. Well done on your win.'

I trembled slightly 'Thanks. It's great to win before a rest day, as it lets you sort of bask in it for the whole next day. Shall we go back to the hotel now?'

I looked hard at her and she looked at me.

It was only a short walk to the hotel from the tournament hall. The snow had stopped falling, at least for the moment, though it had settled on the pavement and made pulling Hélène's case more difficult.

If the Budapest Rightprice Hotel, where I was staying, had been in England, or a bed and breakfast establishment in some English provincial town, I suppose questions might have been asked, and at the very least repressed eyebrows raised, about a lady in a double room having a lady guest suddenly moving in with her, though I suppose it would have been easy enough to have deflected the questions by simply, briefly (and a tad indignantly) explaining that we were friends. After all, ladies often share rooms, and even a double bed, without anything naughty happening.

Of course, in this case I knew that probably wasn't going to be the case, but the great thing about the Budapest Rightprice hotel (and, I suppose, about all other Rightprice Hotels the world over) is that while there are of course members of staff in the breakfast room in the morning, and obviously there are chambermaids in the hotel too, the basic idea of the hotel is to make everything as a robotic as possible, to save on staff. Check-in's automated, and while you could get someone to come and help you in reception if you wanted by making a phone call from a phone provided for this purpose, reception wasn't actually staffed, and so smuggling Hélène up into my room on the fifth floor - which was simply a matter of wheeling her case into the entrance lobby and walking across the lobby to the lift - was about as difficult as picking up a pawn.

We had the lift to ourselves, just us and Hélène's wheeled case and her red bag. We looked at each other, but didn't speak.

And then we were at the fifth floor and the lift doors opened and I wheeled Hélène's case along to my room, 518, and I opened the door and here we were.

Yes, here was my room with its large double bed (which had been made up) and the old-fashioned foreign-looking wooden furniture, including two armchairs and the wooden desk. It was the room I'd been living in for six days, and I was completely familiar with it, but how different it was, now that Hélène was there with me.

I went all the way in with the case, glanced back and saw Hélène confidently walking in herself.

'I adore your room,' she said, looking round it and closing the door behind her. She took off her silver fox jacket and lay it neatly on the nearest armchair.

'I'm glad you're here,' I said, but my mouth was so dry I could hardly speak.

'I'm glad I'm here too, my darling chess champion,' Hélène replied, looking me hard in the eyes.

'I'm not... well, I'm not actually the champion yet, you know. There're still three rounds to go, and I've still only got a score of four out of six.'

'Believe in yourself and you'll win the tournament,' Hélène said, looking at me intently as she said this. She took off her boots, which gave me time to take mine off too, and then when mine were off she came up to me and held my hands in hers.

And then she kissed me.

She didn't suggest we 'talk', or e.g. order cups of tea from reception. Instead, she just kissed me with her lovely mouth with its full lips and as she did she put her arms around me, her hands against the small of my back as she pulled me towards her.

She kissed me hungrily, feverishly even. I felt myself going totally dizzy. We snatched at each other's clothes and, gasping together, tugged relentlessly at them. I unbuttoned her skinny black jeans, she did the same to my own blue jeans and then she began pulling off my pink pullover and then my blue top, then she untied my hair (of course I'd worn it up for my chess game) and let it fall all over my face. She quickly undid my bra at the back (she was more expert at doing this than Tom was), then took it off, and she took her own bra off with great speed.

We fell onto the bed, me onto my back, then Hélène slowly kissed me all over my body, and everywhere, before wriggling on top of me. I simply adored having her beautiful body against mine, and her light but vigorous weight on me. She kissed me for a long time, her lovely lips opening my mouth for me, and, her tongue touching my mouth and teeth in a way that made me feel even dizzier than I did already, and presently she again started to kiss my ears, my eyes and my throat and my neck, and then the kisses she was giving to my throat and my neck turned into licks, and she licked my face and throat and neck and began to kiss my breasts, supporting herself on her elbows. *Mon Dieu*, she knew what she was doing!

We spent most of the rest of that day in bed, apart from when we went for supper; a goulash (of course) which we had at a little restaurant down a little alley not far from our hotel.

The next day, the Sunday, the tournament rest day, was heavenly from start to finish.

Hélène had found a cool site on the internet called *When Sally Met Sally: a gay girl's guide to Budapest* and this made lots of suggestions for what tourist attractions women could visit together on a day out in Budapest and basically we visited many of the things the guide suggested. I suppose I was also drawn to following the advice on the website as it had the same name as my car.

When Sally met Sally recommended we have breakfast at the Gellert Hotel, which is one of the most famous hotels in Budapest apparently, so after I worked out from googlemaps how to get there, we walked to the hotel on empty stomachs in the morning across another bridge, the Liberty Bridge, and wangled our way in as non-residents with Hélène's complete charm doing most of the wangling. Of course we were going to pay; it was just that the breakfast was obviously mostly designed for people who were staying at the hotel, and we weren't.

The weather had turned a little warmer; there was no snowfall and the snow on the streets and pavements was melting. The Gellert Hotel, which is located just on the Buda side by the Danube, is just amazing, with Art Nouveau architecture and an overall look that makes you think it's a Royal Palace rather than merely a hotel.

There were too many delish dishes in the breakfast buffet to list here and I don't remember them all anyway, but I do remember that we had, among other things, lots of different kinds of salami, some lovely roast pork on brown Hungarian rye bread, tangy sheep's-curd cheese, sweet red and green peppers and slices of really amazing big and incredibly juicy and ultra-delish red tomatoes, and then croissants with butter and marvellous strawberry jam, and some lovely fruit tea. We paid, tipped the waiter very well, then left the hotel and held hands almost as soon as we were out of the imposing front doors. We didn't care what people thought; we just wanted to hold hands, and we held hands for most of the day and no-one objected, though we did get quite a lot of teenage men, and older men too, giving us second glances, though maybe they would have anyway.

From outside the Gellert Hotel, we caught a green and cream-coloured number forty-seven tram back across the Liberty Bridge we'd crossed earlier. I think we were both too full to do much more walking for the time being. We got off not far from the Andrassy Ut, another of Sally's recommendations (the gay guide rather than my car), which is basically Budapest's answer to the Champs-Élysées and full of posh coffee houses, smart bistros, interesting museums and swanky shops. Later, we found a coffee-house that had a friendly rather than too imposing look to it and we had lattes there but definitely no pastries.

'I still don't feel that I could ever eat anything else, ever,' I said to Hélène.

She smiled. 'Me neither. So now, well, something that's also in Sally's guide is a four-hour boat trip on the River Danube, two hours up the river and two hours back. I know where the boats leave from.'

I smiled. 'Let's do it.'

The river cruise took us, I would say, about thirty miles north of Budapest. Once we were out of the city we enjoyed a wondrous wintry scenery of little villages, sumptuous churches, and the voyage on the great slowly flowing river. Sitting next to Hélène, feeling pleasantly tiddly (we'd shared a bottle of Bull's Blood wine) and watching the scenery pass us slowly, I felt more relaxed than I could remember feeling, and very happy. We weren't holding hands, but were just sitting, calmly and contentedly, next to each other, on a wooden seat that faced the big long window on the starboard (Vanny the mariner) side of the boat.

At one point, when the boat was heading back to Budapest, I popped to the onboard loo, and when I was in there I put a bit more eye make-up on and a little more lipstick; I found making myself girly for her a strangely disturbing turn-on. As I was finishing doing my lipstick, my phone emitted the single beep it makes to tell you a text has arrived.

The text was from Hélène. It said:

After the boat gets in, darling, I want to go back to our room, have a long bath with you and then make love to you for quite a few hours. xxx

I drew a breath. With my fingers trembling, I texted back:

Let's do it! xxx

41

Monday morning.

A big week ahead.

Three more rounds to play, and each game would be against one of the best women chess-players in Europe. I also knew that with only four points out of six so far, I absolutely had to win every remaining game to have any chance of winning the tournament.

No pressure, then.

After I got up on Monday morning I switched my phone on. I knew it was already on mute. I was surprised to find I was rather hoping for a message from Tom. There wasn't one, though. Of course, he didn't even know of Hélène's existence. I wondered what he'd think if he had.

At two fifteen that afternoon, I found myself *fiiiinally* playing on one of the six top boards that had the games on TV screens behind each board so spectators could see the games.

Best of all, Hélène was there in the front watching me.

I absolutely needed to win this game if I possibly could. Yet sometimes when you badly need to win a game it's much too easy to start fantasising about what your score will be if you do manage to win. But somehow seeing Hélène there with me really helped keep me focused.

That afternoon I was playing Judit Nagy (I knew this was pronounced 'nadge'), the Hungarian women's chess champion. I'd lost once to her before in tournaments, and we'd had two draws. To try to combat Judit, who was known for being an expert at most openings and who was fabled for her amazing ability to recall games, openings and interesting strategic initiatives, I decided to use a fascinating opening called Larsen's Opening, named after the late, great, Danish player, Bent Larsen. Larsen liked to play quirky openings, and he invented Larsen's Opening, where White starts by playing a strange kind of side-move - he pushes his queen's knight's pawn just one move forward. It's a shock technique designed to tempt his opponents to build a really powerful pawn centre and then Larsen would do his best to try to eat away at it from the sides. He often succeeded, too.

I got a promising attack against Judit using Larsen's invention. My attack didn't lead to checkmate but it did lead to the win of two pawns and I found myself, after a really gruelling struggle, in a rook and pawn ending with two extra pawns and that turned out to be enough for me to win.

There was applause among the spectators when Judit resigned - only brief applause this being a chess tournament - but applause nonetheless.

That evening Hélène and I had a quiet time at the hotel, eating at the hotel restaurant, which isn't something I usually do but it suited our mood, which was calm and reflective.

'Vanny, listen,' she said, as we were eating our starters, which were very nice Hungarian salads featuring cucumber, vinegar, paprika and dill, 'I'm not going back tomorrow afternoon as I'd intended.'

Instantly dizzy with happiness, I stared at her. *'You're not?'*

'No. I emailed my boss. I said I was with a woman friend who was doing really well in a chess tournament and I wanted to stay with my friend... my boss doesn't know I'm gay, and he rather fancies me, so telling him the truth, that I'm with a female friend, makes sense... and that I really wanted to be here for another couple of days.'

'What did he say?'

'That it was fine by him and that in fact it's been a quieter week than he expected anyway. I am off until the weekend! On Friday afternoon I will return. That is,' she looked at me flirtatiously, 'if you can bear my company until then!'

I smiled. 'I think I can just about manage it.'

We went to bed early. With my chess aims foremost in both our minds, we were cuddly and kissy rather than as passionate as we had been. But we still couldn't resist making love, this time very quietly and especially tenderly.

The next day, Tuesday, March the twentieth, the day when Hélène had intended to fly home but now wasn't, I played Black against Rosa Morelli. Rosa's a thirty-year-old Italian grandmaster who's something of a female role model in Italy. There's even a short YouTube video of her kissing the Pope, albeit only on his right cheek. He didn't turn the other one.

In my game against Rosa, I was feeling very determined and not at all constrained by papal edicts. Rosa made a bad mistake in the opening and that was enough for me to win. She resigned on move thirty-one.

As our routine of having quiet evenings seemed to be working, Hélène and I pursued it again and ate at the hotel restaurant before having an early night.

I didn't need to check the pairings to know who I would be playing in the final round. My opponent would be the Ukrainian player Galya Roberts.

Galya, a brilliant player, had married an Englishman, Mike Roberts, and they now lived in Kiev where Mike taught English and Galya pursued her professional chess career. I've met Galya and Mike once or twice and they're really great people and Galya's English is completely fluent.

Galya and I were now the only players on six out of eight. If I won our game, I'd be European Women's Chess Champion, which would be the biggest triumph of my so-called chess career, by a long way.

Not surprisingly, and despite all our efforts to stay calm that evening, and even after I'd had a nice hot shower (alone, to promote calmness), I didn't feel remotely calm as I went to bed. But Hélène calmed me down nicely.

42

So on Wednesday, March the twenty-first, with six points out of eight: after my six straight wins, I sat down, at just before two fifteen in the afternoon, to play Galya Roberts in the final round of the Women's European Chess Championship.

The winner would become Women's European Chess Champion and take home the first prize of 30,000 euros. The prize was being paid by cheque in euros despite the forint being the Hungarian currency. If our game was drawn, Galya and I would have to play a two-game speedchess play-off match to decide who won the title.

If the game was drawn, I'd have my second grandmaster norm. I'd discovered, an hour or so before sitting down to play Galya, that in view of her score in the tournament and the scores achieved by my other opponents so far in the tournament, the grandmaster norm for me for this event would be six and a half points.

As Galya made her first move, my body felt to me as if it were suddenly glowing.

I glanced at Hélène, and for once, there in the tournament hall, we did briefly make eye contact.

She knew that this game I was playing now could make many of my dreams come true.

I was playing Black and as usual chose the Caro-Kann defence. I played well enough but Galya played better. In the end, under a lot of pressure from her, I managed to force a perpetual check, and so a draw, on move thirty-six.

The moment I'd forced the perpetual check, my spirits soared within me. I'd got my second grandmaster norm. Just one more norm, at some tournament somewhere or maybe the New York tournament Boris had arranged in the summer, and I'd BE A GRANDMASTER!

Meanwhile, Galya and I had both tied for the European Women's Championship.

I texted Tom while Galya and I were having the hour break that was stipulated by the tournament rules before we played off for the title.

The play-off consisted of two games: both played with each of us having only twenty minutes on our clocks and with one of us being White in the first game and the other being White in the second game.

If after those two games the score was still tied - such as if they were both draws or if one of us had won one game and the other the other game - then there would be a third game which was known as the 'Armageddon' play-off. In this play-off the player with White has twenty-five minutes and Black has just twenty minutes, but White has to win. A draw (or, of course, a loss for White) means that Black is regarded as the winner.

I texted Tom briefly: *check out the internet. I've drawn my game just now and am playing off with Galya for the title. Please send me positive vibes!!! xx*

I got a text back from Tom about a minute later: *Vanny, you played really well. I've been watching all your games on the internet and I'll be watching the play-off too. Good luck and thinking of you. xx*

I texted him: *Thanks for watching all my games. Can you text Lottie and Steve and tell her what's happening? She may know already but text her in case she doesn't. I know she'll want to know.*

Please tell her I can't call as there isn't much time before the play-off. xx

Tom texted back: *of course I wanted to watch your games. And yes, I've already phoned Lottie and told her what's happening. xx*

I texted him: *thanks for everything. xx*

Jaz sent me a good-luck text too.

Then, with Hélène by my side, I went into the tournament hall, where the seating had all been arranged so that Galya and I were playing on a stage at the front of the hall, and there were about two hundred seats. They were, as far as I could see, all full. Well, chess is a very big sport in Hungary.

I'd arranged for Hélène to have a seat at the front. I know I would have been incredibly nervous if Hélène hadn't been there, but because she was, I wasn't.

Well, the first play-off game was a complete disaster.

Before the game started the tournament controller flipped a coin to decide who could choose to be White or Black in the first play-off game. I chose heads but it was tails and Galya decided she wanted to be White. I played the Caro-Kann again. My game fell to pieces horribly soon. My pieces got in a complete mess and on move twenty-eight I resigned.

I felt utterly terrible about this, but in the fifteen minutes before the next play-off game started, I had a cup of coffee and a cheese and salad sandwich and decided I would absolutely do all I could to make Hélène's and Lottie's wish for me come true. Hélène squeezed my right hand, which helped a great deal. I was White in this next game.

Galya played the opening well but I pressed hard for an advantage and eventually we reached an endgame where I had an extra pawn and the more active king. I advanced with my king and I forced Galya's king back and on move fifty-six or thereabouts, faced with my extra pawn queening, Galya resigned.

The organisers only allowed ten minutes' rest between the second play-off game and the Armageddon Final. In this game I would be Black and Galya would be White as she had had White in the first play-off game.

I went to the Ladies quickly and there after having a pee I chucked cold water on my face to make myself as alert as possible and I brushed my teeth as the tension had made my mouth taste pretty yucky. When I came out of the loo, Hélène was waiting for me and this time she squeezed both my hands.

So now I went back into the tournament room to play the Armageddon game.

The spectators' seats were full as before, but while for the first two games of the play-off I hadn't really minded this, the large audience now added enormously to my nervousness as I sat opposite Galya, who looked perfectly calm and whose eyes were bright with scenting victory. I saw that on her clock she had her twenty-five minutes and I only had my twenty. And I was Black.

Armageddon it was. Galya had to win to become Women's European Chess Champion. If she lost or the game was a draw, I won the championship.

The next forty minutes of my life were about the most thrilling I've ever had, or at least except some very special times with Hélène and with Tom, oh, and once with Sven, of course.

I really wished Lottie and Tom and Jaz had been there at the chess tournament to watch me. But none of them were.

Hélène was, though. Yes, there she was, in the middle of the front row of spectators and leaning forward, to be as close to me as she could, my sister in passion, my sister in sisterhood.

Galya sacrificed a pawn in the opening for a positional advantage. But on move twelve, I found a rather cool move I'd never thought of before where I managed to check her with my queen while she was still un-castled and this caused Galya some delay. From then on things began to go my way, and although I wasn't getting enough pressure to win, we reached an ending which was completely level, where I'd given her the pawn back and we both had a queen, a rook and three pawns each. She tried a desperate bid to checkmate me but I found a way of defending it and a moment later I saw a move which would force perpetual check.

My heart beating so fast in my chest I thought it might rip free of its moorings, I played the move which forced the perpetual.

A draw.

Which, as it was an Armageddon game, meant I'D WON.

I looked at Galya. She was in tears.

A moment later the audience sort of erupted in a frenzy of applause and shouting. Hélène rushed up to me and hugged me, then kissed me on my forehead: the sort of kiss, I suppose, which a doting female friend might have given me. But frankly, at that moment, if anyone had guessed the truth, I wouldn't have minded in the least.

Galya was weeping. I felt sorry for her, but not too sorry, because now I was European Chess Champion and if Galya had managed to beat me, there'd have been a strict limit to how much she'd've cared about beating me. That's the problem with chess, no matter how friendly you feel towards people you know in the chess world, when the time comes for you to try to beat them, you have to do your best to do precisely that.

The next few hours were mostly a blur and I still remember them being like that in my mind. I'd never in all my life won such an important event as the European Women's Championship, and not only had I won it but I'd also made my second grandmaster norm. Hélène, wanting like me to keep our personal relationship secret from prying eyes and inquisitive gossip, was restrained in her congratulations, but I could see in her eyes and smile and in the affectionate squeezes she gave my hands whenever she could do this reasonably surreptitiously, that she was delighted with me and just so proud of me.

Now that the play-off games were finished, I could put my phone back on without fear of defaulting a game if it sounded, though in fact I still kept it on mute anyway. The point was, there was so much I needed to do now.

There were lots of journalists from TV, radio and newspapers at the event. They knew me well enough to know that I don't give interviews while I'm actually playing in a tournament as I don't want to lose my concentration or tempt fate, but now that the event had finished and I'd won, I was very much in demand.

Hélène, whose organisational talents I'd glimpsed but hadn't yet experienced, suggested I tell people I was her 'attachée de presse', as she put it, which I took to mean my press officer or publicist. I was perfectly happy to go along with this, it was comforting to let her take charge of things when I was so tired. She courteously arranged with the tournament organisers for a private room to be allocated to me and her for press interviews and she organised a schedule of about a dozen interviews with print, radio and TV journalists who were all given just ten minutes but who had exclusive access to me during that time.

At my suggestion, Hélène arranged the first interview to be with the British international master Richard Palliser, editor of the leading UK chess magazine *Chess*. Richard's an affable and charming chap and a good friend of mine.

I gave Richard about half an hour rather than ten minutes, which rather threw the schedule out of sync from the start, but we had a great interview.

Three hours or so later the last journalist had gone, and Hélène and I were finally alone in the private room, which still had the airless and tangy smell you get when TV cameras and radio recording equipment have been running for quite a long time in a fairly confined space and when sweaty journalists (and a sweaty chess-player) have been there too. Hélène came up to me and kissed me on the lips this time.

She smiled. *'Bien fait. Très bien fait.'*

'Tu es très gentile,' I said, venturing to speak French to her, which I didn't usually do except occasionally in bed during moments of particular rapture.

'Tu es formidable. Tu es vraiment formidable.'

I did at least know that *'formidable'* meant something rather different in French to what in meant in English: that in French it meant something like 'impressive'. I was too modest to acknowledge this new compliment, so I just smiled back.

'I'm so hungry,' Hélène said.

I nodded. 'I'd be too, if I wasn't still so hyper. But you very much deserve a nice late-night supper somewhere and I think by the time we reach the restaurant I'll have an appetite too. Just before we go, I'd better look at my phone and see what's come in.'

'Of course. I'll have some of this water here. Take your time; I need to unwind a little.'

I smiled. 'I won't be long.'

I went to a nearby chair, sat down and glanced at the texts and Facebook messages that had come in. There were too many Facebook messages to count, congratulatory ones from chess-players who were my Facebook friends and lots more from people who weren't. I scrolled down what seemed like an endless list. I knew I'd want to answer them all, even though for obvious practical reasons I'd have to keep most of the replies short. But that was a job that could wait until tomorrow.

There weren't as many text messages; after all, I don't give my mobile number out to people who weren't actually friends. But there were still about thirty of them. The one from Dad said:

You clever clever girl!! You make me feel proud every day, and especially today. Very well done my dear Ivana. I am with Piotr, and he says well done too!

Lots of love, Dad xx

PS The new apartment is very nice

This was from Lottie:

BIGGEST HUG!!! I knew you could do it! Tons of love from me and Steve. xxxx

There was one from Jaz too:

Dearest Vanny, I am SO proud of you. I'm with Mum and we both send all our love. Jazzy xxxx

I replied to Dad and Lottie at once by text, and told them I was sorry I hadn't replied sooner but that I'd been doing lots of interviews with journalists. I just hope my reply didn't seem too pretentious; though probably it did. But I hoped they'd forgive me.

There was no text from Sven, which rather disappointed me. But there was one from Boris.

My dear Ivana, congratulations! I am not surprised at all. I know just how talented a chess-player you are. Yours in admiration, Boris

There was also a text from Tom.

Well done. Please call me.

43

So using the pretext of a visit to the loo, I went downstairs and outside and I called Tom.

I knew I'd have to tell him sooner or later about Hélène, but as I didn't have any reason to think he knew of her existence yet, I vaguely imagined I'd be having that conversation at some indeterminate time in the future.

Tom took more rings than he usually does to answer, and I was waiting for his voicemail to kick in when he suddenly answered the phone.

'Vanny, hi,' he said, levelly.

'Oh, hi, Tom.'

'Well done.'

'D'you mean it?'

'Of course I mean it. Well done. That Armageddon game was just amazing to watch. There was a live camera feed. You played like a genius.'

'That's nice of you to say, Tom. I was lucky though.'

'No more than you deserved to be. We all need some luck in chess if we're going to win. Women's European Chess Champion and your second GM norm! Well, all I can say is, if anyone deserves it, you do.'

Pathetically drunk with life and triumph and excitement and confidently-expected nocturnal passion with the ever-imaginative and resourceful Hélène as I was, I said, little imagining what was going to happen next:

'That's very sweet, Tom. You're very sweet.'

'I know. Who's the girl?'

'What girl?'

'Don't bullshit me, Vanny. I mean the girl with the black hair, who looks a bit like you.'

'She does?'

'Yes. I saw her.'

'You saw her?'

Obviously my dialogue at this point wasn't going to win any prizes for sparkling wit, but I was pretty shattered and... anyway, *you* try playing three incredibly stressful play-off games against Galya Roberts and see how good *your* dialogue is afterwards.

'Yes, Vanny, like I said, I saw her. There's a live camera feed, remember? I mean that stunning girl with the long black hair who gave you an enthusiastic hug and kissed your forehead. I only caught a few glimpses of her face; her hair was in the way and the video feed isn't great quality anyway, but I could see she's totally beautiful. So what's her name?'

For several moments, or maybe more, I said nothing, then I murmured:

'Hélène.'

'Lovely name.'

'How do you know she's with me... I mean, how d'you know we're friends?'

'I do have a brain, Vanny. It was also the way she was leaning forward from her seat as she watched the game. She obviously wanted to get as close to you as she possibly could. My guess is she's in love with you.'

I said nothing. At least not at first, anyway. But he and I had been through so much together, and after all I was and am very fond of him. I wasn't going to lie.

'Oh, Tom,' I murmured, finally.

'Where did you meet her?' Tom asked.

I just couldn't reply at all for a moment. Then finally, I said:

'In Monte Carlo. When I was visiting Dad. She works in the hotel where I was staying.'

There was only a brief pause from Tom before he said, 'I see.' It was his turn to be quiet now. I didn't say anything either. Then finally he added:

'So... has she been staying with you all week?'

I cleared my throat. 'No, just since Saturday.'

'I see.' He paused for a few seconds, then, quietly and softly, asked, 'have you done it with her?'

I didn't reply at once. At last, I said quietly:

'Yes, I have.'

'Just once or twice?'

I cleared my throat. 'No. Many times.'

Another pause, then, 'I guessed so.'

'Then why did you ask?'

'I just wanted to... well, be certain.'

Tom fell silent. I didn't feel like saying anything. A few moments later Tom went on:

'I mean, I always knew you sort of fancy Lottie, and... well, I suppose as someone who thinks women are just wonderful, I shouldn't really be surprised that a beautiful woman might seem attractive to you, too.'

'Tom, does it change things for us, that I like Hélène?'

'Isn't the real question how it changes things for you? I mean, are you going to shack up with her or something?'

'No, I don't think so. She lives in Monte Carlo with her mum. I don't want to live in Monte Carlo.'

'Maybe she'll move for you?'

'Probably not. She likes to live with her mum.'

'I see. So are you in love with her?'

After a pause I said: 'I don't know. I am fond of her though.'

'Vanny, listen. I want you to enjoy this moment, I really do. I mean, winning this tournament is the biggest success of your career. But… I have to look after myself and my own feelings. I mean, when two women really hit it off in bed that must be just amazing for them. I mean, they must both kind of automatically know just how to make each others' bodies feel fantastic. How can a man compete with that?'

I hadn't expected him to see things in this way, but now he'd said what he had, I understood why he'd said it. *He's so right*, I thought, but of course I didn't say that.

'I'm so sorry, Tom. I didn't want to hurt you, I really didn't.'

'I know.'

'I'm so sorry.'

'I believe you, but it doesn't reduce the hurt. Anyhow, I'm going away.'

'Where?'

'To a tournament in Melilla,' (he pronounced it something like *Me-yi-ya*), 'on Saturday for two weeks.'

'*Where?*'

'Melilla. It's a Spanish town on the Moroccan coast, a bit like a Spanish version of Gibraltar. I didn't even know it existed until I got the tournament invitation at very short notice last week.'

'I didn't know Melilla existed until just now when you told me about it.'

'At least it'll be hot. The weather's been pretty awful over here in Britain. I've been invited to a twelve-round tournament sponsored by a rich Melillan who made his money from fish and who loves chess. Who knows - maybe I'll meet someone there who really likes me.'

'*I* really like you. I'm not sure I want you to meet anyone else.'

'Vanny, right now, you really can't expect to have any romantic rights over me *at all*.'

'I realise that. But it's not as if I'm with another man, is it?'

'You mean if it's with a girl it doesn't really count?'

I thought about this, then said: 'Well, maybe not in quite the same way, no.'

'I'm not sure about that,' said Tom. 'But I haven't really digested this, yet. All I know is, I'm feeling pretty cheesed off about us right now, so I'm going to hang up. Don't take it personally. Well done again on your big win.'

The line went dead.

He hadn't even given me a chance to say goodbye.

I wanted to send him a text to make him feel better, but I couldn't think what to say in it.

The next day, the Thursday, Hélène and I spent basically almost entirely in bed.

At one point during that wonderful day in bed I had a wicked and naughty idea.

'My phone has a pretty good video function, you know,' I said. I think it was sometime in the afternoon. We were both naked as usual and had been sleeping for an hour or so. I was feeling definitely amorous again. I didn't, of course, know if Hélène was too, but I had realistic hopes.

She glanced a little sleepily and very beautifully at me. 'Why do you say that?'

I told her why.

'All right,' she said, after a few moments, with another smile, 'let's do it.'

In fact, it didn't turn out to be as easy as I'd expected to wedge my phone upright on the bed, using chess books to keep it in position and from falling over, but I managed to in the end and then I pressed the button to start the video. When I had, we made love concertedly but this time more than a little embarrassedly together, as the video camera on my phone filmed us. I stopped the camera after what I thought was about five minutes as I didn't want the file size to get too big. In fact, the camera filmed our beautiful happy loving for four minutes and thirty-three seconds.

Afterwards we watched the video together, in stunned amazement at seeing ourselves coupled and entwined. It was brazen, almost too brazen to watch, but it was also actually rather beautiful. And it was certainly incredibly sexy.

I still have that video, and while I'm telling you about it now, I've never shown it to anyone except Hélène.

By the time we went to bed on the Thursday night, Hélène still hadn't said anything about her plans to return home and I was wondering happily whether she might want to stay for a day or so more or even already had permission for her boss to do that. I'd got out of bed to have my shower but I hadn't actually showered yet. Naked, and holding my white towel, I glanced at her. She was lying in bed and looking at me, smiling.

'Darling Hélène, I've never had such a fantastic time with anyone in my life.'

'That is nice of you to say.'

'Well, I mean it. Now, Tom, tell me, do you really have to leave today?'

I felt absolutely mortified the moment I'd spoken.

'Tom? Who's Tom?' Hélène gasped.

44

I just knew I was going totally red. 'I'm so sorry. He's... he's a friend of mine from England. I spoke to him the other night after the press session.'

'Why did you call me Tom?'

'I've no idea. It was an accident.'

Hélène sat up in bed and pushed her duvet to one side. I went back to sit on the bed, holding the towel I was carrying around my thighs and trying to look reasonably sensible and convincing, which is admittedly rather difficult when you're completely naked except for wearing a towel.

'People mix up the names of people when they have emotional feelings for both people,' Hélène said, with what I had to admit (though I certainly didn't have any plans to admit it) was considerable psychological insight. 'Vanny, I need to know who he is.'

'He's a friend.'

'Have you slept with him?'

I nodded. 'Yes, I have.'

Hélène shook her head sadly and seriously. 'Well, we've never pretended you're gay, have we? I need to know a bit more about you and Tom, then we can leave the subject. Do you love him?'

'No,' I said, which I felt was true enough, for all that saying it somehow seemed an act of disloyalty to Tom by me.

'All right,' Hélène murmured. 'Well, I'm very pleased about that. I'm not going to ask you *exactement* what Tom is to you, because that's your own business. But there is one thing I think it's fair for me to ask. It's this. When did you last sleep with him? Or rather, I mean, so you certainly know what I'm asking: when did you last make love with him?'

45

Of course I should have been expecting this question, but I wasn't. I was too dismayed I'd mentioned Tom's name at all and had upset Hélène; I wasn't on my guard as I should have been. Also, I had the stupid idea that if I was completely honest with Hélène, everything would be fine.

'It was at the concert,' I muttered.

'At the concert?'

'Yes,' I said, 'in the interval.'

'Where?'

'Behind... behind a thick curtain down a corridor.'

'I see. But... but you told me that was the night before you flew here to Budapest?'

I cleared my throat. 'Yes, it was,' I said.

Now her expression changed abruptly and appallingly into an open-mouthed look of horror.

'You mean you had sex with your Tom only a week ago last Saturday? After we had met?'

'Well... well, yes, but... you hadn't come to Budapest then, and, well, none of what's happened had happened and... I didn't even know you were definitely coming here.'

'So? We were in touch! We were having affectionate conversations! It was likely I would be coming.' Her face fell, and actually became even more open-mouthed. 'Oh, Vanny, *how could you do that?* I absolutely can't believe you could have had sex with him after we had met and were in touch!'

I absolutely didn't know what to say. Then I thought of something.

'Hélène, I have been completely honest with you, haven't I? You should give me credit for that.'

'You think you deserve praise for being completely honest about being disloyal to me? You think you deserve that?'

I was still wondering how to reply when Hélène did something I wasn't prepared for at all. She scurried naked across the bed, snatched away my towel and threw it on the floor, then she grabbed me around my neck with her strong left arm, forced my face down onto the bed and with her right hand began slapping me very hard on my bum like she was some crazy naked young schoolmistress. There was hardly anything we hadn't done to each other's bodies, except this.

It *hurt*. She was strong and hitting me hard and it *reeeeally hurt*. 'Get off! Stop it!' I shouted.

'No, Vanny, you deserve it!'

I tried to wriggle out of her grasp, but her arm around my neck was very strong.

'You will never get out of my grip!' she shouted. 'It's a jiu-jitsu stranglehold!'

I remembered what she'd said about how she could kill with her jiu-jitsu hold. I wriggled and struggled absolutely as much as I could to get free but I just couldn't, and her hold round my neck tightened and my panic increased and I tried to speak and couldn't and she just went on slapping me until my bum hurt like mad, as if a thousand bees had stung it simultaneously. I thought it was perfectly likely she might really be upset enough to kill me, and Hélène seemed to me to be tightening her grasp around my neck so that for all I knew she *was* trying to strangle me now, and that made me panic and in one almighty wriggle and convulsion I somehow finally managed to escape from the pain and the strangling and to slip out of her terrifying jiu-jitsu grasp.

I stood on the carpet, naked and breathless and close to tears. Hélène launched herself at me like a young tigress and began slapping me hard about the face and I slapped her face too and her arms and shoulders and we really did have a fight now and we slapped each other whenever we could and wrestled hard though much more forcibly and mercilessly than the last time we had and the pain made me reckless and I used all my strength in my hands and forced her back onto the bed and she was crying tears of I don't know, anger and dismay I suppose and I was crying too and we were both slippery with sweat and then crazily we found ourselves switching from crazily fighting to crazily making love on the bed in pain and unhappiness and in excitement and love and hate, until Hélène started slapping me again on my sore and no doubt very red bum, though in a kind of exhausted hopeless anger and so not so hard and somehow I squirmed out of her grasp and shot into the bathroom and locked the door. Hélène banged on the door, with a fist or her fists I suppose but I was supporting the door with my shoulder and the lock stayed firm.

There was a long, sudden silence.

I didn't dare to open the door because I was convinced she would just dash in and start hitting me again, this wild and amazing and completely understandably angry lover of mine, who had obviously lost her heart to me just as I had lost it to her.

Maybe ten minutes later, naked, exhausted and feeling sick, I went to sit, half-collapsing, on the cold floor of the bathroom and waited to see what happened next.

I listened hard. I just sat there in silence and pain, breathing deeply and sobbing quietly.

Eventually, exhausted, hurt and completely drained emotionally, I fell into a drowsy sleep.

I don't know how long I slept, but sometime later, maybe after an hour or so, I suppose, I jolted awake. My eyes were bleary with sleep and tears and sadness and shock.

I staggered to my feet, splashed a lot of cold water on my face from the tap, then cleaned my teeth. Now I felt a lot more properly awake. My bum still really hurt.

I listened hard. There was no sound at all. I went to the door and called through it: 'Hélène? I'm coming out of here. Don't attack me, OK?'

I waited and listened. There was no reply. I listened as hard as I could, but I couldn't hear a sound from the other side of the door.

Finally, still hesitatingly, I opened the lock and pushed the door open a foot or so.

I was expecting to see Hélène on the bed asleep or in tears. But she wasn't there.

She wasn't in the room at all.

Nor was her luggage. She'd completely gone.

She'd left her toothpaste and toothbrush behind in the bathroom. The toothpaste and toothbrush were all that was left of her.

Now I noticed that on her side of the bed, on her white pillow, there was a piece of paper. I ran over to it. There was writing on it, in French, with a blue biro. My French was just about good enough for me to understand what the letter said, which was:

Vanny, tu es hétéro. Je ne peux pas croire que tu aies couché avec Tom après que nous nous soyons rencontrées, alors même que nous avions toutes ces conversations romantiques jusque tard dans la nuit. Tu m'as brisé le coeur! Je n'aurais jamais dû commencer tout ça, les femmes hétéros sont toutes les mêmes. Je pars, je vais à l'aéroport. Je ne retournerai pas travailler à l'hôtel donc ne me téléphone pas là-bas, s'il te plaît. Je vais changer mon numéro de portable et mon adresse e-mail. Je suis tellement déçue. Je t'aime vraiment, Vanny, et le temps que nous avons passé ensemble à Budapest était comme un rêve, mais tu es hétéro et notre relation est une erreur.

Je te fais confiance de ne jamais montrer notre vidéo à quelqu'un d'autre.

Au revoir.

That is:

Vanny, you're straight. I can't believe you would have sex with Tom after we'd met and when we were having all those romantic conversations late at night. You have broken my heart! I should never have started this, you straight women are all the same. I'm leaving and I'm going to the airport. I'm not going to go back to work at the hotel so please don't phone me there. I will change my mobile number too and my email address. I am so disappointed. I really love you Vanny and our time together in Budapest has been like a dream but you are straight and our relationship is a mistake.

I trust you never to show our video to anyone else.

Goodbye.

I understood enough of the letter from a quick read to know what it was all about, but I mournfully worked out a translation of all of it the following day. Totally broken-hearted as I was, I loved, all the same, how she'd described it as *notre vidéo*, because that was exactly how I felt about it too.

I got dressed without showering, grabbed my purse and my phone, and raced downstairs and through the lobby. This being a Rightprice Hotel, at least there was no-one to see me in my total distress. In the street outside the hotel, I found a cab and took it to the airport.

On the way I thought *maybe she's still there.*

And in fact she was there, but only in a manner of speaking. Because when I arrived at Budapest airport, paid the driver and ran into the terminal and to the first information desk I found, a uniformed lady I spoke to there told me she couldn't give me information about a specific passenger but that yes, a Slovo-Air flight from Budapest to Ljubljana had started to board and was scheduled to depart at 11.25. I checked the time on my phone. It was 11.07.

I knew there was absolutely no way I could buy a ticket and get through security in eighteen minutes, and even if there had been, it hadn't occurred to me to bring my passport with me from the hotel.

I thanked the information desk lady, walked a short distance from the desk and phoned Hélène's mobile. The call went straight to voicemail. I left Hélène an imploring message, begging her not to get on the plane. I ended by saying 'I'll never show the video to anyone else, please don't worry about that.'

I waited, frantic with hope and despair, for ten minutes or so, but Hélène didn't call me. Short of untruthfully informing the lady at the information desk that there was a bomb in Hélène's luggage and me spending the next few years teaching chess to my fellow inmates in some Hungarian women's prison, there was, very obviously, nothing whatsoever I could do to stop Hélène boarding the plane to Ljubljana.

I found a spare seat some decent distance away from the information desk. I sat down, buried my head in my hands, and cried and cried.

46

I arrived back in Britain at Heathrow Airport Terminal One at - I don't remember the time exactly - early that Monday evening.

As I emerged from air-side and came out through the exit proper into the real world, I was so hoping Lottie and Steve might be there to meet me (I'd texted them my arrival time). They were. I burst into tears when I saw them. I trundled my luggage over to them at double-quick time, left my case standing on the floor near a column of the building and hugged Lottie and then Steve. Steve, gentleman that he was, took my luggage.

For about thirty seconds I managed to pretend that I was elated by my success, but then I gave up pretending and I burst into tears. It was only when we were all in Steve's four-wheel-drive in the car-park (for obvious professional reasons cello players tend to have big cars) that I finally told Lottie and Steve all about Hélène, and everything that had happened.

The hours in Budapest following my win had been a bit of a blur, and what I found now was that the three and a half weeks between my return from Hungary, and Lottie and Steve's wedding on Saturday April the fourteenth, were a blur too. But they were the wrong kind of blur: a blur of total unhappiness, my days were all equally unhappy alike and merged into one, in which I didn't feel I was properly alive at all, but just a sort of nerve for experiencing misery.

Sometimes Jaz popped in to my room and gave me a hug, and other times she made childhood comfort food for me: like fish fingers, pork chops and Heinz tomato ravioli (though not all at the same meal), and quite often we played five-minute chess and that let me forget Hélène and Tom a bit, though not for long. But most of the time I just suffered, and even though I answered my emails and Facebook messages, I did it all in the same fog of misery. I vaguely remember some invitations to international tournaments, arising from my new fame, which I politely declined. I wasn't in the mood for playing chess, though I still found myself able to write articles about it, in viciously unhappy autopilot.

Speaking of which, I'd even, for the time being, lost interest in flying the virtual helicopter.

47

The only really good news at this time was that the Ditrexican did seem to be continuing to work. Lottie had had another scan two days after her poor pathetic lovelorn friend flew home from Budapest, and that drug, the gift to the world of the deathstalker scorpion, had by now reduced the size of her glioma by twenty-seven percent. Lottie was, I knew, still, very worried about dying, but she was looking much better.

Boris and I exchanged emails about every week. He told me he was busy with his businesses as usual but that he was still working very hard on his chess – I liked his optimistic frame of mind. About half-way through those three weeks, I got the following email from Boris, and an attachment.

My dear Vanny

> *My congratulations again on your superb victory in Budapest.*
>
> *Thanks for letting me know about the successful progress of the Ditrexican. I am so pleased that it is continuing to shrink that vile tumour in Lottie's brain and I am very much hoping that the drug continues to shrink it.*
>
> *Thank you also very much for the invitation to come to Lottie's wedding. I'm sorry about the late reply and I am most grateful to you and to her for inviting me. Of course I shall come and I look forward to the wedding very much.*
>
> *I'm also sorry about the delay in letting you know about arrangements for the chess tournament I'm sponsoring in New York, but I can now tell you that it is going to be*

held from Monday June 4 until Thursday June 14 with Monday June 11 being a rest day. I attach the official details about the event.

Looking forward to seeing you at the wedding on the 14th. My dear Vanny, I won't embarrass you at the wedding by pleading my suit so please don't worry about that.

With very best wishes, your friend
Boris

48

I suppose you know how it is at a really great wedding and you're happy yourself; you're in a different state of being, especially (I imagine) if you're getting married. Everything seems incandescent or as if you're standing somewhere on the top of a mighty mountain and all the joy and ecstasy of life and everything that matters about life is burning in your heart and there isn't a shred of negativity or tediousness or humdrumness about it.

Tom was there, looking really smart in a morning-coat he'd rented from Moss Bros. He had a gold-coloured cravat and his hair was brushed for a change: actually he looked really great. Jaz, sitting on his left, was wearing a yellow and cream below-the-knee-length dress with a halter neck. The dress tucked in at the waist and accentuated her curves. She was also wearing a cream-coloured cardigan and accessorising with a black clutch bag and platform heels.

John Hamlyn was sitting two away from Jaz, who was herself next to her mother Lucretia. On Lucretia's other side sat Jaz's brother Brandon, who had a good job now as a junior manager at a shop in Peckham.

Boris didn't arrive in Tenterden until a couple of hours before the wedding began at the lovely old church of St Mildred's. The wedding was scheduled to start at eleven o'clock and would be over by about twelve-thirty, whereupon the congregation who didn't have their own cars would all be ferried off in mini-buses to the reception at Cranbrook Hall.

Lottie walked down the aisle in a splendid white wedding dress to the tune of the 'Queen of Sheba', from the oratorio *Solomon* by Handel. The melody's forever lodged now in my mind and I will always associate it with Lottie. It's such a happy melody and I think it's almost impossible to listen to it without smiling or even laughing at how lovely and wonderful life can be.

I think I succeeded quite well at keeping a happy face most of the day, which obviously as Maid of Honour it was my duty to do.

I felt as confused about Tom as I ever had. I hated having hurt him but I'd emailed him after he returned from Melilla (where he'd come only equal fourth but had earned lots of rating points as his opponents were so strong) to tell him that Hélène had dumped me, and broken off all contact with me, after hearing that I'd had sex with him the night before I'd left for Budapest. So now, as we were both emotionally convalescing, Tom and I had, I suppose, more or less made up. But I was still much, much too upset about Hélène to have any interest in sleeping with Tom, even as a FWB, right now. Indeed, I was fairly sure I didn't ever want to sleep with anyone ever again unless it was Hélène, and if it was, I wouldn't have planned to have done much sleeping.

Cranbrook Hall is in the Weald, about five miles from Tenterden. Early in the evening, when an excellent swing band with a super vocalist was performing 'What a Wonderful World' which of course Louis Armstrong made so famous, I met up with Boris and we went for a chat. Cranbrook Hall is an enormous place and we found a bar on the other side of the building, well away from the wedding. There were only a few other wedding guests in the bar, at the bar itself, and we found a table at the back of the bar and talked there.

'So how's Alexander?' I murmured to Boris after we'd sat down and were waiting for the pot of tea for two I'd asked for to be brought over.

'Oh, he is very well. I thought he might want to explore Tenterden, but he told me he has never seen Canterbury, which is not too far from here, so he has driven there for the afternoon and shall be back in a couple of hours.'

'Shouldn't he be with you, really, him being your bodyguard?'

'Yes, perhaps, but the chance of anyone knowing I am here is so small that I am not worried. Besides, the people who are my enemies tend to be family men… in both senses of the expression. They are not the kind of people who would order an attack to be carried out against me at a wedding, even if they knew I was here.'

'But who would be your enemy, Boris? I mean, of course ever since I've met you I've known you had a bodyguard, but I simply can't imagine you'd have any enemies.'

'My dear Ivana, you are so sweet and good.'

I don't think so, I thought.

'Yes, you are so sweet and good,' said Boris, as if he were disagreeing with what I'd just thought. 'It is, by the way, a very great pleasure to see you again. I'm afraid, however, that there are people who would be only too glad to see me dead.'

'But why? You seem a totally decent kind of person.'

'What you say is very kind, but I'm afraid when one is very rich then one has enemies by a kind of natural process because of course many people would like my money.'

I looked at him calmly but intently. 'Is this anything to do with Henki Oy?'

Instead of reacting in any kind of annoyed way, Boris just nodded slowly and said:

'So you've found out about that organisation?'

'Yes. But I don't know exactly what it does.'

'I can't tell you what it does, because our work is confidential and so are the projects we undertake for our clients. But I assure you there is nothing nefarious about what Henki Oy does to earn its daily bread. It is simply working in the field of advanced medical research and I'm afraid that is all I feel comfortable to tell you. But to other things, how is the Love Fund coming along?'

'Quite well, I think. I have done a few selfish things with the money you gave me, for example I've bought a car.'

'Don't feel guilty about that, please. The money was for you.'

Now it was me who wanted to change the subject. 'I'm very much looking forward to the tournament in New York and I think it's fantastic that you've organised it and want me to play in it.'

Boris smiled. 'I don't just want you to play in it, I want you to do really well in it and get your third grandmaster norm.'

I was truly moved by what he said. I got up from my chair, walked quietly over to him, put my left arm around his large, powerful, manly shoulders, looked into his eyes and gave him a quick kiss on the lips. 'Come on,' I said, 'let's finish our tea and get back to the wedding. Everybody will be thinking we're having a passionate tryst. You know how people gossip. Everyone thinks weddings are the ideal place to meet the person of your dreams.'

Boris smiled. 'For me that is not true, because I met the person of my dreams back in January outside the sports hall where the Hastings tournament was being held.'

'You do say all the right things.'

Boris shrugged. 'When I'm with you, it is easy to say them.'

My gentlemanly oligarch kept himself rather in the background during the wedding supper and didn't come over to talk to me or my friends and in particular didn't come over to talk to Tom. I didn't feel that Boris was deliberately avoiding us but rather he fell in with some business friends of Sir Rupert who was sitting near to the top left-hand corner of the spacious dining-hall at Cranbrook Hall, and Boris looked pretty natural in their company. In the event, he wasn't staying overnight in Tenterden as Jaz, Tom, and I all were but Boris left for London with Alexander at about eleven o'clock in the evening. Boris told me he was staying overnight at Claridge's in London and would be flying back to New York in the morning.

I made sure I said goodbye to Boris of course; I asked him whether he could have stayed in Tenterden but he told me he had to get back to London because he had a business meeting in the morning and was then flying back to New York at lunchtime. I suppose one of the great things about being a very successful and busy businessman is that you can always use the excuse of a business meeting to avoid any difficult situation, and it was only after the wedding that it completely occurred to me that very likely Boris was, deep down, as reluctant to meet Tom as I was to introduce him to Tom.

Tom, Jaz and I stayed in separate rooms in the White Hart pub in the centre of Tenterden. It was a celibate night for the three of us.

I discovered some time later from Lottie that she and Steve were celibate that evening too because by the time they went to bed in the room at Lottie's home in Tenterden, where they were staying for a night before heading by car to Fowey in Cornwall for their week-long honeymoon, they were both so tired from the wedding that all they wanted to do was sleep.

'What a start to our married life, Vanny!' Lottie told me a few days after they came back from their honeymoon. 'We were so completely shattered after the wedding, and it was about half past three in the morning before Steve and I got to bed anyway, so you can make no mistake there was no passion scintillating from our bedroom whatsoever. But we certainly made up for things in Fowey. It was a lovely week. Fowey at night, with the lights of Fowey on our side of the river and the fainter lights of Polruan on the other side, made everything like a dream.'

I felt sure Lottie was getting better, and that the Ditrexican was saving her life.

49

I didn't see much of Lottie and Steve in the week after they returned from Cornwall. They invited me over for a home-cooked Indian meal at Steve's flat, that was now their home, on the Monday about ten days after they came back (I forgot to mention about Steve being a really good amateur cook of Indian food), and we had a nice time, given how unhappy I was.

Lottie said the morning headaches had completely stopped now. She also said she was working hard at her piano-playing. Steve was playing at a big classical music concert in Reading later that week, and Lottie would of course be going too. I knew that now my darling was married, our friendship was going to be different. Still good, but different. I just hoped she kept on getting better and that the Ditrexican went on doing what it was doing.

It wasn't, of course, only Lottie I was pleased for. I'd done plenty of research into brain tumours now of course on the internet and I knew what a scourge they were. As Ditrexican was obviously so effective, many many people who would otherwise have died would be enjoying the return to health – and, I hoped, complete remission – that Lottie seemed to be enjoying.

I wasn't happy myself; all day and every night I ached to see Hélène again.

I was starting to miss playing chess, which may have been a good or a bad sign, I don't know, but anyway, feeling that as I was so unhappy I may as well finally make use of chess's undoubted powers as a mental anaesthetic, and feeling glad that I was in the mood to play chess again, I decided that rather than accept any of the invitations I was being offered to play in major international events, I'd dress down, so to speak, and play in a weekend tournament in Kettering in the Midlands that was taking place on the last weekend of April. The tournament involved playing one round on Friday evening, two during the day on Saturday and two on Sunday. I won my first four games quite easily, but had a tough struggle in Round Five against Emily Green, a talented sixteen-year-old player from Canterbury, though in the end I managed to beat her by a whisker and so I won the first prize of £300 with five points out of five.

I'd driven up to Kettering in Sally and I drove back in her too. When I was about half way back to London - this must have been about seven o'clock on the Sunday evening - a call came to my mobile phone. Using hands-free, I answered it.

'It's Steve,' he said. The noise of Sally's engine made it impossible for me to hear the tone of his voice.

'Steve, hi, how are you?'

'Vanny... Lottie's had a seizure here at our flat and been admitted to hospital.'

'Oh, God. Oh, God.' I did my best to keep calm, I was driving and I was trying to keep calm. It was hard though. 'Which hospital?'

'The Cromwell in Kensington.'

'Oh, God. I'm on my way.'

'Please drive carefully.'

'I will.'

I reached the Cromwell Hospital on London's Cromwell Road about ninety minutes later. When I got to the hospital I went to reception and was politely asked to wait and told that 'Mr

Juselius' would come to see me shortly. I waited in the palatial waiting room but didn't read any magazines or newspapers.

When Steve finally came, he took me outside the building into the hospital's lovely garden at the back so we could talk in private on the warm April evening.

'It… happened at home today… only about two hours ago,' Steve said, breathlessly. 'Lottie's been really well. This is a total shock. Oh God I'm so scared.'

'Steve,' I said, 'have the doctors said what caused it?'

Steve shook his head. 'I'm waiting for a neurologist to come out and tell me. John isn't here because he's doing an emergency operation tonight; there's been a horrible car crash in central London and he's operating on two people this evening.'

Suddenly I felt very very depressed, which is not at all a frame of mind I usually get into. I mean, aching for someone you love makes you feel awful, but it's not exactly depression. How full of suffering the world seemed to me at that moment.

About half an hour later a black consultant neurologist guy with a velvety deep voice came and invited Steve and me into his consulting room. When we were there, he told us, in a deep, sympathetic voice, that another tumour had been detected in Lottie's head and that it had apparently grown very quickly as it hadn't been detected during her last scan, the one she'd had before the wedding. He told us that this other tumour wasn't a glioma but another kind.

Neither Steve nor I spoke for some time. Finally Steve said:

'But I thought Lottie's tumour was shrunken significantly by the Ditrexican?'

'Yes, Mr Juselius, it was. But this new tumour is something different and as it is not a glioma the Ditrexican is having no effect on it.'

'Do you have any treatment for this new kind of tumour?' I asked.

The doctor shook his head. 'Only surgery, I'm afraid.'

A few days later, Steve and I met with John Hamlyn in his consulting room on Harley Street. Lottie was still in hospital at the Cromwell Hospital. She wasn't having seizures any more, but that was only because they'd had to drill into my darling's skull the day before to relieve the pressure inside. She'd had several seizures and fits before that proceedure, and had been in intensive care and only Steve had been allowed to see her. A day or so after the operation, Lottie was moved out of intensive care but she'd been unconscious since the operation. I'd been to see her, but she'd stayed unconscious all the time. Lottie being so ill was so utterly unspeakably awful that I just felt almost as if I'd rather be dead myself than have to experience the idea of my beloved friend going through what she was going through. They were still administering Ditrexican to her, giving it to her intravenously.

'Could you operate to remove the new tumour?' Steve asked John.

John nodded. 'Yes, I could. I could also use radiotherapy. There is no chemotherapy at present for the secondary tumour Lottie has. But radiotherapy or surgery are options. However, there is something you need to know.'

Steve glanced at me, and then at John. 'Tell us,' Steve murmured.

John drew a breath, then said:

'The location of the new tumour means radiotherapy would have a seriously damaging effect on Lottie, and surgery would have an even more damaging effect. The tumour is positioned inside a part of her brain that is known to play a major role in emotions. If we intervened, Lottie would unquestionably lose a large part of the function of that part of her brain. She would most likely become a completely different person; possibly - I need to say this to you – someone who can hardly feel emotions at all.'

Steve and I just sat there in silent horror.

John cleared his throat. 'If Lottie remains unconscious, you, Steve, as her next of kin, would have the right to decide what to do.'

'I can't make that decision alone,' Steve said quietly. 'I need to ask Lottie.'

I felt a very big lump in my throat. I knew I had to say what I needed to say. 'John, what if you don't give Lottie radiotherapy or try surgery?'

John, professional and gentleman that he was, didn't indulge in any dramatic pause before answering a question he must surely have been expecting anyway.

'Without any treatment,' he said, quietly, 'I don't think Lottie will live for more than two or three weeks.'

The following morning, after the hospital had administered a drug which Steve was told had a 50:50 chance of waking her, Lottie became conscious for about twenty minutes and Steve told her what the situation was, and got her answer, before she lapsed into unconsciousness again.

'Lottie was terribly groggy,' Steve told me when he came to see me after leaving the hospital, the flat on Churchill Gardens only being a short walk away. 'She was just so groggy, but she was awake and somehow I managed to tell her the situation without crying. After I'd told her, she just lay back in the bed and closed her eyes. I thought she'd fallen unconscious again. But then, a few minutes later, she opened her eyes again, and she looked at me and she whispered to me: "I know I have my music, but that isn't enough. Love is all we have. I don't want to be a person who can't love. If I can't love, I don't want to live. I don't want any surgery or radiotherapy that stops me being able to feel.'

Steve shrugged slowly, and then he started to cry. I put my arms around him.

He looked at me. 'Before she became unconscious again she told me she loved me. I waited for more than an hour in case Lottie woke up again, but she didn't.'

Steve stood up, wiped his eyes, and said:

'I left the hospital and phoned John's private mobile from my car in the car-park. When he answered, I told him I'd spoken to Lottie and that I wanted to act on her wishes and that consequently, as her next of kin, I couldn't authorise either any radiotherapy or surgery. I know they'll keep giving her the Ditrexican.'

I was in tears.

'Vanny, I'm driving down to Tenterden in an hour or so to see Rupert and Elizabeth. They know I was seeing Lottie today and was hoping to talk to her. They told me they want to hear the news in person, not on the phone. I'd love for you to come with me.'

So I did. Steve and I arrived in Tenterden a couple of hours later, spent the rest of the day and some of the evening with the Richmonds, and headed back to London at about eight o'clock. It was the one of the saddest days of my life, and it certainly put things with Hélène into perspective, though it didn't in the least stop me missing her.

I visited Lottie every day at the Cromwell Hospital, but she was unconscious all the time. On Tuesday, May the fifteenth, Lottie was taken by ambulance to her home in Tenterden. Steve went there in the ambulance with her, accompanied by two nurses.

The following day I drove down to Tenterden in Sally and was given a guest room in the Richmonds' house by an utterly distraught Elizabeth. Hugo was there too. I had my overnight case with enough clothes and stuff for a week or so.

The Richmonds' house seemed to have died. I spent most of the time with Lottie and Steve. Steve was watching over her, his cello and his amazing career completely forgotten.

50

If life were full of justice, Lottie's health would have started to get better.

But it isn't and she didn't. Lottie died at about eleven o'clock on the morning of Thursday, May the seventeenth, the day after I arrived in Tenterden. The poor girl didn't even make it until the weekend.

Of course I can't be sure she was in no pain but I don't think she was. She just slipped from the world without being able to say goodbye, but at least without being conscious of what was happening to her. She slipped from the world we know about and into the netherworld about which we know nothing except that it isn't the world of the living. One moment she was still breathing in a kind of coma and the next moment her breathing stopped and the room was as silent as death.

I glanced round, wondering if the Angel of Death was anywhere in the room, but if it was, that dark angel had more sense than to show its beastly black leathern wings to me, or to anyone else, at that moment.

Somehow, I got out from the room where Lottie died, after embracing Steve and also Rupert and Elizabeth. I said goodbye to the two lady nurses from the hospital and the family doctor, a tall, grey-haired man in a dark suit who looked to me like a doctor from the nineteenth century. I didn't glance at Lottie, that poor, frail, thin being, whom I'd just seen breathe her last. I stumbled out of the room and away from the smell of disinfectant and the horrible musty smell of death. There was also the smell of the salt in my nose from my tears. I was teary and salty and hopeless, doubly grieving now and in such a terrible mourning that I could think of nothing.

The Richmond family didn't need me there anymore. Lottie was different now; she wasn't really Lottie now, but some vague insubstantial shell of the person I once loved, and who had been my very best friend.

The Richmonds' house was so big, it was easy for me to hurry upstairs unnoticed now and into the room I'd stayed in, gather my things together, and quickly pack them in my overnight case. I did so, and then quietly padded downstairs and through the large, wood-panelled hallway with the grandfather clock in the corner and the polished terracotta flagstones on the floor and the stained glass in the windows on either side of the big heavy dark brown wooden front door. Now I opened it and I went out into a gorgeous bright May day with the sun shining, a day that was completely indifferent, as indeed was May itself, to the death of anyone or anything, and particularly to the death of someone who'd passed away far from the daylight.

I closed the door gently with my right hand, my case in my left. With slow, wandering steps, I walked out into the world.

I just wanted to be far from Tenterden. Out of respect for what was happening at the Richmonds' house, I hadn't parked Sally in their drive but in Tenterden's main car-park.

I soon reached the High Street. There are several public benches along the High Street in Tenterden; it's that sort of place. I found an empty one, sat down, put my overnight case down next to me, took out my phone and texted Tom:

Tom, I'm really sorry to have to tell you that darling Lottie passed away about thirty minutes ago. I don't know anything about the funeral, but I'll let you know when I do. Xx

Then I phoned Jaz on her mobile, but there was no reply. I left her a short voicemail. *Jaz, dearest. Darling Lottie died today at about eleven o'clock. Let's talk when you want to. Lots of love from Vanny. xx*

After I'd left that message I sent short, loving emails about Lottie's death to Mum and also to Dad. Then I sat and thought for a while. Finally, not even feeling nervous now, I sent a text to Hélène, whose own mobile number I still had on my phone. I know she'd said she would change numbers, but I didn't care.

Hello. I hope you are OK. I thought I would text you to let you know the terrible news that my friend Lottie died about half an hour ago. I know you won't reply to this and probably won't even get it but I wanted to tell you anyway.

I was about to add just *xxx Vanny* but after a moment's hesitation I added, instead, *I miss you. Vanny xx.* Then I pressed 'Send' with my right forefinger.

Once I'd sent the text to Hélène I thought, OK, Vanny, *now switch the phone off then you won't keep listening and looking to see if she's replied.*

Using an immense effort of willpower, I managed to switch my phone off.

When I got back to Sally there she was, all friendly and waiting for me. I got into Sally, closed the door on the driver's side, wept for poor Lottie for about ten minutes, then wiped my eyes and switched on the ignition.

I just drove.

The endgame

The final phase of a game of chess, when both sides have fewer than seven pieces or so left. Not all games reach this stage.

From *Introduction to Chess* by Ivana Jones
(Checkmate Publications)

51

I didn't know where I wanted to go, except that I absolutely knew I didn't want to go back home to London.

So I decided, on a whim and without any definite plan, to drive north towards the Kent town of Ashford. I'd only ever travelled to Ashford in the sense that I'd been to and from the Continent by Eurostar a few times. I remember the Eurostar had shot past Ashford at about a zillion miles an hour on an overhead line, supported on turrets like a bridge, that side-steps the station.

When I reached Ashford I decided, also on a whim, to drive to Canterbury, which I'd never been to at all and which I reached at, I suppose, about one o'clock in the afternoon. On the way, I'd vaguely thought I might stay in Canterbury for a few days, but when I saw Canterbury Cathedral in the distance, rising above the city's skyline, all I could think of was how cathedrals are full of tombs of dead people.

And so I drove on eastwards and presently, after another hour or so, I found myself in the small seaside town of Broadstairs, and I decided that staying by the sea might be a good idea on such a nice sunny day and I parked Sally in a car-park I found near the sea-front. I put enough money in the meter to cover the parking charge until noon the following day and I took my overnight case out of Sally and went to find a hotel.

The one I found was the Royal Broadstairs Hotel. The lady at reception asked me how long I wanted to stay and I said 'a week' without really thinking. After she'd taken an imprint of my credit card, she showed me up to a nice big room on the third floor with an unnecessary double bed and a wonderful view of the sunny bay that she told me was called Viking Bay and which has a big house on a cliff-top on the left that she said Charles Dickens had used to stay in when he visited Broadstairs. I thanked her for being so helpful and she smiled and wished me a pleasant stay and she left me alone in the anonymous hotel room whose anonymity totally suited my mood at that moment.

After she'd gone, I drew the curtains against the bright daylight - they had black-out backing and when they were closed left the room surprisingly dark - then I lay on the bed and cried myself to sleep.

I woke up maybe two hours later or so, my face salty with tears. I brushed my teeth and had a long bath and washed my hair. While I was in the nice warm water I stroked myself and made myself come by thinking about making love with Hélène, her lovely smooth tanned body lying on top of me and us passionately kissing. Then I got dry and smoothed moisturiser all over my body and got half-dressed and lay down on the bed again and wondered what to do. I couldn't decide particularly, so I plugged my phone's charger into one of the sockets on the wall above the desk, and I keyed the code of the hotel's free Wi-Fi, which was on a small printed cardboard notice on the desk, into the Wi-Fi menu on the phone.

I clicked onto my emails, stirring sugar into my coffee as I did, my heart jolted.

There was an email from Hélène.

I'd actually forgotten she had my personal email address. I ultra-quickly tapped on the email icon with my right forefinger.

Hello Vanny

I'm so sorry about Lottie.

It's been long time since you and I had our terrible argument and fight in Budapest and I have thought about you so so much and have been so so unhappy.

I don't work at the hotel anymore and I'm not intending to tell you where I work because I don't want you phone me there and make me even more unhappy than I am already.

I've got quite a good job as junior manager at a new hotel and it goes with my training quite well and will help my hotel career, but I've been living in a terrible strange way over the past two months but have somehow managed to focus on work and looking after my mum and not crying all the time although I've cried lots and lots.

I've really fallen in love with you, Vanny, and I am wishing I never met you because you're straight and you don't love me and I suppose now you're with Tom and don't give me any thinking at all.

Hélène

I cried.

The whole world seemed even more full than usual of tears and pain and upset.

Then I did what I'd promised myself I would never do again: I phoned her up.

As I waited for the call to be answered my heart was beating so fast I thought it might rip free of its moorings.

I imagined Hélène would be at work and that she probably wouldn't answer the phone but then I heard her voice, her voice that I loved and knew so well.

'Vanny?'

So she hadn't deleted my mobile number, or maybe she knew it by heart.

'Yes,' I said. 'Listen, I want to see you. I really want to see you.'

'I'm not coming to see you, Vanny. You really hurt me in Budapest. You don't know how much you hurt me.'

'You should have let me explain! Yes, I did have sex with Tom the day before I left for Budapest, and yes, that was after you and I were in touch. I was honest about that. But you need to understand, you need to really understand, that when I had sex with him that day, I was already kind of in love with you. It was a very strange day. I was really afraid for Lottie's health and...'

And then I began to talk too fast; indeed I'm amazed she understood me. I told Hélène that because Lottie had died, I'd come on a strange drive through Kent to 'a seaside town called Broadstairs' and was all alone and missing her and I loved her.

What Hélène said was:

'Have you slept with Tom since you and I had our fight?'

'No. *No*. No, I haven't.' There was a silence, then she said:

'I believe you, Vanny.'

'Good. Good.'

Another silence, then she said:

'Oh, Vanny, I am so so so sorry about Lottie. But what happened? You told me the drug was helping her?'

'Yes, it was helping her and the tumour was shrinking, and continuing to shrink. But then she got another tumour, one that couldn't be treated. Things were all just totally awful. I watched her die and it was just so dreadful although I don't think she was in any pain. Hélène, I so much want to see you. I think I'm going crazy here. I want to see you.'

'Oh, Vanny.'

'Would you like to come to see me?'

'You know I would. I think I can get a couple of days off from my work. And listen, I've got money, I've been saving up money. If I come to see you, I'm paying for my flight this time.'

'All right, no problem.'

'So, how do I get to this place "Broadstairs"?'

52

Hélène arrived at Broadstairs railway station at just after half past one, two days later, on Saturday, May the nineteenth.

She'd caught an early morning Air France flight from Nice airport to London Gatwick, then a train from Gatwick to Victoria station and at Victoria boarded the train for East Kent, which terminated at Margate and called at Broadstairs just before reaching Margate itself. I'd looked up this journey plan on the internet and had texted it all to Hélène.

Quite a lot of other people got off the train at Broadstairs, so Hélène and I, by a kind of mutual consent, managed to delay things until I'd walked with her the half mile or so down Broadstairs High Street from the station to the Royal Broadstairs Hotel, pulling her wheeled case with my left hand and holding her left hand with my right.

I didn't want to risk any complications at reception; it was, after all, a medium-sized English family seaside hotel, nothing like the hotel in Budapest, but anyway, I'd already noticed that there was a way onto the main staircase of the hotel through the bar at the rear of the hotel. If you went that way you couldn't be seen from reception going up the staircase. Besides, it wasn't as if I was cheating the hotel of any money; I'd paid a week's rent upfront and the rent was per room, not per person staying there.

We arrived in my room at, I suppose, about two o'clock. The sun was streaming into the room through the opened curtains and so, without saying a word to Hélène, I closed the curtains almost completely. At once the room was almost pitch black again apart from sunlight shining through a gap in the middle like rays of life.

I glanced at Hélène and smiled, she glanced at me and smiled back. She closed the door with a louder bang than, I thought, she'd intended, but I felt a thrill incandescent in my heart at realising how urgently she wanted me.

'I love you, Vanny,' she said.

My heart was racing. 'I love you too,' I told her.

We flung off our clothes, scampered onto the bed, scrambled under the duvet and made love like experts, which I suppose by now we were.

Later that afternoon we explored Broadstairs together. The first shop we went in was a second-hand book shop, which was on the road just opposite the hotel. It was dusty and not very tidy, with piles of books on the floor as well as on the shelves, but she smiled and said to me that it was *'magnifique'* and she went to inspect some books about flowers. Meanwhile, I just went up to some shelves on the left at random, and found a rather shabby edition of a poet, called Rilke, whom I'd only ever heard of vaguely. I found myself looking at some of his thoughts, including this one:

It is also good to love: because love is difficult. For one human being to love another human being: that is perhaps the most difficult task that has been entrusted to us, the ultimate task, the final test and proof, the work for which all other work is merely preparation.

OK, well you might think it was just totally unbelievable that I found that comment at that particular time in my life on that particular afternoon, but what I'm telling you is completely true: I did. I sometimes think that there's a force in the world, some energy, some power, some special kind of gravity maybe which provides us with important experiences at the very moment when we need them. You may of course think this is nonsense and perhaps it is or perhaps it isn't and maybe there was some force taking me to that quotation from Rilke.

So yes, I bought the book, and it's since become part of my small, personal library, including a few chess books that I adore and that I take with me on trips. Hélène bought a newish book, with lovely colour illustrations, of British garden flowers. It was quite a big book, so I suggested to her I pop back upstairs to the hotel room and leave it there before we continued on our stroll around Broadstairs. Hélène thanked me for thinking of this, and after I came back down (having left my Rilke book there too), we went on exploring Broadstairs.

It's a pretty town, and was especially so on that lovely day in May. The walk along the promenade above the bay - we were so high up, we could look *down* on flying seagulls - gave us a wondrous view of the bay and the sea. The path eventually meandered down towards a tiny pier on the far side of the bay, and we had a cup of tea there. The old, fort-like, brown brick house where Dickens had once lived was above us on the cliff-top, and after finishing our cups of tea we walked up to it and found that it was now a hotel and restaurant. So we had dinner there.

I still felt deeply in grief for Lottie, but being with Hélène, there in Broadstairs on that lovely sunny day, felt like being in a dream.

After dinner, over our decaf cappuccinos, we checked my texts and I found I had a brief, friendly, but sad text from Lottie's brother Hugo, telling me that Lottie's funeral would be the following Friday, May the twenty-fifth, at the church in Tenterden, and that Lottie would be buried in the churchyard there.

I also quickly checked my emails, and found that there was one from an Australian tournament organiser telling me about a tournament in August to which he was inviting me. It would last for two weeks and it started in the second week of August. I hardly thought of that invitation at that moment, although I did glance at it.

Later that evening, when Hélène and I were in bed together, she said, quietly, 'I don't think I will come to the funeral, Vanny. I didn't know Lottie and it wouldn't be right. But I love you and I want to be with you. I am sure I can find a job in a hotel in London.'

I just looked at her. 'You mean… you'd like to be in London with me?'

She kissed me, then whispered in my left ear, 'you *know* I would. My mum will be OK about it. She knows I love you. We could visit her sometimes, and she could maybe visit us. Mum's never been to London.'

'Oh, Hélène, of course we can visit her and we'd give her a lovely time in London. Oh, Hélène, living with you would be fantastic.'

I knew there were things that would need sorting out. I knew, for example, that at some point I would need to ask Sir Rupert if it was OK if Hélène stayed with me in the flat and would pay rent. But I knew I would wing it for the time being, and have Hélène stay in my room and, well, I was just so thrilled at the prospect.

Hélène and I spent the next few days in Broadstairs. We knew each other better know than we had in Budapest; we had had our fight there and our estrangement afterwards as mutual history, and when two people have mutual history in a relationship, it usually helps the relationship unless, of course, the mutual history leads them to break up completely.

On Thursday morning we checked out of the hotel and I drove us back to London in Sally. In case you were wondering,

I'd put money in the parking meter every day to avoid getting lots of parking tickets.

When we got to the flat, Jaz was in the kitchen and I introduced Hélène to her. Jaz didn't seem fazed in the least. She just looked happy for me. But then of course Jaz and I hugged and cried over Lottie's death.

Hélène made us tea. It was strange, but I already felt as if she'd been living there for ages.

As we were all drinking our tea and eating some chocolate biscuits, Jaz said:

'Vanny, I need to tell you about Sven and me.'

I just looked at her. 'Oh my God... you mean?'

She beamed at me. 'Yes!'

I just felt totally happy for her. 'Since when?'

'Since the weekend when you played in Kettering. Sven was in London on the Saturday on a course for magazine editors, and I stayed with him in his hotel. I've been keeping it quiet because of Lottie, but I had to tell you. And Hélène too.'

Hélène nodded slowly. 'It is so sad about Lottie, when there is so much love here in this apartment.'

'Lottie wouldn't think it was sad, though,' I said. 'She'd be so happy.'

'I so much wish I had met her,' said Hélène.

'I wish you had too.'

The following day I drove down in Sally with Tom and Jaz to Lottie's funeral.

I didn't tell Tom on the journey down about Hélène having moved in with me: Jaz and I had agreed not to mention it to Tom.

I spent most of my time at Lottie's funeral in tears, but somehow I managed to speak my own eulogy to the assembled

301

congregation of more than a hundred people without crying all the time.

I told them how much Lottie had meant to me, what a great friend she'd been and how she'd completely saved me at Abbey Hall school when I was so lonely and how she was my best friend there and had been my best friend ever and how beautifully she played the piano, and how wonderful and loving she was and how she'd almost fought off, with the help of an experimental drug, the brain tumour that had killed her, but then the other tumour had developed.

I don't remember what else I said. It was a truly beautiful funeral, and they played several hymns including 'I vow to thee, my country' that had been a particular favourite of Lottie's and which I think most of us know.

I vow to thee, my country, all earthly things above,
Entire and whole and perfect, the service of my love;
The love that asks no question, the love that stands the test,
That lays upon the altar the dearest and the best;
The love that never falters, the love that pays the price,
The love that makes undaunted the final sacrifice.

And there's another country, I've heard of long ago,
Most dear to them that love her, most great to them that know;
We may not count her armies, we may not see her King;
Her fortress is a faithful heart, her pride is suffering;
And soul by soul and silently her shining bounds increase,
And her ways are ways of gentleness, and all her paths are peace.

53

From: ijones2412@chessmail.net
To: chairman@russfiduciarybank.com
Subject: Something I need to tell you
Tuesday, May 29 09.28 GMT

Dear Boris

*You'll know from the email I sent you a few days ago
that, to my great sorrow, poor Lottie has passed away.*

*There's no doubt at all that the Ditrexican prolonged
her life significantly and that without it she'd probably
have passed away sometime in March or even February. So
you helped give her two extra months of life. I will never
forget that, Boris.*

*You're a wonderful man and you've changed my life. I
hope we can always be friends.*

*There is, though, something you need to know and
which I need to tell you. And I'm telling you before the
New York tournament in case you decide you don't, after
all, want me to play in it.*

*I absolutely DON'T want to hurt your feelings, but I
need to tell you the truth.*

*Completely unexpectedly I've fallen in love with a
woman called Hélène Dubois. She's French and I met her
in March when I was visiting my father in Monte Carlo.*

*I'm living with her now in London, She's trying to get
a job at a London hotel and in fact later today she has an*

interview for a job at a hotel on Park Lane as a junior manager.

If you'd still like me to come to New York I want to come with Hélène please.

It's not just that I'd enjoy her company but she's really inspiring to me when I play too, e.g. when I played in the European Women's Championship I did very badly at the start as you know but then Hélène came and I started to do better and eventually I won as you also know.

Of course, if you don't want me to come to the tournament now I'll totally understand that.

I'm not saying I've become gay but I obviously do like women as well as men and this is something I need to think about.

I won't say any more because I can imagine that you might be quite angry and I'll just have to wait to see what you say in response to this.

*Very best wishes
from Ivana*

There was no reply for more than a day, which, despite Hélène's company, I spent in a high state of tension about how Boris would reply, and indeed whether he would reply at all - of course I didn't (selfishly) want to lose the chance to go to New York but what I was much more concerned about was that I hated hurting Boris's feelings. After all his great kindnesses to me and to Lottie the last thing I wanted to do was hurt him but I didn't see how I had had any choice but to tell him the truth.

Then around lunchtime the following day, the Wednesday, I got this email from Boris.

My dear Ivana,

Thanks very much for your email.

I totally understand your situation.

I was disappointed and upset yesterday after hearing from you but I woke up today feeling more philosophical.

Indeed I am flattered that you were so open and direct with me, for it means we are true friends.

I would like you to come to New York with Hélène and at my expense (I'll pay her air fare) and I want you both to have a great time.

Your friend, Boris

54

'Why don't you both come round tomorrow evening?' Tom asked.

He phoned me at about five in the afternoon of the Wednesday, the day when I received the email from Boris. When Tom phoned, I was studying chess in preparation for the New York tournament, which started the following Monday. Hélène and I were booked to fly out on a British Airways flight which left London Heathrow at 11.10 am on Saturday morning.

I knew Tom was planning to fly to New York this coming weekend. I also knew that he hadn't yet booked his flight and was planning to make a late booking to keep the cost down.

About a minute earlier, in that same phone call, I'd told Tom that Hélène was living with me in the flat.

'In Lottie's room?' he'd asked.

'Of course not. In my room.'

'What's it like, living with her?'

'Mind your own business.'

'OK. I'll just have to imagine.'

'You really are a pervert, Tom.'

He didn't deny this, but instead he asked his question inviting us both round.

'I'll ask her, Tom. She may not want to.'

'I totally realise that. But please tell her it would be great to see her.'

'OK.'

'So what shall I tell Tom?' I asked Hélène later that evening over supper. She'd made us delicious home-made pizzas, with mushrooms, ham and sweetcorn on them. Jaz wasn't there. She'd gone to Norway to see Sven and they were planning to fly to New York from Oslo non-stop on Saturday, the same day we were crossing the Atlantic ourselves.

'Yes, I'd like to meet him,' Hélène said. 'After all, you've loved him and let's face it, you do still love him in many ways. He sounds like an interesting guy.'

I shrugged. 'Well, yes, he is. But I do worry a bit that he's simply curious to see us both together... I mean in real life rather than on the Budapest chess tournament webcam.'

'If he's curious to see us together then why not let him *see* us together? Everything should be transparent I think and there's no need for stress between people.' Hélène nodded slowly. 'Most stress between people is caused by a lack of communications and a lack of understanding. That's probably also true of wars as well.'

I smiled at her. 'You say some amazing things. It's lovely to be with you.'

So anyway, the following day, we arrived at Tom's at about ten past eight. We were invited for eight. I didn't want him to think we were too eager and besides, lateness is beauty's privilege as he'd often said to me.

I'd gone to see Tom in the past in all sorts of different moods. I'd never before gone to see Tom feeling nervous but I did now. Hélène and I had both dressed down by the way, both of us wearing blue jeans. Hélène wore a plain white tee-shirt and I wore a plain sky-blue one. These were supposed to be friendly, not-too-sexy clothes. They'd been Hélène's suggestion. Certainly it would have been just too cruel on Tom if we'd turned up in sexy tight clingy black dresses but actually as

307

we were walking to his flat it occurred to me that maybe he might find our jeans and tee-shirts pretty sexy anyway, when combined with our mutual trademark long black hair. Though of course I personally thought Hélène would have been sexy even if she'd only been wearing an old sack.

I had no idea what was going to happen that evening.

As we climbed the stairs up to his flat amid the aroma of kebabs (I was carrying a Harvey Nicks bag with my flat shoes in it to wear indoors, and a nice bottle of Bordeaux) I glanced at Hélène and said, 'like we agreed, I don't think we should be too obvious in our display of emotion.'

'Oh I don't know about that,' Hélène said with a smile, 'I think if we both took our clothes off and made love passionately in front of him he'd be absolutely *delighted*.'

'Well, in a way he would, but in another he wouldn't. He's sensitive.'

When we reached Tom's floor and I rapped a couple of times on the door, he opened it very quickly. He was looking good with a nicely pressed clean pair of maroon trousers rather than his usual shorts or jeans and with a very nice long-sleeved button-down shirt with narrow green and white horizontal stripes. I couldn't remember him ever looking so smart.

Tom and Hélène shook hands and she smiled at him and immediately the poor fellow was captivated by her beauty, as anybody would be.

Tom cleared his throat. Just for once, he seemed to be at a loss to know what to say. But a few moments later, he said, in a voice that was a little hoarse:

'Very good to meet you, Hélène. Could I show you round the flat?'

Hélène said she'd love to see round his flat, and I accompanied them.

Hélène seemed fascinated right away by the orc.

'What a lovely cuddly creature!' she exclaimed. And she went up to the orc and gave him/it a hug and kissed him/it on his/its horrible tusked face. And then she proceeded to wind herself around the orc as if she were basically trying to seduce the ghastly thing, though she kept all her clothes on. She did a kind of impromptu, sensuous, slithery, lithe dance around the orc while Tom and I just looked, astonished, at her.

Well, Hélène's dance broke the ice and we had some wine in Tom's living-room and everything was very relaxed. Tom seemed OK. He didn't particularly appear to be jealous. I could tell that he really had accepted the way things were between me and Hélène. In fact he asked us questions about our relationship but they weren't questions that made you think he was being perverted but just genuine questions about what it had been like for us to meet and he also asked Hélène why she thought girls were more attractive than guys but not as if he was contesting that feeling but just because he was genuinely interested.

By the time he'd asked her that question, we were all onto our second glasses of a really nice Chilean red wine which Tom told us he got from the local Sainsbury's especially for the evening which I thought was very nice of him. We were sitting in his small living-room which has two armchairs in it, some large black beanbags, a lava-lamp and an old but still comfy sofa. The lava lamp wasn't on.

Hélène was sitting in one of the armchairs, her lovely long legs straight ahead of her and lying back on the armchair slightly. She gave a measured shrug. 'Why do I like girls? I suppose because they smell so nice and they're soft and they're often just so lovely and their voices are tuneful and, well, because they're girls we seem to know each other's bodies, in a way, kind of automatically.' Hélène cleared her throat. 'Oh, and also, there's the excitement of the forbidden!'

Tom just nodded slightly and said: 'I think maybe the truth is that many men find the idea of girls together fascinating and attractive because it's an area of sexuality they can't be part of. But I also think that when men think of two girls or women together they find it all a bit frightening and intimidating.'

'You think so?' Hélène asked thoughtfully.

Tom nodded. 'When men think of two girls or two women together or maybe see them on a video or a movie – it's amazing how many movies are made about girl on girl relationships nowadays – they find it disturbing because… maybe in a deep and dark kind of way it kind of reminds them of the sexuality of their mum which of course they couldn't touch or be part of when they were younger.'

'That's pretty heavy, Tom,' Hélène said.

Tom glanced at her, 'is it?'

Hélène nodded, 'but you might be right.'

'Well, anyway,' I said, 'I don't think Hélène really wants to hear about your amateur philosophising about gayness in women, Tom.'

Hélène glanced at me, 'No, I'm interested, really. I think what Tom's saying is very perceptive, you know.'

We went on chatting, or rather Tom and Hélène went on chatting and I went on feeling embarrassed. Yet in fact nothing in any way really embarrassing was actually happening. Tom was asking Hélène about being gay. She told him how she discovered that she was gay when she was about twelve and that she'd kissed her first best friend at school and at the age of fifteen had had her first affair, with another girl from her school. Tom and Hélène got on alarmingly well. We decided to go out soon for a Chinese meal, but first we decided to do some web-surfing, as one does. Hélène went onto YouTube and found the scene in what she said was one of her favourite movies, *Emmanuelle 1*, where Emmanuelle seduces her friend Bee.

'It's an old movie and quite silly really,' Hélène said, 'but this scene is very beautiful.'

And she found the scene on YouTube and it was beautiful, too; I mean, the way Emmanuelle, naked and slender and elfin-like and very pretty, dominated the taller and sturdier and also naked Bee by lying on top of her and then vigorously making love to her, the girl elf possessing the queen, though actually you didn't get to see very much. We played the scene several times, and Tom said nothing, he seemed to me to like watching us enjoying it even more than the scene itself.

At the restaurant I finally started to relax a little. Tom and Hélène were chatting about love, friendship and about movies they loved, and eventually I joined in properly.

Over the banana fritters, Hélène asked Tom what flight he was taking to New York and he said he hadn't quite decided yet, as he wanted to get the cheapest deal he could.

'Well,' said Hélène, 'why don't you see if you can get on the flight Vanny and me are going on?'

Tom glanced at me. 'Isn't that the ten past eleven British Airways flight?'

'Stop pretending you don't really know, please,' I said to him. 'You know it leaves then.'

He smiled at me, and then at Hélène, and she smiled at me.

'OK, I'll try to get on it,' he said.

After Tom had paid the bill and we walked back to his flat, we both hugged him goodbye. Hélène kissed him on the lips, although not, I thought, in a really sexual way and Hélène and I walked off and only after Tom had gone back into his apartment block we held hands and went home and felt very happy.

'Believe me, he'll be over the moon that we're happy for him to be on our flight,' I said to Hélène.

'I think he loves you very much,' Hélène said. 'And what makes me feel very emotional is that in a strange way, he is happy that you are happy. I think he is a very good man, Vanny.'

'Yes,' I said. 'Yes, he is.'

'I think it would be fun to fly with him to New York.'

'I think so too,' I said.

The next day Tom texted me in the morning to tell me he'd managed to book himself onto our flight but had had to book himself on Business Class as Economy was totally full. Hélène and I were travelling Economy and I was paying. Boris had wanted to book us into First Class but I hadn't let him.

5 5

The Boeing 777 in which Tom, Hélène and I flew to John F. Kennedy Airport in New York on Saturday, June the second, for the Niklas Bogolyubov World Open Chess Championship, seemed to me like a flying village.

Tom, Hélène and I were in Economy. Tom had swapped his Business Class seat with a rather stout bald man who had been sitting next to me on the other side of the aisle and was more than happy to find himself upgraded by Tom. As for Hélène and me, we obviously felt very impressed with Tom, that he'd given up his posher seat to sit with us.

The three of us were sitting about two-thirds of the way along the Economy cabin and on the right-hand side of the plane. Hélène was sitting by the window, I was next to her on her left and Tom was sitting across the aisle next to an Indian family who were spread out from the seat next to him all along to the other aisle.

I wondered what the next couple of weeks would bring. I knew that the Niklas Bogolyubov World Open Chess Championship (as Boris had styled his event), would be my best chance for my third grandmaster norm that summer and very possibly also that year. I knew that this event in New York was going to be one of the most exciting events of the whole chess calendar that year. For one thing, Sven and Jaz, who were now officially a couple and who had plans to get married the following spring, would be playing. I also knew that Boris was planning on playing, although goodness knows what kind of result he would be expecting. Also, I'd heard on the grapevine that Stuart Conquest and David Howell would be there, as would The Three Vs, and Matti Ots, Fabiano Caruana and the international master Andrew Greet who had held Miklos to a draw so memorably in Hastings. Oh yes, and Miklos would be playing as well.

About half an hour after we'd taken off, the cabin crew served lunch, which was (for non-veggies and non-vegans, anyway) steak with new potatoes, gravy, carrots and peas. I felt quite sleepy after lunch, no doubt helped by the relatively low oxygen level that Tom believes airlines deliberately keep in planes to make passengers drowsy and so render the stewardesses' and stewards' jobs easier. I suggested to Hélène that she might like to change places with me. I said I'd like to have a snooze by the window without disturbing her. She smiled and so we did change places and I used the horseshoe-shaped pillow they provide and I put my head back against the seat and became more and more drowsy.

Something happened in the next hour or so that I didn't really understand and which I saw, peculiarly, through my drowsiness.

I wasn't sure that I went to sleep completely, as after all one doesn't do that very often on aeroplanes with the modest but nonetheless constant noise in the cabin and the little beeps of service bells and the noise of the engines and goodness knows all the other noises that we put up with when we're flying. So I wasn't fully asleep but I wasn't fully awake either. I was indeed very drowsy and what I *think* happened was that at some point - though this might have been a dream and I might have been mistaken - Tom and Hélène got up together and disappeared for at least ten minutes, or maybe longer.

Anyway, they did disappear, but I wasn't awake at the time, not properly. Of course if I had been, I'd have been curious about where they'd gone and what had happened but anyway I seem to have a vague memory of them returning to their seats after those ten minutes or so which I only witnessed in my drowsy state.

If, when they returned to their seats, there was something of a glow about both of them, well, maybe my drowsiness was imagining things and in any case I went back to sleep and slept more deeply for about an hour or so after that. Then I woke, quite completely but in the way you often wake in an airline cabin where your mouth feels dry and there's a time between you waking up and your brain connecting with your body again before you can actually move your body and do things that you're likely to want to do such as go to the bathroom and get a drink.

I sat there in that weird sort of paralysed state, my eyes half open and knowing that I was sort of half-awake and I just felt there was a sort of harmonious aura projecting itself from Tom and Hélène towards me. They both sat innocently reading now: Hélène the British Airways magazine *High Life* and Tom was reading the late, great Bobby Fischer's *My Sixty Memorable Games,* one of the best chess books ever written. I didn't ask them about what I'd suspected, but I did file it away in the library of my mind where I put curious things.

The Presidential Suite, which Boris had reserved for Hélène and me in the Manhattan Ambassador Hotel on Park Avenue, near the corner of East 47th Street, was as wonderful as Boris had promised. I'd decided after all to accept Boris's offer of staying there as I felt he was being very good indeed about Hélène and besides, I wanted to give her a treat, in view of everything she'd put up with from me. We both loved the Japanese water-garden, which was all enclosed and on an extended part of the balcony. Hélène and I also adored the humming-birds, which lived in a spacious alcove on one side of the suite, behind glass in a specially temperature-controlled aviary, and which were attended to every day by a specialist hotel person. The suite, and the Manhattan Ambassador Hotel generally, was such an amazing place that I felt in a dream even more than I did already.

I'd already discovered there's something thoroughly dreamlike about arriving in Manhattan. I'd never been to the US before. It's dreamlike not only because you feel drowsy after the journey, though there is that, but because, when you arrive in Manhattan, somehow *you feel you've been there already*. Obviously, you've seen so many movies that take place in New York that when you're actually there in New York you simply feel you're in a movie and that of course is a kind of dreaming.

Tom's room was two floors below our suite; he showed us his room not long after we arrived. Tom, like all the grandmasters who were playing in the tournament, had his accommodation paid for by Boris, and was allowed to eat anything he liked at the hotel, at any time. This was the big time, and the big time in New York is always, almost by definition, the biggest of all. Tom showed Hélène and me his own room the same evening when we arrived. Tom's room was pretty impressive, with an enormous double bed, beautiful period-type furniture, a TV screen about the size of a window attached to the wall opposite the bed and a general air of utter luxury. I was privately glad he had such a lovely place to stay in; it seemed like a reward for all his hard work on chess so far and all I'd put him through.

That first evening, the Saturday when we arrived in Manhattan, we all went out for dinner at a deli on East 47th Street not far from the hotel, as we were all feeling fairly jet-lagged and we thought we'd eat somewhere nearby. All of us preferred to go out somewhere to experience the ambience of the city's streets rather than eat at Boris's expense at the hotel. We were all captivated by the deliciousness of the pizzas and salad that the deli sold. I'd never had such a delicious pizza in my entire life.

I wanted to spend the Sunday doing chess training, although I was still feeling pretty jet-lagged and in fact I didn't start work until about twelve noon.

Tom said he had done all the preparation he wanted to do and that he wanted to see New York, so I was very happy for him to take Hélène out that afternoon while I did chess practice and played games against my computer at the desk in our suite when I wasn't sleeping. Tom and Hélène said they planned to do lots of New York touristy things e.g. go up the Empire State building, go to Ground Zero, walk through Central Park, have ice-creams, and go to some of the most famous stores.

The tournament opening ceremony took place the next day, not in the huge ballroom that was accommodating the tournament, but in a large meeting-room adjacent to it. Boris was the main speaker at the opening ceremony, which began at noon on the Monday, with play scheduled to start at two thirty in the ballroom.

Shortly before the opening ceremony started, I saw Boris by himself in a corridor of the hotel, so I went up to talk to him.

He smiled. 'Thank you for coming. I hope you and your friends are having a great time. Perhaps you and I will play each other in the event. I'm playing myself. After all, how could I not play in a tournament named after my father? I know there are some wonderful players here.'

'Boris, are you in any danger here?'

'I don't think so. There have been some threats to me, and Alexander and I have been putting strategies into place to minimise the risk to me.'

'That's just so dreadful. Are you saying there are still some people out there who might want to kill you?'

'You could say that, yes. Fortunately, I have Alexander.'

'But then why isn't he here with you now, protecting you?'

'It is as when we were at the wedding. Nobody would try anything in here in full public view.'

'I think you're very calm about it.'

Boris shrugged. 'In a place like New York, where there are usually police close by, and where the police, as in most parts of the world except Britain, are always armed and don't hesitate to shoot, there's always a likelihood that anyone who tries to assassinate someone is going to end up being shot themselves. No, the people who want to kill me operate in much more sordid and secretive ways than that. But enough of me. You know how very sorry I am about Lottie.'

There were some sudden tears in my left eye. I wiped them away. I found I couldn't help reaching out and up and stroking his left cheek. 'Dear Boris, I really hope you find someone who is worthy of your love, someone who is better than me.'

He smiled faintly, then shook his head. 'The trouble is, we don't have any choice about who we fall in love with, now do we?'

'Oh, Boris…'

'Please don't be upset, please don't be sad. Friendship is also wonderful and a union of two sympathetic souls.'

The lump in my throat suddenly grew even bigger. 'Yes,' I said. 'Yes, it is. And… listen, please don't deprive yourself of love and passion and happiness on my account. Please don't.'

I couldn't help myself: I stood on tiptoe and gave him a kiss on the lips, and a big, long hug.

Finally, I held both his hands in mine for a few moments, and then I hurried off to the room where the opening ceremony would take place.

I loved Boris's speech at the tournament opening ceremony, where he was talking to maybe three hundred people including the players, the visiting dignitaries, the media from New York and many chess journalists from around the world. I don't remember everything he said, but I do remember he welcomed everyone to the 'Niklas Bogolyubov World Open Chess Championship' and said, 'my beloved father Niklas, who was himself quite a keen chess-player although he did not have as much time as he would have liked because he was busy building up his jewellery business in Moscow, once told me, in Russian of course but I'm translating it, that chess is the most wonderful game ever invented. *"Remember, my dear Boris, as the great chess player Siegbert Tarrasch once observed: chess, like women, has the power to make men happy."*

Boris looked around at the audience and said:

'But I think Siegbert Tarrasch was wrong in some respects because, seeing all the talented women here who are playing in the tournament, I realise that they would say that chess also has the power to make women happy. I salute you all, and I declare the Niklas Bogolyubov World Open Chess Championship... open!'

56

What Boris definitely didn't have on when he was making the speech was a New York Mets dark blue baseball cap. Now, this was strange, because when he played in the tournament he wore a baseball cap in every round. Quickly it became known that the boss of the tournament, the sponsor, Mr Big if you like, Boris Bogolyubov, the son of Niklas Bogolyubov, Boris Bogolyubov the billionaire oligarch, was wearing his New York Mets baseball cap during his games.

It really wasn't clear why he was wearing it. Certainly, it wasn't cold in the beautiful ballroom where we played. It was, after all a tournament held in late spring heading for the summer and while New York was extremely humid during the weeks of the tournament - I wasn't expecting New York to be so humid and I only now realised why air-conditioning is such a big part of life there - I really couldn't see any rational reason for Boris wearing a baseball cap except that he must have thought he looked cool in it, which actually he did.

I was disappointed that in the very first round I was drawn against Jaz herself. I know that some tournaments program the computer controlling the draw so that it deliberately prevents players from the same country from playing in the first round. But this didn't apply at the New York event, where the draw was based only on rankings and so, as a relatively highly-ranked player - though by no means as highly-ranked as many of the players - I was drawn against a relatively low-ranked player. Jaz and I were just unlucky that we were having to play each other in Round One.

I was White and Jaz knew perfectly well that I had to try very hard to beat her and I managed to, though our game was a tough struggle. In Round Two I played Black against Fabiano Caruana, who is regarded as a potential future world champion. He was at the time of this tournament the fourth highest rated player in the world. I played as well as I could, and I even had something resembling a queenside attack against Fabiano's king which he had put in the far left corner after castling queenside.

But he defended very cleverly and fended me off and then attacked my king with extreme cunning, deadly precision and horrible accuracy.

So after two rounds I had just fifty percent, one out of two. On the other hand, I'd played one of the very best players in the world and I hadn't looked like an idiot even though I'd lost.

In Round Three I was drawn against no less a person than the grandmaster and organiser of the Gibraltar tournament Stuart Conquest, who comes from Bexhill near Hastings and has twice been a joint winner of the Hastings Tournament. I know Stuart pretty well, as you know, but as always when two chess professionals play each other, we have no choice but to put our personal friendship on the back-burner, at least until the end of the game.

I knew playing Stuart would be a tough challenge - he's higher rated than me and a superb player. But I was lucky in this game. I was White and I felt confident and I kept the position closed and slowly I kept improving my pieces. On move fifty-six Stuart resigned.

Well, my next opponent the following day, which was Thursday, June seventh, was none other than... Tom himself!

I was Black and didn't particularly fancy my chances but the strange thing was that over the past few days Tom hadn't really been himself. He often went early to bed and sometimes over dinner he drank a bit more than he normally did – maybe four or five bottles of Budweiser beer rather than just his usual one or two.

Tom was White and he played, surprisingly, very badly. I checkmated him on move thirty-one.

After the game, when Tom and I were analysing it in the analysis room with Hélène with us (sitting next to me), Tom looked at us both and said:

'I didn't play very well, Vanny, I know. I'm just not really in a chessy mood at the moment.'

'Why not?'

'I'm just not.'

Our game had finished pretty early and there were only two other people in the analysis room analysing some way away near the door. Keeping my voice down I said, 'You're not jealous of us are you? I hope not, Tom, because I don't want you to be unhappy.'

Hélène said nothing.

'No, I'm not jealous,' Tom said, 'I really am not. Part of the problem is I... well I suppose I've been playing so much chess this year I've got a bit fed up with chess, to be honest. I'm going to do some writing, I think, at some point. Maybe write a chess book for kids: something I've always wanted to do.'

'You'd be very good at doing that, Tom, I think,' Hélène said.

Tom smiled, for the first time since we'd started playing our game, as he glanced at her. 'Thanks. Nice of you to say so. Yes, it's a book I'd like to write. Maybe I will.'

On the Friday, June the eighth, in Round Five, I was paired against another friend David Howell, the extremely talented British grandmaster. We had a really sharp game but we reached a level endgame. David offered me a draw on about move sixty-five. It had been a completely exhausting game and we were one of the last to finish on the top boards and we both got a round of applause by that point.

So, as I embarked on Round Six, which was played on the Saturday, June the ninth, I had three and a half points out of five and was in joint tenth place in the tournament along with quite a lot of other players. The tournament was at that point being led by Matti Ots, the great Estonian player, and Miklos Steiner, whom you're unlikely to have forgotten about, I think. Miklos and Matti each had five points out of five.

In Round Six, I had to play Matti, who was rated fifth in the world. Maybe I was too much in awe of him, but I'm afraid my play in Round Six, even though I was White, was pretty embarrassing. He basically just overwhelmed me. So after the first six rounds I had just three and a half out of six.

By the Sunday, we'd played six games of chess on consecutive days and, like everyone, I was feeling the strain. Even at night with Hélène I'd simply been too tired for the past two nights to make love and Hélène had seemed to be all right about that which secretly surprised me in a way and even disappointed me a bit.

In Round Seven on the Sunday I was paired against no other than… The Three Vs. As it's been some time since you've met him I'll remind you that he was reputed to be the most crazy member of the international chess tour.

In the event, despite playing Black, I had a comparatively easy victory. The Three Vs, being on the face of it mad, began with a relatively mad move against me: pawn to king's rook three.

The Three Vs lasted until about move thirty. I felt sorry for him really.

He resigned with a disgusted frown on his face, and when I suggested, rather half-heartedly, because I didn't really want to, that we look over the game in the analysis room, he just shook his head and murmured to me, in a heavily Russian-accented English, the rather strange phrase, *'Beneath this face there lies more than a mask.'* Which struck me as being an extremely bizarre thing for him to say because after all he didn't have a mask on at all he just had his face and how could anything that was more than a mask lie beneath his face? I found out since that the quotation comes from *V for Vendetta,* The Three Vs' favourite movie.

57

Thank goodness, it was now Monday, June the eleventh, the rest day, though I knew I would have to work hard on chess all through it. I mean, there was just so much at stake right now.

'Darling, I really need to do chess practice today rather than anything social or go sightseeing,' I said to Hélène, after we'd woken up that Monday morning. 'I hope you don't mind.'

Hélène shook her head, '*Je comprends, cherie.* I want you to do the best you can in the tournament. Besides, Tom's doing really badly and I know he won't mind taking me out today.'

'You really get on well with him, don't you?'

'Yes I do. It's fun. I've never been such good friends with a guy before.'

I nodded. 'Tom's an amazing person. He seems to know almost everything and he's a kind and good friend.'

'Do you ever still wish you were with him romantically?'

I shook my head quickly, aware that despite everything this was potentially dangerous territory.

'No, darling, I don't,' I said. 'He and I are really good friends but if he and I were going to be together romantically he and I would have been together already. I was looking for something else.' I smiled. 'I found you.'

'And I found you, darling Vanny.'

Boris was playing much better than people expected. By the rest day, he himself had four points out of seven and he'd actually managed to beat one grandmaster. I was astonished at how well he was doing. The baseball cap had never come off, at least not while he was playing chess, although no doubt Boris took it off when he went to bed at night. I imagined so, anyway.

In Round Eight, I managed to scrape a draw against the brilliant young Dutch-Indian player Anish Giri. Then, in Round Nine, I was drawn against… Miklos.

Well, in my game against Miklos I had a major stroke of luck.

On move ten, to the amazement of me and everybody else who was watching the game, Miklos left his queen *en prise*, where it could be taken by a backwards move of my white-squared bishop.

It's known that, psychologically, many players, even grandmasters, miss backward captures by pieces because they are so used to the idea of the enemy piece coming towards them.

After I'd seen that Miklos had left his queen *en prise*, I tried to keep my face as expressionless as possible as one needs to in chess; after all you don't want to exult too openly. Also, I looked very hard at the position. Had he seen something amazing which I'd missed? But as far as I could see I hadn't missed anything.

Once I'd realised this, I decided it was time to take a bit of revenge. After all, he'd annoyed me with his arrogance and with his refusal to contact me after that strange night when I'd given myself to him in Odessa. So what I did was, rather than take his queen off the board immediately, I went for a walk outside, and on the way I found Hélène watching Tom's game and we both went outside into the bright sunshine and the humidity of New York as summer approached.

'What are you doing, Vanny?' she asked. 'You're still playing your game against Steiner, aren't you?'

'Yes I am. Haven't you seen what's happened?'

'No, I was watching Tom's game.'

'Miklos Steiner's left his queen *en prise*!' I knew that as she was French, I wouldn't need to explain to my darling what I meant by that.

'You mean… his queen can just be taken?'

'Yes, and it's my move next and I can grab it!'

'Then why don't you?'

'I will. But… I want to make him suffer, at least for a bit.'

'But why?'

I decided to tell her. After all, it had happened a long time ago, unlike the concert naughtiness with Tom and I couldn't imagine she'd be cross about it.

'Oh, I succumbed to him… I slept with him in Odessa last year. It was a terrible mistake. He's very arrogant and he thinks he's God's gift to women. He ignored me completely after what happened. He didn't even send me an email or anything. I don't mean I wanted him to… but you know what I mean.'

'Yes, I do, no-one wants to feel they've just been, well, screwed and then ignored.'

'Exactly. So he's going to suffer now. I've got plenty of time on my clock. Fancy a quick glass of iced tea?'

I didn't get back to my board for almost fifteen minutes. I had plenty of time left on my clock anyway.

When I finally returned to my table, Miklos was sitting there, frozen into a sort of catatonic crisis of stress. He'd certainly seen that his queen could be taken. If he'd had any sense maybe he would have vacated the board himself or perhaps resigned before I played the move. But I actually thought he imagined I was stupid enough not to have seen it.

You could bet the *spectators* had seen it. There was a totally perceptible nervous tension in the first three or four rows of seating and it spread even further back. Quite a few players had seen it too. Anyway, I sat down casually at my table carrying a can of unopened Tango orange that I'd brought with me, not because I wanted to drink it after the iced tea I'd had with Hélène but because I wanted to annoy Miklos a bit more by opening it slowly, which I did, letting the fizz and the orange scent sweeten the atmosphere between us.

Then I glanced at Miklos, met his gaze, smiled at the bastard and with my right hand, I *sloooowwwly* took his queen off the board with my bishop.

Miklos stared disgustedly at the board, as if a decrepit donkey had just that moment had a thoroughly good wee all over it. Then he gave me a look which somehow combined lust with embarrassment, humiliation and fury. About two seconds later he stopped his clock, took hold of my score sheet, signed it, signed his own score sheet and walked away from the board in the biggest huff I'd ever seen in my entire life.

Life can be tough, but sometimes there are sweet moments.

Six out of nine. One round to go, one more win and I would have my third GM norm and would be a grandmaster. The big question was, who would I play in the last round?

The answer was in the last round I was scheduled to play... Boris himself, who by now had reached six points out of nine, as I had.

By this point in the tournament the amazing play of the man who was sponsoring the event had, not surprisingly, caused abundant consternation among the players, the spectators, and the media too. There were some who speculated that he might have even been bribing some of his opponents to lose, but of course whereas in football you can probably arrange for a team to play rather too passively and allow an opposing team to win as a result of some bribe, that isn't easy to do in chess because you can see the score of the game afterwards and you can easily tell if someone is deliberately playing badly.

As Boris and I sat down to play, he beamed at me under his baseball cap, and then gave me a sort of thoughtful nod, as if this game we were about to play could be the only possible destiny between us.

'You've been doing wonderfully well,' I murmured to Boris as we waited, there in front of all the completely full rows of spectator seats, for the arbiter to tell the players playing White to start the clocks.

He smiled. 'I've been inspired, I think.'

I didn't ask him who he'd been inspired by because I was fairly sure I could guess. 'Yes, but your play's miraculous. How can you have improved so much in such a short time?'

He smiled. 'Vanny, I just do what any chess-player does: I use my grey cells.'

A few moments later the arbiter asked the players playing White to start their clocks. I was White, so I pressed the button in the middle of the clock which made my clock start and my time begin to reduce. I glanced at Boris, and then at the board, and I played pawn to king four. Boris still had his baseball cap on. He kept it on throughout the game.

So I was playing Boris Bogolyubov at last! I was playing the man who had confessed his love for me in what many would have considered the most romantic of letters, though perhaps the cheque the letter contained detracted from the romance a little, or - I don't know - maybe it added to it. Well, I had tried to divert his attentions from me by telling him, which was true, at least then, that I could only feel for a man if he could beat me at chess. I was pretty sure by now that this quirk no longer applied in my life, or at least I hadn't had much of an opportunity to test it recently, being with Hélène. It certainly didn't seem to apply as far as she was concerned. Well, OK, obviously she was a woman, but anyway I was pretty sure that, over the past few months, somewhere along the line, I'd lost my quirk.

Why on earth *was* Boris playing so well? After all, it had only been about five and a half months since I'd first met him, and he only had the rating of a reasonably good amateur. But no, he was playing like a top professional. What could have happened? I didn't know. All I did know, as my game with Boris proceeded, was that he was playing like a grandmaster. He'd met my first move, pawn to king four, with pawn to king four himself, so I decided to play the Bishop's Gambit, where after your king's bishop's pawn is taken by your opponent, you move your king's bishop out to queen's bishop four. Boris accepted the gambit and played a variation that is well known for being strong against this opening: he tried to hang on to the Black pawn on king's bishop four for as long as he could.

I tried everything, but he was getting the better of the position, which soon got incredibly complicated. We were both under some time pressure by now and my heart was beating so fast that I think if Hélène had been holding my hand as well it would have definitely exploded.

But while Boris played brilliantly, my experience and my ability to play quite well even when I'm under pressure began to give me an edge. Finally, on move forty-six, Boris used the index finger and thumb of his right hand to knock his king over.

He was the tournament sponsor, he was the boss, he was the billionaire behind it all. No-one applauded in the audience, perhaps fearful for what might happen if they did, and besides there were many other games still continuing. But what happened at that moment was that Boris stood up and he himself began to applaud *me*.

Once he did so, so did most of the spectators.

I stayed sitting down. My eyes were full of tears. I was a grandmaster at last.

I really was.

58

The audience went on applauding loudly and none of the arbiters said anything or did anything to stop it. Hélène came up to me and patted the top of my head in a way that was friendly but gave no definite clue about our relationship. Jaz was there as well; evidently she'd finished her own game. The applause continued, and I felt not on top of the world, but several thousand feet above it.

Later that day, after I'd been interviewed by about twenty journalists, and after I'd been awarded a cheque for $23,000 which included the woman's prize of $10,000 and my one-half share of fourth and fifth prize which I shared with David Howell, Boris invited me, Hélène, Tom, Sven and Jaz - he knew how precious these people were to me - to have supper with him in his private suite at the hotel.

Jaz had done pretty well at the tournament (and, for that matter, in her personal life), but had missed the international master norm by half a point, unfortunately. Sven had done rather badly, and had ended up with only three points out of ten.

Boris's penthouse suite was at the very top of the hotel. It had a fantastic view of the New York skyline and was full of beautiful antiques and blue and black Wedgwood jasperware, which Boris told us he especially liked.

Boris was still wearing the baseball cap. After we'd sat down in the dining room of his penthouse suite, Boris turned to me, Hélène, Sven, Jaz and Tom and said, with a smile that had a great deal of seriousness in it, 'tell me, friends, would you like to know something remarkable?'

I looked at Hélène and she looked at Tom and Sven and Jaz looked at Boris and then at me.

I decided that I was the spokesman for this particular moment and I said: 'I'm sure we all would.'

Boris nodded slowly and looked around at us all before saying:

'My friends, you are about to witness one of the most extraordinary developments in medical science.'

Only now, I mean only now for the first time in the daytime ever since the tournament had started, at least as far as I knew, Boris took his baseball cap off. He turned it inside out and showed it to us carefully. I noticed that on one side, the side nearest the visor, there was what looked like a roughly oblong-shaped piece of black graphite or something like that. It was, I would say, about two inches long and one-inch-wide and it was attached to the green fabric inside the baseball cap by what looked like some little plastic staples. I didn't know how comfortable they would be against his head but if they'd caused any discomfort he'd certainly not said anything about it.

'What's that, Mr Bogolyubov?' Tom asked.

'Oh, please, Tom, call me Boris. "Bogolyubov" is such a mouthful. But to answer your question, Tom, what you are looking at is the first-ever working prototype of the Adaptive Cognitive Enhancer.'

We all sat there, just looking at him.

'I'll tell you all more about it in a moment,' Boris said, 'but first, please, come on, everyone, let's eat. This food is rather splendid, don't you think and it will get cold even here on this lovely warm evening. I'll be mother, shall I? I know that's what people say in England in this situation.'

Boris and I served our friends from some of the many inviting and attractive looking dishes of Chinese food that had been brought in by hotel staff. Boris obviously knew what chess-players liked to eat. As Tom, Hélène, Jaz, Sven and I tucked in, Boris started telling us more about the invention, I was sure (though I didn't ask) that the invention was made, presumably, by the very company Tom and I spent so much effort trying to find out about.

'The Adaptive Cognitive Enhancer is the first inductive brain augmenter ever developed,' Boris said. 'Its development is based on extensive research which a medical research company I own has been undertaking, under my direction, for almost ten years.'

He looked around at us all. Tom was on my left, Hélène on my right, and I felt Tom gently touch my left ankle with his foot. I knew he was telling me he also suspected Henki Oy had been somehow responsible for the invention.

'For much of my life,' Boris went on, 'and certainly ever since I was a teenage boy, I've been fascinated with, among many things, how the brain works. I am especially interested in how the brain stores skills in chemical form.'

Boris nodded slowly. 'Chess is an excellent field to use to study the new and fascinating field of cognitive enhancement. Why? Because chess is independent of language. My organisation Henki has found that studying how the brains of chess players work is an extremely interesting and rewarding field, precisely because it is a non-linguistic ability. Yet despite literally hundreds of man-years of work at my medical research company, we haven't found any way of specifically inserting new knowledge into the brain. That appears to be something that is impossible with our current technology. Also, of course, it would require some kind of invasive physical interface into the brain and that would be extremely risky. When we acquire skills by a natural process they go into the brain via our eyes or ears and are converted into knowledge in some process of digitisation that is, surely, God-like in its complexity. The adaptive cognitive enhancer doesn't need to work like that. It is altogether a much more simple device.'

'Its initials spell ACE,' Tom murmured, saying the word 'ace', rather than the names of the three letters.

'Precisely, Tom,' Boris said. 'They do. And that is the brand-name under which we are planning to market it when it is perfected. The ACE,' (he said 'ace'), 'is powered by a tiny battery which will provide close to a thousand hours of use. The ACE works by an inductive process that is a carefully guarded commercial secret. The ACE does not, as I say, insert knowledge into the brain - I still had to do lots of work to learn openings and new techniques - but what it does is it gives a higher level of energy to the thinking there and it therefore makes the player significantly better at chess.'

Boris fell silent for a moment before adding:

'The ACE is at present only something to help chess players, but I've no doubt at all that it could be developed to help everybody, including people with brain damage or who are born with intellectual impairment. In the world of sports, its applications will be prodigious, for at the highest level of performance in sports, the mind is more likely to produce that all-important incremental edge over one's high-level rivals than the body. You see now,' and he glanced around at us all again, 'why I said it was a most remarkable invention. Now, let's finish this delicious dinner and afterwards, I would like to take you all for a ride over New York. I propose we fly from the helipad here above the hotel out to Long Island, where I have a house and we have some music there and maybe some dancing, and I will fly you back later on. The helicopter we shall fly in is a model that I introduced to Vanny when we met in Hastings last winter: it's an eight-seater Brewster Speedbird BS9. I have one in Britain and also one here in New York. Don't worry, I don't intend to drink any alcohol whatsoever before the flight. I am a fully qualified helicopter pilot, by the way. Oh, and I have asked my bodyguard Alexander to join us on the flight.'

5 9

About an hour later, Boris led us all onto the hotel's rooftop heliport for the short flight to his home on Long Island. I was by now happier than I had been for a long time; the lovely Chinese supper, and two excellent bottles of Chinese beer had contributed to that, certainly, but mostly I think I was so happy because I was so much enjoying the company of the people I most loved in all the world, apart from mum and dad, anyway.

It was dark, but nice and warm though still pretty humid, when we emerged on the rooftop, though there were floodlights to illuminate the rooftop itself and the helicopter too.

I recognised the Brewster Speedbird the moment I saw her. She was a beautiful red colour, just like her counterpart had been at Hastings, except that here at night, in the bright floodlights that chased away the late spring darkness, the Brewster Speedbird actually looked brighter and more glamorous than she had in Hastings, under the dull grey daylight. A strange, but perhaps not completely weird, thought struck me - a thought I'd never had in Hastings - that the Brewster Speedbird was somehow feminine rather than masculine in her sleek beauty and power. *Maybe that's why Boris likes this model so much,* I thought.

Boris went up to her and unlocked her on the pilot side. 'The flight will only last about twenty minutes, and then I will have the great pleasure of welcoming you all to my home on Long Island. Ah, Alexander,' Boris added, in the same breath, 'good evening.'

'Good evening, sir,' said his bodyguard Alexander, in heavily accented English. Hélène, Tom, Jaz, Sven and I all turned round and set eyes on the bodyguard, whom I had seen before of course on that fateful day in Hastings but whom they, to my knowledge, hadn't. I felt momentarily a little scared at seeing him, as I always did, but that's was a rational enough emotion, because even before what happened happened, he was pretty scary. He was so huge, and the very formality of the large black suit he wore made him look even scarier.

Boris opened the door on the passenger side. 'Alexander, please sit next to me. I suggest Hélène and Vanny sit behind us, and then Tom, Sven and Jaz can sit wherever they like in the other four seats. Whoever takes the seat at the back will have the privilege of stretching out, if they wish!'

Inside, after he opened the front door on the passenger side, the helicopter was done out beautifully in beige leather and smelt of fresh leather inside which believe me, I think is the most luxurious smell it's possible to imagine. Alexander, tall, massive and gruff as always, got in the left seat next to Boris on the right at the pilot controls. Hélène sat behind Alexander, I was behind Boris, and Tom, Sven and Jaz organised themselves with Sven behind me, Jaz on his left and Tom at the back, with the privileged spare seat.

'You will all find headphones on the little shelf in front of you,' Boris said. 'Please put them on, as the noise of the rotors makes any other kind of communication other than through headphones impossible.'

We all quickly started putting our headphones on. As we were, Boris turned the ignition switch and the hugely powerful gas turbine engine started revving and within barely ten seconds the sudden oscillation of the rooftop lights told me that the overhead rotors (and doubtless the anti-torque tail rotor too) were moving. Another ten seconds or so, and we all had our headphones on. Boris glanced round to make sure that we did, then he faced forwards again and took hold of the cyclic control rod, which governs the angle of attack, or feathering, of the overhead rotors and so makes the helicopter rise or fall. At once, the large helicopter went up very rapidly into the night air.

I'd already noticed in Hastings that when you're in a helicopter everything seems to be happening much faster than in normal life, which is partly because everything *is* happening faster than in normal life, the helicopter being such a rapid, and of course incredibly unnatural, form of transport.

'We don't need to go out to sea to get to Long Island,' Boris explained through his headphones, 'but I think you might enjoy seeing the lights of New York from out over the water. We will then turn and head for my home.'

Soon we were climbing fast; there was no cloud cover at all and I could see over Boris's shoulder that the altimeter was at just under three thousand feet. Very soon we were well over the sea and the view of the skyline of New York's dozens of skyscrapers and the myriad lights in pretty much every colour known to the prism was stunning and awe-inspiring. Boris, of course, was focused on the piloting, but he kept us informed of what he was doing.

'I hope you're all enjoying the flight. I'm taking her up to about three and half thousand feet. We're around twenty-five miles from the coast now and I'll take us to about thirty miles out, then I'll turn and head for the south side of Long Island and fly along the coast about five miles out before heading to the helipad in my grounds. My helipad there is well-lit by the way so don't worry, I'll be able to find it even at night.'

Botis had just finished saying that, and I was wishing Lottie was there with us to enjoy this, when something very very awful happened.

60

What happened was that Alexander suddenly turned to the right and gave Boris a dreadful punch on his left temple.

Boris cried out with agony. I could hear his cry on my headphones but that was the only noise he made. He slumped forward over the helicopter controls. At once, Alexander, that bear of a man, got hold of Boris by the scruff of his neck and pulled him to the left into Alexander's own seat while Alexander quickly scrambled to change places. Boris didn't move.

I shouted into my headphones *'Alexander, what are you doing?'* But all Alexander did was glance behind at me briefly and say, in his guttural Russian-accented English, *'Shut up, bitch,'* before taking over the helicopter's controls.

I froze. I glanced behind me at the horrified faces of Hélène, Tom, Jaz and Sven. They all stared at me and I stared back. What could we do?

'Listen,' Alexander said, 'you're all friends I think, so say goodbye to each other because this is the end of everything, at least for you.'

'What... what do you mean?' I shouted.

'What do I mean, bitch? I mean that I'm a businessman like this idiot who is about to die with all of you and so as a businessman I work for whoever pays me the most. Bogolyubov pays me to investigate some people who want him dead and I find out more about what they're doing. I meet them and they offer to pay me ten times what he pays me. So I ask you, what would you do? But don't talk to me, talk to your friends. Say goodbye to all of them, say goodbye to each other.'

I didn't know what to say. I just watched Alexander as he reached down below the seat on his left, the seat Boris was slumped on, and grabbed what looked to me, at first, like a rucksack. Removing his hands from the helicopter controls for a moment, he quickly strapped the rucksack onto his back. I suddenly realised two things: that there must be a parachute in the rucksack, and that Alexander must have put it there earlier without Boris knowing. But I still didn't know what was going on.

Then Hélène glanced at me; *'he has a parachute,'* she whispered to me in English.

Alexander said nothing.

We all still just sat there. I felt too stunned to do anything. The whole experience felt completely surreal, but perhaps that's what life feels like when you're very likely soon to be grotesquely murdered. I hadn't even known Alexander could speak English as well as he could. I glanced, horrified, at Hélène, who reached out her right hand and touched my face.

'Je pense que quand nous serons plus proches de la côte, il sautera de l'hélicoptère et lorsque nous nous écraserons dans la mer, personne ne saura qu'il n'est pas mort avec nous,' Hélène said, calmly, and in a level voice, and in French.

'What's the bitch saying?' Alexander demanded.

So he couldn't speak French. But I very quickly pieced together in my mind what Hélène had said just now, which was: *I think that when we are close to the coast he is going to jump out of the helicopter and when we crash into the sea no-one will know that he hasn't died with us.*

I glanced at her. *Oh my God she's right, oh my God she's right,* I thought. *Some people who want Boris dead must have bought Alexander and after he parachutes out and swims ashore and the helicopter crashes and Boris dies, no-one will know Alexander didn't die in the crash.*

In a strange, rapid, quick-fire of thoughts, I realised I was close to a region which Lottie already inhabited. Perhaps in a sense I was already dead. I wondered what it would feel like as the helicopter smashed into the sea.

I saw Hélène glance at me and then at Tom, and then at Jaz and Sven. She did all that, this woman whom I'd met completely by accident when visiting Dad in Monte Carlo and who had entranced me ever since. She glanced at us all and gave a small and barely noticeable nod as if nodding to herself.

And then she moved.

I'd never seen anyone move so beautifully or so strongly or with such purpose. Hélène reached forward and across and like an agile fairy grabbing hold of a giant, put her left forearm around Alexander's neck, and then somehow used her right bicep to press her forearm inside the crook of her right bicep and she yanked Alexander's head, shoulders and body backwards as if the huge bodyguard had been made of balsa wood.

I'd never seen such amazing wiry strength and decisiveness displayed by such a wiry and slender woman. Hélène just kept Alexander's neck in her grasp and she tugged him backwards and now Sven propelled himself over Hélène's seat and, canny Norwegian that he is, reached inside Alexander's jacket and found a shoulder-holster and a large black automatic pistol which Sven immediately drew and pointed at Alexander. I suddenly remembered that Sven had been in the Norwegian army. I know that in most European countries men need to do national service. Anyway, in the incredible confusion inside the cockpit, Hélène and Sven had somehow managed to overpower Alexander.

'He can obviously fly the helicopter,' Tom barked, seeing that Sven had Alexander's gun (I presumed in New York getting a gun licence was a lot easier than in England). 'Make him land the helicopter or we're all going to die!'

Hélène experimentally relaxed her fierce grip on the big man's neck, but the moment she did he started emitting Russian swear words (I assumed) and lashed out with his fists and only just missed Hélène. She instantly tightened her grip again, which at once subdued him. *Sacré bleu,* she knew what she was doing!

The helicopter was still flying levelly towards Manhattan. I realised Alexander must have switched it to autopilot. It would fly, but it wouldn't land unless someone landed it. Tom glanced at Sven; 'you can't fly a helicopter, can you?'

'Tom, no, I'm sorry, I can't,' Sven said, shaking his head quickly.

Tom glanced at me. '*I don't suppose… I mean, the helicopter website you visit, can you fly this bloody thing, do you think? Will you at least have a try? Please don't say no.*'

I made no answer to him. But, inspired by Hélène's wiry agility and somehow feeling that as everything else felt so nightmarish I might as well become part of the nightmare myself, I scrambled over Boris's prostrate form and into the passenger seat which Alexander had vacated. I felt a bit tiddly from the beers but only a bit and the thought flooded into my mind that maybe my being tiddly was giving me some extra courage; I didn't know. Hélène still had Alexander in her grasp, I wondered if she was actually going to kill him. At that moment, I didn't care if she did. I quickly switched the Brewster Speedbird out of autopilot, felt the pedals with my feet and experimentally let me feel my control of the yaw and then, using all I'd learnt from the helicopter flying simulator website. I glanced at the artificial horizon and saw that our altitude was three thousand four hundred feet. I opened the voice channel to New York Air Traffic Control. *'Mayday! Mayday! I am a non-registered pilot attempting to fly this Brewster Speedbird BS9. Our pilot is unconscious. I am heading for the south side of Manhattan and will try to land us safely. Please tell me what altitude to fly at. And please say something encouraging!'*

Almost at once, a reassuring American voice - a man with a lovely New York accent – said, *'thank you, we have your transponder details already and are tracking you. I'm fetching a colleague who's a trained helicopter pilot. Can you fly at all?'*

'Only on a helicopter flight website.'

'Oh, Jesus, I mean, fine, don't panic.'

'I'm trying not to.'

'Can you come down to a thousand feet? We're clearing the airspace in front of you and will guide you to an emergency landing in Battery Park.'

'Is there grass there?' It was a pretty stupid question, I know.

'Yes, there is.'

'Good,' I said, only now sort of realising just how utterly scared I really felt and how silly the question was.

Somehow, I didn't panic.

Somehow, I carefully used the cyclic and the collective controls together to bring us down to the thousand feet I'd been told to use as our altitude, and then I followed the very precise instructions given to me by someone called 'Al' - the trained helicopter pilot whose name I later learned was Al Groman and is one of my Facebook friends now and who is in line for a New York City honour for what he did to help me.

I can't fully explain what the next ten minutes or so of my life were like. They were the most terrifying and yet the most important ten minutes of my life so far, because if I'd not got so many things right as I managed to (many of them with Al's help), they would have been the last ten minutes of my life, and of Hélène's life and Tom's and Sven's and Jaz's and Boris's and of course of that monster Alexander's life too.

During those ten minutes my mind went into... some weird overdrive like the one we'd all been talking about in connection with Boris's invention, and I didn't even have Boris's baseball cap on. I felt totally, totally scared and terrified of dying. But inwardly something else was happening: inside I felt calm and collected and confident that I knew what I was doing. When all is said and done, a helicopter is easy enough to fly if you know what you're doing, and thanks to the hours I'd spent on the helicopter website, I did. Yet it was all somehow a daze, and what's strange is that while I can remember almost all the events of that day and evening really well, when I think of the ten minutes when I was actually flying the helicopter, I can't remember anything very clearly, just being strangely calm inside, and also dazed.

I still don't really know how I managed to get us down in Battery Park safely (though on the way there was lots of juddering and once a very alarming nosedive that I fortunately managed to correct by reducing airspeed and using the collective control to lift the nose again) but somehow I did.

It was a very bumpy landing, and both the skids got damaged. But I got us down. Somehow. No, I'll never understand it, really. Maybe when the Angel of Death leaps into our amidst, we sometimes find resources we never knew we had, and manage to chase that foulest of angels away.

I landed really close to the edge of Battery Park; I mean, I wanted to land just as soon as I could. Of course, Al had told the police - and the ambulance services - and when we landed there were at least six police cars, and three ambulances. What however, I hadn't anticipated, as we finally landed and as Hélène released Alexander from her grip - which she told me later is called rear naked choke, though you don't need to be naked to inflict it - she explained she'd been careful to let him breathe, though after what happened when she tried to release him she was careful to keep him unconscious until we landed - was that the police car which first drove up to the helicopter would contain just about the last person on the planet I expected it to contain.

61

That person was The Three Vs.

He wasn't in his weird black outfit any more but wearing a light blue suit and a red tie.

What The Three Vs was doing there I couldn't imagine, but my concern right now was only for Boris, who was in a dreadfully bad way. I raced to the ambulance and cried out to the medics to please God come and help Boris.

They sprang into action and it warmed my heart to see the four medics, two young men and two young women, all in smart green uniforms. I very quickly showed them Boris and they attended to him and got him into the ambulance. I told them I was coming with them; they said sorry, that wasn't possible.

I said I was coming with them.

Then The Three Vs showed them some identification and told them to let me into the ambulance. 'I'll come too,' he said. Meanwhile the police had arrested Alexander, who was still groggy, but who didn't put up any resistance, which wasn't surprising really as he had four police pistols trained on him. I called out to Hélène, Tom, Jaz and Sven that I was going with Boris and then I was inside the ambulance with The Three Vs and we kept well out of the way while they attended to Boris, whose head was all bloody. He was unconscious. The ambulance, its siren howling, raced to the nearest hospital and got there in only about five minutes. I found out later the hospital was in Greenwich Village. The Three Vs and I said nothing while we in the ambulance, but when we reached the hospital and more medics had taken Boris into the building, The Three Vs and I followed and were asked by a doctor who wore a white coat, and to whom The Three Vs had shown his ID, to follow him.

'The police radioed me to tell me what happened,' the doctor said. 'You can both wait in my own room; you'll be more comfortable there than in the public waiting-room.'

'Thanks,' The Three Vs said.

'Will Boris be all right?' I gasped to the doctor.

'I don't know. He has a fractured skull. We'll do everything we can.'

A few moments later we were in his large, comfortable consulting-room: a desk, chairs, a couch, curtains on an overhead rail, bookshelves with medical books in them, a smell of surgical spirit. Another doctor's surgery with the Angel of Death lurking nearby. *Oh God, don't take Boris, not Boris.*

The doctor left us, and then it was just me in there with The Three Vs.

62

The Three Vs glanced at me and said, in perfectly fluent English and in a New York accent that featured only a light Russian accent, not the manic strong one I'd always associated with him: 'You really landed that helicopter, Ivana?'

I was pretty sure that line wasn't in *V for Vendetta*.

'Yes. But Air Traffic Control helped me.'

'All the same, what an achievement! You're a heroine.' He stuck out his right hand. 'Please to meet you. I'm Vladimir Osadchuk.'

I shook his hand. His shake was firm, yet also gentle. 'Not Vladimir Vladimirovich Vladimirov?' I asked.

'Ah, no. That was, my cover name. I was born and bred in Manhattan, on the Upper West Side. I work for the FBI.'

'You do?'

'Yes. My cover's been that of a psychotic chess-player who's obsessed with the movie *V for Vendetta*.'

I smiled faintly. 'Oh, I see. Am I allowed to ask you what or who you've been investigating?'

'Sure. The arrests have been made so it's all going to be public knowledge anyhow in the next twenty-four hours. I've been involved for more than a year investigating what, for want of a better expression, I'll describe as an international drugs ring that infiltrated the chess world and whose members have been using the easy foreign travel that chess players enjoy to do just about anything they want to do. Miklos Steiner is one of several suspected perpetrators we've arrested. So is his manager.'

'You've arrested Miklos?'

'Yes.'

'But why would Miklos get involved with this? He's well paid as a chess-player.'

'Yes, Ivana, but drug smuggling pays better. I heard on the grapevine, but to my great regret too late to stop it, about Mr Bogolyubov's bodyguard Alexander Brobotnik having been bought by some very bad guys to dispose of Mr Bogolyubov so they can muscle in on his business interests. Boris is a very decent guy. You saved his everyone's life, Ivana.'

'Yes, but I couldn't have done it if my friend Hélène hadn't incapacitated Alexander.'

Vladimir Osadchuk nodded. 'I know. You're both heroines. As for me, I'm glad to be able to meet you both without having to pose as a psycho.'

6 3

Over the next six days Boris nearly died.

64

I told the hospital I wasn't going to leave until he came out alive, and they let me stay in a small guest room in the hospital. I wanted to be close by Boris.

Fortunately he was strong and he had great care at the hospital, and by the following Tuesday, the hospital medics told me he was out of danger, though he would be staying in hospital for at least another fortnight.

'Ivana,' Boris whispered, when I went to see him on the Thursday.

There was no-one but us in his private room at the hospital. The top of Boris's head was bandaged, like Basil Fawlty's in The Germans episode, only this injury wasn't even slightly funny.

I sat down on the chair next to his bed. 'Boris,' was all I said.

'I… I know you've been close by me all the time my life's been in danger. That means a great deal to me.'

'Dear Boris, it was the least I could do.'

'Thank you. I suppose I really can't change your mind on the marriage front?'

I smiled. I didn't want to answer him directly. 'Boris, right now, I want to put my personal life on the back-burner, and make sense of everything that's happened to me. But… I do rather love you, Boris, and I hope you'll always let me know you.'

'Dear Vanny, you can be sure of that.'

He was silent for maybe about a minute, then he said: 'Please tell me: why didn't the helicopter crash into the sea and kill us all?'

So I told him.

After I had, he said: 'Vanny, you and Hélène saved my life. And Alexander, he is arrested, then?'

'Yes. He's been charged with attempted murder.'

Boris nodded. 'Good. He deserves it. I still hardly believe he betrayed me as he did. I had employed him for three years. I paid him a high salary, and gave him many benefits. But enough of him. Well, I am certainly glad I suggested that helicopter flight website to you.'

He lay back on his pillows for some time. I said nothing. Then he sat up again, rather abruptly, and began speaking: 'As I said, you and Hélène saved my life. Anything you both want, and I mean anything, I will give you. How about a private yacht in which you can both roam the world?'

'That's very kind of you,' I murmured. I couldn't help suddenly thinking of Dad's now abandoned yacht the *Ivana* and wondering what would happen to it. 'I'll... I'll tell Hélène what you said. As for me, I don't want a yacht, Boris, not even a really lovely one, as I'm sure it would be if you gave it to me. All I really want to do is to play chess, and spend time with the people I care about, which of course includes you. And also, before too long, but only when I know you really are going to be all right, I'd like to go home.'

Boris smiled. 'Vanny, as I'm sure you can imagine I always hate saying goodbye to you, but if you want to go home, please feel free to do so. My business interests will take me before long to London, anyway. So, yes, go home, my dear friend, and I will see you before long.'

I smiled. 'Only when I know you've fully recovered, Boris dearest.'

65

I didn't go home for another two weeks. I went to visit Boris every day. Tom, Hélène, Jaz and Sven all stayed in New York too. I told Boris that they didn't want to go home without me. He arranged for his hotel to give us all free accommadation and meals.

After the fortnight I was told Boris was out of danger.

The night before we all flew home I mentioned Boris's offer to Hélène. She said she certainly didn't want a yacht but would have a think. In the morning she said, if Boris really did want to be as generous as this, perhaps he could buy a small hotel somewhere in London, and give her half of it and keep the other half and she would manage it and do her best to make it a success. I told Boris what Hélène wanted. He agreed immediately.

I was, in fact, pleased that she was using the opportunity to show Boris, and me, and herself, that she could be successful in her career. I loved that she'd factored a share for Boris in the fruits of any success she won.

I myself, though, was quite sure Boris had done more than enough for me already.

We all arrived back in Britain on the morning of Saturday June the thirtieth, at breakfast time. I don't know if you've ever flown from New York back to Britain overnight and arrived in the early morning. You don't usually get too much sleep on the flight home, partly because sleeping brilliantly on airplanes isn't too easy anyway, and of course your body's on New York time.

I had maybe three hours' sleep; I sat by the window this time with Hélène next to me and Tom a few seats ahead of us in the aisle, but not near Sven and Jaz who were on the other side of the plane, which is where their seating had been allocated. I wondered if there was something symbolic in where Tom was sitting now even though his seat had been allocated by the airline. I wondered whether he was in a way sitting there so he would not be drawn into temptation with Hélène even though I still didn't know what had really happened between them. But I had my theory. I hadn't ever mentioned my theory to Hélène, though. After all, how could I possibly be entitled to complain if my theory was true?

The plan was that Sven would be staying until the following Monday with Jaz in the flat on Churchill Gardens and of course that was where Hélène and I lived, at least for the time being, anyway. So we all got a cab back to Churchill Gardens from Heathrow.

The cab dropped Hélène, Jaz, Sven and me off at the flat on Churchill Gardens at about eleven in the morning. Tom took the cab on to his flat on Gloucester Road. After Hélène and I had snoozed for a couple of hours I got up and had a shower and Hélène and I went to a Pizza Express on the Earls Court Road for lunch.

During lunch I got a text from Tom suggesting that Hélène and I might like to go over to his house for dinner that evening and over the pizza I mentioned Tom's text to Hélène and she said it was a great idea.

As for what had happened during the helicopter flight, this was now very much public knowledge. In New York I'd got quite a few phone calls from journalists around the world; goodness knew how they managed to get my mobile number but they did. I also got plenty of emails too. They all wanted to talk to Hélène too but she said she didn't want to talk to anybody and I could perfectly understand it. I wasn't very keen about talking about it myself but quite a lot of newspaper articles appeared in the press in the US, in England and in other countries, though Hélène had managed to fend off all the requests for TV interviews with me and her.

'Alexander was going to kill us so I did what I had to do,' she'd said to me quietly on the flight home. That was just like her, modest and unassuming but potent in ways that she had to be.

I felt subdued and also felt somehow that I wanted a change and sort of a rest from everything. So that afternoon I sent a message to the organisers of the Australian tournament saying that I definitely wanted to play in the event, which started on Saturday, the fourth of August.

That afternoon I decided how I'd like to get to Australia, and sent an email to see if it could be arranged. An hour or so later I heard back. It turned out that it could.

66

I wasn't sure how I felt about the prospective evening with Tom, especially as I had a feeling it was likely to turn into a night with him.

Hélène and I got there at around seven o'clock. I felt that Hélène and Tom had recovered more quickly from the dreadful experience in the helicopter than I had. I was still thinking about it most of the time and I felt that it had somehow changed me forever.

But we had a jolly enough dinner. Tom had made spag bol for us and we had it with a very nice Australian Shiraz I'd bought. I didn't tell Hélène or Tom anything about my plans to go to Australia, though. For dessert we ate a delicious lemon meringue pie which Tom had bought that afternoon from Waitrose.

By the end of the meal we were all pretty drunk because we'd had not only the bottle of Shiraz but two bottles of Merlot which Tom had in his cupboard.

I was glad to be drunk. It was a relief to reduce my sense of memory and reality for a while. Of course I was delighted about being a grandmaster now and at having survived what happened and knowing that Boris was going to be all right. But I also knew I badly needed a change. Yes, I needed a change and I'd made my plans, but I didn't reveal them to Hélène and Tom.

After dinner we were all nicely sloshed and we went to sit in the living room on Tom's sofa and he put on a DVD of a movie called *Bound*. In case you haven't seen it, this is basically about two gay women who get the better of a mafia thug. I won't say any more in case you want to see it. The movie's frequently incredibly sexy and I found Hélène starting to kiss me and then, to my mild drunken surprise she kissed Tom and one thing lead to another and we basically all ended up naked in Tom's double bed.

Tom told Hélène and me, in a calm, drunk kind of way, that he had a fantasy of wrestling with Hélène because he'd been so impressed by what happened in the helicopter and he wanted her to use her jiu-jitsu on him (I'd told him subsequently that it was jiu-jitsu she'd used on Alexander). I was puzzled, intrigued and excited by what it would be like to watch them both wrestle and also why Tom was so keen for this to happen in front of me.

Well, I watched them wrestle. They were both only wearing their undergarments when they did – that is, Tom had just his black underpants on and Hélène her white panties and white bra. I enjoyed watching them but I was expecting to feel more excited by what I was seeing than I did. It didn't feel wrong; it felt right and fun and sexy and friendly but I just somehow felt that this was not really what I wanted to watch. But Tom, I could tell by the visible pressure against the inside of his pants, was having a fabulous time. Even though actually I didn't feel all that sexy - I was still pretty traumatised by what had happened in New York, I joined in with the wrestling after a while and actually it all got very intense and very exciting. I suppose at some time in the past I might have thought this was something really wonderful and amazing to do, with my girl lover and former male lover in the same bed and yes I suppose it *was* exciting and presently I made love with Hélène and then afterwards with Tom and then Tom asked us both to torture him and we did, Hélène and I grabbing him and forcing him down onto the bed while we tickled his feet and pinched him and did all sorts of other things to him.

By this time there really was a sense of no holds being barred and anything going and I made love with Hélène again while Tom sat on the edge of the bed and watched us, then finally... he made love with Hélène in front of me. It was very weird, sexy and disturbing, seeing him go in and out of her. Tom wore a different condom each time he made love with one of us.

'I'm not suddenly straight, Vanny,' Hélène whispered hotly to me after Tom had, very obviously, made her come at least twice. They then made love again, this time with Hélène on top. Watching Tom and Hélène both completely naked and she astride him and he inside her was a pretty mind-blowing sight. I was puzzled, though, that I didn't feel more jealous.

I don't exactly know what time we all went to sleep, though it was probably around two or three in the morning. It felt gratifying that Hélène slept in my arms rather than Tom's, though Tom was sleeping nearby and he looked incredibly happy, which was hardly surprising, I suppose. And then we slept the sleep of the sexually exhausted and the drunk and I was sort of happy but actually I felt, even more strongly, that I wanted to get away for a longish while.

Well, I was going to.

67

When I woke up at about, I suppose, seven o'clock or so on that Sunday morning, the first of July, I felt surprisingly wide-awake and sober. I glanced at Hélène and Tom. They were both still asleep and sleeping very close to each other.

Before I left the flat I wrote a short note on a piece of scrap paper I found on Tom's desk. I put the note on the bed next to Tom. My note said: *I'm going abroad for about six weeks. Have a great time you two and do everything you want to do. I understand, and I won't be jealous. I love you both very much. Vanny xxxxxx.*

Six kisses. Three each.

I didn't bother showering; I just left and I walked home and I had a shower there and I finished packing my case; I'd done most of my packing the previous evening without letting Hélène know that I was. I'd packed in Lottie's room.

I was planning to embark on the voyage to Australia the following morning from Felixstowe. The ship would leave at nine o'clock, with the tide, so obviously I couldn't travel to Felixstowe the following morning and expect to get the ship. So after my shower and after I'd finished the packing, not forgetting my passport, I left the flat and got a cab all the way to Liverpool Street Station and from there I caught a train to Felixstowe. I planned to find a B&B or a small hotel in Felixstowe.

When I was on the train my mobile buzzed with a call from Hélène. There weren't any other passengers close by me, but I cupped my left hand around my mouth and the phone, and talked quietly, to keep the conversation absolutely as private as I possibly could.

'Vanny, where are you?'

'I'm on a train. I'm going abroad tomorrow.'

'Yes, I saw the note. Where are you going?'

'To a tournament in Australia. I'm going by ship. It'll take me about four weeks to get there. I know you can't come because of sorting out your work in this country and the hotel but in any case I think you should spend time with Tom and see how you get on. I know you like him and I think you probably made love with him while we were in New York, and maybe also on the plane when we flew there.'

I fell silent. Hélène didn't say anything.

'Anyway, if you did,' I went on, surprised at how calm I felt 'don't worry. You've not done anything worse to me than I did to you. In any case, Tom's a really sweet guy and I think you get on better with him than even I did.'

I was sort of hoping she might deny this but what she said, quietly, was, 'You're right about me liking Tom. I do. I've never felt anything for a man before, I mean never but I feel a lot for him and I really loved you watching us making love last night.'

'I know you did. I could tell. Well, it was very exciting.'

'And I loved making love with you, too. I love you too, Vanny.'

'I know, and I love you but I need to go away by myself and sort of digest everything that's happened over the past eight months or so. Also, I think last night was amazing and I really enjoyed it but... well, it's not actually the kind of personal life that I want. I want to be with one person and get to know them. For all I know it might still be you, Hélène, darling. But really you need to... well, I suppose you see how you get on with Tom. I won't be away forever, only until around the third week of August. The tournament starts on August the fourth and it lasts for a couple of weeks. I plan to fly back.'

'I love you, Vanny, you know I do and I love the way you know me and the way you care about me and the way you care about Tom and how you want me to see how Tom and I get on.'

'Yes, I do want you to do that.'

'But you don't hate me?'

'Of course I don't hate you, I love you and I'll keep on loving you but sometimes in life we need to explore what being with someone we're interested in is like and the only way to explore that is simply to do it. That's the only way.'

There was quite a long pause, then she said:

'I think you're right.'

It was a while before either of us hung up but then I decided that I would before she did and I did, after about a minute of wondrous romantic silence between us.

I sat back in my seat on the train from Liverpool Street to Felixstowe and just thought about everything.

I thought about Lottie and about Hélène and The Three Vs and about Tom and Sven and Jaz.

And Boris?

Well, in fact, I haven't quite finished telling you about him and me.

68

The next morning, Monday, July the second, I set sail aboard *The Antipodean*. It was a huge container ship, with a weight of close to sixty thousand tonnes, which actually, I knew, made it bigger than *Titanic*. When fully laden, *The Antipodean* would, as I'd discovered from its website, accommodate more than 12,000 containers.

There were eight other passengers apart from me, and we all had our own spacious and comfy cabins in the passenger corridor. My room was not unlike a luxurious hotel room, and had satellite Wi-Fi and electric sockets and a nice en suite bathroom and a double bed, though I didn't have any plans of making use of that item of furniture other than for sleeping.

The other passengers consisted of three elderly married British couples, a middle-aged Japanese businessman who didn't seem to speak much English, and a lady American travel writer called Shanee in her thirties who, I discovered on the first evening when I sat next to her at dinner, was researching an article about being a passenger on a container ship.

Shanee told me that the reason why container ships took on passengers wasn't for the money (I could believe this; the voyage had cost me £3,250 and I didn't imagine the passengers' fares made any significant difference to the revenue of a ship carrying 12,000 containers) but because the crew liked to have new people to talk to.

I hadn't been on the ship long enough at that point to know whether this was true, but in due course I found that Shanee and I became quite popular among the crew as people to talk to, but that the crew didn't seem especially interested in talking to the other passengers. I didn't have much to do with my fellow passengers apart from Shanee, but she and I quickly became friends, and usually had at least one meal together every day. It was lovely to have a new friendship free of any complications; Shanee had a husband and two children back in San Francisco and missed them a great deal and Skyped them every day.

Otherwise, when I wasn't talking to Shanee or to the crew, I kept myself to myself. I wasn't lonely, anyway. I had my phone and the ship's satellite Wi-Fi and my laptop and I was starting to write about the past six months. I'd decided to call what I was writing *The Mating Game*.

We had five twenty-four-hour unloading and loading stops scheduled for the voyage - at Cadiz in Spain, Athens, Port Suez, Mumbai and Jakarta, before our arrival at the Port of Melbourne in Australia. I discovered when I was planning the voyage that we would arrive at these stopover destinations in the morning and leave mid-morning the following day.

When I boarded the ship I met Captain Graeme Boxall, which seemed to me a highly appropriate surname for a captain of a container ship. I even wondered whether his surname had been a factor in his career advancement. That first evening on board, Captain Boxall invited the passengers to join him for dinner at his table on Saturday evening, but it was still some days before Saturday and in fact our first port of call was Cadiz, which we were scheduled to reach on Thursday morning and would depart from late on Friday morning.

Soon after I got back to my cabin after a lovely lunchtime chicken curry on the Tuesday, my second day at sea, (I learned that there's a tradition on board ship that the lunch menu option includes a curry), I saw I had an email from Boris.

My dear Vanny, I hope this finds you well. I am very pleased to tell you that I was discharged from hospital on

*Saturday. I am flying home to Moscow later today. How
are you and Hélène and Tom? Are you in England? It
would be lovely to see you, I have received your email about
Hélène's request. Thank you for letting me have her email
address. I have passed it on to my operations team who will
communicate with Hélène direct about this matter and
make the arrangements.*

*I am at present in my suite at the hotel and I thought
that before I started packing I would email you.*

I miss you, Vanny. Thank you for giving me life.

Dear Boris

*I am SO glad you've been discharged from hospital.
My dear friend, one of the proudest things I've ever done is
save your life, but please you don't need to keep thanking
me; I am just so pleased you are well again.*

*Guess where I am? Well, you probably can't so I'll tell
you. I'm a passenger on a cargo ship, 'The Antipodean', on
its way to Australia. I'm alone (well, I mean apart from
a small number of other passengers, the captain, the crew
and 12,000 cargo containers). I'm heading for Sydney to
play in a tournament there. We left Felixstowe yesterday.
We have some 24-hour stops planned, so it should be an
interesting voyage.*

Actually I miss you too, Boris.

Vanny.

*Oh, and I think it's time you got two kisses, so here
you are:*

Xx

I knew it must have been quite early in the morning in New York. I had a feeling Boris would reply to this email pretty quickly, and he did. Men, even billionaires, are often pretty predictable, if they really like you. The truth was, though, that I *wanted* him to reply promptly, and I *wanted* him to ask the question he did, in fact, ask.

Hi again Vanny

Is a humble supplicant allowed to ask you where the first stop-off point is?

Xx

I smiled and right away replied:

It's Cadiz in Spain. We dock there this Thursday morning and stay until Friday morning. Xx

69

'Cadiz was the port from where the Spanish once set out to conquer the world,' Boris said.

I didn't doubt it, but on the other hand it wasn't clear to me why anyone would want to leave this place to sail anywhere else. The area around the huge port where *The Antipodean* had docked was mostly commercial rather than picturesque, but we soon got a taxi away from the harbour and were dropped off in the lovely, higgledy-piggledy old town, where everything looked historical and old-fashioned and mostly white and absolutely blazing in the midday sun. Some way inland, on the left, was the stunning cathedral with its two beautiful white towers. Boris had said that the cathedral, which we were planning to visit later, was a 'mix of baroque and neoclassical'. I'd nodded, happy to agree, though the only buildings I know much about are rooks in chess.

I hugged him very warmly when we met and gave him rather a nice kiss too. We walked together, close by each other yet not holding hands or anything, but very happy to be together, down into a wonderful old-fashioned warren of little passageways, few more than about six feet wide, so you couldn't have taken even a small car down them.

'This is the old heart of the city,' Boris murmured.

I nodded again. I supposed he'd googled Cadiz, which was of course just what Tom would have done.

Boris had been waiting for me as I stepped down the long gangway and onto dry land for the first time since Monday morning. We didn't hug, but we did shake hands in a really warm way, with both hands, and I was so happy to see him I let my hands stay clasped with his for a minute or even two.

He looked very nice. For the first time since I'd met him he wasn't wearing a suit. Instead, he was wearing a pair of blue Levis, a short-sleeved white button-up tee-shirt that wasn't tucked into his trousers, and a white Panama hat.

I smiled, still holding his hands. 'I like the hat.'

'My dear Ivana, it's a practical necessity in this heat. Also, I still have a large plaster where Alexander hit me, and my head is shaved on that side.'

I was wearing a hat too, of light-brown straw, which Shanee had lent me when she heard I was going ashore for most of the day. In a sort of sartorial echo of what Boris was wearing, I had short sky-blue denims on and, like him, a tee-shirt, but mine was long-sleeved and not button-up, and sky-blue.

'No bodyguard?' I asked him.

'No bodyguard,' he said. 'I've not recruited a new one yet. I may not need one… I'll tell you about this later. Let's go and explore this beautiful city.'

Sitting next to Boris, in the back of a taxi, I realised that being with him felt very different now to how it had ever felt. Even before the nightmarish events in the helicopter, we had been through so much together.

Suddenly I had an amazing thought. *I helped save his life. That means that, in a way, he belongs to me.*

That thought never left my head for the rest of the day… and evening… and night.

It didn't leave my head as we spent about an hour exploring the warrens of Cadiz, then were driven indoors by the heat and had an early lunch at an inexpensive *tapas* restaurant, where I introduced Boris (who, to my surprise, had never been to

Spain before) to the delights of *boquerones* and *jamon Serrano* (wind-dried ham) and *gambas al ajillo* (shrimps cooked in olive oil and garlic and served sizzling hot). We had all this with lots of lovely fresh Spanish bread. We ate at a cosy little table in an alcove at the back of the restaurant and shared most of a heavenly bottle of Rioja. And, sometime over this delightful lunch, Boris, lowering his voice, said:

'Vanny, I shall tell you now why I am travelling nowadays without a bodyguard.'

I nodded in a confidential kind of way. 'Please do.'

Boris quietly cleared his throat, then, still keeping his voice lowered, said:

'About a week ago, when I was still in hospital, I made a private call, when I was alone in the ward, to my main business rival, also an oligarch, who is a former friend of mine. I suspect him of being behind the corruption of Alexander. Needless to say, I have not confided my suspicions to the New York police. My dear Vanny, I must ask that you don't either if you are asked to testify at the trial of Alexander, though I think that unlikely, as I am sure Alexander will be, shall we say, induced, by his paymasters, to plead guilty and not talk. They will hire top lawyers and he will serve, I am told, about five years in gaol. After he is released, his paymasters, no doubt, shall give him enough money, as a reward for his silence, for him not to have to worry about money for a long time to come. But yes, I must ask you to regard everything I have told you as confidential.'

'Yes, I know. Please don't worry, Boris, I will treat everything you say as completely confidential, obviously.' I wasn't at all happy at the prospect of Alexander only getting five years, all the same.

'Thank you. So, yes, I spoke to the oligarch I mentioned. The matter at dispute between us for some years is a very large aluminium factory near Ekaterinburg, a big city at the gateway to Siberia. My rival claims that under an agreement he says we made six years ago during a drinking-session at a Moscow hotel - I was not always as sober as I've become these past few years - I agreed to give him an interest in half the factory. In fact, I remember the drinking session well: I made him no such promise, though I have to admit that when I was negotiating the purchase of the factory about eight years ago, he gave me considerable help with the negotiation.'

'How do you know it was him who bribed Alexander to try to kill you?'

'I don't know for certain, and I never will. It is at least possible that there are one or two other people, also former friends of mine and now confederates of his, who may have been responsible. But in any event, the essence of what I said to him was this: "the time to cease our warring has come. I point no finger, I cast no blame, and you can be assured that I shall never mention your name to the police. But yes, the time to cease our warring has come. If someone wants to kill *me*, so be it, but I have to act to protect those who might be with me and who might themselves be in danger if there is an attack against me, as there was in New York." I asked him what he thought of what I was saying. All he said was that he understood. He did not, of course, admit to the crime, but yes, he did say he understood.'

'So what happened next?'

'I said that I would sell him, not give him, sell him, a one-half share in the aluminium factory for... well, I don't want to contaminate our lovely time together by mentioning sums of money, but perhaps I can say that the offer I made to him was an extremely generous one. He accepted at once, and I think it fair to say that we have made our peace.'

'Does that mean no-one else is going to try to kill you?'

'I can't be sure of that, for people in my position are much envied - not always necessarily rationally - and we may easily create enemies without even knowing the people who decide to become our enemies. But I do not now think I shall face any more attempts to kill me from the man I mentioned.'

He picked up his glass and drained it. I smiled, and drained my glass too.

You probably know that beautiful, calm, beguiling song 'Perfect Day' by Lou Reed. Well, my time with Boris in Cadiz felt like that. After our lunch we decided to head for the magnificent cathedral, which became more magnificent the closer we came to it.

We spent an hour or so inside the cathedral and on the outside, exploring its stunning beauty. When we had, we walked down the hill to the old town, and as we did I gently and quietly took hold of his left hand with my right. I don't remember much else precisely about that afternoon, but I do very vividly remember taking Boris's hand in mine, and the shiver of electricity, or something, that I felt in his hand as mine entwined itself with his.

I also remember that we shared a plate of *paella*, and had another glass of Rioja each, at another restaurant near the harbour. Afterwards, by which time it must have been I suppose about six o'clock, as it was getting dark, Boris said, his voice sounding rather hoarse with love and passion (we had been getting on so very well, and there was a nice cosy and romantic atmosphere between us):

'Well, I think I should take you back to the ship.'

I don't remember exactly what I said in response to this, but it involved me asking him where he was staying. Now, as you'll have gathered, Boris is usually the kind of man who likes to stay in very smart hotels. What impressed me very much that evening was that he hadn't booked himself a room in one of Cadiz's top-notch hotels (I didn't see any when I was there, but I presume there must be some). Instead, Boris had booked himself a room in a small hotel - even smaller than the Hôtel Anglais. The hotel Boris had chosen was in a pretty street, with orange trees, a hundred yards or so inland from the warren. His room was on the second floor, and had quite a spacious balcony - there was space for us both to stand there next to each other, holding hands, anyway - with a fence around it made of black iron tracing.

I know that because I spent the night with him there.

Boris had wanted me for so long, it perhaps wasn't really very surprising that he was comically and desperately excited about me finally yielding to him; I mean, I remember that as we were going up the stairs to his room, this normally calm, collected and delightfully manly man kept accidentally colliding with the walls and the sides of the staircase in his excitement.

I feel I've told you so much about the details of my life, and my passions, that perhaps I've earned the right to observe a certain confidentiality about that night with Boris, and if you don't mind, I'm going to. All I'll say was that our night together was so full of the most intense emotions, there were many times when we hardly spoke.

Boris came to see me when *The Antipodean* docked at Mumbai, too.

70

And so here I am now, writing the final words of this, *The Mating Game*, as *The Antipodean* sails onwards to Australia.

Boris will be visiting me in Sydney, and I'm looking forward to seeing him there.

Right now, I don't exactly know whether I want to be with him, or with Hélène, or Tom, or even with someone I haven't met yet. All I know, right now, is that for the time being I don't, in fact, necessarily want to be with anyone, but just to get to know myself better and experience being alone. Yet I know how much Boris loves me, and I know what an extraordinary and marvellous man he is and after all we've been through so much together, including two helicopter flights, and after the second one... well, yes, in a way, as I did help save his life, he does belong to me.

So here I am looking out from this comfortable deck-seat over at the sparkling sea. I do my writing in my cabin; it's far too sunny out on the deck for my laptop screen to be clearly visible. Shanee, who's become a close friend of mine (she knows all about my adventures in chess and romance, including my recent times with Boris) is lying sun-bathing on a deck-chair about fifteen feet away.

Jaz and Sven are getting married in June next year. The wedding is to be in Norwegian Lapland. I'm so looking forward to going, even though I don't know, right now, whom I'll be going with.

But I think most likely I'll be going with Boris.

As for my father, God, I had the wonderful news about halfway through my voyage that he'd returned to Britain and had moved into a flat he had bought for my mother and himself. My mother, needless to say, was delighted about this development in her life, but I told Dad by email that he mustn't get back with Mum if he ever thought he would dump her again and he said he understood and that he had no plans whatsoever to be with anyone else, ever, but her.

John Hamlyn's reputation as one of the leading brain surgeons in the UK and indeed in the world continues to grow. Today I know he's an even closer friend of Sir Rupert and Elizabeth. Hugo, who had frankly always been a bit directionless in his career before Lottie's death, has started to knuckle down now and has decided to become a barrister and is studying for the Bar and somehow I feel he'll make a success of it.

I made arrangements during the voyage to make over the rest of the Love Fund to a charitable trust I would run for brain tumour sufferers to continue to develop research and to provide respite care for their carers. I felt I was doing something very useful with the money. Darling Lottie, how I will always love you!

And me? Your Vanny?

What is it Johnny Depp says at the end of *Pirates of the Caribbean*?

Yes, I remember. '*Bring me that horizon.*' What a wonderful line! Surely he means not only the literal horizon, but also the figurative horizon of our futures. And my own future? Well, we'll just have to see. But even if, most of the time, I've only been muddling along, I do at least think I can truthfully say that I've always meant well.

Pawn to king four... no, I think from now on I'm mostly going to start with pawn to *queen* four.

My dear friend, it's your move.

THE END

Acknowledgements

Our grateful thanks to Annelisa Christensen and to Lilly Hamon for their editorial acumen, and also to Paul McCracken and Jo Bavington-Jones for their eagle-eyed editing. The first draft of Chapter 32 as it is now was written by Lilly.

Our warm thanks also to Charlotte Mouncey for her magnificent help with the proofs, to Jacqueline McBride and Margaret Dowley MBE for their hard and dedicated work on the Dictaphone transcriptions, to Fiona Godfrey and Helen Komatsu for their help with dictation, and to Sandra Koutzenko for the French translations.

Many thanks in addition to Andrew Greet IM, David Howell GM, Stuart Conquest GM, Danny Gormally GM, Mark Hebden GM, editor of *Chess* Richard Palliser IM, Matt Read and Tao Bhokanandh.

- J.H. and J.E.

My love and gratitude to my husband, Arne Hagesaether, for supplying the Norwegian which Sven speaks to Vanny, and for being *my* sex god.

- J.H.

My thanks to my brother Rupert Essinger, Briony Kapoor, Francesca Garratt, Laurence Green, Amy Cohen, Chris Stampe, the Reverend David Moulden, and also to Kieran Minshull and Akile Tahir of my optician L.K. Leon & Co., and to Maxine, Harley, Remi, Gemma, Lisa and Alex at the Camomile Rooms in Canterbury, and to Robert and Colin at Print Matters in Canterbury.

My special gratitude to Jo Smith, and to Damian, Rowan and Freya Smith.

-J.E.

How *The Mating Game* came to be

by James Essinger

I'm a chess-player, but not a very good one. However, I like being involved in the chess world, and I enjoy writing occasional articles for *Chess* magazine. I'm also proud to have some super friends in the chess profession, including Jovanka Houska.

The origins of *The Mating Game* go back to about 2005, when I paid a visit to the famous annual Hastings chess tournament and had a memorable dinner with Jovanka - whom I was meeting around then for the first time - and also with her then boyfriend (now husband) Arne, who like Sven, is Norwegian. Andrew Greet, the international chess master, was also with us and was as witty and urbane as ever. Jovanka was talking about her life as a professional chess-player and presented the profession as being a mix of extremely hard work at chess, the inevitable stress of competing at a high level and a social life which could sometimes become, let us say, rather heated.

I'd been to the Hastings chess tournament in the 1970s as a junior player and played in some of the events there, but I wasn't really involved in the chess world from about 1977, when I went to university, until about 2003, when I began to play for a chess club in the village of Bridge near Canterbury. I played a few times for my college at Oxford University in the late 1970s and I played in a tournament when I was in Finland in the early 1980s but apart from that I pretty much gave up chess for about twenty-five years.

Being with my new chess friends in around 2005 made me think, eventually, that it might be fun and exciting to write a novel set in the chess world. There was something about the Hastings tournament in the winter that I found curiously engaging and in a way romantic – romantic, that is, in the sense of being glamorous and poetically meaningful rather than in the relationship sense. The idea of a movable community of enthusiasts filling the Horntye Park sports centre with their competitive fervour and with their strong sense of community during the dead of winter - and Hastings is a particularly cold and windy town in the winter - somehow struck a chord within me and I decided that the novel, when I wrote it, would start in Hastings.

In fact, Vanny is not very much like Jovanka. Jovanka is a really super person, full of life, an extremely good chess-player and, as anyone who has met her or seen pictures of her will testify, a lady of great beauty. I hope Vanny is all those things too, but I wanted Vanny to be different to Jovanka: troubled, at least when we meet her, by something of a complex about only being able to fancy guys who could beat her at chess. I also wanted Vanny to have a confusing and complicated personal life, which Jovanka doesn't have.

Jovanka told me, by the way, when we were working on the story of *The Mating Game*, that she was 'gutted' that Vanny didn't end up with Sven, but I good-humouredly reminded her that this was a novel, not an autobiography, and in any case I felt that Vanny would probably have a more complex resolution of her personal passions than to marry Sven, whom

I felt from the beginning was never going to be quite right for her, and much more appropriate for Jaz.

A major aspect of the story that I didn't foresee when I set out to write the book was Vanny's relationship with Hélène. I felt that by the time Vanny was in Monte Carlo, she needed to be taken out of her comfort zone somehow. I felt this was really important as otherwise it wasn't clear that enough was going to be at stake for Vanny. By definition, characters in a novel need to be dealing with difficult problems, or the momentum of the story evaporates. So the idea that Vanny would fall in love with a beautiful and deep-hearted woman and have a physically passionate and emotionally intense relationship with her appealed to me, as indeed it appealed to Vanny. It seems to me likely that whom one fancies and loves may be more to do with what that person is like rather than what sex they are, and certainly that's what Vanny finds. At first I thought of ending the novel with her basically living life as a gay woman, but I decided in the end that I wanted to give her another kind of ending, and that the most loyal, and in some ways the nicest, character in the entire novel was someone who should be involved in that happy ending.

George Orwell remarks in his essay 'Why I Write' that he doesn't understand why people write novels and that at heart, the reason is basically, as he puts it, a 'mystery'.

For me, my novels often have their source in a close friendship with someone who comes to mean a lot to me and who fires my imagination into creating a fictional version of that person and exploring the tendrils of their engagement with life and their energy for it.

This is perhaps the right time to say that there was an original of Charlotte too: a fantastically beautiful and life-loving lady who introduced me to Tenterden, to Waitrose, to rural France, and to many other of life's joys. She eventually left me, and perhaps, in order to move on from the version of her I had loved so overwhelmingly, I had to create a fictional version of her who died young. I'm delighted to say that the original didn't, and that I'm good friends with her and her husband.

But of course Jovanka was my primary inspiration for *The Mating Game*. This is, I suppose, another way of saying that *The Mating Game* would not exist if I'd never met Jovanka, even though, as I've said, Jovanka isn't very much like Vanny. What's been lovely throughout the writing process - I wrote the book but Jovanka and I collaborated extensively on defining most of the characters and much of the story - is that writing the novel has made my friendship with Jovanka and Arne even stronger. Writing books is a joy in itself, and all the more so when it wins us new friendships, or better friendships, in the world of reality in which we all live our lives.

IN MEMORIAM

KEVIN SMITH (1962-2010)

Kevin Smith was a musician and songwriter of genius, a tall man with a big heart, a love of entertaining an audience, a powerful, beautifully melodious voice and a tremendous stage presence.

I first saw him perform at the Canterbury pub, Caseys, sometime early in the first decade of this century and subsequently saw him there maybe a dozen times. The evenings some of my friends and I spent as Kevin's audience were utterly memorable. He had tremendous virtuosity and versatility on several instruments and his act combined many songs he'd written himself, including 'Drink Down' and also traditional folk songs. As well as this, Kevin liked to vary the pace and tone on occasions by playing other music, including Pachelbel's marvellous 'Canon', which he played on electric violin using a CD to provide the backing track. I can still see Kevin playing this beautiful piece in Caseys, in a corner of the front room, surrounded by his instruments and entrancing his audience.

I began writing The Mating Game in the autumn of 2009. At first, my progress was slow, and it wasn't until 2011 that I wrote chapter 19, where Vanny goes to visit Tom. By this time I'd got to know about Kevin's tragic and untimely death. The only reason I didn't attend Kevin's funeral was because it was only a few months after Kevin's funeral that I had learned he had passed away.

I decided that I wanted Kevin to feature in The Mating Game and so I used some lyrics from my favourite song of his own composition, 'Drink Down', in chapter 19. Tom is disconsolate about Kevin's death and Vanny does her best to cheer him up.

I naturally wanted to make contact with Kevin's family to ask permission to use the lyrics. I was able to contact his widow, Jo, who has been most helpful. For both legal and ethical reasons, I would not of course have included the lyrics in chapter 19 had Kevin's widow, Jo, not approved of them being used in the chapter, which Jo read and said she thought Kevin would have loved it. I should say that I have paid a fee to Kevin's family for the use of the lyrics.

I suggested to Jo that she might like to write some biographical details of Kevin to feature in a tribute page at the end of The Mating Game. Jo supplied me with the text below, which I have only edited very lightly. It was written by Jo herself, with the musical parts of the biography being supplied by Kevin's best friend Charlie Higginson.

Thanks, Jo, and thanks, Charlie, for supplying the following moving account of Kevin's life.

Above all, thanks to you, Kevin.

Please note: if you would like to enjoy listening to Kevin singing 'Drink Down', a search on YouTube for 'Kevin Smith+Drink Down' should find the video. If you can't find it, please message me via the Facebook wall for The Mating Game and I'll send you the link.

James Essinger November 2016

A Tribute To Kevin Smith

by Jo Smith and Charlie Higginson

Kevin was born at home in Deal, Kent.

He picked up a guitar at the age of sixteen and didn't emerge from his bedroom until he had completely mastered it. This was to be his learning style with the numerous instruments he learned to play over the years to come. When people told him he was talented, he would reply by saying, 'it's not talent, mate, just sheer hard work.' I would disagree with this to an extent, as there was also a big dollop of determination in that recipe and definitely a considerable amount of raw talent! In his late teenage years he spent many years practicing in pubs and smoky bedsits. Music was his love, his passion, his everything.

Most of his early playing was in rock and blues outfits performing on lead guitar.

He developed a unique ad lib style that exploited every corner of any 12 bar groove. He transposed this ability, later, to the many instruments he played throughout his career.

The ever so non-conformist Kevin bought a violin around 1990 and after experimenting with a few riffs, took it to a few gigs – which went down very well with the audience.

His natural nose for entertainment kicked in and Kevin started to explore music outside rock/blues which took him towards the Celtic genres and the formation of The Original Fling.

Mandolin, accordion and flute soon followed, and in around 1991 and 1992 he wrote a plethora of songs and tunes, often championing the underdog in his writing, producing three albums in quick succession, the third one being titled Drink Down.

Kevin continued his band with several different line-ups, and eventually settled for a solo act, which gave him the freedom to explore music in his own way… just as he had done in the beginning!

Original Fling 1990 – 1997
Fling duo 1993 – 2002
Fling Solo 2002 – 2010

As well as his music his other two loves were the great outdoors and his three children. He would love nothing more that climbing a snow-peaked mountain alone, with his friend Charlie or his wife Jo. His two sons, Damian and Rowan, gave him so much pleasure and he was a father who was determined to teach his children about the magic of the outdoors and hoped they would also learn to love music. In 2010 his third child, Freya was born. Tragically, five months later Kevin was diagnosed with terminal cancer. He called Freya his 'sunshine girl', as she was such a smiley baby, which helped him so much, as did his two boys, through his darkest days.

While out walking one day in the snow, he collapsed and later died. The man who loved winter so much, ironically died, on the winter solstice of December 21 2010, aged just forty-eight. A packed church said their goodbyes to Kevin Smith, local music legend and much loved father, son and husband. Of course, Kevin's music featured in the service.

As his coffin was brought into the church, a rainbow appeared and filled the sky with colour. A fitting accolade for such a colourful, energetic, life force of a man. And, as Kevin's coffin was led out of the church to his final resting-place in the pretty churchyard of St Nicholas Church in the village of Ash in Kent, the music accompanying Kevin's departure was the song 'Drink Down'.